THE
SACRED
SPACE
BETWEEN

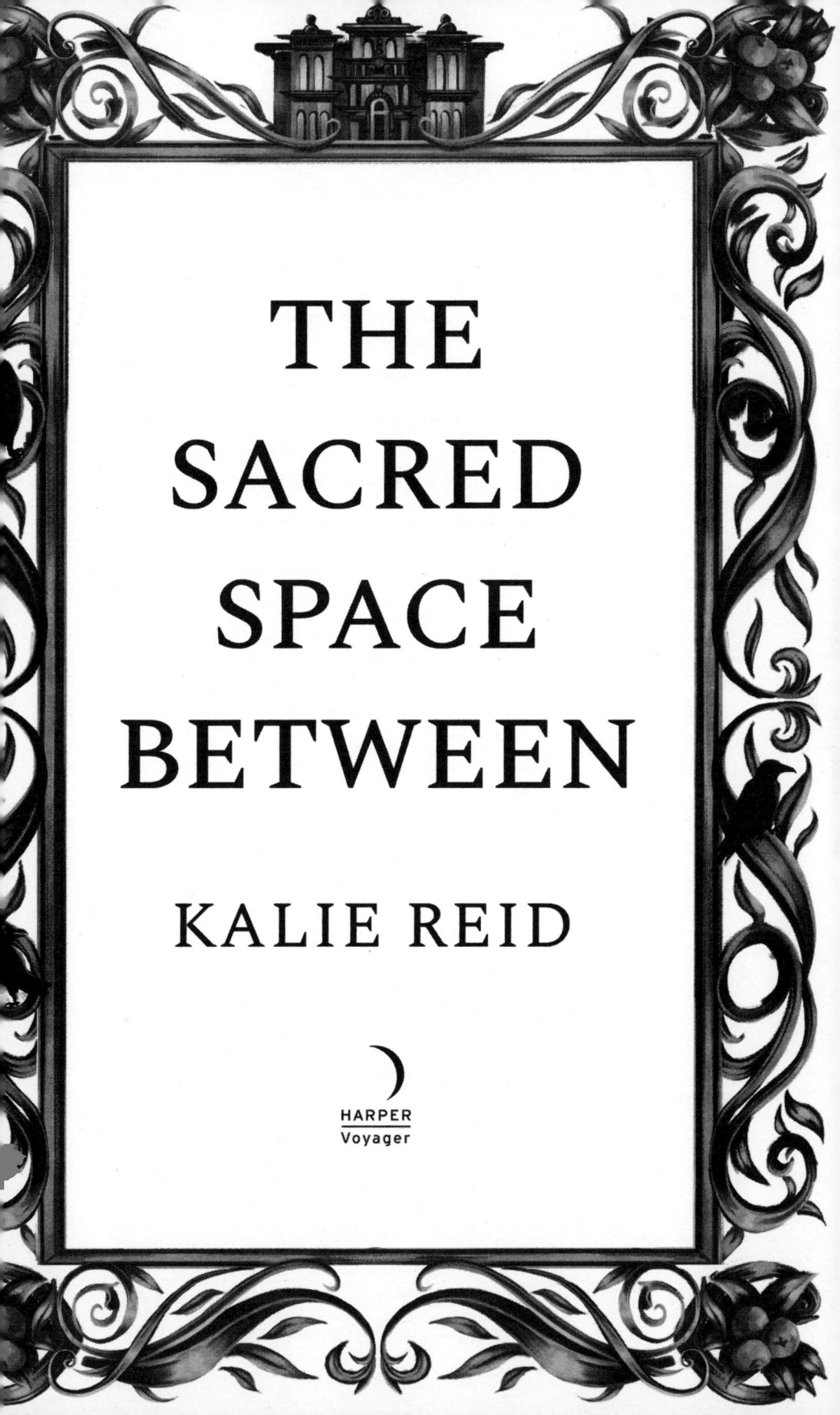

THE
SACRED
SPACE
BETWEEN

KALIE REID

HARPER
Voyager

Harper*Voyager*
An imprint of
HarperCollins*Publishers* Ltd
1 London Bridge Street
London SE1 9GF

www.harpercollins.co.uk

HarperCollins*Publishers*
Macken House,
39/40 Mayor Street Upper,
Dublin 1
D01 C9W8
Ireland

First published by HarperCollins*Publishers* Ltd 2025
1

Set in Fournier MT Std by Palimpsest Book Production Ltd, Falkirk, Stirlingshire

Printed and bound in the UK using 100% renewable electricity by CPI Group (UK) Ltd

For Gregg –
In this, and everything else.

Ánhaga: a solitary being, one used to dwelling alone.

PROLOGUE

Jude

Two blackbirds streaked across the sky – a bad omen if Jude had ever seen one.

Dappled storm clouds gathered where the moors glittered with hoarfrost, the edges already blurred with rain. He checked over his shoulder to ensure he was alone before refocusing on the sky. His breath hitched in the back of his throat, fingers trembling deep in his pockets.

Jude would do anything to see a third bird cutting across the tumultuous horizon.

The winged shadows moved with sinuous fluidity, there one moment and gone the next, whipping black feathers through the mist like hounds seeking blood. The scent of the slender firs lingered in the empty spaces between his ribs and stuck beneath his tongue. The air was quiet. Too quiet. He didn't realize how much he missed birdsong until winter stretched its fingers and silenced the world around him.

He'd started this ritual of the birds as a child, alone on a frigid windowsill, staring out at the sea with a weight in his belly. Back when he was still whole. Before exile, before sainthood. Before he'd been unmade and hastily put back together again. The old, clung-to superstition whispered through his mind like a melody he couldn't escape.

One for courage. Two for despair. Three for hope.

Fucking birds.

Giving up, he trudged back towards the house. Paint chips clung to his fingers as he shoved open the door to the cellar. He wiped them off on his jacket, ignoring the mud staining the once-fine linen. Like all his clothes, the sleeves were too short, the trousers fitting more tightly around his thighs than he would've liked. They'd been made for a fifteen-year-old. It was only natural they no longer fitted at twenty-three.

The door closed with a shuddering groan behind him. He winced. In a half-hearted apology to the rotting wood, he locked the bolt gently. He'd need to spend some time mending the patches of wet rot before the temperature dropped entirely for winter. The house existed in a constant state of decay, but he tried his best to keep it comfortable. He needed it to last, down to each spalling brick and squeaky hinge.

Still, Jude couldn't help but wonder which of them would crumble first.

A boom of thunder shoved him from his thoughts. He scoured the roll of clouds through the smudged window, weighing up the bruised purple of the sky. It wouldn't be long until the rain hit. Already, the hills were disappearing into the mist. He could smell it on the air, the dampness of soil and the low hum of lightning.

He turned away just as a black shape left one of the apple trees, stretching out on feathered wings towards the encroaching storm.

A third blackbird.

1

Maeve

The toll of the Abbey's bells cracked through the silence. Maeve lurched upright.

Fractal sunlight arched across the basilica's ceiling like the ribcage of a great leviathan. This late in the morning, she was alone in the colossal room, a fact she was secretly thankful for. Praying was a vulnerable practice, with her knees aching and the nape of her neck prickling with cold. She preferred privacy with the icons to the other acolytes' whispered requests.

Her icons.

Her chosen saint, a middle-aged woman called Siobhan, stared down at her with her usual lack of emotion. The wall before her held the Abbey's hundreds of icons, each neatly framed and hung from long lengths of silken rope stretching from one end of the room to the other. Despite all the options Maeve could kneel in front of, she returned to Siobhan because she liked the colour of her robes. Cadmium yellow was so hard to get lately.

She studied the stone floor under the kneeler, the spot of red beside her left knee. She scraped it with her nail, examining the flakes stuck to her thumb. *Oxide red*.

The guard stationed at the door to the basilica tutted at her tardiness as he eased open the double doors for her to leave. Maeve dropped her eyes, ignoring the heat in her cheeks and the weight of the guard's gaze as she passed. She'd overstayed her allotted time. Acolytes could only enter the basilica alone under strict supervision, but her status as an iconographer granted her some level of leeway. Even so, she shouldn't make a habit of abusing it.

A briny layer of seawater coated the corridor leading to her studio. The room occupied a lonely corner of the Abbey, far from the other acolytes. Maeve liked the seclusion; painting was an act best done alone, in her opinion, but the walk to and from the basilica often felt never-ending.

Her boots slipped on the wet stone as she quickened her pace. She needed to return to her studio before the oil paint hardened beyond use. Ezra's temper might burst if she let more paint go to waste. She'd already begged her mentor for coin to buy more onyx and ochre twice this month.

Besides, Felix might be early, and she couldn't stomach the idea of the saint waiting for her.

Gaining an audience with Felix was a privilege earned through years of devotion, study, and dedication to her craft. Though she was trained to paint an icon with little more than a vague description, the honour of having a saint sit for her was one she didn't take lightly.

Felix was her first in-person sitting, the first saint of his stature she'd put to oil and canvas.

She couldn't help the dart of hope shooting through her chest – maybe it was more than an honour. Maybe it was a sign.

Brigid, the lead iconographer, hoped to retire in the next few months. The position would be open.

It could be Maeve's . . . *possibly.* If she kept her wits about her and proved her devotion, she could move up in station and have her voice heard in the strictly regimented Abbey hierarchy. She would be allowed to form friendships with the other craftsmen, a seat at the monthly conclave of elders and senior craftsmen where every moment of Abbey life was decided. After fifteen years of living in the limestone halls, she would finally see behind the curtain. Her life would no longer be one of questions and sightless trust. Purpose and belonging: two peaks she had long pointed herself towards, finally within reach.

If her icon of Felix met Ezra's ruthless standards, of course.

Simple tasks, really.

The stiff set of her shoulders finally relaxed at the sight of her empty studio. No Felix yet.

She lowered the scarf from her hair and toed off her boots, stepping into a pair of soft-soled slippers. The studio was small, barely more than a closet, but it was *hers*. It was more than many people held claim to, and she was grateful for it.

A draught from the half-closed window slunk through the space, skating down her neck with icy fingers. She crossed the room to close it fully. It was usually open to air out the ever-present smell of turpentine and oil, but as winter sharpened its claws, she'd need to put up with the fumes. That, or freeze.

Would the room be comfortable enough for Felix? Wherever he spent his time when he wasn't at the Abbey, it was sure to be lavish.

If he lived at the Goddenwood, she could only dream of the luxury and comfort he was used to. The secluded village where the holiest of saints lived in community with each other was a fabled mystery in its own right. She'd never been tasked with painting it herself – her talents lay more in portraiture – but she'd studied depictions of it enough to picture its gabled, gold-tipped roofs and jewel-toned buildings with perfect clarity. Outside of the Goddenwood, saints lived in isolation, sequestering themselves to better focus on the prayers only they could answer.

Maeve aspired to their piety, dreamed of it, even, but she found the idea of such a lonely existence hard to grapple with. Maybe that was why only the holiest of saints were allowed to live in the Goddenwood – community truly was the highest reward.

Monasticism might have been a virtue, but loneliness . . .

The Abbey was isolating enough as it was. Hundreds of people lived in the limestone halls – acolytes, craftsmen, elders, guards, household staff – yet interaction between them was kept to a bare minimum. Sometimes, Maeve went days without speaking, longer without touch. Coupled with the Abbey's strict censorship of information from the outside world, the solitude often felt like a physical weight on her chest. Impossible to breathe around.

The saints were worth every bit of the sacrifice living at the Abbey called for. Maeve was grateful for the life she had been given, the life her parents had chosen for her at seven years old. Always, *always* grateful for the opportunity to pray and to paint.

The icons she dedicated her life to creating were more than just portraits – they were objects of focus, symbols designed to connect the intercessor to the saint. She didn't take her role in the sacred practice lightly, nor the prayers sent dutifully to the saints she so carefully depicted.

Carefully, Maeve traced the edge of Felix's profile with the tip of her paintbrush. A heady tremor passed through her fingers. A slow-burning peace, undercut by the steady thrum of devotion, not unlike what she felt during prayer or hymns. Warmth, bright and golden and consuming, threaded through her chest.

She'd already completed the underpainting in preparation for Felix's sitting. Hopefully, the remaining work shouldn't take more than four or five sessions, though oil painting was a fickle beast and might take longer than she'd mapped out. The detail work could be done without the saint, of course, but a part of her was tempted to extend it as long as she could to keep herself in his presence.

Her hand twitched, smearing a line of burnt umber across his jaw.

Maeve dropped the brush.

No questions. She needed to stay professional. *Only* professional.

Just as she was collecting her brush from where it had dropped on the floor, a knock sounded at the door. With a stern word to her nerves to stay in line, she moved to open it.

Felix stood on the other side.

The reality of him forced the breath from her lungs.

A saint. Here, in her studio.

Felix was tall and imposing, with dark brown skin and a finely boned, carefully blank face. Perhaps five or six years older than her. He stared down at her for a beat before his gaze fixed somewhere over her left shoulder.

Words formed and died on her tongue. She'd seen him at a distance before, but never so close.

The thick brocade piping on his black robes shone silver as it swirled over his shoulders and down his chest. A swathe of shiny scar tissue ran up the left side of his neck to spider over his cheek and jaw, dragging down the corner of his eye. A medallion hanging at the centre of his chest glinted as he breathed, revealing a hollow centre. It wasn't a relic, a medallion that signified an elder's connection to a particular saint, but it resembled one. Enough for her to take an unconscious step forward to examine it closer.

She was sure she had seen something *wrong* in the light refracting off the metal.

Felix cleared his throat.

Maeve flinched, stepping aside to let him into the room. 'Apologies. Thank you. Welcome.' She cringed, swallowing another rush of mindless words as Felix moved past her.

'Where do you want me to sit?' he asked. His voice was low, scratchy.

'There. Please.' She pointed towards the stool she'd set up by the window.

He complied, angling himself to face almost entirely in profile. The scarred left side of his face wasn't visible from Maeve's position by the easel. Usually, saints faced fully forward, one hand raised, the other on their lap. Her preliminary drawing had posed him that way.

She picked up a brush and tried to think around the heavy

silence. She needed to ask him to move, but would it offend him? He seemed wholly absorbed in staring out the window. If it weren't for the stiff set of his shoulders or the subtle movement of his fingers under the cuff of his robe, she'd wonder if he was aware of her at all. She couldn't paint him as he was. Ezra wouldn't be pleased, and she needed Felix's icon to be perfect.

'Felix?' Maeve hedged. Her knuckles bleached white around the paintbrush. 'Could you . . . I mean, please, could you move to face me?'

His eyes flicked briefly to hers. 'No.'

'I need to see your entire face for the icon,' she said, voice petering softer with every word.

His fingers moved faster beneath his cuff – a frenetic rub of his forefinger with his thumb. 'This will have to do,' he replied after a bloated pause.

Maeve dipped her brush in the paint. It was doable, she reasoned. She could follow her sketch from the neck down and still keep his face turned away. A thought occurred as she limned the curve where his neck met his shoulder in gold, lining out the halo's contours surrounding his face – did he want his scar hidden?

The texture was unlike that of the scars on her own body or ones she'd seen on any of the men she met in the town – though she'd rather not dwell on her secret dalliances right now, worried that Felix might somehow know what thoughts swirled in her head. She was painting his icon, after all, and outside of answering prayers, his saintly abilities were largely a mystery.

The Abbey didn't know she liked the occasional night away in someone else's bed, and she wanted to keep it that way. Some things were a private indulgence just for her, sweetness tinged with shame. A constant teetering between letting the guilt suck her down or pushing back against the Abbey's rhetoric around chastity. As an iconographer, purity was expected. Her personal feelings didn't matter under the weight of her title.

Her thoughts spun out the longer she painted, the deeper the silence grew.

She had a saint in her studio. Would she ever have the honour again, an object of her devotion at such close range? *Alone*, with no listening ears at the door?

If she gained Brigid's position, certainly. If not . . . Maeve didn't know what shape her life would take. She tried to shove the gnawing thought from her mind. So much of the Abbey was kept from her. If she became lead iconographer, perhaps that would change—

Slowly, her eyes rose to Felix.

A saint in front of her. Questions on her lips.

Long-fermenting wonders about sainthood, his holy magic, the mystery surrounding his very existence. Her own prayers cast doggedly into the world. Forbidden questions and even more insidious doubts.

But she couldn't ask him. She *couldn't*.

Not Felix, not Ezra . . . no one. There was no one she could ask, no one who would reassure her.

She forced her eyes back to the painting. Lifted her brush. Pressure built just behind her eyes.

Waves drummed outside her window, urging a comfortable looseness to Maeve's limbs. The action of sliding her brush across the canvas rode on instinct. The weak sun shifted into shadow, shadow into dusky blackness. Her gaze strained to focus only on what the bristles touched. An ear. The fold of a cloak. The arch of his cheekbone highlighted in raw sienna.

Minutes, maybe hours, ticked by.

Her breathing grew shallow, muscles tensing in her shoulders and wrist. Nothing else remained but him. Nothing could exist but what she formed by paint and brush. Gold-tinged candlelight flickered at the furthest reaches of her vision. Perhaps it was a mistake keeping the window shut as paint fumes filled her lungs.

A deep hum trickled into her ears.

With it, a voice. A whispered suggestion.

Maybe she *could* ask him whatever she wanted. Maybe she could beg him to answer her prayers, to call upon his glorious abilities and grant her every petition. If she could paint an icon worthy of him, an icon that would propel her into lead iconographer, she could have the security she wanted so desperately. All Maeve wanted was to belong. To be acknowledged. To be trusted with the Abbey's secrets. She wanted to be carved into their history as securely as the icons she depicted. All she had to do was her best, and everything she wanted could be hers.

Everything.

She sat at the cusp, the precipice just before the fall. Wind beat at her back. Never before had she stepped so close to the edge. How would it feel to jump? To break all the rules and *ask, ask, ask.* To shatter the mirror and open the door. To fully see the glory of the Abbey she'd so readily given every particle of unflinching faith she had to offer.

A shivering wash of pain coasted down her arm to the fingers clamped tight around the brush, skating up to linger behind her eyes. Her vision began to blur.

In the space between breaths, Maeve tipped backwards on her stool.

She blinked slowly, slowly.

High above, the ceiling swam and dipped as the world shifted to glimmering, gauzy metallic. Reality unspooled like yarn. Warmth moved up her arms, down her shoulders and ribboned around her spine. A soft space of welcoming nothingness. Dreaming without sleeping.

A push on her shoulder. Fingers on her pulse—

Maeve returned to herself with a choked gasp.

Felix stood above her, an unmoving and spectral figure. She lurched upright from where she'd been lying flat on the floor. Nausea surged as her vision continued to spin. A fine layer of dust covered everything in the room, soft and shimmering like powdered gold.

How long?

How long had she been passed out on the floor? The dryness of her eyes and the pain at the small of her back told her it had been a while. Her stomach curled in, clenching at nothing. She pushed clumsily to her feet.

'Felix?' Maeve's voice was a choked rasp in the heavy silence.

He didn't reply, only stared. But not at her – at his icon.

She turned.

Staring down at them from her easel with an imperious curl to his mouth was Felix in oil, fully formed. Slowly, she reached towards the fine streaks of white daubed in the corner of the canvas – her signature, an M, the edges curling to circle around the letter. The oil paint was hard to the touch. It should have taken days to finish and weeks for the oil paint to fully dry.

She was *dreaming*. She had to be.

She pressed her fingers harder against the dry paint to prove she wasn't imagining it. Gold dust gilded her hand. She had painted the shadow under Felix's jaw less than an hour ago, keeping the time from the track of the shadows across her lap. The thick coats of oil paint peaking like meringue on the canvas.

Yet, it was *dry*.

Impossible.

Maeve turned to Felix. The same gold dust that coated her skimmed across his shoulders and the high points of his face. A holy figure, demanding her unflinching respect.

But yet, but *still—*

'Did you do this?' she asked, voice hoarse.

Felix's throat bobbed. 'Not me.'

She stared at him in disbelief. 'You didn't?'

'No,' he replied, just as short, almost dismissive.

His tone rankled something deep inside her, a part that stretched its limbs every time an elder ignored her when she spoke or Ezra denied her request for more supplies. The note of condescension wasn't an unfamiliar one, but that didn't make it any easier to swallow.

His gaze dropped to the floor. Maeve's frustration sparked higher, shifting steadily towards anger. Who else could have done it? He was the one with magic flowing through his veins. *He* was the saint. Somehow, he'd dried her painting, taking hours of her life in the process, and dared to try to convince her he wasn't behind it?

'Felix,' Maeve began steadily. She needed to confront him somehow. He'd involved her in his act of magic, involved her *work*, and that surely warranted answers, but finding the words to do so without offending his position proved difficult. 'I think I—'

'Ezra,' Felix interrupted. 'We need to find Ezra.'

She shut her eyes briefly, trying to swallow the thorns in her throat before turning towards the door. A hand on her wrist stopped her. 'No. I'll do it,' Felix said with a shake of his head. 'I'll find him. You stay here.'

Something surged in Maeve as he moved to leave, stronger than any impulse she'd ever harboured. A blistering, phantom heat upon her skin. A question on her tongue that she couldn't remember placing. Her mouth gasped open like it searched for air after drowning.

'Your scar,' she croaked. 'It's from a fire, isn't it?'

Felix froze with his back towards her. Slowly, he turned. His eyes met hers.

Before he could reply, a knock sounded at the door.

A wall-mounted oil lamp haloed Ezra from the shoulders up. His dark brown habit was wet with seawater at the hem. 'Felix. Maeve,' he said. 'I was finishing my evening round and heard your voices. Is everything all right?'

Before either of them could reply, his eyes widened at the state of the room, the gold powder covering every surface. Felix's icon watched from the corner. Ezra stepped past them to approach the painting. He ran his fingers lightly over the dried peaks, tracing her signature in the corner. 'It's finished already?' He turned to Maeve, confusion in his pale blue gaze. 'Didn't you just start this?'

Maeve opened her mouth to respond when her gaze caught Felix's.

His eyes levelled hers with a maddening intensity. Every moment he had previously refused eye contact coalesced into his stare now – something so fervent she felt like he was trying to speak directly into her mind.

Indignation and something like confusion rolled in her stomach. How could Felix put her in this position? What was she meant to say to Ezra? As much as she couldn't allow whatever magic Felix had deployed to finish his icon to compromise her career, equally, she couldn't be seen disrespecting, *doubting*, the saint in front of her.

The truth, then. Her only option.

She turned to Ezra. 'I started with the oils today. I was working, and there was this gold light, and the dust—'

Felix stepped closer. Maeve glanced at him. Something like panic crested his expression. Was it her imagination, or did he shake his head at her?

Abruptly, fear surged within her. Why was he nervous? What had he *done*?

And was she about to be blamed for it?

'Maeve?' Ezra prodded. She tore her eyes back to her mentor. To his placid, encouraging expression. He laid his hand on her shoulder, squeezing gently. 'Whatever happened, you can tell me.'

Maeve sucked in an unsteady breath. 'Well . . . My head started swimming. I think I fainted, and when—'

'Sounds like you might have been unwell,' Felix cut in. 'A spell. Women have that sometimes. Hysteria.'

'I don't think so,' Maeve forced out through the anger limning her throat. 'How would that explain the paint drying? Besides—' she paused, weighing her words. 'You were here. What did you see?'

Felix shut his eyes briefly, breathing out hard through his nose.

'What, indeed, Felix?' Ezra murmured.

She wanted to ask more, demand that Felix tell Ezra the full story. It was her career on the line, after all. But what did she have to gain by angering a saint?

The gravity of her thoughts hit her full in the face – maybe she was the one in the wrong.

Who was *she* to question a saint?

Maeve ducked her head under Felix's pressing stare. Guilt surged in her chest.

'It's getting late,' Ezra continued. 'Perhaps you ought to go to your room, Maeve. I need to speak with Felix. We'll discuss this first thing in the morning.' He pulled her around by the shoulder, a smile on his face. 'A good night's rest will surely offer clarity.'

Felix disappeared down the opposite hall as Ezra guided her from the room. His footsteps echoed like bells in her sluggish mind.

'Maeve,' Ezra said quietly. She dragged her gaze back to his.

Torchlight flickered, licking long stripes of flame up the Abbey's limestone walls. The weight on her shoulder increased. Ezra's smile seemed to grow softer in response. Warmth filled her chest. An early summer berry, sour on her tongue. When he spoke, his voice sounded muffled and far away. She'd expected anger for her questions, her impertinence. Not . . . this – the gentle smile, the guiding hand.

'Let me walk you to your room,' he said.

Soon, Maeve sat on the edge of her bed, worrying the edge of her skirt between her thumb and forefinger. Shadows trailed Ezra as he moved around the room. The darkness undulated in the liminal space between her slippers and the doorframe. Thicker than air, thinner than water. When she lay back against her pillows, the light behind her eyes faded into night-pressed blackness. She covered her face with the crook of her elbow.

Ezra closed the door behind him. The lock slid home with a metallic click.

2

Maeve

The vicious beast of worry struck as soon as Maeve awoke the following day.

Her questioning was concerning. She'd entertained the odd doubt over the years – who wouldn't? The Abbey was all she'd ever known. Her parents had chosen to give her up and offer her life and talents to the saints. It was an honour and a privilege she'd do well not to squander. There was no room for questions, not when the saints had given her so much. Besides, once she was made lead iconographer, she'd have no need for questions.

The nausea grew teeth, guilt biting down.

Questioning showed a lack of devotion, and Maeve was nothing if not devout.

She'd spent years bundling up her questions into neat parcels and shoving them into the furthest recesses of her mind, hoping to forget the truth that underneath the surface she presented as an acolyte, as a *believer*, she was cracked. Crumbling and drying out.

Soon, her questions would ruin her.

If she attained lead iconographer, it might allow her to pick at the secrets that shrouded the Abbey, like the saints' ability to answer prayers or why their community needed to remain separate from the outside world. Maybe she could even convince them to loosen their rules around friendships between the acolytes. Unpicking their rigid confines wouldn't be easy, nor could she do it alone, but as lead iconographer, she could encourage the process.

But not yet.

She couldn't question *yet*.

Maeve shifted off her bed to kneel. She pictured Felix as he'd looked in his icon. Paint and canvas and not flesh and blood. Someone who couldn't see her in her entirety. Someone safer at a distance. The prayer for forgiveness came easily to her lips.

All too soon, the bells for the morning meal split the air.

Ezra was an early riser. Why hadn't he come to see her yet? He had said a good night's sleep might offer clarity, that he'd talk to her tomorrow, now *today*.

Yet . . . nothing.

She pushed up to her feet and rubbed the ache in her back as the bells finished their chiming. She kept her space neat and orderly. Jumpers, coats, and dresses in the wardrobe. Shoes under the desk, laces tucked inside. Freshly cleaned brushes in a glass jar she had salvaged from the sea. Coins stacked in a neat pile, one on top of the other.

Sitting in front of the small mirror, she smoothed her pale, thick hair with a boar bristle hairbrush before braiding it down her back. She leaned closer to the mirror, touching her fingertip to where the thin skin under her eyes shifted to a bruised purple. Another mark of a sleepless night and too little sunlight.

She tried the door, finding it unlocked. Maybe she'd imagined the metallic echo of Ezra bolting it shut last night, or maybe he'd told her to meet him in his study and she'd forgotten. Either way, if she didn't hurry, she was going to miss breakfast. She stepped into the hall, casting a final look at her bedroom. Water beaded on the iron-webbed window like pearls, tracking down the glass in slick rivulets. Sunlight illuminated swirling dust motes.

For a moment, the dust flashed gold.

Her steps faltered. She blinked once, twice, as a shudder coursed through her body. Emptying her thoughts, Maeve kept moving. A cold rush of sea air swept through the corridor as she approached the stairs leading to the courtyard below. Despite the early hour, the courtyard was half-full of acolytes milling about. Though each acolyte kept to a schedule of meals, prayers, and hours designated for study or craft, interaction between each other was minimal in the extreme. Even after over a decade at the Abbey, Maeve wasn't sure if she could count any of her fellow acolytes as true friends – exactly as the elders wished it to be.

She scanned the courtyard for Ezra, instead spotting Brigid heading towards the open doors of the dining hall. She let out a relieved breath. Just the person she ought to speak to. If there was anyone who might know what strange phenomenon had completed the icon, it was the lead iconographer.

The stairway down the courtyard was crowded this time in the morning with the youngest acolytes leaving the basilica. Maeve gazed over their heads as she reached the ground floor, searching for Ezra's familiar cap of thick grey hair. Had he taken the early prayers, maybe?

A bright wash of light cut from the gap between the massive doors leading to the basilica, momentarily flooding her vision. She blinked. The sound of the acolytes pattering feet disappeared up the stairs behind her.

Suddenly, a shout cut the air.

Two elders wrestled a young boy from the basilica before throwing him bodily onto the rough flagstone. One knelt, wagging a finger in the boy's face. Maeve was too far to see what was being said but close enough to see how his face paled as he gazed up. His mess of blond curls flung back from his face. A tear, vivid against the bright blue of his eyes.

She started forward, to intervene or to watch closer, she wasn't yet sure.

She'd also been thrown from the basilica in her younger years for gossiping, picking at the pews, lagging behind on the prayers. Still — he didn't deserve the rough treatment. Her heart clenched at the startlingly red blood streaking down his temple.

Maeve froze mid-stride.

Something was strange about the boy's habit.

His collar flapped in wide points that covered his shoulders, the edges intricate with embroidery. She hadn't seen that style in years, and maybe only in icons. It had to be at least twenty years old. Perhaps older. They were given new habits each year, some subtle differences marking the year's style. Always in dark grey for acolytes. As the previous years were taken to be remade . . . there was no reason for the boy to wear something so markedly old-fashioned.

The boy reached out, clasping his hand on one of the elder's shoulder. The elder jerked back, his hand flying towards the boy's face in an open-palmed slap.

'Maeve! *Maeve.*'

Maeve whipped around. Her legs were shaking, a stitch in her lungs like she'd been running.

No one was there.

An ink-black raven sprang off the arched cloisters above. Wingbeats filled the air as it ascended towards the pearl-grey sky, disappearing amongst the clouds.

Her pulse pounded unsteadily in her throat.

Slowly, she turned back to the basilica's firmly latched doors. There was something she'd been watching, a reason she had stopped . . . wasn't there? A finely pointed headache throbbed behind her eyes as though she'd been staring at the sun. Maeve closed her eyes, pressing her fingertips to her lids. Her ears echoed with a phantom scream.

Suddenly, the pain left as quickly as it had come.

She opened her eyes. Her back was pressed tight to the wall, the jut of a stonework digging into her spine. The Abbey was still and silent around her. It was breakfast. She was here to meet someone, wasn't she? *Brigid*. She'd seen the other woman making her way to the dining hall.

Slowly, Maeve peeled off the wall, giving her head a rough shake. Pushing past the strange uneasiness swirling in her stomach, she stepped inside the hall. The room was half full, the platters set up in the middle of the long tables almost empty.

Brigid's hand trembled slightly around a piece of charcoal as Maeve sat beside her and picked up a piece of toast. She was midway through some kind of still life – of what, Maeve wasn't sure. An empty breadbasket, maybe, though it looked like blankets were trailing from the lip.

Maeve cocked her head and looked closer. She choked on her toast, hurriedly washing it down with a sip of lukewarm tea. Not a breadbasket. A bassinet.

Brigid dropped her charcoal. 'My goodness, Maeve. Must you cough so loudly?'

'Sorry,' Maeve managed. She forced her gaze from the bassinet and took a moment to collect herself.

'Did you need something?' Brigid prodded. She glanced over her shoulder. 'You shouldn't be sitting so close.'

'Yes. I . . . well,' Maeve paused. She didn't want to be too hasty with her questions. Or too revealing. 'Did you know Felix is here?'

Brigid replaced the charcoal in its tin and snapped the lid shut. 'Of course.'

'I'm surprised you weren't the one to paint his icon.'

'I declined the offer,' Brigid said. Watery daylight streamed in from the window across from them, sinking into the creases of her face. 'My time as iconographer is coming to an end, as I'm sure you know.'

Maeve took another sip of tea to hide her awkwardness. 'Have you painted him before?'

Brigid's lips twitched downwards. 'Yes.'

Saints. It was like drawing blood from a stone. 'What do you think of him?'

'Why do you ask?'

'He's the first saint I've met with, just the two of us,' Maeve replied. 'I wasn't sure what to expect. About him or his abilities. I've never considered that he could—'

'That's enough,' Brigid interrupted, harsh enough to make Maeve jump. She looked around, lowering her voice to a whisper. 'Have you no sense, Maeve?'

Brigid's dark eyes were wide under their hooded lids. *Fearful.*

Maeve swallowed. 'I'm sorry,' she replied convulsively.

Doubting, even voicing questions aloud, was strictly forbidden. Every acolyte knew to search for answers from prayer and study alone. Never from each other. Brigid was afforded more freedom as the lead iconographer . . . but not Maeve. Not yet.

But she had to ask *someone.*

'I know it's not my place to ask, and certainly not of you,' Maeve whispered. Brigid's eyes narrowed. 'But something happened, and I think . . . I think Felix lied to me about it.'

As quickly as she could, and before Brigid could protest, she told her about the strange buzzing that had suffused her body, how she'd passed out and woken to find the painting finished and the room cast in gold. How Felix had *denied* it.

Brigid made a rapid motion with her hand, an urge for Maeve to stop speaking, but now that she'd started, she couldn't quite seem to stop. 'Felix wanted to leave immediately to get Ezra, but he arrived before he could and saw the icon. Felix tried to convince him I had a hysterical fit or something. But *Felix* did it, whatever it was that finished the icon.' She took a breath. 'Can a saint's abilities work that way? Do you know if—'

'*Maeve,*' Brigid interrupted. 'Please. *Please* stop talking. Now.'

Pain sprang up her jaw from how tightly she clamped her teeth together.

Slowly, the other woman shifted to face forward once more.

She stared out the window. In the distance, the chimneys and gables of Whitebury blurred with morning haze. Maeve continued to try to breathe. Panic tied knots in her chest.

'Did you tell Ezra about the gold?' Brigid asked carefully.

'He saw it. The room was covered.'

Brigid nodded. Opened her mouth. Closed it. Nodded again. 'Some things aren't for us to know,' she said, a note of finality in her voice. 'Or to tell.'

Maeve's heart sank deeper as Brigid opened her charcoal tin and drew out a stick. She sketched a symbol on the crisp white paper. Maeve knew what it was going to be even before she started.

A half-circle with three lines fanning from the top. A pared-back version of the Abbey's insignia of two hands holding a cupped sun. One of the first symbols every new acolyte was taught.

Each ray held a meaning. *Piety. Belief. Devotion.*

The symbol of the sacred distance between saint and intercessor. The glorious magic of the Abbey; an unknowable force for them to believe in. Not to doubt. Not to question. Even if Brigid knew more than she was letting on, she wouldn't tell Maeve. She needed to believe. To trust fully, even without answers.

Maeve straightened her fingers on her thighs, wincing at the stiffness.

'Do you understand?' Brigid asked. 'You might be taking my place soon. I need you to tell me you understand what I'm saying.'

'Yes,' Maeve whispered. 'I understand.'

Brigid closed the notebook and moved to her feet. She bent to collect her bag pushed under the bench, dust swirling through the buttery sunlight. Maeve kept her eyes dutifully forward, breathing slowly through her mouth.

The whisper pressed against Maeve's ear was unexpected. 'Ezra will summon you tonight. You must agree to whatever he asks.'

Maeve turned towards Brigid to ask what she meant, to see her face—

She was already gone.

The vast dining hall was empty.

3

Maeve

Ezra came for her as the sun was setting.

Maeve was in her studio. Felix's icon was no longer there. Neither was the gold. Every speck of something amiss had vanished so completely she wondered if she had imagined it entirely. Only the gold-dusted soles of her slippers reminded her that her memory wasn't faulty. Somehow, Felix had finished and dried the icon. And soon, Ezra would ask something of her that Brigid demanded she agree to.

The knock came. Maeve moved to the door. Her hand hovered over the doorknob. Gritting her teeth and summoning every last drop of confidence afforded to her, she opened the door.

Ezra wasn't a tall man, only a handful of inches more than Maeve, but when he drew himself to his full height and donned the air of an Abbey elder, he sketched a formidable silhouette. He fixed her with a calculating look in his pale blue eyes. 'You're needed.'

She nodded, letting the door close softly behind her. Her breathing, shallow and quick and far, far too loud, echoed through the maze of halls as Ezra led her to the basilica.

A hushed reverence shrouded the colossal space like a burial shroud. Maeve turned her eyes upwards reflexively. High above, the rose window turned the pale stone and endless parade of portraits multicoloured with the setting sun.

The entirety of the wall to her left was covered in icons, some hundreds of years old. The golden haloes undulated the longer she looked, water-gilded surfaces burnished in glittering metallic. She recognized dozens of her own icons staring down at her.

The style of her work had changed drastically over the years. She'd begun her specialized training in iconography at thirteen after six years at the Abbey, but her icons hadn't been deemed good enough for the basilica until her seventeenth year. Even still, seeing her earliest paintings hanging on the walls made her cringe. She'd been a little *too* obsessed with motifs at the beginning.

But, like all things, practice, patience, and sheer determination to be the best had grown her abilities. Now, her paintings were so lifelike they almost breathed. Close enough to touch, as though mere proximity could win holiness. If that was the case, Maeve might've been a saint herself given how many icons she'd rendered over the years.

Ezra led her to just beneath the rose window, sun-bruised light streaming over his shoulders in crimson and azure, gold so bright it hurt to look at. Shadows obscured his expression.

Maeve bowed her head and waited for him to speak. If she knew him at all, he'd make her wait for a few tense minutes before putting her out of her misery. Just because he could.

Although saints were the highest echelon of Abbey power, the elders were the ones truly in control. The ones who decided the rules and regulations, who ran daily life, who monitored the veins connecting each and every acolyte to the beating heart of the Abbey.

More importantly, elders venerated acolytes into sainthood through holy visions. A sacred ability held only by the elders, kept just as secret as the saintly power to answer prayers. All she knew was that once they saw a sign in a person, a saint was marked with a tattoo – a vertical line bisected with three horizontal. The rune for *saint* forever inked beneath their left collarbone.

She often wondered what the first signs of sainthood were in a person. Was it like an icon, a corona forming around their head that only the elders could see? Did it come to the elder in a dream, or did it happen in real time?

Finally, Ezra cleared his throat.

Maeve lifted her head. The silence of vast, empty spaces pressed in on all sides. Ezra's hands were clasped in front of him so tightly that his knuckles were entirely bloodless.

A thought occurred, the accompanying strain of hope damning in its intensity.

Maybe she hadn't been summoned here for a punishment. Maybe it was a reward. Had whatever happened between her and Felix been a test of Maeve's loyalty, a stepping stone on her way to the lead iconographer position?

Or . . . had she ruined her chance at advancement by asking Brigid?

She should've stayed silent.

Lead positions weren't easily come by, especially in iconography. Illuminations, scribing, masonry . . . all were important, hard-to-master jobs, but none held the status iconography did, nor the level of isolation. If she were made lead, that would all change. She could stretch the limits of her art like never before. Maybe she could visit other painters in the surrounding towns and learn new techniques. Perhaps she could paint something other than icons. Waves and birds and rolling, endless hills.

Maybe, just maybe, she could shrug slowly out of her loneliness, inch by inch.

Even one single friend would be enough. One person she could talk to openly without fear.

Maeve scanned the wall across from her. She focused on an unfamiliar icon. A boy around fourteen or fifteen with dark hair curling around his temples, vivid against the paleness of his skin and a curiously devoid gaze. She silently prayed to the saint that she hadn't ruined everything.

'Maeve,' Ezra said. 'As you're aware, Brigid will soon be retiring as lead iconographer. She's devoted over forty years of service to the Abbey. Painted hundreds of icons, many of which adorn our walls today.' He swept a hand towards the wall across from them. 'I recognize a few of yours alongside hers, yes?'

'Yes,' she replied. Her voice shook only slightly.

'I thought so. You're very talented . . .' he paused. Maeve shifted on her feet. 'I brought you here tonight to inform you we're considering you for Brigid's role. But there is something we'd like you to do first. An *assignment*, of sorts.'

There was something cold to the way he regarded her. Suddenly, she wondered if the anger she'd thought he'd shown last night was resurfacing in an entirely different way than she'd expected.

'Anything for the Abbey,' she murmured, drawing her spine up straight, shoulders back.

Ezra angled his head towards the boy saint she'd prayed to mere minutes ago. 'Do you recognize him?'

Maeve studied the icon. Once more, his eyes struck her. Devoid, like a candle snuffed out.

An image pushed forward at the furthest recesses of her mind, hazy with age and distorted around the edges. A boy – *this boy?* – with his face turned away, kneeling at a man's feet, both hands extended in front of him. A thin piece of twine across the boy's palms, blood welling around it, dripping towards the floor. Dark hair, damp with sweat at the nape.

As quickly as it had come, the recollection faded.

Recollection . . . if she could even call it that. It was too hazy to be a memory, too unsteady to be her imagination. She tried her best to force it from her mind, the ruby blood splattering on the flagstone, vivid against the greyscale of dreams.

'No,' Maeve managed. 'I don't recognize him.'

At least, she didn't think she did.

'His name is Jude. A saint, as you might have guessed,' Ezra said. 'He's no longer welcome at the Abbey or within our fold. Put simply, he's been exiled.'

She rolled his words over in her mind, not liking their sound. Saints were encouraged to live isolated lives, but this sounded like something more. *Exiled?*

It didn't sound like a punishment; it sounded like a sentencing.

'Why?' she asked, praying the question would be allowed. 'Did he . . . do something?'

'A good question,' Ezra murmured, the brogue of his accent thickening. 'Jude took the power of the saints, the sacred ability to answer prayers he was blessed with, and uses it outside its design. A corruption that we fear he might use to harm those who pray to him. A recent development, we believe.'

'How?' Maeve breathed.

'We don't know. Not yet. That's where we need your help.'

'My help?' Her voice was meeker than she would've liked. She glanced at Jude's icon. He'd be close to her age now based on the date under the indiscernible scratch of a signature. The painting was almost entirely done in greyscale except for the corona haloing his face. Despite its age, it remained as brilliantly gold as though it was painted yesterday.

'We'd like you to go to him and paint an updated icon,' Ezra said, drawing her attention back. 'We'd like you to report any findings you may encounter in his home.'

'You want me to spy?' Maeve asked before she could stop herself.

Ezra winced slightly. 'Not spy. More like carefully observe. And let us know what you find.'

So, spy.

Questions bubbled up thick and fast. She desperately wanted to put voice to them but wondered how much prodding Ezra would allow. Would she even be permitted to say no? Even if she wanted nothing to do with this *Jude* and his corruption of what she held most dear, most sacred?

She wet her lips. She had to ask. She had to be certain.

'Why an icon?' she asked. 'If he's been . . . exiled, why do you need a new painting of him?'

Ezra moved closer until they were mere feet apart. The sun had left the rose window. Inky shadows stretched across the space between them. 'Icons bridge the gap between saints and petitioners. We pray to their image, and it *works*.' He let out a slow sigh. 'A holy mystery.'

Her jaw clenched. Did elders like Ezra not know exactly how the saints' magic worked? Did that mean she wouldn't, either?

Piety. Belief. Devotion.

Maeve swallowed the words like a stone, felt the weight keenly in her stomach.

'I've spent years studying your art,' Ezra continued. 'Learning how the saints' power works. Some days, I feel closer than ever. Others . . . it's as though I'm standing on a cliff, straining to see past the horizon. Whatever exists beyond my eyesight is unreachable, no matter how far I swim. Do you ever feel the same?'

'I do,' she breathed, soothed by Ezra's unexpected candour, despite how it surprised her. She often had the same wonderings around prayer. She'd experienced small moments of the saints' magic in her own life. A lost hair ribbon found the next day. A day out in Whitebury. Burns on her arm, healed far faster than was natural. 'I do feel the same.'

Ezra smiled softly. 'The man Jude is today is unknown to us. A new icon will help us assess the damage he has wrought to his sacred ability and place measures to prohibit he doesn't . . . harm any petitioners.'

'I understand,' she replied.

She'd always felt a connection to the saint she was painting, like she was creating a bond between her brush and her heart that existed long after the icon was finished. It felt similar to praying, in a way. Like something lasting was being built, even if she couldn't see it at the time – a connection both invisible yet solid as stone. It was heartening to learn her abilities could be used to protect the Abbey, even if the prospect of going to Jude's, of *spying*, was one she found uniquely frightening.

At first glance, Ezra's mission looked like exactly what she had been praying for – freedom. Fresh air on her skin. A glimpse of the world despite how she'd been taught to see life outside the Abbey as one fraught with turmoil and darkness.

Freedom as a concept was intriguing, but as a reality . . .

Maeve swallowed. Perhaps the illusion of choice was a shallow one.

'I'll go to Jude's if that's what you'd like of me,' she replied, exactly as Ezra expected to hear.

He reached out, laying his hand on her shoulder. 'I would trust no one else but you. You know that, Maeve, don't you?'

'Yes,' she murmured, trying to convince herself that it was true.

'Even more than our lives, our very *safety*, the saints' abilities must be protected. The sanctity of their magic must be upheld. Perhaps you can be the one to provide the information needed to stop what dirty thing he's made of it. You can do that, can't you?'

'Yes,' she repeated, louder, more sure. 'Of course.'

'He knows you're coming to paint an icon, but that's it. You'll leave tomorrow and travel across the moors. Shouldn't take more than a day by horse. His housekeeper will be there to greet you. You won't be alone.' Ezra paused and considered his words. 'It's near the Goddenwood.'

The smallest seed of excitement grew in her chest, and she fought to keep it from showing on her face. 'How close is it?' she asked. She wouldn't be allowed to visit, but even a *glimpse* of its existence would settle her immensely, the promise of its nearness like sunlight on her skin.

'A few hours away,' Ezra replied. 'Let its proximity be a reminder that the Abbey rewards loyalty. A paradise Jude could avail of if he repents and turns back from his corrupted ways.'

She drew his words tight to her chest, revelling in them. Why would Jude want to risk his future at the Goddenwood? Why would he reject a life of peace, of community with his fellow saints? Somehow, the idea that he'd willingly turn his back on it was more jarring than anything Ezra had told her yet.

She clenched her hands into fists at her sides. Maybe she could convince him differently. The Abbey would certainly see fit to reward her if she brought him back like a lamb to the fold.

'How long will I be gone for?' she asked.

Ezra moved closer. The hem of his robes brushed the stone floor with a faint whoosh. He gathered her hands in his. His touch, warm and solid, familiar enough to make her heart ache, steadied her immensely. 'As long as it takes, my dear girl,' he said. 'As long as it takes.'

4

Jude

The oncoming storm chased Jude inside.

His footsteps clattered on the tiles in the main hallway, tracking mud with every step. Much had changed in the eight years he had called Ánhaga home, though sometimes he still felt a jolt of childlike fear walking the halls alone. Especially nights like tonight, when the storm sought entrance through the cracks in the stone and rain battered the windows. He'd need to wrangle the ancient mop from the cupboard, scrounge up a bucket and—

Jude stopped.

A letter sat on a low table by the door. Even from a distance, his name stood out starkly black on the envelope.

Elden, his grumpy housekeeper of the past three years and keeper of the kitchen, hadn't mentioned any post arriving this morning. Jude hadn't received a letter in eight years, at least not one addressed directly to him.

He approached it slowly, trepidation settling in his stomach.

There was only one place it could be from. Only one hand tight on his throat.

Jude picked it up, ignoring how his fingers trembled. The envelope was pristine, unmarked by rain and travel. His name was scored precisely across the front, the familiar contour of the sigil just as damning.

The cupped hands and sun of the Abbey.

The Abbey which, until his fifteenth year, had been the only home he had ever known. His grip crumpled the sharp edges of the expensive vellum, and his heart felt like a slow-to-start fire, reluctant to pump blood down the lengths of his limbs. Steeling himself – he refused to flinch, even if they weren't watching – he ripped open the envelope.

His lungs caught between breaths.

In a handful of sentences, his forgotten existence turned on its head.

The Abbey was sending an iconographer. One they were considering for the lead position, apparently – a woman called Maeve. Something about the name sounded familiar . . . perhaps they had been at the Abbey together, but he no longer remembered. It didn't matter either way. She was coming to paint an icon.

Something Jude could *not*, in any circumstance, allow to happen.

Hatred surged up in a vicious lash. Both for her, and the Abbey that haunted his every step, looking for some new way to control him. They wanted to ensure he kept to himself, holding himself in check. Alone and abandoned.

And to send an iconographer, of all people . . . there had to be a reason they wanted an updated icon of him – an exiled saint. Why send her now?

He reread the letter. Underneath the prickling rage and the raw vulnerability that he refused, *refused*, to acknowledge was the smallest spark of something he was too pessimistic to call hope. An inkling, maybe – grey instead of black.

Over the past year, Jude had been picking at what allowed the Abbey and its insidious band of elders to hold the reins to his magic, to all the saints' abilities.

It had started with a book he'd found shoved behind a shelf in the dusty confines of the library: *Iconography and the Saints*. Despite the title and the fact it had so clearly been hidden, the gold-dusted fingerprints on its spine had piqued his interest. Whoever Ánhaga belonged to before Jude had taken up its tenancy had read the book and left their mark behind.

The cramped text within had confirmed something he'd long suspected – the icons were how the Abbey controlled the saints they so dutifully brought up and sent into exile. His last icon had been painted just before he left. If its power was growing weak with age . . . a new icon of him would allow the Abbey to renew their hold on him.

And if, *if* the iconographer succeeded, if a renewed icon of Jude was made—

The Abbey's connection to him would be restored. All the measures he'd taken to protect himself and his memories . . . gone. He wasn't sure he had the strength to fight his way free yet again.

Jude pressed the heels of his palms into his eyes until lights popped and flashed behind his lids. Memories swam at the furthest recesses of his mind, begging for entry in honeyed voices. A familiar pang of worry wormed its way into the tender space between his ribs, growing stronger with each ragged inhale. He rubbed the spot with the palm of his hand, feeling the rise and fall of his chest.

But. *But.*

That damning thread of hope.

The book hadn't told him how the elders accessed the magic held in the icons, nor how to restore the memories and magic to the saints they were stolen from.

Maybe the iconographer would know.

She, who formed the icons, who knew of the power between artist and subject . . . was it too much for him to wonder if she'd share her knowledge? If the Abbey hadn't sunk its claws in deep enough to keep her from seeing the truth amidst the lies?

He crumpled the letter as the feeble flame of hope began to wane.

She was an iconographer. Fully trained. Deeper in the Abbey's clutches than he'd ever been, comfortable in its hold. The danger far outweighed the potential of breaking himself free. Of curing himself of the Abbey's grip on his magic, a poisonous taint that turned it into something that wasn't his own. Of running as far as he could from the Abbey and ensuring they could never touch him or his magic again.

Maybe then his life would finally be his own.

Jude had done what was needed when he agreed to leave the Abbey. He'd donned the title of saint just as they asked. A perfect fucking icon for anyone looking for something to pray to.

And still, it wasn't enough.

'What else can I do?' he whispered to the house, voice cracking on the syllables.

He forced a slow breath in between his teeth. In and out, in and out, until the rapid fluttering of his heart settled. The Abbey suddenly remembering his existence couldn't be anything but a threat to the fragile peace he'd managed to forge for himself. Redemption couldn't be something he still hoped for.

It *couldn't*.

He smoothed the letter back out. His focus landed on the iconographer's date of arrival.

Two days from now.

Jude shoved his letter into his pocket and made for the front door. He couldn't stay here, cooped up like a man in a cell. Not tonight. If he had anywhere else to go to that wasn't the house *they* had sent him to, that's where he would go. But he didn't. There was nowhere he would be safe from the Abbey, nowhere they wouldn't find him. Every cyclical worry and half-suppressed fear chased him outside like a shadow he'd never outrun.

He'd run once, and he could do it again. Forever, if that was what it took.

He strode towards the entry gate, palming the back of his head to protect against the whip of winter cold. Short hairs tickled the skin between his fingers. He'd kept it shorn close to his skull for eight years, never allowing it to grow long enough to grab.

Flickers of memories coloured the backs of his lids.

Blood and iron and salt. The edges of his vision glinted metallic. He'd need to visit his library and sate the magic inside him before she arrived – but not tonight.

Jude only allowed one thought to find harbour as he ran for the neighbouring village of Oakmoor. He wanted to get completely and utterly *sloshed*. Forgetting had never been a problem for him, but tonight, he wanted his thoughts free of anything but the bottom of a cup.

He kept his head down and his feet moving as he entered the town. Consisting of only two major streets, though even that was being generous, Oakmoor was shabby and startlingly poor, its population dying out with every passing year. It was almost empty this time of night, which suited him perfectly. He didn't want to be recognized. Not when he had one stop to make before the blessed oblivion of the pub.

Too soon, the village shrine stared back at him.

It was small enough that he could wrap his arms around it and pull it free from the wall if he tried. Other villages had churches and cathedrals, grand places of worship with room for hundreds, but Oakmoor only had the shrine. Small and forgettable, though not to Jude.

The base was carved wood, the saint's visage above worn by time and clawing, desperate fingers. Frost turned the metal luminescent in the moonlight. A slot was cut in the base for coin. Something to urge the prayer along, or some other brainwashed claim they liked to spew to the poor souls who still believed.

He blinked back the gold, the murmur of memories knocking against the back of his skull.

Hollow eyes watched him turn and walk away.

He was glad he made the stop. He needed the reminder that the Abbey wasn't returning to his life – they'd never left. The arrival of the iconographer would simply be a step closer. Jude tucked his hands into his pockets, squeezing his nails into the soft meat of his palms until the rolling mess inside him quieted.

He rarely visited Oakmoor, fearful of the Abbey's long-fingered reach. They would know if he tried to weave himself into the community, of that he was certain. Abbey members visited often enough – to collect the shrine's coins, to sell pilgrim's tokens, to preach in the streets. Tucked away in a wild corner of patchwork towns and surrounded by the bleak moors of the Wold, it was an easy place to be forgotten.

But they hadn't forgotten him, a needling voice whispered. Why else would they be sending the iconographer?

Jude made a vicious promise to himself – he wouldn't think of the Abbey anymore tonight, even if it took a whole bottle of whisky to achieve it.

The bell above the pub's door chimed his entrance. The smell of burning peat and souring pints filled his lungs. He'd been coming here for a little under two years, ever since Elden convinced him leaving his cage was not only possible but could be good for him.

Still, he never quite got the sense he was welcome. The bar was small, with squat windows and walls decorated with clumsy paintings and tacked-up village notices. A handful of patrons were tucked around tables, nursing pints and glasses of indeterminable liquid. Jude quickly scanned the space for the old woman who usually kept him company during his visits, but even she was absent that night.

'Heya.'

Sean, the barman, smiled at him from behind the scored wooden counter. He raised an empty tankard, and Jude nodded. Lowering onto a bench tucked against the wall, he watched him work, trying very hard not to think of anything but the barman's swift, practised movements.

Setting a pint next to Jude's elbow, Sean knocked his fist on the table in two abrupt beats. Jude moved his arms under the table so Sean wouldn't touch him. 'Alone?' the barman asked.

Jude nodded. It was rare he visited the pub without Elden. His housekeeper was fond of the ale, though perhaps the barman and his upstairs bedroom was the real draw for Elden. 'Sorry to disappoint,' he murmured.

The corner of Sean's mouth ticked up. He tapped the side of Jude's tankard. 'Want me to keep them coming?'

Carefully, Jude extracted an arm and downed half the pint in one go. He stifled a grimace at the bitter aftertaste. Beer wasn't usually his drink of choice. Once, it had been cider. Sweet and tart, a glass passed between young mouths. 'Whisky, please.'

It'd do the job quicker, at least.

Sean studied him for a lingering moment. They weren't friends, not even close, but Jude couldn't be sure what Elden had told the bartender about him. Not that Elden should have said a word, but Jude suspected he might have let a few morsels slip.

'Now,' Jude grumbled. Guilt flooded him when Sean jerked away from the table. Before he could dredge up an apology, the barman was gone, a glass of whisky appearing a minute later.

His throat burned in protest as he gulped it down. Warmth suffused his face, whether from the curious gaze of the bar's patrons or the whisky, he wasn't sure. Coming here was a risk, but one he was willing to take. He'd better get used to it. The iconographer would soon be watching him just as closely. Closer.

Jude raised his hand in the air, signalling Sean for another drink. Whisky or beer, he didn't much care as long as it fulfilled its end of the bargain. He'd regret the indulgence in the morning, but he would be a mess either way. Might as well make it miserable by his own hand.

'C'mon. You can't stay here all night.'

Jude peeled back his eyelids, one at a time. Light danced in his vision, multiplying into a shattered dance of fire and spinning faces. His tongue stuck to the roof of his mouth. He tried to speak, but all that came through was a distorted murmur. Everything was so *bright*.

'Ungh—'

'Yep. That sounds about right.'

Someone slid their hands under his armpits and hefted him to his feet. He struggled to focus on their face. Pale eyes leering closer. A glint of a sliver chain—

'No! *No*—' Jude flailed, kicking out. He needed to get free. He couldn't let the man touch him. Not his hair, not his back, not his wrists or hands. 'Stop it!'

'Okay,' the voice murmured. Softer. 'You're okay.'

Jude looked up from where he'd crumpled onto his knees. The face swam into hazy focus. Familiar. *Safe*. 'Sean?'

The barman nodded, unsmiling. 'Time to get you home.'

This time, Jude let himself be pulled to his feet and guided towards the door. He couldn't feel his legs, and his eyes were gritty with sand. Gold flashed disconcertingly bright with every blink. Alcohol influenced his control over his unruly magic, which was why he usually abstained. His loss of control was another point against the iconographer.

The freezing wind felt like a bucket of water had been dumped over his head, diluting the numbing effect of the alcohol. He blinked. 'What happened?'

Sean propped Jude up against the side of the pub. 'Had a bit too much, mate. You all right?'

'I've got him.'

Elden materialized from the gloom with a flat cap pulled over his sandy hair. He smiled at Sean before peeling Jude off the wall, careful to keep his hand light on Jude's elbow, knowing how he shied away from touch. 'Let's go.'

They made their way slowly from the village. The first curls of nausea swarmed in Jude's belly as the house came into view, joining with his embarrassment at Elden having to *fetch* him like an unruly child. He stopped at the gate, bracing his hands on the iron. A small, rusted plaque was mounted at the centre. Jude ran his fingers over it, feeling the shape of the letters. The name of the house he'd been condemned to.

ÁNHAGA. Solitary being. A dwelling for one.

Tears pricked the corners of his eyes as he turned his messy focus to the moors behind him. Dawn was still hours off, the sky a deep blue indigo. The old oak tree stood proud, not too far in the distance. A spectral figure with hulking branches like shadows given substance.

A wave of drunkenness swept over him, as infallible as the tide. Fear chased it, pummelling against all his sharpened edges until they softened with weary reluctance. His body felt weightless. Not entirely his own, like he could float away at any moment. A restlessness in his veins that felt at once both untenable and wholly unfamiliar.

'Elden,' Jude asked, 'what's wrong with me?'

The question was quiet, hardly more than a suggestion between exhales. But still, Elden paused. Their eyes locked. Something in their light blue depths gave Jude pause. He wondered if he would ever truly know the other man. Even after three years in the same home, he still sometimes felt like a stranger, a fault that didn't lie with Elden. Warm, friendly Elden. Jude only had himself to blame.

'Let's get you into the house,' Elden murmured.

Jude bit the inside of his cheek until he tasted blood. He pulled his gaze away from his housekeeper and back towards the oak, further, *up*. He searched the horizon for guidance, for birds. He would allow himself that much. A desperate moment of pain and fear, a prayer sent towards an uncaring sky, before he turned and trudged back towards Ánhaga.

5

Jude

Jude awoke as the sky gradually lightened to a stormy, limpid blue. There would be no sunrise today – no hazy shafts of russet and ochre illuminating the patchwork shape of the moors. Mist fogged the edges of the orchard where it met the far wall, dew coating each lichen-webbed branch. A delicate lace border of frost ringed his window.

The rain might as well have been a thunderstorm with how his head ached.

He downed the cup of water Elden had left on his bedside in three gulps. It left a stale aftertaste, but anything was better than whisky. At the edge of the bed, his cat Olive gave a luxurious stretch. She padded up to him, butting against his arm with her tail held high. At least someone would still look him in the eye after last night's antics.

He flopped back in bed. Fucking hell . . . what had he been thinking?

He never got drunk. *Ever.* Not only for how it affected his loose-fingered grip on his magic but for how it made him feel the following day. Something he'd clearly decided to disregard last night. He'd wanted to think of nothing but how the whisky was slightly smokier than his preference. Easy thoughts. Ones that wouldn't drag him down or fill his head with hazy, half-remembered fears. Jude pressed his fingertips against his closed eyes. Maybe he could push his eyeballs back into his skull and summon a quick death.

At least he hadn't vomited. Small mercies.

Stifling a whimper, he forced himself out of bed, into the bath, and finally down the stairs. The house creaked around him. The acrid smell wafting from the kitchen told him Elden was cooking.

He stopped in the doorway, scrubbing at an eye.

Elden was lying on the floor, poking at the coals lining the bottom of the cookstove and grumbling under his breath. Even from his position in the doorway, Jude could tell the coals were too hot to make anything palatable. His stomach churned at the charred smell emanating from the open hatch at the top. If Elden would just let *him* cook, none of this would be happening.

'Is all this truly necessary?' Jude asked with a sigh.

Elden grunted. One hand slapped the flagstone by his hip, searching the ground. Loosening the rigid set of his legs, Jude leaned down to grab the poker and slide it into his waiting palm. Elden's huff sounded vaguely thankful this time. An improvement.

'I'm going to make something,' Jude told him, pushing back to his feet before Elden could argue. He took up the knife and a handful of carrots, chopping them into equal pieces. Some of the tightness banding around his ribs loosened. He liked to cook. Perhaps he'd make a stew to have later. He moved on to the onion. At his feet, Olive wound around his ankles. Jude dropped a piece of chicken. She hunched over it, black fur glinting amber down her spine.

'Jude,' Elden growled, finally freed from the stove. 'Let me do it.'

Jude rolled an undersized parsnip under his fingers, inspecting the discolouration around the base. He'd need to spend some time in the garden to get it ready for the colder temperatures on their way. The women who ran Oakmoor's market wouldn't be pleased with a half-rotted and shrunken selection. He pushed the parsnip aside, holding up a sprout for inspection next. Sheena would be having words with him the next time he hauled himself down the road, of that he was certain.

Elden cleared his throat.

Jude sniffed at the burnt air. 'What were you trying to make? Bread? Or the memory of it?'

Elden slid the knife out from between Jude's fingers. 'Go make yourself useful elsewhere. Leave me and my kitchen be.'

Jude didn't have the energy to argue today. He poked Elden's ribs as he stepped back from the butcher's block. Elden flinched, his grumbling hiking up a notch. Kitchen control had been a constant battle between them in the years since Elden had showed up. In all fairness, the other man was better than he used to be.

Elden picked up the knife and cut a parsnip clumsily in half, barely missing his fingers in the process. The end of the parsnip rolled promptly to the floor.

Maybe Jude's assessment had been too generous.

Rain splattered the windows lining the kitchen. A fresh bout of nausea found a home in his stomach as he brushed aside a hanging bushel of garlic, tracking droplets as they raced down the glass. Outside, the sky had darkened to near black. The pane rattled with a gust of wind. A day to be indoors if he'd ever seen one.

Light fluttered at the edge of his sight. Jude blinked.

Abruptly, he remembered — *the iconographer*.

He dug his nail into the soft, damp wood lining the window, thinking. She'd be here tomorrow. He needed to control the situation. Alongside her assignment to paint him, he had no doubt she'd be reporting back to the Abbey like the dutiful acolyte she was. His movements, his words, his house . . . all of it would be under her watchful eye. He needed her to see only what he chose to reveal and nothing more.

He turned back to Elden. 'Have you seen the keyring?'

Elden dropped the knife blade first into the chopping block and rooted in his pocket, drawing out a ring of well-worn keys. 'Here.'

The force of the gold swirling in Jude's vision momentarily blinded him as he reached for the keys, far too late to stop the momentum of his already moving body. As Elden's hand accidentally brushed his, Jude's world spun out from under him.

He sat at a scuffed wooden table, sticky with the liquor remnants. Too loud voices echoed around him, the candlelight overly bright to his feverish mind. He only recently had begun to feel stronger after his sickness, but not enough to leave the house willingly. His trembling fingers jostled his half-full pint. He wanted to leave. To be back under the open sky or tucked under a quilt on his sofa. Anywhere but here. He'd left the limestone halls for a reason. Even a half-day's ride away was too close for comfort.

But he was meeting someone. Someone who promised the medicine he needed to cure the sickness that had been wracking his body for months. He needed his health back if he wanted to return to work, if he wanted to maintain his freedom.

Footsteps sounded behind him, louder than the tread of patrons who maintained a wary distance from his brooding figure. He stilled, taking a deep breath before turning. He didn't know what to expect. His eyes fell on the dark hem of a cloak. Strange, given the summer's heat. He looked up, barely making out the curve of the stranger's jaw—

Air came thin to his lungs as Jude fought to clear Elden's memories from his mind. They lingered like glimmering smoke, gold-tinged and agitated. Panic turned his movements jerky as he hastily stepped back.

Did Elden realize what had just happened?

Jude met the other man's eyes, worried what he might see. The pale blue was hazy, irises glinting almost metallic before he blinked. Elden rubbed one eye with the back of his hand. When his gaze met Jude's, it was clear once more. 'You all right?'

Jude took a moment to reply. Elden had never mentioned battling sickness before. He'd never seen him with so much as a running nose. And . . . perhaps more importantly, had Elden honestly not noticed his memories had just been *invaded*?

At least, it was a rare occurrence for the most part. It had only happened twice before with Elden and once, very briefly, with the barman Sean, nothing more than a hazy memory of a bare back and rumpled sheets. Never on purpose, and always when Jude was feeling particularly strung-out, his grip on his emotions tenuous.

It didn't make sense. *Nothing* made sense.

For the hundredth time since leaving the Abbey, Jude wished for answers. Instead, he was left stumbling in the dark with only his unwieldy magic to guide him, tainted by the Abbey's touch. More broken than it was whole.

'Jude?' Elden's voice brought him back to the present. 'Are you? All right?'

His brain chugged slowly into action— 'I'm fine.'

'You'd forget your head if it weren't attached,' Elden said fondly.

He tried to smile as Elden returned to the sprout he'd chopped into a near-mashed state. 'Probably.' With that, he slunk away from the kitchen and headed towards the front hallway.

He needed to visit the library and release the poison from his blood like a leech held to his skin. Keep the magic from ruining his carefully maintained sense of stability. If he didn't . . . well. Elden wasn't the only one at risk of having his memories viewed without his consent. Jude's magic loved memory, even if his own resembled a moth-eaten sheet. Threadbare and rendered useless with holes.

Before Elden arrived three years ago, he'd been a woodsman somewhere up north. Whenever he spoke about his past, which wasn't often, his words were stilted and awkward on his lips like he was dredging them from somewhere deep within. Stories about the moors and highlands, the perils of the ever-mercurial weather, and conversations with strangers under a star-filled sky. He painted a picture of a quiet life. A simple one.

Jude had long nursed a poisonous, tenacious worry that the reason Elden couldn't remember much of his life before Ánhaga was because Jude had stolen his memories. An accidental touch that had taken far, far more than he could control.

Elden was only a few years older than him. Had he grown up as Jude had, with prayers and bowed heads, salt in his nose? Jude guessed he had some connection to the Abbey – who else would've sent him? It had made him suspicious initially, but the other man's quiet patience and kindness had worn Jude down in time. If the Abbey had sent Elden for some nefarious reason other than keeping him alive, keeping him somewhat functioning, he would've acted by now. The Abbey needed him whole if they wanted to continue using him. A pig kept healthy for slaughter.

Jude shuddered.

Elden might not have been working under ulterior motives, but the *iconographer—*

He needed to lock the house down. There wouldn't be a room, a single *cupboard* available for her to pry into that he wasn't aware of. Especially the library. The secrets he kept there were for him, and him alone. In no world would she ever be permitted inside his library.

His study, the dining room, the drawers on the empty sideboard he'd never used. Even the broom cupboard was sealed tight, home to little more than a mouldering mop and a handful of spiders. He breathed easier with each lock click.

Rolling out his shoulders, Jude walked up the stairs to the first floor and opened the door to his library. The scent of books and magic hit him with a gust of heated wind, the subtle smokiness of a candle blown out, underpinned with a faint metallic edge that stuck to his lungs when he inhaled.

He locked the door behind him and rubbed his chest with the flat of his palm. He'd put off coming here a few weeks longer than he should have. It was painful, sometimes, going back to his knees, though Jude had never shied away from what hurt the most.

The days where he wished himself back towards devotion

were the worst. He was never sure if he missed the person still haunting the rose-tinted halls or if he grieved a life already decided for him. The urge to bow his head and pray wasn't easily fled from. It'd worsen once *she* was here. A constant reminder of everything he'd left behind, both stolen and forgotten. He stared at the tall expanse of books, unable to dismiss the feeling he'd lifted his head in the wrong direction.

His mind wasn't as boggy as it used to be, in his earliest days away from the Abbey. Each day, each month and year brought more clarity, like the Abbey's grip on him was at the end of an ever-fraying rope he still felt the tug of. He would never lose it completely as long as they still held his magic. As long as icons still existed.

Gold flickered with growing intensity in his peripherals. The voices grew louder in his ears, shifting from hum to chant as he crossed the space towards the window, searching for one final, desperate sign of reassurance.

He found it in a small robin perched on the sill. Its reddish-orange chest was vibrant against the grey stone and even greyer sky. The robin cocked its head. Jude took a deep breath.

Then, a flutter of movement from the library behind him. A stirring as if the room drew breath; the soft pad of footsteps.

Jude whirled.

Nothing.

He rubbed his chest again. It wasn't the first time he'd felt a presence in the library. Like it held memories of its past occupants written into the walls. Shaking off the feeling, he pulled a book off the shelf and knelt, arranging it open on the floor before him. It wasn't one of the tomes on Abbey sacraments or history left behind by whoever the house belonged to. Instead, the pages were still blank. Snowy white and deceptively innocent for all it took from him.

He closed his eyes and placed his hands on the book.

It didn't take long. It never did.

6

Maeve

As one day of travel bled into the next, Maeve had quickly realized that the thrill of leaving the Abbey hadn't been all it was cracked up to be. In the last hour, as she urged the horse up one hill and down another, she'd had to stop twice to vomit.

The unforgiving scenery hadn't helped. Not the heather whipping at her calves nor the headache cropping up somewhere between crossing a frigid mountain stream and skirting beside a darkly forested valley that she *swore* she felt eyes watching her from.

To distract herself, she'd tried to picture the Goddenwood lurking just between the folds of the hills. How she would crest one rocky foothill and see the fabled village like a pearl, all gleaming roofs and tidy streets. Though she wasn't a saint, a warm bed would be waiting for her surely – wouldn't it? There would be bakeries and bookshops and expansive windows she could paint in front of. Every wish would be answered. Every secret prayer a reality. She'd find a sense of *home* in the Goddenwood that over a decade at the Abbey hadn't been able to provide.

Somewhere to belong. Fully and truly. *Finally.*

But even her strongest imaginings couldn't free the weight from her belly, as much as she tried.

The Abbey was counting on her skill and abilities to fulfil her assignment. Failing wasn't an option, not if she ever wanted to see her home again.

Maeve had never considered herself particularly courageous, but as she crossed through the open gate onto Jude's property, she couldn't help but feel her anchor had been pulled away, leaving her to face the storm alone without Ezra to guide her.

She *had* to be brave.

No other option remained.

Her foot sank into the mud as she slid off the horse, suctioning her right boot straight off. 'Oh, by the *saints*—' she grumbled, reaching for the gate to the imposing house, no more than a shadow silhouetted against the bruised plum sky.

A name was etched into a plaque – *ÁNHAGA*. An unfamiliar word in a language long forgotten.

The horse trailed behind, nosing between her shoulder blades as she tied him to the fence. Maeve shivered as the wind slapped the exposed skin of her neck and wrists. She tilted her head back to face the house. She had to see what was waiting out here in the middle of nowhere.

Ánhaga stared down in greeting, dark but for a single candle flickering in a downstairs window. A blackbird launched off eaves into the sky. It hovered in place, suspended by wind and rain, before changing course for the roll of the moors barely visible through the mist. The only hopeful sight in the otherwise desolate, foreboding image introducing itself to Maeve as her new home.

The sooner she finished her painting, the sooner she could leave.

Months, the storm seemed to howl. It could be months before the paint was dry enough to travel, longer if she factored in the sketching time. And who knew how long it would take to deliver the Abbey Jude's secrets . . . or what she might find in the process.

Fear burned up, hot and bright.

She shoved a hand into her pocket. The smooth contour of a

coin greeted her. An icon, though she wasn't sure of what saint. She ran her fingers over it, working a prayer into the motion. Strength, guidance. A shoulder to lean on. She had to believe it would be answered, even here in this forgotten place.

She approached the steps leading towards the door. Stopped. A silhouette waited in the shadows.

Silence pulsed like the hum of energy before lightning struck. An animal fear launched her heart into her throat as she took one step closer, then another. For a moment, she could have sworn she'd met him before.

The intensity in his knife-sharp features sent a curl of fear racing up her spine. This stranger couldn't be Jude. A saint, even one such as him, wouldn't come out to greet her like this, in an ill-fitting coat and mud-scuffed boots. Didn't Ezra mention someone else living here? A housekeeper?

'Get inside.' His voice was a low grate. 'I'll take care of the horse later.'

The blackness lingering behind the half-open door swallowed him as he disappeared into the house. Maeve forced herself to follow, tracking mud on the rug spread over the hall as she shrugged off her waterlogged cloak and single remaining boot, leaving them crumpled by the door. She was too off-balanced by his animosity to do anything else with them. Her fingers trembled with a mixture of cold and pounding, tremulous energy.

He reappeared like a spectral figure in the corner, carrying an oil lamp and a blanket.

'Thank you,' she murmured, wrapping the blanket around her shoulders. 'It was a long journey. I'm a bit . . . damp.' She tried for a laugh. Anything to dispel the horrible tension. 'As you can see.'

The housekeeper ignored her, his gaze fixed just over her left shoulder. Hostility radiated from him. 'Your room's this way.'

She prickled. Not that she'd expected a warm welcome, but the barely leashed fury in his eyes was unwarranted and entirely unwelcome. Gritting her teeth, Maeve followed him towards a staircase tucked in the corner. Like its exterior, the inside of the house was cold, draughty, and reeking of neglect. Her breath fogged in the frigid air. Why didn't the housekeeper do something about the state of the home? Wasn't that what he was here for?

And where was Jude?

She hadn't expected him to greet her at the door with biscuits and tea, but surely he was curious about who the Abbey had sent to his home. Though hopefully not *too* curious, given her task.

'Will I be meeting the saint soon?' Maeve asked as the house-keeper led her up another flight of stairs. His steps faltered for a heartbeat before he continued. *Silently.*

She scowled.

Another staircase, several dark-panelled halls and shut doors later, and the housekeeper stopped, shoving open the door to a small, sparse room. A window between a wardrobe and the wall let in a weak flash of moonlight as the clouds shifted across the sky. He placed the oil lamp on the bedside table, illuminating the space as Maeve stepped inside.

It wasn't dissimilar to her room back at the Abbey. The rough-hewn floorboards and bare plaster walls were a little foreboding, but nothing she couldn't work with. A faded blue quilt covered the bed, reminding her of the sea. The endless ebb and flow of the waves she could hear from her room were gone, replaced by a whistle of the wind and a creak of floorboards.

Maeve peeled the blanket off her damp skin before it could soak through, grimacing at the heavy weight of the dress plastered to her skin. Her hair hung in a matted rope down her back. She didn't think she'd ever been so cold and miserable. She pulled at the dress's collar as she considered asking the house-keeper if he could help her draw a bath.

Exhaustion hazed her senses. Sleep first, bath later.

Somewhere behind her, she heard a wooden scrape – the housekeeper opening a drawer, or maybe shutting the door. She decided she didn't care. The dress needed to come off. *Now.*

She wrenched at the buttons, loosening just enough to scrape the dress over her head, dropping it in a puddle at her feet. Her stockings came next. The damp slide of the wool against her saddle-sore legs was unbearable. Her chemise wasn't much drier, but at least she was free from the dress.

'Do you *mind*?'

Maeve whirled.

The housekeeper stood wild-eyed before he schooled his face. 'At least wait until I leave before disrobing. Self-awareness is clearly a difficult concept for you, but I implore you to try.'

She crossed her arms over her chest, half in embarrassment, half in defiance. Darkness from the hall swept over his frame, coaxing the blackness of his clothing into something deeper as he levelled her gaze. The light from the oil lamp swelled, expanding around him. Her tongue felt unwieldy in her mouth.

'I don't—' she tried. 'The dress . . .'

The light spread wider, like sun through widening curtains. Gold flickered at her peripherals.

'Go to bed,' the housekeeper said. His voice was muffled and far away.

The edge of the bed hit her thighs. It welcomed her down, feather pillows pooling around her face as exhaustion consumed her senses. Far above, higher than she thought possible, the wooden slats of the ceiling expanded and condensed. They curved, forming a circle. Hands. A sun. As Maeve closed her eyes and let sleep claim her, the image settled over her like a heavy blanket. Stifling and comforting all at once.

The morning dawned even greyer than the day before. Maeve stared up at the ceiling with her palms flat on the mattress, her heartbeat in her fingertips. The linen was soft with age and warm from her body. She wasn't sure where her bag had gone. Perhaps the housekeeper had left it sitting outside in the mud. Her paints would be ruined, a fact that was more concerning than everything else put together.

She sat up.

The quilt wasn't fully blue as she'd thought last night. Squares of cobalt and cerulean bordered emerald and olive, each patterned with a subtle white fleck. Idly, Maeve considered the blackbird she had seen last night. Oil-slick feathers had featured in her dreams. She'd dip her brush in black iron oxide to mark its shadows if she painted it. She'd use the same for the housekeeper.

Overnight, her chemise had dried in sticky patches against her sternum and between her shoulders. Mildew filled her nose when she brought the neck of it to her face. She'd need to find her bag and bathe, which meant leaving the fragile safety of her room.

Her memory of the previous night was hazy with exhaustion and embarrassment over how brazenly she'd shed her clothes, but she somewhat recognized the dim hallway and the staircase at the end as she stepped from the room. Silence lingered like a vapour. Unlit sconces were placed at even intervals down the walls, one between each closed door.

More bedrooms? A washroom? Closets? The house was far larger than it had looked from the outside; too much space for just a saint and his housekeeper.

She stopped at the last one and tried the handle. It held fast. When she crouched to peer through the keyhole, only a long stretch of empty floorboards greeted her. Moving on, she took the stairs down a level, stopping when they tapered off to a wide expanse of checker-boarded tile. Paintings of the surrounding moors and other pastoral scenes hung on the walls. They were rudimentary in style, but something calming lingered in the desolate depictions.

A door in the middle of the far wall caught her attention, urging her closer.

There was no sign of the housekeeper. She was alone.

Anticipation slicked her palms. Perhaps this was a good place to begin her prying. Slowly, she knelt, wrapping her fingers around the brass handle. It was warm to the touch.

Eight years ago, she'd knelt beside another closed door like this one, hadn't she? She'd been alone in her wing of the Abbey, the other students off attending their designated areas of study. She hadn't been feeling well and had been given special permission to rest, a rare treat in her regimented life. She remembered smoke seeping under her closed bedroom door.

The door handle had been hot enough to make her flinch back and inspect her palm before she'd put two and two together and screamed *fire*. Shuddering now, she ran her hand up her forearm, knowing the skin there was unmarked despite her memory of burning flesh. Either her injuries hadn't been as bad as she remembered, or the burning flesh had been a nightmare.

She tried to turn the handle again. Locked. She looked closer. Was it *glowing*?

Something hummed in the back of her skull, a begging to open the door.

If only she could turn the handle; if only it weren't locked. She needed to get inside, she must—

Hands shoved her from the door. 'Get *back*.'

Maeve gasped as someone pulled her upright and pushed her against the wall so hard her teeth knocked together. She closed her eyes against the light that marred her vision with streaks of black and blue. Hands held her against the wall as she fought to peel open her lids, finally succeeding.

The housekeeper stared back, eyes wild.

'What the *fuck* are you doing?'

7

Jude

Jude wasn't sure what had compelled him to leave his armchair that morning and head upstairs. He'd been sitting in what Elden liked to call a state of *forced peacefulness*, staring out at the moors and counting the birds with Olive curled up on his lap, when a prickle had started at the back of his neck. A prodding to investigate the whereabouts of his unwelcome houseguest. Since he'd deposited her in the spare room last night, he'd been trying very hard to forget her existence. Unfortunately, the sight of her soaked chemise and furious dark eyes had trailed him into sleep.

The house felt different with her in it. The silence felt louder. Heavier.

He liked his privacy. He liked routine and predictability. What he didn't like was meddling iconographers picking at the seams. He imagined he could hear her footsteps even through the layers of wood and stone separating them.

He couldn't take it any longer. Jude shoved to his feet and made for the stairs.

Panic overtook him as he found her room empty. Surely . . . *surely* she couldn't already be—

There, kneeling in front of the door to his library, was the iconographer. Her head was bowed over her hands braced on the wood, pale braid trailing down her back. Foreboding gripped his heart in an iron fist as he approached. There was no valid reason he could dream up that would compel Maeve to kneel at the door to his library. No reason she'd be so focused as to ignore his presence.

Unless. *Unless*—

He strode forward, grabbing her shoulders and pulling her back from the door. She went easily. Her eyes flashed wide, then squeezed shut, lips forming words he couldn't hear. Jude shoved his hand between her skull and the wall as her head jerked backwards. Fear dug claws into his spine at her slackened expression.

'What the *fuck* are you doing?'

Her raspy mumbles filled the space between them. He repeated his question louder, shaking her slightly. Maeve came back to herself with a sharp inhale. For an agonizing heartbeat, they stared at each other. Touching from chest to toe. Her face was so close he could see himself reflected in her near-black eyes. A vivid flush spread up her pale cheeks and down to the gaping collar of her nightgown.

He couldn't quite seem to separate his mind from his body – and his body was wholly preoccupied with the iconographer pressed against him. An insistent voice reminded Jude that it had been a very, *very* long time since someone he didn't know had touched him.

Maeve raised her hands, planting them on his chest, and shoved. 'Get *off*.'

Her braid whipped his face as she elbowed out of his hold. Without entirely thinking it through, he caught her by the upper arm and spun her back to face him as she tried to leave.

The back of his mind itched as he took in her face for the first time in the daylight. Her haphazardly braided hair, the skittishness in her darting eyes and heaving breaths familiar in a way he couldn't place. He could practically picture her on her knees again, an icon held to her lips.

Hate boiled his blood. What a perfect representation of the Abbey she was.

'What were you doing at the door?' Jude hissed.

She folded her arms over her chest, chin held high. 'Where are my clothes?'

He pulled his gaze to the ceiling. That thin white chemise was decidedly *not* typical Abbey attire. Especially not when the material had been near-translucent with rain the night before. He focused on the bite of his nails in his palm, remembering she didn't know who he was. Last night, she'd asked when she'd meet the *saint*, and he'd nearly laughed at the irony of it.

'How should I know?' he asked.

'Where. Are. My. Clothes?'

'An answer for an answer.'

Ire glinted in her eyes before she looked away. Like a moth to a flame, her gaze flicked back towards the door. Her chest rose and fell with a rough breath. 'What's in there?'

Her curiosity was like a hammer straight to the back of his skull. His skin prickled. It had to be a coincidence. She had to be interested in the library because it was locked, because it was a mystery she wanted to pry into. Because she was a fucking *spy*.

Not because of the magic. Anything but the magic.

Maeve brushed roughly past his shoulder, stirring his thoughts.

'You didn't answer me,' Jude said to her retreating back. He followed her two steps down the stairs and stopped. Her braid swung between her shoulders, thicker than his wrist.

'Neither did you,' she called

'Your bag is in the kitchen downstairs,' he said. 'Elden washed your clothes last night. You ought to thank him.'

Maeve stopped midway down the stairs, face ashen as she turned to look back at him. 'Elden?'

'The housekeeper,' Jude replied. He folded his arms across his chest as he waited for her reaction.

'The housekeeper,' she repeated, swallowing roughly. 'You're the saint . . .'

'I am.' His name hung in the space between them, heavy in the silence. 'Jude.'

'Jude,' Maeve echoed, softer than he thought she might. Her chest rose and fell with an unsteady breath. She gripped the railing tighter.

'Stay away from this floor,' Jude commanded when she didn't respond.

She gave a slight nod in acquiescence. Something small and miserable cowered in him at the sight of her lowered eyes. But as much as he hated his title, hated the way her eyes fell in deference, seeing her squirm wasn't a hardship.

Jude left before he could see her take another step away, heading back up the stairs. She could find her own way to the kitchen. Elden was sure to be waiting for her, probably with some half-burnt but doggedly well-meaning breakfast prepared alongside her bag.

The housekeeper had carefully gone through its contents that morning, washing her sodden clothes and arranging them by the fire to dry, carefully laying the paintbrushes on the windowsill so their bristles wouldn't bend.

And Jude had scoured through the rest.

Elden's disapproving glare had heated the back of his neck as he flipped through her sketchbook and opened a small enamel box containing a string of beads and several metal, coin-sized icons, the faces sloughed smooth from her touch. No doubt one of multiple coined icons. He used to find them everywhere at the Abbey, scattered like breadcrumbs.

Perhaps most importantly, he'd found a closed envelope tucked in a small pocket on the outside of the bag. He'd held it to the light, trying to read the contents with little success before tucking it into his jacket pocket when Elden wasn't looking.

He'd open it later – once he felt justified enough by her spying to do some prying of his own. Or once the rawness of the Abbey's violation grew too much to bear without striking back.

After glancing over his shoulder to ensure the iconographer had disappeared down the stairs, Jude opened the door to the library and stepped inside, locking it firmly behind him. The subtle flap of imagined wingbeats echoed in his thoughts as he closed his eyes.

The library drew a slow breath around him.

He was being inhospitable, but what did he care? The Abbey stood for two things: control and coercion. Despite their claims of offering their followers answers to prayers, they were little more than dressed-up executioners, pretending to set you free while tightening the noose. There was no other way to look at it – Maeve was naive and weak-minded to remain devoted.

Ánhaga curled tighter around him. He was still here, still alive. It might not be much, but to him, it was everything. He had his house, his cat. Elden. The smallest number of freedoms imaginable, but he wouldn't give them up without a fight. Even if he wanted to be free from the Abbey altogether, he'd settle for a return to his life before her arrival.

Jude would survive the Abbey's prying eyes. He would survive *her*.

He had to.

Much of his time at the Abbey had been lost to memory, but not everything. There were some things his mind refused to relinquish. The words pressed to his ear as a boy while hands held him flat to a stone floor, the smell of blood in the air, was one of them—

'*You have made your choice, Jude, and now you will reap the consequences.*'

8

Maeve

Maeve sagged against the wall at the foot of the stairs and shoved her hand into the pocket of her chemise. She just needed a little bit of comfort. Even a touch of the metal icon would be enough to soothe – until she remembered her favourite icon was in her cloak pocket, the rest still in her bag. She'd left it in a heap by the front door, hadn't she?

Embarrassment surged in. She couldn't *believe* how she'd treated Jude. He was still a saint, no matter what he'd been accused of. Every particle of her being screamed at her for the blatant disrespect she'd shown him. And in his own home, of all places. Whether or not he expected her piety – he had turned his back on sainthood, after all, let his magic become tainted – his position required deference. Her behaviour was a reflection of the Abbey. She couldn't bear the thought that she'd already displayed its image in such a sacrilegious light.

What must he think of her?

She'd tracked mud into the house and left the horse for him to care for, even asked him when she'd meet *the saint*. She refused to think about the reverence that had no doubt suffused her voice with that particular question.

Maeve shuddered. She'd *disrobed*.

The memories from the night prior were waterlogged and hazy, but she was confident he'd admonished her for her lack of self-awareness. A rebuke she'd most certainly deserved.

At least her chemise wasn't as sheer as it'd been last night.

She shoved the reminder firmly away as she peeled herself off the wall. If she was going to accomplish her tasks here, she couldn't allow herself to get caught up in mistakes she couldn't change. She could only move forward.

With that thought in mind, she followed the faint sound of rattling pots towards the kitchen.

The room was snug and humid, with warm wooden cupboards and an iron range topped with something faintly smoking. The fogged window looked out to a vegetable patch beyond and a greenhouse silhouetted against the gentle slope of the heather-laden moors. Beside the range, a man had his back to her, his entire focus on a knife clamped tightly in his left hand.

Maeve cleared her throat. 'Hello?'

He turned, knocking into a precariously balanced pitcher in the process. Milk slopped over the side of the blue and white ceramic. Maeve rushed to steady it, smiling at his hasty thanks.

He wiped his hands on a dishcloth before presenting one to her. His palm was warm and dry, enveloping hers completely. Sandy blond curls flopped over blue eyes as he smiled. She smiled back. He wasn't much taller than her, with shoulders broad enough to take up a doorframe. He looked around thirty, if not younger.

'Maeve, I'm guessing?'

She nodded, remembering the name Jude had given her. 'And you're Elden.'

'That I am.' He squeezed her hand one final time before releasing it. 'You've met him?'

'Last night,' she replied, not wanting to get into the specifics. 'I, ah – arrived quite late. He let me in. I think he stabled the horse, as well?'

Elden frowned. 'Don't have a stable. He must have taken it to the neighbours.'

Last night?

Maeve chewed her lip, remembering the intensity of the storm. She hadn't seen another home for miles. A dart of guilt ran through her stomach.

'How are you finding Ánhaga?' Elden asked, his thick northern accent rolling off the word.

'I haven't seen much of it so far. But it's, ah – very cosy.' Maeve paused awkwardly, wondering how to word her request. 'But I need to find a room to set up my things. Did Jude tell you I'm here to paint his icon?'

Elden nodded. He rolled his lips, studying her for a long moment. Abruptly, he turned away. 'I'll leave finding a room up to him.'

Somehow, she doubted the saint would be very helpful – not after their previous interactions, at least.

If Ánhaga had secrets tucked between its walls, she would have to do all the digging herself. Her first letter was due to Ezra before the end of the week, and if she knew him at all, tardiness would not be tolerated.

Maeve leaned against the butcher's block behind her, studying the stacks of colourful ceramic bowls, the chipped mugs. 'What does it mean, Ánhaga? I don't recognize the language.'

Elden picked up a spoon and swirled it into the pot on the range. 'It's an old language. I don't know much of it anymore.'

She noticed he didn't answer the first part of her question . . . had she offended him with it?

Once again, she cursed herself for her hasty tongue. How many times would she misstep before she found her footing? Her social skills were woefully rusty, grown almost entirely by brief interactions when she was allowed into Whitebury or short, monitored conversations at the Abbey. It was no wonder she could barely manage a straightforward exchange without putting her foot in it.

'Smells good,' Maeve said, drawing closer to peer into the stew cooking in the pot. 'I'm not a bad cook, you know . . . if you ever need any help?' Her voice drew embarrassingly high at the end.

'He won't.'

She spun around. The saint – *Jude* – leaned against the doorway, arms folded.

How long had he been listening in?

His resemblance to his boyhood icon was uncanny in the daylight, something she had missed in the exhaustion of last night. The same knife-sharp features and dark hair, shorn close to his skull, where it'd once been long enough to hold a curl. The same shifting hazel eyes, now bright with animosity where they'd held a careful blankness before.

Her gaze lingered on the slightly too-short crop of his trousers, the tightness of the material around his thighs as he moved towards her. The way the sleeves of his deep green knitted jumper were not quite long enough to reach the jut of his wrists.

A black cat swept in behind him, tail held high. Jude reached down and scooped her up against his chest. Without a word, he drew a spoon out of a cluttered drawer next to the range and swirled it through the broth, bringing it to his lips.

'Nice of you to introduce me to your guest,' Elden said. He sent a wink in Maeve's direction. She relaxed enough to smile back. She hadn't completely offended him, then.

Jude sprinkled in salt from a dish on the counter. 'She is *not*,' another pinch of salt, 'my guest.'

Her smile faded as fast as it had come.

She didn't know how to behave around him. Not even a little. He was so unlike Felix with his sweeping robes and unwavering distance. Nothing like the other saints she'd painted off description alone – always stoic, like they existed on some higher plane she hadn't a hope of reaching.

As they should be, in her opinion.

But Jude . . . he shocked her with the unabashed *humanness* of him. There was no other word for it. The way he moved, face twitching with displeasure as he tasted the stew. The irreverent words coming from his mouth, even the cat – none of it was as she'd expected.

He had betrayed the Abbey, Maeve reminded herself. The man before her had corrupted the magic he was *lucky* to be blessed with. She had made a promise to find out how. A promise she intended to keep.

'Jude's right,' she said, daring to draw her voice loud enough to break over their quiet bickering about the salt. 'I'm not his guest. The Abbey sent me to paint an updated icon.'

Jude deposited the cat on the floor with a pet down her back. He rose slowly, cocking his head as he considered her. 'An icon . . .'

'Yes. An icon.'

'Yet, you've spent your morning snooping around my house instead.'

Her first reaction was anger at the accusation in his tone. She stifled it quickly. She needed to tread carefully with him, that much was obvious. She didn't want to offend . . . well, maybe not *Jude*, but his position. His sainthood. Nor did she want him to question why she'd been kneeling at the door earlier, asking questions she herself didn't know the answer to.

Maeve dropped her eyes and lowered her voice, just as she'd been taught. 'My apologies. I was just trying to find my clothes.'

Elden pushed past Jude to hold out a large bag in her direction. Jude watched the bag pass into her hands with narrowed eyes. Her whole body relaxed at the touch of the worn leather.

'Thank you,' she murmured. She opened the bag, loosening a sigh of relief at the sight of her still tightly sealed palette. 'I was worried about my paints.'

'*Paints*,' Jude scoffed under his breath.

Elden ignored him. 'I gave your clothes a wash. The storm had done a number on them. They're drying on the rack by the fire, but I put some of Jude's old clothes in there you can wear in the meantime.'

Maeve's cheeks flushed at Jude's answering sound of derision. She looked closer at her bag now that some of her panic had subsided, running her fingers over a soft navy wool cardigan. It was a kind gesture, but in *no* world would she be wearing Jude's clothing.

'Thank you. I appreciate it.' She took a half step towards the doorway. 'Is there somewhere I can bathe?' she asked, directing her question towards Elden.

'Outside,' Jude replied.

'For the *love*—' Elden groaned, surprising her with his comfortable familiarity with the saint. 'I'll take you, Maeve. There's a bath near your room you're welcome to use.' He offered Jude an unimpressed glare as he moved towards the hall.

She met Jude's steady gaze, ignoring how it burned to do so. 'I'd like to begin your icon tomorrow. Does after lunch suit?'

'Tomorrow?' Jude tapped his chin. 'No, I have plans.'

Maeve tried to keep her expression neutral. 'The day after, then?'

'Let's make it the end of the week.'

She blew out a short breath from her nose. 'Fine. Yes. Good.'

'Wonderful.' A sharp-edged smile played at the corner of his mouth. 'I cannot wait.'

'Thank you,' she mumbled under her breath. The acerbity in his voice rankled.

To her surprise, Elden was grinning as he led her towards the front of the house. 'Jude likes to joke, but he's harmless.'

'It can't be easy having a stranger come into your home,' she offered as they ascended the stairs.

'No. Especially not for someone like him.'

'How do you mean?' Maeve asked, hoping her desperation for insights into Jude didn't show in her voice. More bare floorboards, empty walls, and closed doors surrounded them. Elden pushed open one near the end to reveal a clawfoot bath. She'd never seen such a welcome sight in her life.

'He's been here a long time,' Elden said, pulling open a cupboard and unearthing a towel. He paused, still facing the cupboard. His shoulder moved with a sigh. 'Well. Jude likes his routine.'

'Nothing wrong with a routine,' Maeve replied lightly. She liked Elden so far, but something told her his openness might recede if she pried too far. But she had a job to do. She needed to push him as far as she could. 'How long has he been here for?' she asked.

Elden glanced towards the open doorway, taking a half step towards it. 'Eight years, give or take.'

Eight years?

Did that mean he'd been, what . . . around fourteen when he'd been marked as a saint?

Veneration wasn't unheard of at such a young age, but their ability to answer prayers typically surfaced a bit later, closer to twenty. Intense study and mental pressure sometimes made it appear earlier, however. She wondered if that was what had happened to Jude. What elder had been the one to see the first signs of sainthood in him? Who had pushed the tattoo into his skin?

She pictured the last time she had witnessed a saint's veneration. A young woman. Her hair had been riotously curly, the light streaming in from the basilica's rose window catching on strands of gold amongst the deep brown. It had fallen across the elder's arm holding her down for the ritual tattooing. Her mouth had fallen open as the needle touched her skin, eyes closing. In bliss or agony, Maeve still wasn't sure. Maybe both.

She blinked the memory away. She hadn't seen the woman since. Hadn't even learned her name.

Sometimes, the newly marked saints stayed at the Abbey for months after veneration, other times they left right away. If they stayed, they no longer attended meals, prayers, intercessions . . . anything that allowed them a modicum of normality or community was stripped away. She always wondered what they were told to convince them to enter into such isolated lives, whether the exchange of community for sainthood was an easy one or simply a necessary sacrifice on their way to the Goddenwood where it would be repaid a hundredfold.

Maeve drew her attention back to Elden. 'Jude's been here the whole time?' she asked. 'Since his veneration?'

Elden fidgeted with the edge of the towel. 'Yes, I believe so. Although I've only been here a few years. I don't know what life was like for him before then.'

'Was he alone before? Do you know?'

Elden's face shuttered. 'Can't say I do.' He set the towel on a low stool by the tub. 'Need to get back to the stew before Jude ruins it.'

'Of course,' Maeve murmured, angry at herself for pushing too hard. She'd need to work more carefully next time. The last thing she wanted was for Elden to suspect anything. Jude's watchful eye was trouble enough. 'Thank you,' she repeated. 'For the bath. And the hospitality.'

Elden nodded, stepping into the hall. He held the door just before it closed. 'Perhaps it's best if you do your job and go home. Let Jude return to his routine. Yeah?'

Maeve flinched. 'Of course.'

Elden shut the door behind him. Maeve shut her eyes, lifting one hand to her chest to feel the movement of her breath. It didn't matter if she was wanted here. Didn't matter if she was liked. What mattered was the Abbey. Her tasks. Her icon.

She moved her hand up to cup her throat. No matter how practised she was in the motion, swallowing her desires never came any easier.

9

Maeve

The following days bled quickly from one to the next, and Maeve had yet to see Jude.

She'd caught glimpses of him. Remnants, like a smudge of ash after a fire. The edge of a black coat trailing around a corner. A half-finished cup of tea, still warm. His mud-covered boots left in a heap by the door. She told herself it didn't matter that he was avoiding her. It was the end of the week. He'd promised to show for his first sitting. She'd get her share of observing him then.

And observe him, she would.

She'd slept later than normal that morning. The small black cat, Olive, as she'd learned, had made a home curled at the foot of the quilt. She'd found a tray with slightly burnt toast, gooseberry jam, and cold tea waiting outside her door. Elden, no doubt.

Writing her initial letter to Ezra hadn't taken long. She didn't have much to report back yet besides the information she'd gleaned from Elden and her assurance that she was starting Jude's icon straight away. She added a few sentences detailing her journey and how she was settling in despite a small part of her whispering that Ezra would probably skip those parts, so why bother? She'd yet to sign it, hoping she'd have more to add after Jude's first sitting.

She'd spent the majority of her first week doing her best to search the house, partly to look for information and partly for a room to use as a studio. To her frustration, she'd only found one nearly empty room on the first floor that was unlocked, next to the mysterious door Jude had found her kneeling beside.

Inside, she'd pressed down on all the floorboards, picked at a loose curl of wallpaper, and examined every inch of skirting. There had been nothing more interesting than a child's worn rabbit toy tucked into the corner and a series of scratches on the windowsill that looked like words scrawled out. It was just her, a three-legged stool, and her paints.

Maeve placed her hand on the cold glass of the lone window. A band in her chest slowly loosened at the view before her. A stream cut steadily through two windswept hills, a lonesome oak silhouetted against the steel-grey sky. A formation of birds high above.

The cramped confines of the Abbey had always choked her, as much as she hated to admit it. She needed the cool air to ghost her skin unencumbered. It nurtured a certain wildness that all her years in the Abbey hadn't quite managed to stamp out.

Typical that she'd find that need for freedom sated *here* of all places.

She straightened her row of brushes on the windowsill as she waited. She'd completed dozens of paintings over the years. Most with little more than a short description.

Yet, the prospect of painting Jude seemed impossible.

A vindictive part of her wanted to paint him as some hideous beast rather than a man. Another pettier side of her wanted to paint him *just* off enough to make him doubt his appearance. Perhaps if she made him believe his outward looks matched the prickliness he'd shown her so far, she'd finally be satisfied.

Maeve sighed, pulling back from the glass. Her hand left a fogged print behind, fading more with each passing second. It had taken her longer to set up the makeshift studio than she imagined. Nightfall wasn't far off, and still no Jude. The light was starting to fade from the hills, ushering in a bruised purple dusk, highlighted with the deepest ochre.

The sight made her ache. A deep yearning for something she didn't have words for.

Maeve wondered if she was homesick.

She didn't like it here, didn't enjoy the unsettled feeling Jude's home forced upon her. She missed her room back at the Abbey, with all its familiar corners and smell of sea-soaked lavender. Perhaps that was what homesickness was – an itching desperation to return to steadier ground.

When she had left, she hadn't had time to consider how she would feel to be so far away from Ezra and the Abbey. It was like losing the heavy weight of a collar around her throat. Freeing, somewhat, but frightening. As though she could stumble at any moment.

She leaned her forehead back against the glass. It was time to face reality – Jude wasn't coming. She doubted he ever planned to.

A secret part of her was glad. She didn't want a repeat of whatever strange force had gripped her the last time she'd picked up a paintbrush. The buzzing in her skull, the liquid slip of time and memory . . . had it truly been Felix's magic at work? Was Jude capable of doing the same?

She considered the differences between Felix and the saint she'd been sent to paint. Was it blasphemous that she couldn't picture Jude as the saint he was? That maybe he wasn't so special after all?

Maeve shoved the thought from her head, feeling sick. She could not allow herself to harbour such thoughts, such doubts. Whatever had happened with her painting had been Felix alone. Felix the saint, with power too great for her to understand, its glory unknowable to an acolyte like her. Who was she to doubt how it worked? Who was she to claim blasphemy?

She pushed off the window and stumbled to her knees. Her breaths came in frantic pants as she shuffled forward until her bag was within reach. There was only one way to find the comfort she was so desperate for. Only one way to repent. She fished out one of her coin-like icons from her bag and held it to her lips, closing her eyes. The tattered edges of her heart chafed with guilt.

It's natural to question, Maeve told herself. *As long as it goes no further than questions.*

Picturing Felix's face, she asked for clarity. For peace of mind to finish her task and return home. To avoid the temptation to allow her questions to develop into doubts. To trust in *him*. In the Abbey, in Ezra and all the saints.

Almost all the saints.

A sudden wash of sunlight stained her vision red. She squeezed her eyes shut, bowing her head.

'You won't find what you're looking for here.'

Maeve jerked upright.

Jude leaned against the doorway. His lips curled in a sneer as he watched her scramble to her feet. 'Waiting a long time, were you?'

Saints, how he rankled her. She yanked her gaze to the window before she said something she'd regret. Why did he continue to defy her every expectation? Was it not enough to curse the power he was gifted, he needed to turn his back on sainthood all together? Had he no respect, no piety left in him? Not even towards the Abbey, but towards his position. His *gift*.

'You're late,' Maeve said in a low voice. Her nails bit into her palms.

Jude's prowling steps were silent on the wooden floor. 'Why are you *here*? In this room.'

Her heart rabbited in her chest. What was so special about this room? 'Am I not allowed here, Jude?' He flinched at his name on her lips, and Maeve wondered how often he heard it.

'No,' he replied. 'You're not.'

'Why not?'

'It's *my* house. You're not welcome here. Especially not this room.' His eyes pierced hers as he moved closer. 'You come to my house, believing your lies, cradling your beliefs to your chest like they're something sacred, but you know nothing about me and nothing about sainthood. And I want you gone.'

'That's just too bad, isn't it?' Maeve hissed. 'The Abbey sent me here to paint you, and—'

'The *Abbey*,' Jude spat. 'Fuck the Abbey.'

Shock suffused her chest, as breathtaking as ice water. The fact he was a saint was lost on her. At that moment, he was nothing more than a man stoking the coals of her anger with careless abandon. He didn't respect his position, *fine*. If he didn't respect it, why should she? What demanded that she bow her head towards a station he eschewed with every fibre of his being? When he mocked not only the system they were both a part of but her entire life?

'Do *not*—'

'And another thing,' Jude interrupted. Spots of colour bled into his pale cheeks. 'Don't pray in my home. I don't want to *see* your icons, let alone come into *my* room, in *my* house, and see you on your knees like some perfect acolyte, willing to do whatever the Abbey asks just to reassure yourself that you're doing the right thing. Keep it away from me.'

He shook his head in a way that seemed both patronizing and pitying all at once. 'Aren't you just so obedient? Running when they call. Painting whoever they ask. Such a good little acolyte, to pray when commanded.' He stepped closer, the space between them growing remarkably short of air. His hazel eyes glinted with barely restrained fury. 'Is it really devotion when the fear of refusal is woven into every verse? One misstep, one question too far and it's gone. And you're left with nothing and no one.'

Maeve froze for one long, horrible second.

Nothing, *nothing* could have prepared her for him.

She drew in a breath. 'Just like you, then?'

Jude flinched. Hurt crossed his face one moment, gone the next.

Maeve held her icon up between them. '*This* is none of your business. I don't care why you hate the Abbey. I don't care that you hate yourself more. I have every right to be here.' His nostrils flared, but she wasn't finished. 'I'll paint your icon and leave. You'll go back to being alone.'

Suddenly, the harsh edges of his face briefly softened into something like baffled shock. He took a quick, uneven step back. Maeve lurched towards him in response, thinking he was stumbling. Her reaching hand froze in mid-air.

'Don't,' Jude said, the softness in his voice more shocking than the sharp edge before. 'Don't come any closer. Don't touch me.'

Before she could reply, he turned on his heel and left.

10

Jude

The moors weren't providing the solace they usually did. The edges of the orchard transformed into a skeletal forest in the purpling dusk as Jude fought to keep his jacket on his shoulders against the wind. He ripped it off and crumpled it in his fist after the corner of his collar snagged on a bough for the third time.

Fuck.

The vision of the iconographer staring up at him with those night-pressed eyes, the icon held between them like she was trying to ward him off, wouldn't leave his mind. It was a simple request: don't pray in his home. Her reaction had been entirely uncalled for.

He hadn't planned on attending the portrait sitting. That icon would *never* be painted if he had anything to say about it. He'd rather return to the Abbey himself and face them head-on than let the elders renew their link to him.

Even if seeing her paint could provide answers on how the elders accessed the saints' magic or how to get it back, two questions he desperately needed to work out. But Jude had become extremely adept at ignoring that cloying voice of reason. He'd ask her questions when he was ready and not a second sooner. And preferably by not risking his mind and his magic.

No, it wasn't his rational side that had urged him upstairs, but the restlessness under his skin at the thought of her waiting for him at all.

Finding her in the room where he had spent his first few years of exile had been an unwelcome surprise. Her things arranged beside the small plush toy he'd spent hours talking to because there was no one else. The windowsill where he'd carved his name over and over because he was afraid of forgetting it, only to scratch over it the day after. The window that had reflected his tear-stained eyes on countless lonely evenings. He'd left that small bedroom behind when Elden had arrived. The sight of Maeve in it had been a shock. Seeing her on her knees even more so.

'I'll paint your icon and leave. You'll go back to being alone.'

Frustration lined his throat. He'd spent too many years convincing himself he was okay for her to shake him like she was. Walking the halls of his home like he was searching for meaning, his footsteps against the dust the only sign he had a body.

At first, he'd waited, sure that someone would come for him, to return him to the Abbey, to the only home he'd ever known. A little over five years ago, he began having entire conversations aloud. He had three years of isolation under his belt by then. Formative, crucial years. Years when he grew taller, his voice deeper, his moods unwieldy and confusing. He'd stopped hoping, stopped waiting. His hope had eroded, slowly and steadily, into hatred.

No one was coming for him.

He'd spent years tallying the days on the wall to prove to himself the passage of time. Sitting by the gate for hours on the days food was delivered, hoping to have a brief conversation with the farmer who brought his provisions. Eventually, he'd taken to marking the months on his skin.

The tattoos had helped at the beginning. An upside-down symbol for saint pushed into his forearm to mirror the one on his chest, gone over so many times with the needle and thick black ink that it took weeks to heal, only for him to open it back up again. Tallies on his stomach for each month he continued to spend alone. Signs for piety and devotion, for commitment and loyalty.

Jude was Abbey-trained in illuminations, after all. Scribing was in his blood.

Finding the library had helped somewhat. It had answered some questions. The collection of holy tomes inside rivalled that of the Abbey itself. It was there Jude first learned how to forge a connection between his tenuous magic and the seemingly endless supply of blank-paged books, the paper thicker and more textured than the Abbey texts. Books that his magic had slowly filled up with memories transcribed into runic words only he could read.

During the darkest years of his tenancy, when he felt like his mind was a bed of quicksand, eager to swallow him whole, the library was the only place that made him feel safe. The only place he felt like he wasn't an abomination.

The year he turned twenty, he'd had enough. He'd refused to pray, taking to paper instead. Writing to the Abbey had cost him something, but he knew he wouldn't survive another year if he didn't beg for company, for a looser rein.

He'd tried to run, once. Five years ago. The farmer who brought his food had stopped him an hour into his trek into the moors. Beaten him so severely he hadn't been able to bear weight on his right leg for months. His ribs still ached when the weather grew cold.

Jude never saw that farmer again. His food was delivered by someone else, their eyes just as watchful, just as cold. Whether or not the new stranger worked for the Abbey didn't matter, the lesson was the same: if he ran, the Abbey would find him. The punishment would be swift and merciless.

He had braved his first journey to Oakmoor on the day he

mailed the letter, checking over his shoulder so often he'd developed a crick in his neck. Up until then, he'd been too afraid to visit the village – terrified of being recognized, of being sent back. He'd been stared at, as any stranger would in a small village, but nothing more, to his relief. The Abbey had taken their time with a reply, but Elden had shown up shortly after.

After Elden's arrival, Jude was able to leave Ánhaga for longer and longer stretches. He could visit Oakmoor, walk in the surrounding moors. His mind felt clearer, too. The press on his memories less intense.

Another reason Jude suspected Maeve was here to spy. If the Abbey's hold on him was slipping, they'd do anything to renew their grasp on his magic.

His thoughts settled firmly on the iconographer. More specifically, what he had seen at the end of their confrontation. For a moment, as she had stood before him, practically vibrating with anger, she'd *glowed*. It had pushed the tide of his fury back long enough for him to look at her not as an interloper or an Abbey spy but as a woman set adrift.

As the shape of her body had been limned with gold, he saw himself reflected on her face.

Jude had been that devout once.

He'd believed in the saints as much as every other Abbey acolyte. He'd spent his days in the scriptorium, copying the texts and learning the art of illuminations. Prayer had been his closest companion. He'd waited eagerly for the day a saint would be venerated, hopeful he could be the one to copy it in their history books. He'd been no less devoted than Maeve. Until the world started glowing gold, he'd expected to live and die at the Abbey.

How stupid he had been to believe at all.

Jude turned back towards Ánhaga. His refuge, his prison. He rubbed over the tattoo on his chest, staring at the bright windows on the second floor. If he looked close enough, would he see her there, in the bedroom that was so close to his? Would she be watching him just as he watched her?

He didn't regret the altercation in his former bedroom, but avoiding her had been a mistake.

Entering the house, Jude followed the smell of cooking towards the kitchen. Their voices hit him first, and he paused in the shadow of the doorway to listen. Maeve's voice came through first, clear as a bell, that perfect enunciation just as grating as the first time he'd heard it.

'How did you end up here?' she asked over jostling pans.

Elden didn't reply. Jude breathed a sigh of relief.

Footsteps, light and careful, before Maeve continued, 'Sorry. How did—'

'I heard you.' Elden set down the pan with a rattle. Jude wrinkled his nose at the smell of burning onions. Elden didn't have the patience for caramelization. 'Only . . . well. I don't remember, exactly.'

Jude tensed. He eased closer to the doorway.

'You don't *remember*?' Maeve prodded. 'How long have you been here?'

Elden sighed. Somewhat concerning that Jude recognized the sound as his resigned sigh rather than his frustrated one. 'A little under three years, maybe?'

'And is that usual for you? Not remembering things?'

No. Absolutely not.

Jude strode into the room, focus immediately landing on the iconographer. 'Making yourself right at home, aren't you?' he asked. She whipped around to face him, a guilty look in her eyes. *Good.* She should feel guilty. 'Would you like to search his bedroom while you're at it? Maybe follow him into the bath?'

'Jude—' Elden started.

He shoved open the door leading to the garden. 'What a lovely few days you've had, getting your meals brought to you, your clothes washed. Sleeping late into the afternoon.' Jude pointed towards the far corner of the vegetable patch in the distance. Last night's rain had turned it into more a mud patch than anything fit for growth. 'Elden and I are going out. Go pick some potatoes.'

Maeve shut her mouth with a snap. To his surprise, she picked up a trowel from a bucket beside the door. Vivid red spread from her cheeks down her throat, disappearing down the neck of one of those *damn* chemises. Clearly, his clothes Elden had given her weren't good enough.

'Is that all?' she asked, lifting her chin.

'Some parsley. From the greenhouse.'

'Wonderful.'

Maeve turned on her heel and disappeared into the rain, trowel tight in her white-knuckled grip. Jude watched her go. A small spark of admiration lit his chest, quickly extinguished.

'Well,' Elden said, chuckling. 'That didn't go as you planned, did it?'

Jude shook his head. 'Come on. Let's go to market.'

'The *market*,' Elden repeated, sceptical. 'What for? I was already in Oakmoor this morning.'

Jude slid the cover off a basket on the counter, a small smile tugging at his lips at the sight of the potatoes he'd harvested a few days prior nestled alongside a neat pile of foraged mushrooms. 'I have a few things to sell.'

The weekly market in Oakmoor was a sordid affair Jude usually left up to Elden. He had a knack for fetching the best prices on their produce and tea blends – probably down to his glowing personality or ability to hold a conversation without wanting to run away. At any rate, he seemed to enjoy the gaggles of grandmothers picking at his business more than Jude.

Jude sifted through the mushrooms, all too aware of the eyes tracking his every movement. If he bruised a single wood blewit, Celia would have his head. He selected the largest and presented it to the elderly woman. She peered at it through milky grey eyes. 'Hm. Small this year, no?'

'Small? It's bigger than my hand.' Jude lifted the mushroom higher to examine it. *Small.*

Celia raised a sparse brow. 'As I said.'

He laid another mushroom beside the offending one. 'Two for one, then.'

Celia had them tucked away and was shuffling over to Elden before Jude could even blink. He sighed, picking up the coins and watching her laugh at something the other man said.

Another customer approached the stall. Jude's gaze immediately alighted on the Abbey sigil swinging from the man's neck as he pointed to a mushroom in Jude's basket.

Sweat slicked his hands, trembling as he wrapped the mushrooms carefully in parchment paper and handed the man his change. Ruddy hair fell across his brow, a deep crease between his eyes.

A villager, Jude told himself. A pious stranger. *Nothing more.*

'The frost looks early this year, eh?' the man said. His smile faded when Jude didn't reply. 'Well then. All the best.'

Geoff. His name was Geoff. Jude had seen him before at the pub. He played the fiddle.

He watched Geoff walk away as disgust rolled in his belly. Why did he have to be so fucking *skittish* all the time? It was off-putting. He turned his face to the sky. Rain misted his skin in a clarifying baptism. What a mess he was.

He blew out a rough breath. He knew exactly who to blame for his heightened nerves.

She was ruining him. Finding the paranoia he thought long buried and unearthing it, one agonizing inch at a time. She'd already consumed his thoughts; soon, his mind would go, his tenuous grip on self and purpose. Nothing was sacred. Nothing was his own.

It was only *her.*

The iconographer, the woman sent to torment him.

A sudden clamour across the square pulled his attention from his rolling thoughts.

A man had pushed himself up on the lip of the long-dormant fountain, his hands waving in the air as he shouted. 'Pilgrimage ampulla! Pilgrimage ampulla sold here,' he cried. Jude stiffened as he reached into his bag and held out a scuffed metal object cupped in his palm – a tin vessel containing a small measure of holy water, marked with the Abbey's sigil. 'The winter intercession is mere weeks away. Get your name on the attendance list today. Do not delay!'

Jude spun, putting his back to the Abbey man before he had to see the crowds rushing forward. Even still, he heard their rising voices, the sound of money exchanging hands.

A squeal of pain had him glancing over his shoulder. A fair-haired woman had pushed the Abbey man against the wall and was begging him – fervently, *desperately* – for something. She no doubt thought the Abbey member could answer prayers. She dug her nails into the man's neck, drawing a ruby flash of blood. He finally succeeded in throwing her off him and onto the muddied ground. She cried out as someone's foot landed hard on her arm.

Jude winced, returning his focus to the wall behind his stall and tried to focus on his scorn and not the insidious press of fear. Her fanatical beliefs would only bring her more pain. He couldn't help her, couldn't help *any* of them, even if he wanted to.

Still – her squeal of pain echoed in his ears.

He never should've come to the market. It wasn't safe; nowhere was. If the villagers reacted with near-violent interest to a mere Abbey layman, how would they treat Jude? Would he find himself slammed against the wall, pummelled until he answered their prayers? Something even worse?

He'd never seen a pilgrimage guide in Oakmoor. He knew

what they were, of course – Abbey members who travelled from town to town gathering people who wished to make the trek to the Abbey for the seasonal intercessions – but try as he might, he couldn't remember what happened at the intercessions. Based on the zealous reaction from the crowd, it must have been something important.

Jude closed his eyes as the voices grew louder. He hadn't realized so much of Oakmoor's feeble population was devout. His fragile sense of safety cracked even further.

A hand touched his shoulder.

Jude shuddered, ducking out of it to see Elden watching him, his hand hovering in the air. He cocked his head. 'Ready? We should leave before things get more . . .' he frowned at the tightly packed crowd. 'Aggressive.' When Jude didn't reply, he lifted a jar of fogged amber honey. 'Your favourite. Celia gave it to me for you.'

Jude looped his basket over his arm. 'Why not just give it to me directly?'

'Maybe the endless glowering put her off,' Elden replied, softening his words with a smile.

The rain had slowed to a ponderous drizzle as they made their way back, the noise of the crowd slowly fading behind them.

Jude was stewing. He couldn't help it. Despite the atmosphere he'd just left, no part of him wanted to return to the house. He knew he should pick at Maeve a little more, see what he could find out from her iconography knowledge, but the thought of spending time with her made his skin crawl. He didn't like the perceptiveness in her dark eyes.

Didn't like it *one bit*.

Elden snagged the sleeve of Jude's coat as they came across the low stone bridge that marked the final leg of the walk back to Ánhaga, pulling him to a stop. Jude raised a brow, carefully extracting himself from Elden's touch. 'Yes?'

'Maeve,' Elden began, voice as slow and steady as ever. 'The iconographer.'

'I know her name.'

Elden's expression pinched. 'You know she's been . . . exploring. The house, that is.'

Jude crossed his arms as tension skittered down his spine. He clenched his jaw. He wouldn't dignify Elden with a response.

Elden seemed to be of the same mind. He studied Jude, brow raised expectantly. His oilskin coat was misbuttoned, longer on the right side than the left. Jude's chest cinched tighter the longer he looked at the man he'd tentatively begun to view as an irritating older brother.

The silence stretched. Jude shifted, uncomfortable.

Finally, Elden sighed. 'Every room you didn't lock, she's been inside.'

Jude turned his gaze to the hills. Geoff was right. The frost would come early this year.

'Jude?' Elden prodded.

'I know she has,' he replied.

'Does it not bother you?'

Jude huffed out a laugh. 'Of course it does.'

'I think . . .' Elden paused for a long moment. 'I think her being here is a good thing. Maybe.'

'*How?*' Jude asked incredulously.

'You've been away from the Abbey a very long time,' Elden replied. 'You've been *here* a long time.'

'So have you.'

Elden nodded. The line between his brows deepened as he stared down at his feet. Worry suffused Jude's chest. The Abbey already had their claws in Jude, and he would be damned if they dug them any deeper into Elden. He couldn't allow Maeve's questioning to continue.

'So have I,' Elden echoed. 'But that's not what I mean.'

Honestly. Jude started walking. Mud splashed up his legs with every step.

'She's fragile,' Elden called. 'More than you think. It reminds me of you when I first arrived.'

Jude stopped walking. Closed his eyes. Without quite thinking about it, he placed his hand over his right hip and squeezed. The symbol marked there – BELONGING – was one of the first he tattooed.

Elden laid a hand on his shoulder, the kind of casual touch Jude usually only allowed after careful consideration. Now, it just made him grit his teeth.

'She's searching for a safe place to land. Whatever happened at the Abbey to make her leave, whatever she's searching for here, I don't think it's just information on you. I don't think it's just to paint an icon, despite what she might say.'

'You think she's searching for something?' Jude retorted, turning to face Elden. The other man's hand dropped off his shoulder.

'Of course she is,' Elden replied. 'Whatever she's putting in those letters—'

'Letters?'

Before Elden could elaborate, Jude spun on his heel and made for the postbox nailed into the gatepost. It would be collected tomorrow morning if he had his dates correctly. If Maeve *had* left a letter there for the Abbey, it would still be inside. Vaguely, he heard Elden call his name as he wrenched open the metal door to the little cubby.

A single white envelope lay inside.

Jude shoved it in his pocket.

Elden arrived, breath puffing in a cloud in front of him as he stared down at where Jude's hand disappeared into his coat. 'Show it to me,' he said, nothing in his voice a question.

For an agonizing second, Jude debated ignoring his demand and leaving, but the last thing he wanted was for Elden to be on the spying iconographer's side and not his. Sighing, Jude pulled out the letter and flipped it over to read the address. 'Maeve's letter to the Abbey. It's addressed to a man called Ezra. Probably her mentor.'

Elden didn't reply. His gaze was fixed doggedly on the envelope.

Jude scowled. Leave it to Elden to disapprove when he was the one who had given him the idea in the first place. He turned back towards the waiting house. 'I'll let you know if I find anything interesting,' he called.

Elden's reply was lost to the wind.

11

Jude

Candlelight cast long shadows over Jude's desk late the following day. Each score across the wood stood out in sharp relief. Crude etchings, mostly of what he saw from his window. Apples and blackbirds and falling leaves.

Jude smoothed his hand over the crisp white envelope before turning it over. It was different than the letter he'd stolen from the iconographer's bag, the one he'd yet to find the courage to open. It had taken him nearly a day to work up the nerve to open this one as it was. The paper was thicker, the edges neatly creased. *Ezra* was written on the front above the address. No surname, no craft delineation. Just a name. Most likely her mentor, as he'd told Elden. An Abbey elder.

Abbey members abandoned their surnames when they entered as children. Jude didn't remember what his had been, let alone anything about his parents or childhood before the Abbey. He might as well have been born there for all he could recall, carved from the walls themselves.

If Maeve had been writing to a fellow acolyte, their craft would have been written below their name. If anyone had thought to write to him during his years at the Abbey, it would've arrived labelled *Jude — illuminations*, to mark his years learning the craft of embellishing manuscripts. A title that had been stripped from him the second he was shunted from their fold.

Unlike the letter he'd stolen from her bag, he didn't hesitate to pull this one free of its envelope.

She'd written it – written about *him*. He had every right to look. He lined the bottom edge up neatly with the edge of his desk. He would read what she reported and decide where to go from there. Nothing rash. Nothing without thought.

Nodding to himself, Jude focused on the page and began to read.

Ezra,

I hope you're doing well and the preparations for the winter intercession have not been too tiresome. I dearly hope to be home for it, especially if you are leading some of the hymns this year.

Jude rolled his eyes. She might as well get down and lick his boots herself at this rate.

Despite the rain, the journey went smoothly. I've started on the preliminary sketch for Jude's icon and hope to begin the underpainting next week. He's not been the easiest to work with so far, but I am confident I will have his icon ready for you before the end of the year.

In regards to my other task—

Jude is very isolated and appears markedly lonely, with little contact with life outside his home. The house contains no icons, no Abbey sigils or symbols, and no obvious signs of his ability. The housekeeper, a man called Elden, seems to remember little from his time before Jude, outside of a few years spent as a woodsman, though I am sure he is purposefully concealing things from me. I will do my best to find and relay more information on him and Jude.

While Jude's daily routine holds little variety, he frequently disappears to a room he always keeps locked. I'm curious to discover what lies inside, as I fear it may be important. I aim

to discover what's inside it before my following report – hope-
fully, it holds answers to how he's corrupting his magic.

The paper creased with the force of his grip. The magic *Jude*
corrupted? Was that what they'd told her? That he had been the
one to taint his abilities? Not the Abbey with their greedy fingers,
their poisonous touch? Fury pulsed in his chest at the blatant lie.
Somehow, they kept finding new and creative ways to surprise
him.

He blew out a slow breath, forcing himself to keep reading.
His eyes skimmed down the page. Her handwriting abruptly
changed from even, albeit messy, penmanship to an outright
scrawl. Ink splatters marred the page.

Jude shows a remarkable lack of respect towards the Abbey
and the saints' glorious magic, bordering on outright hatred.
I'm more convinced than ever that he's hiding something. I will
report back within the week.
    By the saints—
    Maeve

Well.

Jude leaned back in his chair. So, his suspicions were correct.
She was a spy, after all. He shouldn't be surprised. Of course,
her presence here would serve a dual purpose.

Iconographers were fundamental to the Abbey, perhaps even
more so than just as artists. They would never force one away
unless they were desperate . . . and they must *really* be desperate
to have an updated icon of him to choose Maeve, of all people.
At her age, she would've completed all her training to be a fully
fledged iconographer, and the Abbey didn't have many of those.
To send one all the way out here . . .

But why now? Had something changed to renew their interest
in him?

His eyes returned to the page.

Jude is very isolated and appears markedly lonely.

He pushed to his feet and paced from one end of the room to the other. His lungs felt tight, his throat constricted. He yanked the collar of his jumper roughly to the side and peered down at the tattoo just below his left collarbone, tucked into the soft hollow where his shoulder met his chest. A vertical line bisected by three horizontal.

SAINT.

His first tattoo and the only one he hadn't inked himself.

The memory of its inking was another that refused to leave. The hands holding him down, the burning pain. The praying and chanting and fevered voices—

Jude traced the symbol with shaking fingers and resisted the urge to get the supplies to push it deeper into his skin.

If he was lonely and isolated, it was because they made him so. If he was bitter, it was *their* doing.

Instead, he reached beneath the lip of his desk for the tin box he kept wedged there, full of cigarettes he stole from Elden, the dried plant inside one he grew in their greenhouse. The flame from his match sent wavering pools of gold into the furthest reaches of his vision. He'd smoked regular cigarettes before, in a previous life where filching them from townspeople was the height of rebellion. Elden's didn't taste as he remembered, nor did the swirling wave he had come to associate with the herbal taste lend itself to tobacco or clove.

The pressure under his skin slowly receded, just as he had hoped.

Once his mind settled, he would confront her. He needed to approach her carefully, and a repeat of the heated argument in his former bedroom was the furthest thing from careful.

Jude tipped his head back and exhaled a stream of smoke into the air.

Ideas swirled and dipped on a gust of wind. He took another

drag and thought of a bird as it plummeted towards earth, safe in the confidence of its wings.

He set the cigarette on the tin's lid.

It had done its job – he was ready to open the second letter.

Maeve hadn't noticed he had stolen the letter from her bag. It had been tucked into a pocket along the side, the buckle stiff with disuse. Maybe she hadn't even known it was there at all, secreted away for her to find on her arrival.

Pity, Jude thought as he laid it atop her letter to Ezra. It was his now.

Only her name was written across the front, no craft. The envelope was crinkled and water-stained but still sealed with the Abbey's sigil of hands cupped around a sun.

He wanted to open it – badly.

But something stopped him. Not quite the jaded sense of morality that still lived inside him, but close. A recognition that the letter wasn't for him to read, at least not yet. The one he'd stolen from the mailbox had been about him. He'd been right to open it. But this one . . .

Discomfort tightened his chest. It crawled up his throat and lingered heavy on his tongue. The smoke swirling in his thoughts made cutting through the chaff easier than normal, erasing the ever-present edge of anxiety that hounded him like a hungry dog.

Had he reached the point where he wanted to take a step he couldn't draw back from?

He wasn't sure. Not yet, at least.

He wasn't regretful he had taken the letter, but equally, he wasn't ready to open it. Not while he still had his own questions. Questions around her craft, around her beliefs, her reliance on prayer.

The smallest embers of hope stirred freshly in his chest.

If he could discover how the elders accessed the magic within the icons, he would be one step closer to breaking the link. He wouldn't need to protect his mind or his memories, wouldn't have to live in fear of losing control. His life would be his own.

Perhaps the iconographer had the answers.

In the edge of his vision, his reflection wavered.

Jude spun slowly to look himself in the eye. For a moment, the candlelight formed a corona around his head. A golden halo of light, marking him as something holy. A vision he only saw when he let himself smoke. He could never decide if he loved it or hated it.

He blinked, and it was gone.

Was that how she'd paint him if she had the chance? Would she pick up her brushes and show him not as he was, a ghost of a man who trod too lightly to leave footprints behind, but as a saint? She was sure to be talented. All Abbey iconographers were.

It would be a masterful rendition, even if it was blasphemous.

He wanted to pick her apart. Parse through the shroud of devotion and misplaced faith until he discovered what she knew.

Was she aware of the power she held when she put brush to canvas? Was there something *purposeful* she did when she painted that linked the saint's magic to their icon, some process he could disrupt that would free his magic from the Abbey's hold?

If the Abbey had an icon of a saint, they could access their magic. In return, the saint would lose their memories, draining them like water from a well. The iconographer had a part to play in it; so did prayer. What it was, he wasn't yet sure.

Jude drifted his fingers through the candle's flame as the smoke fogged his mind.

His magic flew restlessly under his skin, searching for an outlet. He hadn't visited the library for more than solace since Maeve's arrival. He should, he *needed* to, but the idea of allowing himself that kind of vulnerability while she was mere walls away was unfathomable.

Light flashed behind his closed lids. If he accidentally touched

Elden now, his magic would eat into his memories with a voracity Jude couldn't control.

Corruption of his holy magic, indeed.

If only Maeve knew the truth – he wasn't the one doing the corrupting.

He scrubbed his eyes, loosening a groan. He couldn't move smoothly until he dealt with her.

First, he needed to destabilize her foundation. The idea made him feel strangely guilty – he didn't *like* having to poke and prod at her beliefs. But she wouldn't help him look for answers if she was still confident in the Abbey, in what she'd been taught. Jude needed to be certain of the solidness of her beliefs before he sought to shake them.

He rose to his feet, extinguishing the cigarette on the tin lid.

He could give her a few choice bits of information if it would help him discover if she knew anything about the link between her craft and prayers, her paintings and magic. As long as the Abbey didn't catch wind of his library, of how he'd learned to store his memories somewhere they couldn't be reached, he would be safe.

Nothing, *nothing* was more important than getting her out of his house.

Whatever it took.

12

Maeve

Maeve was back in the room she'd commandeered as a studio when Jude materialized in the open doorway. Olive wound between his legs. She set about sniffing her painting things with her tail held high. Maeve stiffened at the sight of him. It had taken ages yesterday to dry her hair after the potato debacle. 'What do you want?'

'May I come in?'

She swept her hand across the space. 'By all means. It is *your* house, after all.'

To her surprise, Jude walked to the centre of the room, bent his knees, and sat right in front of her stool. Flickering light from the oil lamp licked at his features. Olive jumped onto Jude's folded legs and began kneading at his thigh.

They stared at each other, neither willing to break the tenuous silence.

Maeve leaned forward to rest her hands on her knees, wondering what he saw when he looked at her. Not the bedraggled traveller the storm had spat onto his doorstep. Not the furious acolyte holding an icon to his face. Not even the woman kneeling before a locked door, her mind awash with gold. She didn't want to be any of those things. She wanted to be a portrait, distant and untouched by worry, doubt, or fear. Something she would never be.

Sometimes, when Maeve felt weak and alone, she wondered

if she knew herself at all or if she was simply a combination of everything people had told her she ought to be.

'I have a few questions, if you don't mind,' Jude said into the quiet.

'Politeness doesn't suit you.'

The corner of his mouth quirked up. 'I beg to differ.'

His mood had shifted dramatically from the tightly wound frustration she'd seen in the kitchen. Something was different about him. He seemed . . . lighter. She noted the redness lining his eyes and how he pressed his lips together as if forcing himself into silence. He looked towards the ceiling as though trying to avoid her scrutiny. The movement reminded her of a guilty child, and she found a raspy laugh bubbling to her lips. '*What* have you been smoking?'

Jude blinked rapidly, one hand pressing against the centre of his chest. 'Me?'

She fought a smile. She'd seen behaviour like his before. Growing up, some of the older boys at the Abbey had made a habit of sneaking back from trips to Whitebury with faces just like Jude's – a little too happy, a little too loose. She'd questioned them once, suspicious at their seemingly uncontrollable laughter and jealous of the obvious, and *illicit*, friendship between them. One of the boys had drawn the offending substance from behind his back and let her try for herself. Maeve didn't like how it had made her feel, but clearly, that wasn't a problem for Jude.

She found she liked this improved version of the saint.

'I'm just happy you're not shouting at me again,' Maeve said.

For the first time, Jude smiled fully. He had dimples on either side of his mouth. Charming things that softened the harsh lines of his face into something almost handsome. Shame she'd never see them again. His skin was smooth in the warm light, emphasizing the cut of his cheekbones and his closely shorn dark hair. Stubble lined the edge of his jaw. Maeve begrudgingly admitted he had a certain appeal if one was partial to sharp-edged men with soft mouths.

Which she was not.

'It'll wear off soon,' he said. 'Best enjoy it while it lasts.'

She nodded. 'What is it you'd like to ask me?'

'It's about the Abbey.'

Maeve tightened her hands into fists on her knees. 'If you're going to make fun of me again, you might as well just leave.'

He shook his head, lifting his hands out in her direction. His palms bore faint white scars scored through the middles. 'No. No, I just want to clarify a few things, if I may.'

She didn't *want* to say yes, not when she knew how touchy Jude could be with Abbey-related topics, but they needed to have this conversation eventually. She didn't like feeling as though he hated her. If she were to spend any length of time in his home, she'd rather it be in a state of tentative truce.

Maeve smoothed both hands over her thighs. 'Fine.'

'I'm curious about your prayers,' he said. 'I'd like to know how you've seen them answered. And how you make your requests when you pray.'

'Shouldn't you know, considering you're the one who receives the prayers?' Maeve asked, surprising herself with her candour. 'Besides, you made it *very* clear I was not to pray in your home.'

'Because I'm asking nicely,' Jude offered with a smile.

She huffed a breath. 'I pray by first choosing an icon—'

'How?' he interrupted. 'How do you choose which icon to pray to?'

What he was asking felt private. Exposing. 'I just do. Whichever one I feel like that day.'

His brows shot up. 'Not the same one every day, then?'

'No . . . Well, sometimes. It depends.'

'On what?'

At this, she finally gave in to her frustration and tossed her hands into the air. 'I don't see how that's relevant. I let the saints lead me, okay? I listen to which icon calls to me. Sometimes, it's because of their expression – if I'm searching for peace or reassurance, I'll pray to someone who looks inclined to give it. Is that enough information for you?'

Jude's eyelashes cast long spikes down his cheeks as he tilted his head back. 'And how do they answer?'

'How?' she clarified.

He nodded. 'A specific instance, maybe. Anything that comes to mind.'

Discomforted by his questions and determined not to answer, Maeve studied the stretch of his legs occupying the space between them, counted the slats of the floorboard between his thighs. His black trousers were a shade too short on his long legs, the hems splattered with mud. Jude shifted under the weight of her eyes. Olive jumped off his lap, clearly unhappy with his fidgeting.

'Maeve.'

She didn't want to answer him.

The silence stretched.

Maeve shifted, uncomfortable. Finally, she sighed. 'I can't see why that's important, or why you need to know. You're not a part of the Abbey anymore. The saints answer our prayers everyday. There is always food on the table. Droughts never last for long and the waves never breach our walls. Even the influenza steers clear.' She met his penetrating gaze with one of her own, vowing to be just as sharp, just as unyielding. 'That's enough for me. Faith is believing in the unexplainable. That includes both the mundane and the miraculous.'

'Specifics,' Jude pressed, ignoring everything she just said. 'What do you pray for specifically? And how do the saints answer? *Specifically.*'

'Why should I answer you?' Maeve snapped, trying desperately to quell her underlying panic. She soothed herself with the reminder that she could give him an answer if she really wanted to. She *could*, but she just didn't want to. 'It's about faith. About the power of the saints. About the knowledge that my prayers have been answered at all. I had the faith to believe as a child, and I still have the faith to believe now.'

Jude tucked his legs under him and stood, swaying slightly from whatever he'd smoked. As he leaned down, a chain slipped free from the loose neck of his jumper. A shining gold key dangled in the empty space between them.

Her heart jumped. *The locked room.*

'I want you to consider every moment of answered prayer you can remember,' Jude said. She dragged her gaze from the key to his face. 'Remember the saint you prayed to. Remember how and *if* they answered. As specifically as you can.'

'Why?' she asked, voice a choked whisper.

He didn't reply, only continued to study her.

This close, Maeve could see a faint spray of freckles across the bridge of his nose. The shade of his eyes was a swirl of green and brown and grey. Just below, the gold key shimmered and swayed.

She *needed* that key.

The sole letter she had sent Ezra had barely contained anything useful. She knew it hadn't been good enough. His lack of reply told her she needed to try harder, and she was certain that locked room held the answers she so desperately wanted. She couldn't risk Ezra's disappointment.

'I want you to remember every moment you believed your prayer was answered and ask yourself if your recollections are a true, perfect account. Memory is a funny thing. I know better than most how the devotion of an acolyte can skew faith into blindness. Think on it.'

He straightened.

Maeve rose, too. Her heart hammered in her chest. Almost subconsciously, she rubbed her hand over the miraculously healed stretch of skin on her arm. She could tell him about that answered prayer, but why should she? Why did he deserve her unearned secrets?

'Why? Why should I *think on it*? I know what I believe. I know what foundation lies beneath me. My faith is *not* blind.'

Jude paused in the doorway. Slowly, he turned to face her. Darkness lurked deep in his impenetrable gaze as he cocked his head. 'Isn't it?'

She'd had enough.

Maeve pushed past him into the hallway. Air came thin into her tightened chest. The walls of the house closed in as she fought for breath. She couldn't bear it anymore. Couldn't bear *him*.

Ignoring the heavy weight of his gaze on the back of her neck, Maeve hurried down the stairs and outside into the heavy near-dark beyond. The moors were vast and empty, soothing the rolling anger consuming her every thought. She pushed open the gate and strode towards the oak tree in the distance.

There, and only there, could she finally breathe.

Until she heard him call her name.

13

Jude

Jude followed a flash of pale hair in the twilit distance, grumbling under his breath. Maeve was perhaps fifty metres ahead, pushing past the gate and heading into the fields beyond. The last thing he wanted was to chase after her like some sort of *dog*, but she didn't know the moors like he did. They weren't safe off the path, especially in the dark. Bogs pitted the heather in unseen patches, crawling roots arching from the earth like fingers. Never mind the rain sluicing down his face and freezing the air in his lungs.

What was she thinking, leaving the house on a night like this?

Blood pounded furiously in his ears, turning him into a pummelling wave. He would crash against the shore, crash against *her*, one way or the other. Whether or not she would erode against him or push back remained to be seen.

'Maeve,' Jude called. '*Maeve!*'

He moved faster. The scrape of the wind drew tears to his eyes. Rain scoured across the exposed shape of the land, blurring the figure ahead of him.

Finally, she stopped. Her eyes widened as she caught sight of him.

The thought occurred almost lazily – he'd been so preoccupied with ensuring she stayed clear of danger that he'd neglected to watch his own feet. If he'd stopped for even a breath, he would've noticed the distinctive moss, the swampy water licking at his ankles. If it hadn't been for the blasted *woman in front of him—*

Too late.

Water and freezing mud filled his boots and sluiced up the back of his jumper as his left foot sank to the knee. The other jerked forward in an attempt to steady himself. His arms pinwheeled through the air as the mud stopped him in his tracks.

'Jude!' Maeve cried.

He barely heard her as razor-sharp panic consumed every thought. The bog wrapped fingers around both ankles, forbidding all movement. Soon, the whole lower half of his body was cemented in the mud. Fear surged through his chest as he clawed at the surrounding reeds. The more he struggled, the faster he sank. He desperately searched for anything solid, finding nothing. He was trapped.

Suddenly, Maeve loomed above him.

'Stop,' he tried to warn her, his words harsh and fearful. She would slip into the bog with him if she took another step. 'Don't come closer. *Don't*, Maeve—'

He tried to force himself into stillness and remember what Elden had taught him about escaping the bog's tenacious grip, but suddenly, her reaching hand was all he could see.

'Stay still,' she said, dropping to her knees and crawling forward. 'You're making it worse.'

Jude *tried*. He really did, but the claustrophobia wouldn't release its hold.

All he could think about was his trapped body and Maeve inching ever nearer. Strands of marshy grass snapped off beneath his grasping fingers. Water brushed his chin as mud hit his tongue. It couldn't end like this – earth down his throat, water in his lungs.

'Hold on—' her voice cut through the panic. He tried to focus on her face as his right arm slid deeper into the muck. He forced the left high above his head. His breathing was a wrenched, choking gasp.

'You need to relax, Jude. Please try to relax.' She slid forward on her belly towards the last of the firm ground before it gave way to the bog, her reaching hand barely visible in the dark. 'Take my hand.'

His fingers brushed her wrist, slipping off before he could get a firm grip.

Gold leapt in his peripherals. Jude shoved it back with all his strength as Maeve shimmied forward, both arms extended towards him now. Her hands scrabbled up his arm, against his neck and down around the collar of his jumper, searching for purchase. Rain sheeted between them in a veil of silver, obscuring everything that wasn't the vivid red staining her cheeks and her frantic dark eyes.

With a grunt, Jude freed his right arm from the mud. He reached both hands towards her, securing them around her wrists. His magic jumped eagerly to the surface. He loosened a half-scream, half-groan from between his teeth as he tried to fight it back.

Her memories flooded his mind before he could stop them.

Gold hazed the room in a rush of fine powder. High above, a portrait watched her with knowing eyes. The paint was dry – fully dry in mere seconds. How? How had he done it?

Maeve gripped both his wrists tightly and paused. She blinked rapidly, tipping her head like she was clearing water from her ears. Gritting his teeth, Jude finally succeeded in leashing his magic.

Abruptly, her eyes cleared as the memory left his mind and returned to hers. He squinted against the final strains of gold.

Maeve's hands convulsed around his wrists. 'Okay,' she panted. 'Okay. Start with your legs. Try to loosen the muscles.'

He tried to do as she said, to view his body as separate from his panic-strewn mind. He'd done it before. He could do it again. He focused on his ankles, his calves, his knees, up to his hips. Soon, the lower half of his body felt as weightless as if he was floating.

Slowly, the mud loosened its grip.

'That's it,' Maeve praised. She pulled on his arms, sliding herself backwards. She grimaced, pain flashing across her face as she worked them both backwards. 'Just stay still.'

His torso cleared the bog first. He saw Maeve fully now. She was lying partially on a fallen tree, one leg hooked over a protruding branch to lever Jude out of the bog. Her dress was torn to mid-thigh, exposing a black stocking and a slash of vivid red halfway up her leg.

'You're bleeding,' he gritted out, the words coming out angrier than he'd meant.

Maeve shook her head dismissively and pulled harder.

All at once, the bog released him. He slid out enough to catch his knee on the edge of the solid ground, pushing himself the rest of the way out. The peat was blessedly firm under him. Maeve released his wrists and rolled off the tree and onto her back. They lay there panting, mud-stained and soaked with rain.

'How,' she gasped. 'Do you find yourself in a *bog*?'

'It found me,' Jude muttered, scraping his clean hand over his face. 'Thought you'd be more grateful that it didn't find you instead. You're welcome for that, by the way.'

To his surprise, Maeve laughed. Clear and bright and louder than he expected. He turned to look at her, catching the edge of her smile. Something deep in him shuddered.

He shakily sat up.

Every part of him ached. He'd lost a boot, his sock halfway off and heavy with mud. He pulled it free with a sigh. He'd liked those boots.

Maeve extended one leg, gingerly pulling back her sodden skirt. Her stocking was pushed down around her ankle. Blood streaked down her inner thigh in muddy, blotchy rivulets.

His eyes fixed on the jagged gash. 'Does that hurt?' he asked uselessly.

She gently prodded the edge of the cut. Already, the blood

had stopped. 'I think it's from the tree branch. I probably shouldn't have anchored myself so . . . aggressively.' She tried for a laugh.

Jude didn't find it remotely funny. Up close, it wasn't as bad as he'd thought, barely more than a scrape, but *still*— 'You shouldn't have got hurt at all.'

Maeve met his gaze. 'What, no thank you for saving your life?'

'Not at the cost of your own.'

Surprisingly, he found the words rang true. He wanted her gone, yes . . . but dead? Perhaps not.

'Jude,' she replied firmly, catching him still glaring at the blood on her leg. 'It's a scratch. It will heal in a few days. Your life is far more important.'

Slowly, he extended his hand and brushed the smooth skin around the cut with the back of a knuckle, careful to keep his writhing magic in check.

Maeve shivered at the touch. He pulled back. 'Because I'm a saint?' he asked, not looking away from where his hand hovered a hair's breadth from her skin.

He took his time returning his focus to her face. Her golden hair hung in matted tangles, her eyes huge and softly dark. Her gaze roamed him like she was searching for something hidden, something only she could see.

'No,' she said, 'not because you're a saint.'

For once, Jude didn't have a reply.

14

Maeve

Jude's remaining boot swung from his hand as they entered the house, tracking muddy drips on the wooden floor. He stopped, scraping a hand over the short crop of his hair. 'I'll draw you a bath. Get some oats for it. For the...' his gaze raked down her body, landing on the tear in her dress and the leg beneath. 'For the inflammation. It'll be ready in a few minutes.'

Without waiting for her response, he turned the corner and disappeared towards the kitchen.

Maeve gazed up into the dark confines of Ánhaga.

The tangled mess of her hair would take hours to wash and detangle, and she didn't even want to *think* about the state of her poor dress. She rubbed her fingers absently over the wound on her thigh. Pain pulsed up her leg and curled around her hip, burning faintly. She still felt the ghost of his unexpected touch – surprisingly gentle and alarmingly cold.

The scratch was the least of her worries.

She didn't know *how*, but when his fingers first brushed her wrist, she'd felt the abrupt stirring of a memory, similar to the uncanny feeling of remembering somewhere you'd never been. After, a fine layer of gold had covered her vision for a heart-wrenching second before she'd blinked it away.

She hadn't missed the shock flying across Jude's face when it happened, the careful way he searched her eyes after.

Had he somehow pried into her head? Was that the corruption of his magic Ezra had warned her about? And, perhaps more importantly, how had he done it?

A slippery sense of vulnerability coated her limbs. More than vulnerability – *violation*.

Slowly, she reached for the smooth contour of the key tucked beneath the neck of her dress. She was surprised Jude, cautious, paranoid Jude, hadn't noticed her slip it from his neck when she pulled him from the bog, a move born more out of opportunity than anything else.

If he hadn't noticed already . . . he would soon.

She needed to break into the locked room.

Now, with pain still pulsing behind her eyes, the memory still ripe on her tongue.

Now, with Jude preoccupied elsewhere.

Guilt wriggled in her chest. He'd fallen into the bog trying to protect her from the same fate. He'd followed her into the storm, trusted her to help him free from the earth's hold. Even now, wet and covered in mud, he was drawing her a bath first.

But . . . would she get another chance? How long did filling a bath take? Not long enough.

She had minutes – if that.

Maeve took one step up the stairs, then another. Soon, she was racing towards the top, keeping her steps as quiet as she could. That infernal itch picked up as she approached the door. An urging to keep walking, to lay her hands on its worn wood frame, its shiny brass handle. This time, she obeyed wholeheartedly. She wasn't thinking of Ezra waiting for her updates, or the advancement she desperately wanted. She wasn't even thinking of Jude, who would be coming to find her in mere minutes.

There was only the door and whatever lay trapped behind it.

The lock gave with a faint click. Maeve stepped inside.

Whatever she'd been expecting, it wasn't this. Bookshelves rounded the room, covering the walls until they reached a window at the far side, each crammed with more spines than she could count. Gold glittered on every surface, falling through the air. Like dust, but finer and less substantial. Slowly, she turned her palms skyward to collect the powder on her fingers. The room was gilded light and spun-sugar gold, awash with something strange and beautiful.

She turned in a slow circle.

The gold was the same as in her studio. Was it a mark the saints' magic left behind? Had Jude been exercising his abilities in here? She froze, gazing at the falling powder as a thought occurred.

Had he been answering prayers?

She moved around the room, inspecting the books. A mix between fiction, Abbey tomes, and clothbound, title-less volumes. Her touch left a clean streak across the spines.

A book laid open across a desk pushed under the window. Jude must have left it there, ready to be picked up again the next time he visited. She stepped closer. The pages bore the same texture as her sketchbooks, the shape of the letters unfamiliar. Runes, maybe?

At her sides, her fingers twitched. The pages seemed to shiver in anticipation.

And she knew: the book wanted to be touched. It wanted *her* touch upon its gilded surface. She glanced over her shoulder towards the open door. From a floor up came the faint sound of water, the creak of floorboards. Would Jude wait until the bath was full to find her, or expect her to meet him there?

Either way, she didn't have long.

Her heart rabbited in her chest as she hovered her hand over the pages. Warmth buffeted her palm. She wanted more of it; wanted the book in its entirety. Consumed, like a gulp of air before a fall.

She dropped her hand onto the page. All at once, the world spun out from underneath her.

Shelves swirled into windows, dropping through levels of bedrooms and hallways and windswept moors as Maeve fell from one world into the next. Nausea surged up with a lash of vertigo. She tried to scream, but her lungs wouldn't draw air, the sensation so unlike anything she'd ever experienced that it filled her lungs with pure panic.

She was standing at the edge of an unfamiliar room when the world stilled.

Some parts of it were hazy, like a painting that had been smudged before it could fully dry. Other elements were as crisp and detailed as her vision. Her body felt weightless. Not fully corporeal; more ghost than human. She looked down, seeing nothing but floorboards under her. The slightest hint of smoke layered under the sea salt when she breathed in.

Sweet and familiar – she was in the Abbey.

Was she in a memory?

The bedroom was smaller than hers and so messy she felt the low-level panic that emerged in places that didn't subscribe to her particular level of tidiness. She looked around, heart lurching into her throat as she spotted the boy standing by the open door. Though he was younger, around the age he'd been when his icon was painted, it was unmistakably Jude.

Somehow, she had to be in a memory. *His* memory.

Jude closed the door behind him, crouching to shove a triangular piece of wood between the bottom of the door and the floor, effectively locking himself in. Cursing under his breath, he kicked aside piles of misplaced items to throw himself onto the bed. His legs were overly long and thin, ankles and wrists delicate where they poked out from his ill-fitting clothes. His hair grew in wild curls to his jaw.

Suddenly, he clamped his hands over his mouth and screamed.

An animal noise, one that sent Maeve skittering backwards into the door. Before he could shout again, a knock sounded on the closed door. The handle rattled, the wood groaning as whoever was on the other side tried to shove it open, stopped by the wood jammed at the bottom.

Jude remained on the bed. His breath quickened as the door-jamb squealed on the stone floor.

Another knock, louder this time. 'Jude—' the stranger said. Their voice was fully textureless.

Maeve flinched at the sound of it. It was as though Jude's memory had fallen short creating the voice, like he'd forgotten who was behind the door in the first place.

'I know you're in there. Open the door,' they grunted. The door didn't budge. They drummed their fingers on the wood in a rapid staccato. 'Fine. Have it your way. I thought you'd like to know that a decision has been made.'

Jude stood up. His eyes were wet. He took one step towards the jammed door and stopped. 'I don't want to go. Please. This is my home.' His voice cracked. '*Please.*'

The stranger's sigh trickled through the door.

Was Maeve seeing his final day at the Abbey? In the memory, he looked midway through his teens, he was in his maybe early twenties now. Elden said he'd been exiled for over eight years.

Nearly a decade. He'd just been a *boy* when he'd been sent away.

She had recognized the truth in theory, but the reality was so much worse than she ever could've imagined. The thought of this version of Jude wandering Ánhaga alone was too horrifying to consider.

'It's too dangerous for you to stay,' the stranger said. Jude stumbled back to the bed. He sat heavily, fingers curling over the edge of the mattress. 'Keeping you here endangers everyone. The whole Abbey will suffer if you remain. You don't want that, do you, Jude? To hurt anyone else? Not after what happened.'

Who was this stranger to ask Jude, a boy barely out of child-hood, to give up his home? Maeve might not have understood what Jude had done to deserve punishment, deserve *exile*, but no child should be made to believe his very existence hurt people.

Her left hand gave a sudden pulse of pain. She looked down, finding angry crescent moon marks pressed into her skin from her nails. Pressure built steadily in her throat. She trusted the Abbey. She'd given her life in service, an act she didn't regret. A decision she would make again and again. But this . . . she didn't know how to reconcile Jude's tears with her long-held beliefs.

Perhaps she wasn't seeing the whole picture. This was just a slice of a memory, after all. And from an unreliable source at that. Jude had his own biases, held nearly as strongly as Maeve's loyalty. That was bound to impact his memories as much as it leaked into his current reality. He didn't even remember the identity of the voice behind the door, she reasoned. Of course, the memory would be filled with inconsistencies.

She took a steadying breath and tried to focus on the stranger's voice and not the muffled sound of Jude crying into his clasped hands.

'We're sending you somewhere you will be safe,' they said, voice softening. Though the voice was still strange in its anonymity, the cadence reminded Maeve of the interactions she'd had with the nurses at the Abbey any time she felt unwell. Straightforward, yet still caring. Was that who was on the other side of the door?

'You won't hurt anyone ever again. Is that not what you want?' the stranger asked.

'The Goddenwood?' Jude choked out. His eyes were fever bright with a sudden dash of hope.

'No . . .' they replied, slow and careful. 'Not there. Somewhere else.'

Jude's lower lip trembled. He scrubbed his eye with the back of his fist. The slender slice of his wrist she could see was wrapped in a bandage, blood seeping through the edges. Hardening the soft lines of his face seemed to take effort. It was the same stubbornness Maeve saw in the present Jude. 'I don't want to hurt anyone. I *never*—'

'Shh,' the voice soothed. 'All that matters is that it doesn't happen again.'

'Is . . . all right?' Jude asked. The space a name would fall came through as a buzz.

Silence hung in the air. Jude stared blankly forward as he waited, fingers drumming on his thighs. 'Time will tell. What matters is there isn't a repeat performance.' Another pause, this one longer. Then '. . . is missing. But you knew that, didn't you?'

A strange buzz obscured the name. Did Jude not remember that, either? Maeve studied him, cataloguing the way he flinched at the missing name. Why would he have forgotten such a fundamental detail?

'Okay,' he whispered. 'I'll go.'

A light tap on the door, like the stranger wanted to convey their approval. 'You've made the right choice.'

As the memory faded, she caught the tail end of Jude's expression as he listened to the footsteps leaving his door. The young lines of his face, both familiar and not, shifted from heartbreak to anger to resignation, settling there. He scraped both hands over his head, pulling at the hair around his temples until long strands released into his fingers. The other hand rose to his mouth, forming a fist.

Maeve came back to herself with a gasp.

She was lying flat on her back on the floor of the library. Gold dust shimmered in the air, casting the room in a sense of unreality. Jude's stifled whimpers still rang in her eardrums as warmth ran from her eye to slide down her jaw. She didn't know how she could face him again after what she'd just viewed, knowing she'd see the echo of his boyhood self, broken and pleading. Her heart rattled unsteadily at the thought of it.

Suddenly, the soft pad of footsteps sounded from the corner of the room.

Maeve shoved to her feet, heart pounding a dangerous rhythm

as she turned towards the door, already knowing who she'd see watching her.

And there he was: Jude, bandages and a jar of poultice in his hands. Eyes fixed firmly on the book open beside her feet.

15

Jude

The scent had been the first sign something was amiss. He recognized its sharpness: a candle freshly blown out, a hearth fire left to smoulder. But the power behind it wasn't its own. The edges were unfamiliar.

It hadn't taken him long to realize his key was missing once he'd pulled off his muddied jumper and slid on a fresh pair of trousers to tide him over until he could bathe, the bandages and poultice for Maeve's injury already in hand, her bath filling just down the hall. She must have slipped it from his neck while he'd been waist-deep in the bog.

He had been desperate and vulnerable, and she had stolen from him.

Jude drifted down the stairs in a half-conscious daze, knowing, *dreading*, what he'd find once he arrived, only to have his worst nightmares confirmed. Maeve, in his library. His book, open beside her. His memories, laid bare for her viewing.

The only sound was his heart beating in his ears and her rough, panting breaths. His attention skated between the part of her lips and the flush settling high on her cheekbones. The hem of her muddied skirt, faded blue and white checkered gingham today, opaque throughout, stirred up a cloud of gold.

Distantly, he recognized the screaming cry of violation battering against his walls. He should be shouting, raging at her for the egregious misstep of breaking into his private space, but instead, Jude was calm. Coldness swept over every still-smoking coal as he stepped towards her.

'Jude,' Maeve begged, holding out her hands as if to ward him back. 'I'm sorry. Please, I didn't know. I didn't realize—'

He reached forward with both hands, fingers curling around her wrists.

His magic sighed in relief.

It breathed in, then clamped down.

Gold hazed the room in a rush of fine powder. High above, a portrait watched with knowing eyes. The painting was finished, seemingly in mere seconds. How? How had he done it? She struggled upright as the last humming chants left her ears. Her rasped cry of his name hung in the gold-dusted room as the saint turned to face her.

How like his icon he was, she thought as she reached for the canvas. The paint was dry under her searching touch, just as she feared. Impossible, but yet—

'Did you do this?' she breathed.

He had to have done it. His whispered denial shot terror into the deepest confines of her heart.

Who else could have?

Surging pain lit her skin as words formed before she could stop them. She tried to swallow, tried to clamp her teeth around the question, but it was too late.

'Your scar,' she asked. 'It's from a fire, isn't it?'

The saint's eyes met hers.

She'd seen those eyes before.

Jude stumbled back as Maeve lurched free of his grip. Her eyes were fiercely dark as they bored into his. She rubbed her wrists with frantic motions. 'How . . . What—'

Shame and vicious, poisonous hurt surged with a vengeance, transforming quickly to anger. She'd stolen from him while saving him from the bog. Violated his memories while he was in the middle of drawing her a *fucking bath*.

'You stole from me,' Jude said, control hanging by a thread. 'I returned the favour.'

'What is it? The gold. The memories.' Maeve keened, her chest heaving. 'Please. *Please* tell me. Don't lie like he did. I know . . . I know you have no reason to tell me the truth. But – *please*.'

He took one step back, then another. An untangling started deep in his chest at her words. Biting dread ate at his anger. Maybe it was the pleading in her voice, or maybe it was her naked desperation for answers, an anguish he knew intimately. Either way, his fragile sense of stability peeled away completely, leaving him unsupported against the reality of her.

Maeve had seen the gold.

And still – the Abbey had sent her here. To *him*.

The memory he had stolen changed something between them, like a fire had been lit in his head, obliterating everything he thought he knew about her and replacing it with ash. He needed to sift through it and see what he could pull free.

He could start with the truth. As much as he could afford to give.

'The gold is a mark of magic, Maeve,' Jude said. 'Memory tampering. Whatever happened before the memory in my book, the events that caused the Abbey to exile me, was because of my magic. Because of something I did. Something I can no longer remember.'

He paused. He didn't trust her, wrapped up in the Abbey like she was . . . but did he have a choice?

If her memory had showed him one thing, it was that she was more like him than he'd thought, than he'd feared. And if she was, he needed her to be open with him. Needed her answers more than anything.

Jude drew in a breath. 'The gold is why the Abbey sent me away. The magic that has the ability to tamper with memories, change others' perception of reality. Magic that can dip into other people's minds.' He worked the words over on his tongue. 'Magic that can write memories into books just as easily as it can into paint. It's why I was sent away from the only home I'd ever known. And why you were, too.'

16

Maeve

Maeve's tenuous grip on reality seemed, for a moment that felt too long and entirely too short, to comprise of a dusty library, gold dust upon wooden floors, and Jude's hands slipping from her shoulders. The back of her skull buzzed like a bee had been set loose somewhere between her ears, left to dart through bone and brain matter in search of escape. If she could move, she would have turned and run. Left his home and his life and his secrets.

But, as it was, she couldn't feel her fingers.

In a terrifying shift of time and vision, Jude's face momentarily flickered between his current appearance and the painting of him in the Abbey. Long hair that held a loose curl, thick lashes that brushed his brows. The strange deadness to his gaze.

Pliable, innocent.

Jude as an icon, a boy. Jude as a man, a *saint*.

He reached for her once more, pulling back when she flinched. The expression softening his face spoke of pity and regret, and she couldn't bear it.

'I was sent away?' she asked, her voice small and choked. 'But the Abbey . . . my mentor – he wants me to come back. He said I was being considered for lead iconographer.'

She refused to believe it. She *couldn't*.

And whatever this . . . *magic* was – the gold dust. The memory tampering. She closed her eyes. Felix's finished icon stared back at her from behind her lids, vivid, watchful. Jude said the magic could alter perception, play with time. Cast the world in bright, gleaming gold once it had finished its terrible course.

Something he claimed prowled in *her*. Under her skin and in her blood, foreign and unwelcome.

Maeve took a step back. Another. Swallowed. Words locked in her throat. 'You're wrong.'

The closed library door hit her back. She reached for the doorknob. The metal was hot to the touch, almost burning. It shocked her into action. She couldn't stay here. She *couldn't*.

For the second time that day, Maeve fled.

Jude followed as she left the library and headed for her bedroom. 'Maeve. Maeve, please listen to me,' he asked, voice muffled and far away.

She watched her hands throw items into her bag as if from above. Dresses, tubes of paint, a half-filled notebook. Her fingers slipped on a glass jar of hair oil, spilling the liquid down her wrist. A scrap of fabric cleaned it off, Jude's presence too close as he gently wiped the bandage down her arm. His hands shook in fine tremors against her skin.

Maeve pulled away, shoving the half-closed jar into the bag and wrenching the straps tight. 'Leave. Please leave,' she whispered, hating the tears in her voice. 'I need to be alone. I need to think.'

His lips parted. 'Maeve.'

She shut her eyes. Asked again— '*Please.*'

The door shut softly behind him. Then, silence.

Maeve lowered herself onto the bed and dropped her head into her hands. Uncertainty clouded around her, thick enough to drown in. She longed for the steadiness of the Abbey. A surety that she was on the right path, that her steps were watched and measured by those who knew better. There were no surprises, no gut-wrenching upheavals. Not like here. She'd been set adrift, dropped in the open sea without a sail to guide her.

And she wanted to run. Desperately. To go *home*. Back to safer waters.

Like she had so many times in her life, Maeve tilted her head to the ceiling as a prayer formed on her lips. For answers, for guidance. A desperate plea for a candle in the dark to show her the way. She wasn't expecting an answer, wasn't even sure she wanted one, exactly, but it settled her to ask all the same.

She opened her eyes to a startling realization.

It was Jude's face she'd pictured as she prayed.

'Fuck,' Maeve sighed, the word unfamiliar on her lips. '*Fuck.*'

A gentle knock at the door startled her out of her thoughts. A second later, the door creaked open, revealing Elden. She pulled upright in surprise. He'd never come to her room before.

'Maeve?' he asked. 'May I come in?'

She nodded, curiosity outweighing the simmering turmoil in her stomach. The blackness of the hall beyond obscured his expression as he stepped inside. A cream knitted jumper was pushed up around his elbows, a streak of mud on his forehead underneath a hank of rain-soaked hair. He scanned the room. 'Are you packing?'

Maeve fiddled with the strap of her bag, tucked up against her hip on the bed. 'Maybe.'

Elden cocked his head. 'You all right?'

'A very good question.' Her voice cracked pathetically at the last word.

Elden's eyes softened, and that was all it took.

She banded her hand across her mouth and wrenched to her feet, heaving breath after breath through her nose as she crossed the room to the window. Footsteps sounded behind her. A hand gently touched her shoulder, and, like a cast-aside dog, she turned to the first kind touch offered.

'Shh,' Elden hushed into her hair as he folded her into his arms. 'I promise you he's not *that* awful. At least not always.' She loosened a damp laugh, letting herself be held for another heartbeat before pulling back. 'It's not easy for Jude. He spent too many years alone, I think,' he said, pity clear in his voice.

Maeve nodded, wiping her eyes. She directed her gaze back out the window. Watery moonlight illuminated droplets racing down the glass. The silence between them had the air of the confessional. She was far from its sacred quiet and velvet bench, but the weight on her soul and words on her tongue felt just as heavy. Just as impossible to resist.

'Has Jude ever . . . I mean, does he—' she pressed her lips together. 'I went into his library.'

'Ah.' Elden's gaze drifted over her head, becoming unfocused. 'What did you find?'

She didn't know whether Jude had shared the memory with Elden, but, like in the confessional, she couldn't have stopped the words if she tried— 'A book. A memory was in it, somehow. Written in runes. I couldn't read it, but I . . . I didn't need to. It sucked me in. I saw the memory like I was there. It was of the day he was sent away from the Abbey. Sent here, I think.'

Elden's face didn't betray any emotion as he stared out into the wilds beyond. His chest rose and fell slowly. 'Were there more books? With more memories?'

'I think so. I don't know.' She weighed her words, debating whether to ask Elden some of the questions she longed to ask Jude. 'What are they? The books.'

He didn't reply for a long moment. Finally, he rubbed his brow. 'They're memories, as you said. A record of sorts. He keeps them stored in books. Puts them there. I don't know how.' He blinked once. Twice. 'He doesn't like anyone in his library.'

'Maybe it's to hide the books. The memories,' Maeve said, thinking of how furious Jude was when he found her. 'Somewhere only he can view them.'

A shiver coursed through Elden's body. 'Hide them – yes. That makes sense. Keep them safe.'

'Safe,' Maeve echoed. There was something odd in his expression, as though he searched for answers from her just as eagerly as she probed the truth from him. Perhaps Jude was in the habit of keeping secrets from everyone in his life.

'Well. Anyway,' she said. 'It was disconcerting, to say the least. Jude thinks I'm the same as him. That the Abbey sent me away because of this . . . this *magic*.'

Elden's gaze shot back to hers. 'And if they have?'

'If the Abbey has sent me away? If they—' she paused. The lump in her throat grew too large to ignore. She thought of Jude's memory. His magic had hurt someone. 'If they think this magic I have is dangerous and expelled me because of it, I don't know what I'll do.'

Other acolytes had disappeared over the years. Not many, but enough to send fragmented gossip through the limestone halls like ripples across a pond. The speculations around the disappearances were never very well formed. A sickness the saints didn't want to cure. A wrongdoing so egregious the member couldn't be allowed to remain. Sometimes, there were rumours of members running away. Those were always stamped out the quickest.

But never for magic. Never for golden dust and stolen memories.

'Yes,' Elden replied. 'If the Abbey has cast you out, what then?'

'I don't know.' Maeve tried to ignore the rapid pace of her pulse, the rising panic. 'I was sent here to paint Jude. That hasn't changed. I think . . . above all, that remains my priority. I'll finish it and then . . . go back to the Abbey. If they don't want me to stay, they can tell me.'

She sounded much braver than she felt, but Elden couldn't see how her legs shook beneath the hem of her muddied dress.

Elden took a step closer. 'If you were sent here, same as he was, maybe it's best if you stay for now. Maybe that's what the Abbey wants. You're one of their own. And you need to finish his icon, as you said.'

'Yes,' Maeve breathed. Her fingers tightened around the strap of the bag hooked over her shoulder. '*Yes.*'

If she truly did hold the same magic Jude did, Ezra knew, and the Abbey had sent her anyway. Jude might have his own ideas about why they'd sent her, but she needed to trust what she had been told directly. She was to paint Jude, to spy on him, and then return to the Abbey. No matter how much she wanted to give in to the panic, to pack her things and *run* – she still had a purpose here. A purpose she needed to unravel with the one man she wanted to avoid. Whether or not she decided to continue reporting on him . . . she needed the truth, and she needed it directly from Jude.

'Go speak to him,' Elden said quietly. 'He might tell you more than you expect.'

Maeve nodded, blowing out a breath.

Elden gave her one final smile as Maeve moved towards the door. Questions still lingered, clinging like early-morning frost. They wouldn't dissipate until the sun rose and light was shed – light only Jude could provide.

She buried the last of her panic too deep to reach for without effort, without pain, and left the room. Her footsteps echoed down the stairs.

Each step brought her closer to Jude.

To answers or to more lies, she wasn't yet sure.

17

Jude

As soon as Jude heard the footsteps, he shoved his hand into the pocket of his jacket. Checked the letter was still there. Took a single, clarifying breath. He wouldn't think of the other letter of hers he'd taken, tucked away safely in his library unread.

The door creaked open.

He kept his attention on the window, tracing the shape of the moors in the distance, feeling the weight of Maeve's eyes press hot against his back. Blue and grey and devouring black. He closed his eyes for a single, unsteady heartbeat before turning to face her, taking her in like he was seeing her for the very first time.

A bright wash of colour bled down her neck; her hair tangled nearly to her waist. Her muddied *fucking* dress, torn up her thigh. In the hour since the bog, she'd viewed one of his worst memories, and he'd stolen one of hers in return. He'd realized the same magic in his veins ran in hers. A secret he'd given unwillingly, knowing he had to but baulking all the same.

A secret she'd looked at and ran from.

Running had never been a luxury afforded him; he hadn't been brought slowly into learning about the Abbey's manipulation. Not like what he thought to offer Maeve with his carefully chosen words, his house that wasn't much, but at least it was *safe*.

And still, she'd run. And Jude couldn't take it. Couldn't joke, couldn't tread lightly—

'You wanted to leave.'

Her breaths sawed raggedly out of her— 'Yes.'

Slowly, Jude drew the letter from his pocket and made a show of reading down the page. Maeve's panting breaths abruptly cut off as she recognized what he was holding. He flipped the page over to check the back with an unhurried glance. 'You're hiding secrets of your own, aren't you, Maeve?'

She took an unsteady step back.

Immediately, his eyes were on her.

Her expression wavered, fear, then indignation. 'Perhaps I should give you some context first.'

'Context?' He raised a brow. 'Is that needed?'

'It is.'

Jude didn't reply, just stared at her. Waiting.

She nodded – to herself, to him, he didn't know. 'I've been studying iconography for almost as long as I've been at the Abbey. My entire life, it feels like. Painting, studying faces, learning the craft . . . It's everything to me. *Everything.*'

Something fervent and steady swirled in her dark eyes, lit by a shaft of wavering moonlight. In that heartbeat of connection, Jude saw a profound devotion to her art threading through her, perhaps longer lasting than her commitment to the Abbey. Her purpose, possibly even her entire being, was wound up in her craft.

'I'm up for a promotion. Something I want desperately,' she continued. 'Ezra, my mentor – the one I wrote that letter to – knows this. He knew I would do anything to get it.'

Jude held the letter up. 'Including spying?'

Surprisingly, her voice remained calm. 'They said the position would be mine if I agreed to come, paint you, and report back. That I just needed to do this one thing for them. A test of my loyalty.'

Jude harboured no lingering disillusionment about the lengths the Abbey would go to manipulate their followers, but to hear they had taken something so sacred to Maeve, so fundamental to her being, and held it over her head like a reward for good behaviour was abhorrent – *even* if she had agreed to spy on him.

'During the weeks prior,' she continued, 'I had been preparing to start my icon of Felix. He's a saint at—'

'I know who he is.'

'Oh?' Her brow furrowed.

Felix. He'd been studying at the Abbey during Jude's time there, years before he'd become a saint. Full of self-importance and with a perennially sore neck from how high he kept his nose in the air, Jude had hated him on principle; at least, he thought he had.

His memories of the other man bore some mark of being tampered with. In what direction, Jude wasn't sure. He wondered why he could remember parts of Felix with near-startling clarity when so much had been lost along the way.

When it became apparent that was all Jude would offer, Maeve continued, 'After what you saw in my memory, I awoke on the floor, and everything was gold. Felix's icon, which had just been a sketch and a basic underpainting before, was *finished*. Fully dry. I thought it was Felix who did it. He claimed he didn't, that it was *my* magic—'

Her voice cut out. She took a shuddering breath and ran her thumb under one eye. 'Ezra found out. Felix told him. The next day, I learned I was being sent to paint you. They wanted an updated icon. And they wanted information on you.'

'An updated icon?' Jude asked. 'The old one . . . it's in the basilica, then? With all the others?'

Maeve nodded.

Just as he'd suspected. Their ties to him, forged by his icon, must have been wearing thin, and they had sent Maeve to renew it. In a way, hearing that they still had his icon was a relief. It meant they were still trying to take his magic, his memories. That his books were *working*.

But questions still remained. Namely, how to break that bond completely.

He reached out, pressing the crumpled letter into Maeve's hand. Her fingers curled around it. 'Are you going to send any more letters?' he asked. 'If I tell you everything I know, if I explain the gold, the books – all of it. Will you tell them?'

Her eyes skittered across his face, down to his mouth, the line of his throat. The seconds stretched, becoming bloated, unable to hold up the weight of the one word Jude was waiting to hear. The word he *needed*.

The longer she remained silent, the worse the pressure grew, until he could bear it no longer.

Jude took a single step towards her. He reached out, brushing the inside of her wrist with the tips of his fingers. The fingers clenched around the paper gripped tighter. 'Maeve,' he whispered.

Slowly, her eyes rose to meet his.

Somehow, he already knew what she was going to say.

18

Maeve

Maeve weighed up the set of his jaw and the steady determination in his gaze, undercut by something raw, almost vulnerable. Unable to bear it, she moved towards the chairs near the unlit fireplace and sat, crumpling the letter in her fist. Jude knowing she'd been sent here to spy should have unmoored her, but instead, she felt oddly relieved. Like unlacing a tight corset or taking off a pair of ill-fitting shoes.

Jude wore a restlessness to his movements as he sat in the chair opposite. The lazy cross of his legs, the careful way he'd thrown an arm over the side of his chair. All of it orchestrated to seem unbothered. All of it betrayed by the unwavering intensity in his eyes.

The air pulled somehow tighter around them. He waited patiently for her to break the silence, but he wouldn't for much longer.

'I want to say no. I want to trust you,' Maeve said slowly. 'Everything I know is the Abbey. I can't just . . . throw away everything they told me, including why I was sent here.'

He didn't move, his gaze remained locked on her. She wasn't even sure he was breathing.

'However—' her throat clicked. 'I don't think I can. Report on you, that is. At least not right now.'

His shoulders curled in with an exhale. 'You do realize that's a complete contradiction.'

'I know. But for now, it's all I can offer.'

He studied her for a long moment. 'How about I start at the beginning, then?'

At her nod, Jude drew a book from his pocket and flipped it open. His eyes moved rapidly across the page, a strange blankness lurking behind them like a mist. Maeve leaned forward to look. Runes, just like the book in his library.

Suddenly, he snapped the book shut. 'The memory is fully in here. My head only has a shadow of it. If I read it, I can recall what I saw for a few hours after. What's left of the memory, anyway.'

She furrowed her brow. '*In* the book? How does that—'

Jude held up a hand. 'I'll get to that. May I continue?'

She quirked a brow. 'By all means.'

A ghost of a smile pulled at his lips, disappearing just as quickly. 'When I was fifteen, I altered someone's memory for the first time.'

'What?' she breathed. 'How?'

He shot her a *look*. Maeve pressed her lips tightly together in response.

'It happened right before the memory you saw in the book — a few weeks, maybe,' Jude said. 'I'm not certain. But I remember a fellow acolyte and I going to Whitebury. We were picking up a pile of freshly altered habits for the elders. I remember going to the tailors clearly, but only flashes of what came next.'

He paused to skate his palm restlessly over his head. 'We went to a pub. The barman took us to a cellar beneath it. The other acolyte I was with . . . he was my friend, I think.' The furrow between his brow deepened. 'He handed over the coin. Lots of it, too. Far more than alterations cost. For what, I don't know. Not habits, at least. Whatever happened for the rest of the afternoon is gone, but I remember waking up the next day, back in my bedroom, and my hands . . . my clothes—' he spread his hands wide. 'They were soaking wet. And I had this black powder smudged all over my fingers.'

'What was it?' Maeve asked.

'It smelled like the oil used in lamps. Kerosene.'

She hissed in a breath. 'Why would you be covered in oil? Isn't it extremely flammable?'

'It is.' Jude flipped his hands over to study his palms. 'I returned to the pub the next day. The barman had no recollection of us being there. He wouldn't even look me in the eye, just kicked me out before I'd barely come through the door. So, I went around the back to the cellar, thinking maybe I could find evidence of the kerosene. Evidence of *anything*. But all around the alley, covering the cellar's trapdoor leading, was gold dust. Like in my library and your memory.'

'How did you know you did it, though?' Maeve prodded. 'The memory tampering.'

'An elder found me as soon as I returned to the Abbey. He was furious.' Jude paused. His voice roughened. 'He told me it was my fault, that I was lucky he'd taken care of the barman. He said I'd done my part to erase the memory, and he would fix the rest.' His throat bobbed. 'The barman was found dead the next day. And when I went to ask the elder about it, he—'

Jude's voice cut out. He closed his eyes tightly, massaging the space between his brows. A fluttering began behind Maeve's ribs as she watched him try to collect himself, a fragile beating of wings. Panic, maybe, or something closer to fear.

'All I can remember is falling backwards. I think I collapsed, fainted, maybe. When I woke, the elder was standing over me, holding something in his hand. Gold dust filled the air. I couldn't tell what he held, only that it was small enough to conceal in his palm. It seemed significant at the time, but when I woke, I couldn't seem to remember. My clothes no longer smelled of kerosene, and my memories of the day before . . .' he waved a hand through the air. 'Almost gone. All that was left were fractured bits and pieces, but enough to know that I had been the one to fuck up. The barman had died, and I was to blame. It was *me* who had taken the first step to tamper with his memory. And the Abbey had killed him in retribution.'

Maeve didn't have a reply. Her mind cowered at his words.

The Abbey *killed* someone?

The prospect was too large, too overwhelming to consider. She'd drown under the weight of it.

Jude's eyes met hers. Haunted and searching. 'That was the first time I noticed the Abbey could influence memory. That I could, too. And somehow, they could use my magic against me, stealing my memories in the process. I don't—' he shook his head. 'I don't think they know that I'm aware they can influence memory. If they were . . . I don't think I would've just been sent away. I think I would've disappeared.'

'Like – like the barman?' Maeve's voice was hoarse. 'Disappeared? Or . . .'

Jude didn't reply. He simply stared at her; the word left unsaid.

She dropped her gaze to her hands, twisted up in her lap.

'From then on,' Jude continued, softer this time. 'I sensed it whenever the Abbey worked its memory magic. I *felt* it, like a weakness in my muscles. I'd see flashes of gold at the edge of my vision whenever the magic was being done. The gold dust is a mark of the magic. Only those of us who have the memory magic can see it, or anyone tampering with memory themselves.'

'Like the elders,' Maeve whispered. She remembered Ezra's expression as he'd taken in her gold-dusted studio. Brigid's quietly asked question if Ezra had seen the gold. Had she known what it meant, too?

More importantly – was Ezra actively using memory magic as Jude claimed?

Maeve filed away the question. Even considering it sent a surge of panic through her limbs. Was it not enough to shake her foundational trust in the Abbey without bringing Ezra into it, at least not yet? She couldn't bear the thought of losing him, his hands on her shoulders, keeping her steady.

Forbidding her from straying, or keeping her from falling?

'And the memory I saw in your book?' Maeve asked, returning her focus to Jude. 'Was that the fallout of whatever happened with the barman? With the kerosene?'

'Part of it, anyway,' he replied. 'It feels like there was something more, that something else happened. Something *bigger*, and that was why the Abbey no longer allowed me to stay. But by the time I learned to store the memories in books for safekeeping, there was so little left to save to know for sure.'

He leaned forward, gaze sharpening. 'But, Maeve... whatever happened, my magic was to blame. It's unwieldy. Dangerous. The Abbey didn't want me there as long as it flowed in my veins. They wanted me somewhere far away, somewhere they could still—'

His mouth slammed shut.

And Maeve knew, *knew*, he was still hiding something.

She weighed his words, filed them away, and chose not to press. He was being open with her, sharing vulnerable pieces of himself. She needed to proceed carefully if she wanted answers.

'That's what the gold magic is?' she asked. 'The ability to tamper with memory? And the Abbey, the elders . . . they can use it too?'

Jude nodded.

'How?'

'I believe icons have something to do with it. They help to form a link between—' he paused. 'Between those of us with memory magic and the elders who seek to use our abilities. The icons function like a capstone. Our magic touches one side of the stone, the elders touch the other. The magic bridges both.'

'Icons?' Maeve choked. '*My* icons?'

'I believe so, yes.'

'How?' she repeated. 'I just paint. It's paint and canvas, nothing more.'

'That's what I need to discover,' Jude replied. 'There's something that allows the elders to access the magic, something that captures it. And something that fuels it. And you, Maeve – an iconographer. I think you help to bridge that gap.'

'But icons are of saints,' Maeve argued. 'Are you saying there are icons of normal people like me, who can't answer prayers?'

'Well, they would just be called portraits, in that case. Not icons.' His smile didn't reach his eyes. 'But, yes.'

She weighed up his story, his admittance of magic and how the Abbey had altered memories. The icons. *Her* icons. Something so precious to her, something holy, repurposed in a way that went against the very core of their creation.

'Why? Why alter memories?' she asked.

'To protect themselves. If a situation threatens the Abbey's authority, they bend it until it snaps. It's how they maintain their followers.' Jude levelled her with a look that was both assessing and charged. 'And us, Maeve? Those of us who can see what they're doing and can do it ourselves? They get rid of us as quickly and as quietly as they can. They can't have people running around who know the truth, now, can they? Not when everything they believe is at stake. And not when they can use us for their gain. Not when they take our memories from us to fuel their stolen magic.'

Maeve's view of the Abbey, of *herself*, seemed to break apart and reform, messy and haphazard, with each damning word Jude spoke.

How could it make sense? Even if what he said was true, why did it have to be a malevolent thing? The Abbey, Ezra, and the other elders could still care for their acolytes and followers while protecting their interests.

Couldn't they?

'What if my interests and the Abbey's are the same?' Maeve

asked. Jude's eyes flared as he leaned forward to speak, but she held up a hand to stop him. 'I *am* their own. Even if you were marked a saint, you still left—'

'Sent away,' Jude interrupted. 'I didn't leave. I was *forced*.'

'I've always been loyal. Even if I can see the gold, why is that—'

'Do *not* presume they care about anyone who isn't an elder. They didn't care about me, not when I was fifteen and scared, nor when they shoved me here to live the rest of my days alone. And they didn't care about you. Not if they sent you here.'

Maeve shook her head. She couldn't accept it, couldn't even *think* of the Abbey as anything that wasn't home. 'I . . . How could they know I have the memory magic too?'

His look was part pity, part frustration. 'Even without the incident with the icon, they knew long before you did, Maeve. I guarantee it. And if they know . . . they sent you away because of it.'

Saints, it hurt. Maeve parted her lips and took a deep breath.

'The Abbey asks for piety and devotion, for trust from its followers. Why influence their memory? What do they gain?' She shook her head. 'I'm sorry,' she whispered, agony in every word. 'I wish I could just believe you. Believe everything.'

Jude studied her for a long moment before pushing to his feet. 'There's someone I want you to meet.'

'Tonight?' She blinked, mind spinning at the abrupt topic change. 'Meet who?'

'No,' he shook his head, loosening a raspy chuckle. 'It's been a long day. I need to sleep. And we both need to bathe.' He looked pointedly down at her muddied hem. Their socked feet. 'Tomorrow.'

'Who is it?' Maeve couldn't help but press as she rose from the chair. But Jude was already turning, walking towards the door, holding it open for her to pass through. Too soon, he was locking it behind them and leading her up the stairs.

This late at night, the only noise in the vast house was the creaking of the floorboards. The air was cool and damp against her skin, prickling at the thin layer of nervous sweat collecting at the base of her throat. She gazed at the slashes of moonlight playing in the exposed line of Jude's neck, the hollow at his nape.

He stopped in front of the bathroom and turned towards her, only a few inches away. He didn't move. Instead, he tilted his head to the side, meeting her eyes from behind lowered lashes.

A sudden urge to reach for him rose with a vengeance, clanging warning bells in her head. If she didn't turn and put her closed door between them, she'd do something she'd regret. Like press her fingers to where his pulse beat in his throat as rapidly as hers.

His steady inhale broke the silence. 'Goodnight, Maeve. Enjoy your bath.'

She stared at the space he'd vacated for long after he left.

19

Maeve

Jude waited for her at the front door early the following morning. The night had been a restless one, full of half-formed dreams and waking hours where Maeve had searched her memories for holes with a fine-toothed comb. For anything that felt . . . *off*. Too shiny, too perfect.

And she wondered . . . if she found any, would she know?

There was something else she'd been forced to consider. Over the years, Maeve had dealt with the occasional nightmare. They were always the same. She stood alone in a vast room, staring up at the Abbey's rose window. The stained glass wasn't its usual pattern. Instead, it showed a person. A saint, one arm raised with fingers curled inwards, the other hovering close to their chest. Their eyes were screwed up with pain. Mouth gaping open. Every piece of stained glass in the window, from the saint to the ornate frame surrounding them, was made of bright, arterial red.

In the nightmare, the glass shattered inwards with a deafening explosion. Shards covered the ground around her like a halo, like the rays of a sun. And always, just before she woke, she looked down at her hands to find blood dripping from her wrists to the tips of her fingers.

Her blood, or the saint's?

Maeve had scoured that nightmare last night, running over it again and again, searching for meaning. By the time the sun had risen, she felt like she'd hardly slept at all. And the answer still evaded her.

Jude didn't look much better. Wordlessly, he handed over her coat and a red scarf. She drew the soft wool to her nose. 'Isn't this yours?'

'It's more of a house scarf,' he said as he opened the front door. A gust of cold wind swept in, chasing away the last fuzzy vestiges of sleep and replacing them with a sharp tinge of trepidation.

Maeve stepped outside, tucking windswept strands of hair behind her ears. 'Where are we going?'

'Oakmoor. There's someone I want you to meet. She's usually at the pub, but sometimes she wanders.'

'She? Is *she* a friend? Something . . . more?'

Jude barked a rusty laugh as he opened the gate and gestured for her to go through first. 'Yes. I love eighty-year-old women. How did you know?'

She buried her face in her scarf to hide her blush, catching his eye as he smiled. He'd slid a deep green knitted hat over his closely shorn hair, his hazel eyes vivid against the thick fringe of his lashes. She looked away first, but not before she noticed the faintest hint of pink dusting the tops of his cheekbones.

It didn't take long to trace their way through the moors to the small village tucked between the hills like a cupped palm. Immediately, the village made her uneasy. Curtains twitched as they passed, the wood-slatted and plaster buildings shabby and timeworn. High above their heads, gossamer clouds raced across the watercolour sky; a sharp contrast to the muted greys and browns of the village.

Watched – that was what the feeling was. Whether it was pure community nosiness or something more malevolent that drew villagers' eyes to her, she wasn't yet sure.

Jude stopped in front of a building aptly labelled *PUB* and pushed inside. Maeve followed him, loosening the scarf from her neck as she looked around, surprised to see it so busy in the early hour. The warm scent of peat and malty pints lingered pleasantly in her nose.

'She's in the corner,' Jude said, bending to bring his mouth close to her ear.

Maeve scanned the room for the elusive *she*. Most patrons were men, tucked around tables with mugs of milky tea between them. To her surprise, the barman, a tall man with a mop of untidy dark curls and light brown skin, pushed out from a door near the back, holding three plates of cooked breakfasts — sausages, eggs, toast, and beans. Her stomach growled.

A woman sat alone at a table in the corner, her back to the rest of the room. For a moment, Maeve could only make out a pile of intricately knitted scarves layered over an even more masterfully woven cloak. It flowed from the woman's narrow shoulders in a fall of bright yellow wool and fine gold thread, the colours as vivid as a field before harvest.

Jude reached her table first, bending over to say something before pulling a chair out for Maeve. She lingered, still on her feet as the woman slipped off her knitted hat and let out a low, grating laugh. 'Oh! My, my, my. Sit here next to the old girl.' She rattled the chair Jude had pulled out. '*Sit.*'

Maeve sat.

Was Jude behind her?

The ground seemed to sway beneath her feet as she met the woman's gaze. Her eyes were still a bright, vivid blue, shadowed by sagging lids and a scraggly cap of white hair. Pressure started suddenly in Maeve's chest. The name was there, right there on her tongue. She wanted to say it; she *couldn't*—

'Oh, dear, dear, dear,' the woman said, swiping a hand over her nose. Her knobby fingers came back red with blood.

'Siobhan,' Jude said, reaching forward. 'Let me clean that for you.' He gently wiped her fingers with a handkerchief. Siobhan watched with an unsettling blankness behind her eyes.

Maeve's gaze fell to the pooled contours of her cloak. The bright yellow yarn, the shade so familiar—

Cadmium yellow.

'Siobhan,' Maeve echoed softly. She knew that name. How did she know it?

'*Siobhan*,' the woman trilled, tilting her head back and forth. 'A lovely name for a lovely old girl. She liked it once when the sea was ripe and the sky a pearl.'

Maeve cautiously turned to Jude, finding him already watching her. 'Is she okay?'

'No,' Jude said, 'but you should still talk to her.'

'Talk to who? Talk to me?' Siobhan asked. She sat up straight and tipped an imaginary hat. 'Many people used to talk to the old girl. Many, many people. So many years. So many tears.' She giggled, the sound bright and girlish. 'Leers and jeers and cheers. The old girl got it all, oh yes.'

Jude gentled his voice to a tone Maeve hadn't heard before. 'What do you mean by that?'

She shot him a look far keener than any previous. 'Saint Jude. Don't play with what you don't understand.'

Maeve's mouth felt full of cotton wool. Desperate, she looked around the pub. Tucked back in the corner as they were, none of the other villagers could see what was happening. Or if they could, no one seemed to care. Maybe Siobhan's strangeness was commonplace.

A finger was suddenly in front of Maeve's face, inches from her nose. 'She has questions for the old girl. I can feel it.'

Jude laid his hand on Maeve's wrist, pulling it forward. 'Show her, Siobhan. What you showed me. On your scarf.'

'Her *scarf*?' Maeve asked. Her voice sounded very far away.

Siobhan shoved back from the table and leered over them. From the folds of her cloak, a pendant slipped free. Gold flashed in a rhythmic sway. Maeve had no choice but to look.

Two hands. A sun.

'The Abbey,' Maeve breathed.

'*No*—' Siobhan cried. Jude's hands flashed forward to grip her flailing arms as she lurched backwards, stumbling on the leg of her stool. 'Not them. Not them. No more. No more for the old girl,' she blubbered like a child, fat tears falling down her wrinkled cheeks and off the tip of her reddened nose. 'No more. *Please*. No more for the old girl.'

'No more,' Jude confirmed, his grip sliding down to curl gently around Siobhan's frail wrists as he helped her back to her seat. 'You're safe here.'

'Safe,' Siobhan repeated softly. 'No such thing.' Her eyes flashed to Maeve's as her voice hardened, growing more coherent. 'No such thing. Not for the old girl. Not for you, daughter of memory.'

Maeve could do little more than stare, aghast.

'Can you show her, Siobhan?' Jude urged. His hands hadn't left the old woman's wrists, thumbs stroking circles on the translucent skin on the backs of her hands. 'She needs to see.'

Siobhan stared at him for a long moment before dipping her chin in a jerky nod.

Trepidation swam through Maeve as the woman reached for one of the slender scarves wound around her neck. Each one wasn't just a random pattern, but a picture. A story. The one she slid free started with the blues and greens of a sea before it shifted to what looked like a stained-glass window, to a lush forest before it ended in stacked rows of grey houses.

Siobhan's hand was clammy and cold around hers as she extended Maeve's arm. She began to wind the scarf from wrist to elbow like a bandage.

'Don't be afraid,' Jude murmured.

'Why would I be—'

Then, the pub melted away in a sickening slide of colour and light. The spinning behind Maeve's eyes intensified with the touch, like the vertigo she'd experienced in Jude's memory but worse. She fought for clarity, for control over her body as she fell forward—

Straight into a memory.

The first thing Maeve noticed was the smell, slightly sweet like apples left to rot. It coated every breath and stuck beneath her tongue. The golden haze obscuring her vision began to recede like a thick mist rolling off sea cliffs, leaving a rush of dizziness in its place as the world around her solidified. Dense forestland stretched out in every direction, an opening between the trees revealing a jewel-box town on the banks of a crystalline river.

The sheer beauty of it was like nothing she'd ever seen. A sense of peace washed over her like a wave, filling her chest until she wondered if her heart might burst. Maeve had heard of somewhere like this before, hadn't she? Somewhere wholly perfect, where community flourished and prayers were answered. Somewhere meant as a *reward*—

Suddenly, something hit her just between the shoulder blades, throwing her onto her knees.

Maeve yelped as thick mud met her hands, sluicing up her arms to splatter her face. The ground wavered, flickering like fingers banded over her eyes as the forest transformed into an endless stretch of churned black mud and back again, so fast it hurt to look at. She shut her eyes as she scrambled back to her feet. The earth sank beneath her, loamy and damp.

As soon as she righted herself, the scenery stilled.

She fought for air. Was there something wrong with Siobhan's memory?

A metallic squeal caught her attention. She spun to look, her gaze alighting on a nearby tree. Each leaf was immaculate, a uniform oval quivering perfectly in time with its neighbour. The longer she looked, the worse the ache around her temples grew.

Look away, she commanded herself. It took effort, it *hurt*—

Maeve grunted, forcing her eyes from the leaves and down to a sign on the trunk.

THE GODDENWOOD.

Surprise jolted down her spine. Ezra had told her Jude's home wasn't far from the fabled town, hadn't he? Maeve had been excited at the potential, at the very nearness of the sanctuary. Somewhere the Abbey's favoured saints spent their days — a reward for piety and devotion. A place so perfect that even the paintings of it had hurt to look at.

Strange that Siobhan had managed to visit. Why hadn't she stayed?

Once more, the sense of unrelenting peace stole over her as she gazed down at the jewelled town. Even the colours were brighter, the ridges of the roofs sharp against the cerulean sky. Just like the depictions of it hanging in the Abbey, down to the last shining window and reaching spire.

Distantly, she registered a low thumping, like the thrum of a heart or waves hitting the shore.

Maeve drifted towards it.

Her steps came effortlessly as she moved through the wood. Reaching the clear river bordering the neat wall of pastel houses, she knelt to rinse her hands clean of mud, only to spring back with a choked gasp at the acidic-green sludge coating her fingers. The water still looked crystalline and perfect, but when she reached out to touch it again, only cold slime met her fingers.

Slowly, Maeve got to her feet.

Gold stained the backs of her lids with every blink.

The town was too perfect. Too silent, as she picked her way through its immaculate streets. Every door was closed, every window covered. The town was empty, not a saint to be seen. She could've been inside a dollhouse, or some exhibit in a travelling circus.

The thought gave her pause.

Maeve lifted a hand. Shutting her eyes, she traced the contour of a lamppost. It was rough and curved under her fingers, the jagged edges of what felt like a gouged hole pricking her skin.

When she opened her eyes, it was back to smooth and crisp black iron.

Odd. Very, very odd.

She continued feeling around with her eyes closed. Each wall and window, even the cobbles beneath her feet felt dilapidated and filthy. Maeve brushed against a bench tucked under the shady cover of another too-perfect tree. Her fingers skimmed over its rugged armrest when, suddenly, her hand sank through something soft and mealy. She pulled back in disgust, opening her eyes to find her hand wrist-deep in a basket of rotten apples.

Then, in a horrifying unfurling, the town's perfect veneer peeled back into something else entirely.

Thick layers of dirt blanketed every surface, from the sagging rooftops to the uneven streets. Weeds burst through every crack in the earth. A sickly yellow-grey haze hung heavy in the air, smelling sweet and sulphurous. For a moment, she thought the sky itself had decayed.

Surely, *surely*, this couldn't be the Goddenwood.

As if hearing her thoughts, the town began to reform back into its visage of false tranquillity, like a fresh blanket tucked over wrinkled and stained bedclothes, hiding the horrors beneath. Disbelief, maybe closer to denial, washed over her. The Abbey had told her this was a perfect town, a reward for the most loyal of saints.

But yet. *But yet.*

Bending, she peered closer at a slender chain wrapped around the basket handle. An icon swung from it, shining pure gold against the greyed rot of the town. Maeve cradled it in her palm. A woman's face cast in metal stared back at her. A face she knew. A face she had prayed to, hours and hours of praying, knees to stone, head bent as she begged, as she wept, as she cried out for someone to *hear her*—

Siobhan.

The woman in the pub was a saint. A saint whose icon hung

in the Abbey, whose mind was fading day by day, leaving her to live in fear, in wretched paranoia. And the Goddenwood—

Siobhan's memories revealed a town far from the idyllic haven the Abbey promised. The Goddenwood wasn't a reward, Maeve realized. It was a punishment.

She came back into her body with a sickening jolt.

20

Maeve

The walk back to the house passed in a blur. Maeve was vaguely aware of Jude pulling Siobhan's scarf off her arm, of guiding her from the pub and onto the muddied streets of Oakmoor. She remembered checking her hands almost compulsively, scraping them up and down her sides until Jude trapped her wrists together in one of his hands.

The ghost of his soft reassurances was like a lost melody, like something sweet she'd once tasted – the product of a half-formed dream, where the rest was a nightmare.

It came in flashes and starts, disappearing just as quickly.

A verdant forest made rotten. A town left to crumble.

Maeve rubbed her hands up and down her thighs until her chafed skin began to burn. Jude's face wavered into focus as he held them down, stilling the frantic motion. She was sitting in a chair with him kneeling before her. Books surrounded them. Fine gold powder spun in the sunlight, as vivid as the water gild she used in her paintings. A mark of his magic or of hers?

He was his icon for a heartbeat of a moment – a holy replica, perfect in its distance.

Then, the sun shifted, and Jude returned. The catalyst for every painful moment of deconstruction she'd felt since entering his home. He had been marked as a saint in name, yet Maeve was beginning to believe he was anything but.

Still – she couldn't look away.

Gold dust coated his hair and the tops of his shoulders. The bow of his lips. She eased free of his hands to brush the top of his cheekbone with her fingertips. He inhaled sharply, something soft and begging in his eyes before he pushed to his feet.

'I need you to tell me what you remember,' he said without preamble. 'Quickly.'

'Of what?' Maeve breathed, still staring up at him.

Jude made a frustrated sound deep in his throat. He began pacing around the room, stirring up a cloud of gold as he went. 'Siobhan, Maeve. The memory she showed you. Was it of the Goddenwood?'

The Goddenwood . . .

Memories of the fabled town slipped away faster every second. Water from a drain, smoke in the wind. There one second and gone the next, too fluid to grasp and too swift to chase.

'We went to the pub, she wasn't — her mind,' Maeve choked. 'She didn't seem okay. At all.'

'She's not.' Jude stopped walking. 'Not at all.'

Maeve closed her eyes. She used to pray to Siobhan's icon in the Abbey, didn't she? She'd liked the colour of her robes — cadmium yellow. 'She's a saint,' Maeve said, her voice cracking.

'Was,' Jude corrected. '*Was* a saint. The Abbey broke her mind when they discovered she had the memory magic. She lived in the Goddenwood for years before she escaped.'

Maeve swiped fretfully at her damp cheeks. 'How? How did they break her mind?'

Jude studied the sky from the window. The subtle rise and fall of his chest drew her attention. Maeve brought both hands to her sternum, just below her collarbone. Right where the tattoo marking sainthood would go if she were one.

'The Goddenwood,' he repeated, turning to face her. 'What do you remember?'

'A forest, a river. Cold water. The village was . . .' she shut her eyes. 'Perfect. Clean, silent. No one was around, but it felt

— peaceful?' She gritted her teeth as pain glittered behind her closed lids. She'd been in Siobhan's memories less than an hour ago. It shouldn't be this difficult. 'No. Not peace. Frozen, almost.'

She opened her eyes to Jude holding out a torn page from a book and a stump of charcoal. 'Sketch it.'

Maeve took the items. The texture of the charcoal was comforting in its familiarity. 'Sketch the Goddenwood? Why?'

'I use books to trap memories. Siobhan knits. I think your painting, or drawing, in this case, might be how your magic controls its outbursts,' Jude said. 'Memories are fragile things our magic loves to eat, whether that's by our own hands or the Abbey's. The books are how I both siphon off the excess and preserve my remaining memories.' He took a deep breath. 'Before I skim off the unruly bits, even after, if I'm not careful, my magic has outbursts. Times where I leap into someone else's memories, when my . . . emotions become hard to handle. I think painting is your version of that.'

'Outbursts like when you grabbed my wrists or pulled me from the bog?' she asked.

'Something like that.' Jude considered her. 'And it can show you the truth of a memory if it's different from what you might believe. Your painting might be an even greater link between memories and the Abbey than my books or Siobhan's knitting. There's a connection there, something I've been exploring. I've been researching it here—' he cast his hand across the expanse of the library. 'Not all of these are my memories. Many of them are books. Abbey books. Your icons might allow the Abbey to control those of us who hold the memory magic and—' his throat worked. 'And those of us who are saints.'

Saints—

Despite their similarities – the memory magic they both held, the gold dust, the expulsion from the Abbey – he could answer prayers where she could not. He bore a mark on his chest. The Abbey had chosen him, seen the power in him and venerated him because of it, only to send him away when they learned of his ability to influence memories. Had they sent him away so they could use him? And did her icons help in that manipulation?

Suddenly, Jude rounded her wrist with his fingers, pulling her hand into a shaft of sunlight. 'Will you?' He skated his thumb over the edge of her forefinger, rough from holding a paintbrush. Maeve fought a shiver. 'Sketch Siobhan's memory. Sketch the Goddenwood. See if the theory holds true and your memory magic manifests through your art.'

The weight in his gaze, in his touch, was too much to bear. Maeve pulled away. She moved towards the small desk under the window. 'I can try.'

She'd done a little sketching since her arrival. Quick, messy studies of the moors, of Olive and blackbirds and turbulent skies. Of anything she could see, save Jude. She'd tried not to think too hard about why she'd avoided pressing him to sit for his icon. She'd told him she wasn't sure if she would continue reporting on him, that her clawing belief hadn't decided what to latch onto. But that wasn't true, not anymore. At least not entirely.

She wasn't choosing Jude or the Abbey. She was choosing the truth, no matter where that lay.

Maeve set her charcoal firmly to the paper.

By the time she straightened, dusk had deepened the library into a study of shadows and fading orange light. Her stomach cramped with hunger. She sat back and studied her sketch. Her whole body ached. Her shoulders from hunching, her fingers from gripping the charcoal. The soft hollow of her wrist where it had dug into the tabletop. She dug her thumb into the offending muscle as disappointment filled her.

'As I said.' Her voice cracked unsteadily. 'A perfect town.'

Jude brushed his forefinger over the edge of a building. Charcoal blackened his skin like a bruise. 'Is that what you see?'

Maeve studied her drawing. The peaked roofs, the glistening river, the uniform pattern of shadow and light. Exactly like the paintings she'd seen of the Goddenwood hanging in the Abbey. 'Yes?'

'That's not what I see.' Warmth coated her back as he leaned down. 'Look again.'

The paper shivered. She ran her fingertips over the edges.

'Look at it from the corner of your eye,' Jude murmured.

She obeyed. The drawing changed shape slowly, moving faster. But when she returned her gaze to it, the town was perfect once more. She sighed. 'Maybe . . . maybe my memories are false, somehow. Like there's a distance between what I remember and what I draw. Drawing the town — it just felt like sketching. I don't know what I'm doing wrong. What the secret is.'

The sketch wasn't her best work, admittedly. Maeve had never enjoyed drawing anything that wasn't people. It felt so lifeless. Mechanical.

An idea occurred.

Immediately, she tried to swallow it.

She must have made a sound or stiffened in her seat, *something*, because Jude dropped to his knees beside her, putting their faces level. 'What is it?'

'I need to sketch her,' Maeve said. 'Siobhan. What I experienced in her memories, I won't find it in a drawing of a town. I'll find it in *her* — a saint.'

'An icon,' Jude repeated.

'Yes.'

He stood, pulling a book free and tearing out a page near the back. She cringed— '*Jude!*'

'The book's empty,' he said, dropping the page before her. 'I wouldn't ruin it if it were not.'

'Still,' she grumbled. She picked at the corner of the paper. 'What if it harms her? If icons allow someone to drain magic, wouldn't this put Siobhan at risk?'

'We're not elders,' Jude replied. 'I don't think someone can unintentionally steal magic. There has to be a process behind it.

I'm sure of it. Otherwise, it could happen accidentally...' He paused, frowning down at the paper. 'Right?'

She met his eyes, seeing a flash of anxiety there before he dropped his gaze.

He cares for her, she realized. Despite the saint's eccentricity, Jude genuinely cared for the elderly woman, with her scarves and her cadmium yellow. The thought of bringing Siobhan harm pained him.

'I'm sure the elders have their own way of accessing the magic,' Maeve agreed. 'I don't think it could happen accidentally. Their harm feels... deliberate.'

Jude nodded, exhaling heavily. 'Even so, I worry that even the very act of creating the icon will drain her.'

Maeve turned back to the paper. She hated what she was about to say. *Hated* it. She didn't want to see Siobhan harmed, didn't want her actions to drain the saint even more. But she couldn't see a way around it. Whatever Siobhan had shown her was important, and Maeve needed to recall it.

'Is it worth it, even if it is a small risk? To remember what Siobhan showed me. To see if there's something there that could help her far more than it could hurt her.'

Jude searched her face for a long moment before drawing in a short breath through his nose. His gaze moved to the window. 'Just destroy it after. The sketch.' His lips tugged down as his voice dropped. 'The icon.'

He returned to his window-side vigil as she picked up the charcoal and tried to forget about her pounding heart. Tried to leave everything behind that wasn't her memory of Siobhan, both as she was in her icon in the Abbey and the version of her Maeve had met that morning.

Maeve's hand moved quickly over the page. The slight curl to the edge of her lips. A precise crosshatch of shading under each eye. Each fine detail sprang faster and faster into existence.

And, *there*—

A low buzz. Faint at first, growing louder as gold settled finely across the desk. A swirling tide, drawing closer with every feature that fell into place. Distantly, she heard her name being called. A frantic plea, one she had no choice but to ignore.

Siobhan's voice trickled into her ears.

No safe place, daughter of memory.

Maeve's head tipped slowly forward.

21

Maeve

The dark of the forest gave way to the black of mud, the crisp edges of the buildings and the golden gleam of the clock tower falling into ruin as a soulless rot crept across the Goddenwood. From the outskirts of the memory, Maeve watched as Siobhan wandered through the town. She looked to be around twenty years younger. Tears tracked messy lines down her face. She was alone.

Suddenly, she stopped. Turned her head towards the sky.

In a macabre transformation Maeve wished she could look away from, Siobhan shifted from middle-aged to her current state, black hair into white, her back stooping, skin sagging around her face and neck. Her loose dress drooped to the side with her sudden frailty, displaying the sharp edge of her shoulder and the flash of a black-ink tattoo on her skin. Blankness settled behind her eyes as both hands rose to wrap around the icon swinging from her neck. She tore at it so hard that a line of vivid red opened up on the sides of her throat.

'You took it from me!' Siobhan screamed. 'Everything. *Everything.*' She dropped the necklace to slap both palms over her ears. 'Stop it. Stop speaking. Stop asking. Stop it!'

She froze, staring forward. Her eyes had lost all lucidity. 'They'll find the old girl,' she muttered as she slowly lowered to her knees. 'She hears their prayers. No safe place.'

She drew something from inside her cloak, holding it aloft. A rugged wooden frame surrounded a scrap of canvas, small enough to fit in her palm. Maeve's heart skipped a beat as her gaze caught on the distinctive shine of a painted gold halo. The icon's cadmium-yellow paint was faded, the features blurred and clumsy, but Siobhan's likeness was unmistakable.

Then, Siobhan did something Maeve wasn't expecting – she bent over her own icon and began to pray. Her words were too soft for Maeve to make out, but she recognised the lilting tone, the tightly clamped eyes and bowed head.

The town seemed to flicker as, just for a moment, it returned to its former illustrious state before falling back into ruin. Siobhan looked up as prayers continued to tumble from her lips. The jumbled words became clear: she was asking for clarity, for her mind back, to be released from the Abbey once and for all.

For a moment, it *worked*.

Siobhan's eyes were clear, fully alert as they pierced Maeve's. It was impossible to tell, but Maeve knew her memories were there, fully there in a way they perhaps hadn't been in years. As long as Siobhan's lips were moving, as long as she continued praying to her own icon, her mind was her own.

The saint got slowly to her feet. Her arm lifted, pointing directly at Maeve as her voice changed to something low and guttural. 'Turn. Turn around, daughter of memory. Open your eyes.'

Unable to do anything but obey, Maeve turned.

Suddenly, she was back at the Abbey. The vision lasted less than a minute, but it was enough for Maeve to see what Siobhan wanted to show her. An iconographer Maeve didn't recognize was bent over a painting, her hand moving in careful strokes across the canvas. On it was Siobhan's face, almost perfectly formed.

A wash of cadmium yellow.

A dust of gold.

Across from the iconographer sat Siobhan. She looked around

a decade younger than she was currently, her body fragile and skin liver-spotted. She was propped up against the wall. Her eyes had rolled back in her head, displaying a strip of white beneath her lashes.

The iconographer stood, staring at her painting. Her young face was screwed up in pain. Slowly, she reached out and dusted the gold from the canvas, the suddenly *dry* paint. She pulled back to examine her fingers, flipping her hand around to gaze at the back of her wrist. Vivid yellow paint stained her dark brown skin beneath the layer of gold. She rubbed them together on her wrist, mixing the gold dust in with the paint.

Then, she left.

An elder entered a moment later, jostling Siobhan awake. She came back to herself with a gasp, looking around wildly. 'Where . . . where am I? What happened?' Her unsteady gaze swung to her icon. 'No! *No* – not another. Please, no more, no more. Don't let them pray. Please, no more prayers. I can't take it—'

Abruptly, the scene cleared, the Abbey was replaced by Siobhan. Her head was bowed, hands folded in prayer. Her icon rested next to her bent knees. No words left her lips.

A horrifying picture snapped into place. Siobhan's begging for *no more prayers* echoed in the sudden silence, and Maeve wondered . . . were the prayers sent up to the icons, to the saints themselves, damaging their minds?

If so . . . then why was Siobhan praying to herself so fervently?

The Goddenwood was a haven left to rot, just like Siobhan: drained until nothing was left. The Abbey had taken and taken and taken – her mind, her safety, her youth. She'd been left in the Goddenwood to die until she'd escaped to Oakmoor. The Abbey had shoved her far from home and hung an icon in her place.

Jude was right.

The link between the Abbey and memory lay somehow in her icons. Somewhere in the prayers connecting them with the intercessors, with the elders, with the very Abbey itself.

Maeve lurched backwards as the realization shoved her from the memory and back into her body. She choked, eyes flying open as her arms pinwheeled, trying to slow her fall as the world shuddered around her in a mirage of golden light.

Jude caught her before she hit the floor. He lowered her down to the gold-dusted library floor, eyes wild and searching. 'Maeve. *Maeve*. What happened? You were shaking while you sketched. I couldn't break you out of it. Then, you fell—'

Her back protested as she tried to sit up. How much time had passed?

'Where's my sketch?' she asked. Her throat felt scratchy, as though she'd been screaming. Light refracted in glimmering shards across his desk. The library sat in inky blackness outside of the surrounding cocoon of candlelight.

Jude didn't seem to hear her. He scanned down her body, lingering on her charcoal-smudged fingers, the gold dust sticking to her dress. He gave himself a brief shake. 'It's still on the desk.'

Maeve retook her seat at the desk. When she turned the drawing over, it was perfect. *Finished.*

The level of detail was far greater than anything Maeve could accomplish in even a few hours. The saint's face was flawlessly rendered – each hair, wrinkle around her eye, and fold of her cloak real enough to touch.

She'd done it again. Maeve remembered everything from Siobhan's memory. *Everything.*

'It worked,' Jude breathed, leaning over her shoulder. 'Your magic had another outburst.'

She couldn't wrench her eyes away from Siobhan's sketched icon. Slowly, she brought it to the flickering candle. Watched the flame devour it until it was gone. *There.* It was destroyed. Hopefully whatever magic she'd conjured up in it wouldn't affect Siobhan.

Could icons be destroyed?

Maeve dismissed the thought as soon as it occurred. She needed to recount Siobhan's memory as quickly as she could, terrified that she'd lose it again.

She turned to face Jude. 'The Goddenwood . . . it's not real, is it? We were told it was a kind of utopia. A reward for the saints, but that's a lie. I see that now. And praying – praying makes it worse. Praying is what drains memories.'

Jude shook his head. 'The Goddenwood *is* real. I can't go to it. I doubt you could, either. I tried not long after Elden arrived. We went together. Neither of us could get past the initial boundary of the trees. I could barely see with a headache, and Elden started vomiting. I think . . .' a wave of trepidation crossed his features. 'I think it's where older saints are sent. When their minds are no longer useful to the Abbey.'

'I've never painted a saint over . . . fifty, maybe,' Maeve breathed. 'If that.'

'I can't bear to think of it,' Jude muttered, more to himself than to her.

'Do all iconographers have memory magic?' she asked, voicing the thought as it occurred. 'There was an iconographer in Siobhan's memory. A young woman. She'd just finished painting Siobhan and the room was . . .' she swallowed. 'It was covered in gold. The iconographer saw it. Touched the gold dust. And her painting – it was newly dried, just like mine. Does that mean she had memory magic, too? Is that why we're chosen to train in painting and not any of the other masteries?'

Jude blinked. His mouth parted. 'I . . . I hadn't considered that.'

'You said they knew of my magic long before I did,' Maeve continued, words tumbling from her lips. 'Maybe I was chosen. But when my abilities surfaced fully, they thought it time to send me away.'

The words burned. She couldn't deny the blasphemy in them. The blatant questioning, the distrust – she wasn't the woman who had left the Abbey on that cold winter morning, thoughts of devotion and obedience ripe on her tongue. Not anymore.

Brigid mentioned the gold dust in their final conversation, didn't she?

Maeve reached for the memory, the process of dredging it up more laborious than usual as it worked its way to the surface. Had Brigid known what it was because she herself had experienced it? If so, why had she been allowed to remain at the Abbey for so long?

Jude pressed his fingertips into his temples. 'I'm not an iconographer. I don't know the first thing about painting.'

'Maybe they didn't notice it in you early enough,' Maeve replied. 'If they had, maybe you, too, would've been trained in iconography.'

Jude didn't say anything. He continued to pace across the library, back and forth and back again, both hands linked behind his head. Maeve watched him. 'Jude,' she said. He paused immediately, turning to face her. 'If all iconographers have memory magic, maybe prayer harms more than just the saint. Maybe it hurts the artist, too. What if the elders can harness the magic in both the saint and the artist at the very same time?'

A flash of frustration crossed his face. 'Maybe,' he allowed.

'The loss of memories,' Maeve continued. 'Will it be the same for you? For the iconographers too, if my theory is right?'

It *was* right. She felt it in her bones. She'd always felt a closeness in her icons, a connection she never felt with anything else she'd ever painted or sketched. Hadn't she just affirmed the link when sketching the Goddenwood hadn't worked to recall Siobhan's memory, but drawing her icon had?

'I imagine so, yes,' Jude replied. 'My memories will be forfeit as long as the Abbey has an icon of me that they can use.' His lips twitched into a scowl. 'Same as the . . . iconographers. If they're linked to the icons, as you said, they – *you* – will experience the memory loss, too.'

'A different memory cropped up near the end,' Maeve said, changing the subject. She could tell by his expression alone that he wasn't convinced of her theory. 'Of Siobhan getting her most recent icon painted. It looked to be around a decade ago. She begged the iconographer to stop, for no one else to pray for her. She seemed to believe praying made her condition worse.'

Jude nodded. 'Like adding fuel to a fire. Prayer is one of the Abbey's core sacraments. How often are the acolytes required to pray every day?'

'Twice,' Maeve replied. 'And always in front of an icon. If we want to pray outside the set times, we must have a coined icon to pray to.'

'In the basilica, it's not *all* the icons you pray to at once, is it?' he asked. 'You choose just one to pray to at a time, don't you?'

Maeve's lip trembled. She bit down on it hard. 'Yes.'

Jude crouched before her, putting their faces level. He had a wild light in his eyes she couldn't parse out. 'The Abbey does nothing without reason. Praying – it affects the icons. It fuels them, harming the saint in return—'

'And the iconographer,' Maeve interjected.

His throat bobbed. 'And the iconographer.'

'Although,' she continued, 'it might take longer for the iconographer to feel anything, as we paint so many icons. The effects from the prayers would be more spaced out, I think. Less concentrated.'

The frustration in Jude's eyes only grew. Maeve didn't know why her idea seemed to irritate him.

She shifted in her seat. 'There's more. Siobhan prayed to her own icon in her memory. It gave her lucidity. It returned her memories, at least some of them. I don't know how I know . . . just that she looked into my eyes and I saw *all* of her staring back.'

Jude blew out a slow breath. He rose from the ground, settling himself on the stool beside her instead. 'She prayed to herself?'

'Praying empowered her, somehow,' Maeve told him. 'But not . . . not praying in general. Only to her own icon.'

She paused, taking him in. His utter stillness on the stool, the watchfulness in his hazel eyes. The undeniable *humanity* in the man before her, something she had once seen as a contradiction, even an attack on everything she'd been taught to believe, now made it all the more difficult to voice what she knew needed to happen next.

He would hate it.

But she didn't see another option.

Jude sat on his chair with one knee bent, the other extended in front of him with a certain lazy grace she'd grown accustomed to. Candlelight played in the hollows under his cheeks, the line of his jaw. Turned his hazel eyes more green than grey. Despite her trepidation, Maeve itched for a brush. The need to capture him was like nothing she'd ever known.

Jude wasn't devout, but he was a saint.

'I'm going to paint your icon,' Maeve breathed. 'But not for the Abbey. For you to pray to. Maybe that's how you get your memories back.'

'That's a risk. To both saint and artist, as you said.' A muscle in his jaw ticked. 'What if creating an icon truly does harm the saint? Or . . . or what if the Abbey gets their hands on the icon, Maeve?'

Her hands clenched into fists on her lap. 'You mean if I take it to them?'

Anguish flashed across his face at her words, yet he didn't refute them. Maeve took a breath. Let it out. 'You'll have to trust me then, won't you?'

Jude shook his head. 'I can't risk the memories. Not after I tried so hard to hide them. To *save* them.'

He rubbed the flat of his palm over where the mark for his sainthood was tattooed on his chest. Rubbed it like he wanted to forget about it. Like he *couldn't*.

'Will you show me?' The words left her tongue before she'd fully considered them.

Jude's throat bobbed roughly. His hand slowly rose to his shirt collar. He pulled it aside just enough for the top of the mark to show, starkly black on his skin. So fresh that it looked like it was inked yesterday.

Maeve pressed her lips tightly together as some unknown emotion rose within her. Pity at the thought of a child held down while the tattoo was pushed into his skin. Guilt for making him show her. Or maybe it was deeper; maybe part of her had never *truly* believed Jude was a saint until this moment, with the evidence clear before her.

Showing her was an act of trust – one she didn't take lightly.

Tears burned in the backs of her eyes. She yanked her gaze off his skin and down to her hands, digging her nails into her palms until it hurt. Her next question, should she choose to voice it, would push her over an edge she couldn't crawl back from.

'Is the risk worth getting your memories back? Worth learning how to sever yourself from the Abbey completely? Can you trust me enough to try?'

The words shocked her. The blasphemy in them, the betrayal. The Abbey might have been her safe harbour, the very foundation of her soul . . . but could she continue, complicit in their harm? Could she ignore the devastation they'd wrought to Siobhan? To Jude? Could she continue serving a lie?

No, Maeve decided. No, she could not.

Jude scanned her face, looking for what, she didn't know. The vulnerability leached from his expression as slowly as the setting sun, replaced with breathtaking determination. 'We'll start tomorrow.'

22

Jude

Jude hated sitting still.

It felt like days had passed since Maeve had positioned him by the window in his library. She'd arranged his limbs *just so*, adjusting the fall of his coat to slide in a particular, artful way across his thigh. She hadn't heard his breath catch as her palm had slid up his leg, imbuing warmth into his skin. If it weren't for the memory of her trying to smooth the short crop of his hair, he'd have got up long ago. As it was, the feeling of her nails against his scalp was fading faster than he'd like.

Moving slowly enough not to draw her attention, he looked at the window. He'd been shouted at a dozen times throughout the morning for fidgeting, and while he liked the stern set of her brow when she scolded him, he thought it best to keep her happy in the meantime. Even if the movement helped distract him from the steadily building pressure behind his eyes.

It was just as he feared. The painting of his icon was affecting him.

He couldn't deny the headache any more than he could forget about the slow meander of his thoughts, as though each word needed to cross a lake of molasses to fully form. Despite Maeve's assurances, he'd expected to feel muddled as she worked on his icon, but not like this. Not this quickly.

He wondered if Siobhan had noticed a new icon of herself had been created or if she was already too far gone. Had she felt it when Maeve had burned it? And, perhaps more importantly, had burning really destroyed it? He turned the idea over in his mind. Another question to look into.

Outside, the clouds lay thick on the horizon, heavy with the promise of snow. It had yet to extend down from the moors to dust his house, but it wouldn't be long. Soon, the hunched boughs of the apple trees and the scrubby grass would be covered in white. His gaze moved to a spider's web in the corner of the window. It shone pearlescent, threads of silk dipped in iridescent starlight.

Three winged shapes moved towards the moors in the distance. The tense line of his spine relaxed at the sight. A thought swept in as they disappeared over the horizon—

Would this work? Could he pray to his icon?

Maeve's theory didn't convince him entirely, even after she'd described what she'd seen in Siobhan's memory. Surely, after years and years of Abbey power, someone would have thought to pray to their icon outside of Siobhan, alone and desperate.

And it hadn't even worked for her – at least not entirely.

A swish of Maeve's brush through paint drew his attention back. The library sat still around them. Something in him relaxed as he allowed himself to stare freely at her face. The vision in front of him – Maeve at her easel, fair hair hanging loose over her shoulders, brush gripped between her fingers – had haunted him recently in the dark space where his dreams ought to be.

She drew her lower lip between her teeth, humming beneath her breath. Jude flipped the corner of his coat over his lap and smoothed it down, black wool scratchy under his palm.

'Stay still,' she murmured. Her brows lowered, giving her the appearance of a disappointed schoolteacher as she looked up. 'How many times do I have to ask you?'

Helplessly, Jude felt like grinning. Something had eroded in him when he decided to trust her to paint his icon. He pressed his hand harder to his thigh.

Maybe not an erosion, but a softening.

'How long has it been?' he asked.

'Almost two hours.' She leaned over to dip her brush in a splotch of brownish-orange. *Burnt sienna*, she'd called it. 'The underpainting is almost done.'

'The *underpainting*?' Jude didn't like the sound of that.

Maeve snickered.

He returned his gaze to the window just as another wave of fogginess crested over him. He swayed slightly on the stool. The three birds had disappeared. Jude found he'd forgotten why he'd wanted to see them in the first place.

'Are you feeling okay?' Maeve's voice sounded very far away.

A knock sounded on the door. 'I'll get it.' Jude moved unsteadily to his feet, thankful for the diversion. He caught the tail end of Maeve's exasperated groan as he passed.

Elden stood at the door, a tray with a teapot, three mugs and a plate of biscuits in his hands. It looked out of place next to his oversized frame. Jude eyed the biscuits sceptically. He imagined they would do the job if he needed something to hammer in a nail.

Elden harrumphed. 'They're not for you.'

Maeve placed her hand into the crook of his elbow to lean around him. The top of her head brushed his chin. 'Oh! Elden, how wonderful.' She smiled, the corners of her eyes crinkling as she examined the tray. 'Are these the shortbread biscuits I gave you the recipe for?'

'Aye.' Elden smiled back at her. 'Gave me a spot of bother, but I reckon they're all right.'

He looked inordinately proud of himself as he watched Maeve take a bite. Her lips pressed tightly together as she chewed. Jude could practically see the lump of shortbread move down her throat as she swallowed.

'Lovely,' she said, coughing slightly. 'Thank you.'

Elden's smile widened as he tried to peer around them. 'What are you doing? Can I come in?'

'I'll be taking that,' Jude interrupted, prising the tray from Elden's grip. 'Goodbye.'

He shut the door firmly, fighting the need to brace against it as nausea swirled in his stomach. Gathering himself with a stern word, Jude turned, somewhat concerned that Maeve hadn't complained about him shutting the door in Elden's face, only to find her bent over, coughing into her palms. Her hand shot out. 'Tea. Tea – please. By the *saints*.'

Jude hurriedly poured her a cup, thrusting it into her outstretched hand. She straightened, gulping it down in three swallows. Her face was red, eyes streaming. She smacked her palm against her chest as she continued to sputter. 'I think he mixed up the salt and sugar.'

He couldn't help the laugh that tumbled out of him. She'd been so kind to Elden, eating the biscuit with feigned relish, complimenting him until he smiled. Jude laughed harder when he caught her bending to refill her cup, tipping it back into her mouth. '*Oh*—' he fought to catch his breath. 'Your *face*.'

'Just be glad you didn't have to eat one,' Maeve muttered darkly. 'I fear I'll never get the taste from my mouth . . .' she trailed off. 'Jude.' Her voice rang with false sweetness.

He took a slow step back. He didn't like the way she was eyeing him. 'Yes . . .'

'How would you like to no longer sit for your portrait?'

He blinked. That was not what he'd been expecting. 'Why, going to use your magic to finish it?'

'No.' Maeve's mouth tightened even further. 'But I don't *really* need you here for it anymore today. Sure, it would make my life a little more difficult without you, but I've done more with less. Only . . .' Her expression turned almost predatory. Something low in Jude's stomach tightened. He wasn't sure if he loved the look on her face or feared it. Perhaps some unholy combination of the two. 'I think I need some sort of – *reward* for letting you leave early.'

He cleared his throat. 'Reward?'

'Mm.' Maeve nudged her toe against the discarded tray on the floor. Amidst the tea rubble, one final piece of shortbread lay untouched. Jude studied it, contemplating the merits of choking down one overly salted biscuit if it meant his freedom.

'You want me to eat it.'

She smiled.

Dammit. He wanted to go lie down. Go outside and let the fresh air loosen the cobwebs. He did *not* want to spend the rest of the day sitting still, even if it meant watching Maeve work. He bent down and retrieved the biscuit. Gearing himself up, Jude shoved it whole into his mouth.

Somehow, it managed to be both teeth-meltingly salty and textured like clay left to dry in the sun. He prised his molars apart, forcing himself to chew and swallow. She watched the entire debacle with eyes bright with mischief. When it was gone, Jude wiped his lower lip clean of crumbs, licking his thumb after. He kept his gaze level on her as he did it.

Maeve blinked once, twice. Her eyes snapped back to his as she smiled, killing whatever quip he'd been preparing to make. 'You have crumbs on your face.' Her fingers brushed the corner of his mouth. 'Just here.'

23

Maeve

The following week passed in a comfortable rhythm.
Maeve's magic didn't seek an outlet as she painted, which
both concerned and soothed her. She wasn't sure if she
was ready for another episode, but equally, she worried if the
icon would work as she hoped if she did not. It brought a skittishness to her thoughts, as if they didn't know where to settle.
Coupled with the increasing desire to be around Jude as much
as possible . . . she didn't know how to feel.

She wondered if the restlessness under her skin was an effect
of painting his icon. The connection between her and her work
was there as usual, but the strung-out tension, the awareness that
coloured their every interaction . . . that was new.

Something was changing in Jude, too, the longer they
progressed. He smiled more often, touched her more easily, met
her gaze for longer. Small acts of trust that didn't go unnoticed.

They'd spent most of their days in her makeshift studio, a
room she'd learned Jude had lived in during his earliest years
at Ánhaga. She would paint while he read or watched her work,
stopping only to eat or to stomp around the yard when he grew
fed up with sitting still. She'd insisted he sat for her each day
despite not technically *needing* him in front of her to work.
Surprisingly, he hadn't questioned her request, which worried
her more than anything else.

She wished that was all she noticed about him.

Sometimes, between the smiles, there was a blankness behind his eyes that reminded her of Siobhan. A stilted quality to his movements. More than once she'd caught him reaching for something only to stop halfway, or leave saying he was off to get a cup of tea or something to eat, only to return empty-handed hours later. He was docile and softer than the Jude she had first met.

The strange behaviour wasn't constant, but it was enough to give her pause. She wondered if the icon was to blame.

Not wondered . . . she *knew* it was. But yet, they'd both decided the risk was worth it, even if it pained her to see him with all his sharp edges sloughed away.

Maeve traced her way across the fields towards the orchard. Her breath puffed out in white clouds, frost crackling under her feet. In the distance, the moors were dusted with snow like powdered sugar. The sun barely seemed to crest their slice of the world before setting again, leaving their post-lunch walks to take place in a soupy, bruised dusk more often than not. Even on a morning walk like this one, the heat of the sun was weak and insubstantial on her skin.

She squinted towards Jude's figure as he wove between the apple trees. His coat swept against his ankles, catching on the patches of hardy grass that clung on through the frost. The low light of winter cast a long and meandering shadow behind him. He'd been quiet today. Brooding, even more so than usual.

She didn't want to admit how his stern glare affected her.

Maeve wondered how his contained intensity transcribed to other parts of his life, thoughts she hid like a stolen toffee, sweet under her tongue. She pictured how the tendons in his neck would stretch tight, how his eyes would grow hazy with pleasure. How she'd press her palms flat to his back and pull him closer, how he'd dig his fingers into her hip in a hold just the right side of pain.

Her dalliances back at the Abbey were hardly common occurrences, maybe a handful of times a year when she felt particularly trapped within its limestone halls and craved human connection. They had never been more than a satiation of lust made thrilling by the fact they were so forbidden. As an acolyte, celibacy was expected, even if it wasn't always maintained – Maeve knew she hadn't been the only one who occasionally sneaked out to sample what Whitebury had to offer.

The drifting heat she felt towards Jude was different. She'd rarely experienced want directed at a specific person. It was strange and unwieldy in its refusal to abate. Not when he stretched his arms over his head at his desk to reveal a narrow strip of stomach marked with ink-black tattoos in symbols she couldn't make out. Nor when he tapped a pencil against his lips, the wood scored from his teeth. Especially not one memorable time she'd been reaching for a flat of paint tubes that had somehow ended up on a high shelf, and he'd come close behind her, chest brushing her back as he stretched to retrieve it. She felt the ghost of his touch for hours later. Remembered it that night when she was alone with her face pressed into the pillow.

She ducked her chin into the collar of her coat to hide her flushed cheeks as he neared. All her belongings had begun to lose the salt-soaked, dusty smell of the Abbey and take on the scent of the house. Hearth-fire and windswept moors. Apples and sloe berries.

The tip of his nose was pink, lips reddened. His red scarf had unwound from his neck. Behind him, clouds tumbled through the sky on a far-off breeze, bringing the faintest strain of salt.

Maeve shivered, her teeth clacking together. As he brushed by her and headed back towards the house, he draped his scarf around her neck. It smelled of him, warm from his body.

She watched the hunched outline of his body as he stepped carefully over a half-frozen puddle, unable to stop her heart's transformation into a warm, desirous thing. Made useless with hopeless longing.

She returned to her makeshift studio alone. The scarf slid slowly off her neck to pool in a puddle of red wool on her lap. Maeve stroked her fingers over it, thinking of hazel eyes turned bright, of the brush of fingertips over her pulse. She draped it carefully over the stool Jude normally sat on and picked up her brush.

The icon was nearly complete, but something was missing.

A familiar sense of heady devotion found a home behind her sternum as she touched her brush to the canvas. She'd missed this: the act of worship that was painting. The most honest part of her, the truest commitment she would ever make. More than the Abbey, more than her prayers offered up to saints, more, even than her desire for a hand guiding her as she walked through life, was Maeve's love for painting. Ever since she'd first begun studying iconography as a girl, as she'd moved through training and honed her abilities to a fine point, she'd known that her craft was entirely separate from her faith, despite the similarities.

There was a steadiness to her devotion, a surety. She could sit in front of her easel and release every part of her to the canvas, knowing it would take her faith without judgement. Her anger and her despair, her confidence and her joy. Her work welcomed everything the same. And no matter where she found herself when her time with Jude had run its course, if she fell back to her knees at the foot of the altar or decided to fend for herself without the saints to guide her, she would always have her craft. She couldn't find it in her to be upset at the linking between her painting, her iconography, and her magic. Picking up a brush had always felt like a transcendent experience.

And that was the difference between faith and devotion, Maeve thought as the first stirring of gold began in the corners of her eyes, as her fingers started the tell-tale tremble on the brush.

Her faith in the Abbey was the foundation she had been placed upon as a girl, its branches threading upwards into her thoughts, her beliefs, even her memories. Branches that helped her grow, yes — but also branches that choked.

Her devotion to her craft was her faith made manifest. A deep commitment that required action and intent. It was something she'd chosen again and again. Something that made her feel powerful. Capable. Accepted for who she was. A talent she had fought to make hers and hers alone.

The Abbey could rock her foundation, her very faith, but they could never take her devotion. She could hold tight to her art – what made it sacred, what made it divine – and call it entirely her own. Something the Abbey could never strip from her, as much as they may try.

With that thought swelling in her chest, she set her brush to the canvas and finally gave her magic the freedom to sweep her away into the vast and gold-hued unknown.

24

Maeve

The faintest strain of gold lingered in the air as Maeve set down her brush and examined her work. As in life, Jude looked stern and forbidding, his angled face and intelligent eyes seeing through every guard she'd erected against him. She'd depicted him on a wooden stool with his legs outstretched. One hand on his thigh, his fingers long and elegant against the blackness of his clothes. The other hand was upraised in the sign of the saints. Thumb and first two fingers outstretched, the last two curled inwards towards his palm.

Finished and fully dry thanks to her magic.

Would this work – having Jude pray to his icon?

The idea that they were missing something wouldn't leave her alone. What did it mean if it *did* work? Not every person who had their memory tampered with was a saint, herself included, though she still held firm to her idea that her iconography linked her to the icons as much as sainthood did. Would Jude's prayers restore any memories Maeve might be missing too?

She tipped her head back and screwed her eyes shut. So many questions and not enough answers. Every step shrouded in darkness with little more than a candle to find a path through the mire. She sighed, digging her knuckles into her lower back. A haziness lingered behind her eyes.

The door holding back her doubt grew thinner by the day. It wouldn't be long until it disappeared entirely. When she had first come to Jude's house, she'd been committed to fulfilling her Abbey-given goals and returning home, ready to claim her spot as lead iconographer.

And now . . . Now, Maeve could only think of finding answers.

She leaned forward and scribbled her signature onto the corner. Her abdomen twisted with the motion, a low ache starting between her hips. She ignored it as an uninvited mixture of trepidation and anxiety swirled in her stomach. It was like she'd suddenly become privy to the structure of a house when previously she'd only seen the outside adornment. Nearly her whole life had been dedicated to maintaining the facade – it was high time she saw in full what she had worked so hard to build.

The pain in her back had spread further into her lower stomach, cramping her muscles with a vice grip as she got to her feet. When her belly gave another painful twist, she quickly did the maths. As usual, her monthlies had arrived with nothing less than stellar timing.

Feeling distinctly hard done by, Maeve left the studio and trudged up to take a hot bath. Water helped, usually. Heat compresses even more, but she wasn't about to find Elden to help her scrounge up some rice and an old pillowcase.

Once she was done in the water, her skin red and fingertips pruned, Maeve curled into a ball under her quilt. She wished she had Bronagh's tea to help with the cramping. Tears pricked at the corners of her eyes. She hadn't even got to say goodbye to the older matron when she left her home. Would she ever see her again?

Loneliness cinched her chest. She felt suddenly like a child. Alone, weak, missing a kind touch. Wiping dampness from her cheeks, she pulled the blanket over her head and tried her best to sleep.

She awoke hours later to something soft butting against her chin. Olive stood by her head, staring at her with a luminous yellow gaze. Maeve reached up to pet her, returning to her curled position when her abdomen gave a painful cramp. 'How'd you get in here?' she asked the cat. Olive blinked slowly in reply.

'I let her in.'

Maeve jolted, groaning when the movement sent another lash of pain through her lower belly.

Jude hovered at the foot of her bed. The light slanting through the room was orange-tinted and mellow. Sometime between lunch and sunset. She'd slept for maybe five hours. Jude swept his gaze down her curled form, concern lighting his expression as he moved around the side of the bed towards her. 'Are you hurt?'

'Get out,' Maeve mumbled, turning to press her face into the pillow. She wanted to cry at the egregious betrayal of her body when she most needed its compliance.

He sat. The bed dipped with his weight.

'*Jude.*' She pulled the covers over her face. 'Please leave.'

He peeled back the quilt enough to see her face. She must look a fright. She'd tumbled into bed immediately after her bath, barely keeping her wits about her long enough to dress. Her hair surrounded her in a tangled mass of half-damp clumps. She'd have panicked over having it in such a state if she'd been in less pain. She valued her hair more than most of her possessions.

'Are you okay?' he asked. A line appeared between his brows. 'Did something happen?'

'No, perfectly fine,' Maeve grumbled, snatching the blanket back from him and pulling it up to her chin. 'Clearly.'

Jude didn't reply. He merely continued to look at her, tracing his eyes down her body like he was searching for hidden injury. His gaze locked on her arms crossed over her midsection, the shape visible under the quilt. 'Ah.'

'Yes, *ah*. It's what happens to women once a month, Jude. Not like you'd have much experience with that.'

His eyes flicked back to hers. 'Monthlies?'

'Women.'

The corners of his mouth twitched as he pushed back to his

feet. Maeve closed her eyes and listened to the muted sounds of him pottering about her room. She didn't have many possessions with her, a fact she'd winced at when she'd unpacked again after deciding to stay at Ánhaga. A few bits of jewellery, her scanty wardrobe comprising of long dresses and hardy knitwear. Ink pots, and hair ribbons. She heard a drawer slide open and wondered if he was sifting through her underthings. The thought sent a rush of blood to her cheeks.

She tried to sit up. 'What are you looking for?'

Jude's footsteps moved closer to the bed. 'Lean forward.' He sighed. 'Just let me . . .'

She obeyed with a stifled whimper as he sat down behind her. His reflection showed in the mirror across from the bed. He drew his lip between his teeth, worrying the edge. Her belly clenched with something that wasn't quite pain. For a long moment, neither of them moved. The silence between them felt intimate in a way she wasn't quite ready to dissect.

She knew how men usually reacted when confronted with something . . . *inconvenient* in a woman's body, and it wasn't pleasant. Whenever she'd needed to take time off for her monthlies in the Abbey, back before Bronagh had started supplying her with tea that stopped them altogether, Ezra had made it clear he didn't think the pain was worth missing work over. Maeve remembered several occasions when he'd demanded she work through it. He'd worked while inconvenienced, and she'd do well to display the same commitment.

Now that she allowed herself to admit it, he was a bit of a bastard.

The bed shifted. Maeve's attention snapped back to Jude.

He gently slid the tangled mass of her hair out from under her back, draping it over the covers behind her. His eyelashes cast long shadows over his skin like spikes of the sun. Carefully, he began brushing her hair, smoothing through the ends until they were dry before working his way up to her scalp. Drowsiness overtook her the longer he worked. He ran his fingers through the fine hair at her temples and nape, detangling so gently she barely felt it.

She pressed her lips together and shut her eyes. She tried to tell herself it was her heightened emotions and not the fact that no one had ever taken care of her like this that drew tears to her eyes.

Glass tinkled, and the smell of her rosemary hair oil drifted over the room. Splitting the hair into three sections, Jude slowly began braiding, starting over several times when the hair tangled or slipped through his fingers. Little noises of exasperation rumbled from his chest every time he made a mistake.

Maeve kept her eyes closed. She didn't want to think about the softness of his care. She *couldn't.*

He tied the end off with a ribbon. Before he stood, he ran his hand down her hair one final time. Slowly, reverently, as though touching her like this, like she was precious, was something he didn't want to forget.

Maeve allowed herself one last look at his face as he moved to his feet. The line between his brows was back, deeper than before. His hand twitched at his side as though he was stopping himself from reaching for her again. She waited. Her pulse thrummed under her jaw.

He turned and left.

It took her a long time to fall back asleep. When she did, it felt like only moments had passed, but the room had darkened with nightfall. Moonlight cut a clean white streak across her rumpled quilt.

Jude stood over her again.

'Dammit, Jude,' Maeve exclaimed, sitting up. 'You scared me.'

He chuckled, setting something down on her vanity before lighting a candle. Warm light licked up the walls, lingering in the hollows of his cheeks as he eyed her over his shoulder. The concern had yet to leave his gaze. 'How are you?'

'Better.' Thankfully, the cramping rarely lasted more than an afternoon.

He fussed with something on the vanity, his back to her. 'Rest as long as you need.'

She shuffled up to prop herself against the headboard. As she moved, her braid fell over her shoulder and down her chest. She brought the end to her nose, breathing in the earthy smell of the rosemary. The gesture had meant something to her.

'Here.' Jude turned from the vanity and handed her a chipped clay mug.

Maeve brought it to her nose. It smelled somewhat familiar to the blend Bronagh used to make her. The matron had made the brew for those who requested it, but she kept a close guard on her recipe. 'Jude . . .' she hesitated. 'What is this?'

'Elden makes it for one of our neighbours when she asks. Bethan says it helps with her monthlies. And, it ah—' He looked away.

Even in the dim light, Maeve could see his blush. 'Prevents pregnancy?'

'Or so I've been told. If you – that is, well.' That expressionless mask she'd thought long abandoned fell over his face as he inched back towards the door.

'Thank you,' Maeve said, bringing the tea to her lips to cover her grin. Elden had cut through some of the bitterness of the yarrow with a dash of honey. 'Glad to see his kitchen skills aren't transferable to herbalism.'

Jude smiled, finally making it to the door. 'No. In that, he's surprisingly accomplished.' He gave her one final look of concern. 'And you're feeling better?'

'I am. Thank you for the tea, and—' she gestured towards her braid. Jude didn't reply, his hand going towards the doorknob behind him. Maeve couldn't resist one final attempt to crack his carefully laid mask. 'And thanks for ensuring I don't get pregnant.'

Shock crossed his features. 'That's not — that's not what I meant by it.'

'I know,' she laughed. 'I'm just teasing.'

The shock melted away as he leaned against the doorway and crossed his arms over his chest. He eyed her speculatively. 'You certainly are feeling better,' he murmured. 'Maybe you *should* get back to work.'

Maeve rolled her eyes, shooing him from the room.

25

Jude

Morning found Jude seated in his usual spot in the front room, Olive on one knee and a botany book open on the other. He flipped through it idly. Bethan and her mother were bound to arrive in the next few weeks, as they did once a season. Bethan was a keen forager, and Jude and Elden often helped her comb through the property for the ingredients she needed. Winter brought hawthorn and sloe berries, wood blewit mushrooms and the occasional crab apple. Chestnuts for roasting and nettles for tea. With any luck, she would bring a batch of gin from last year's sloe harvest. She knew it was his favourite.

He let his eyes drift back to the window. A writhing headache pulsed behind his eyes. He tried to ignore it. What it meant.

In the distance, Maeve picked her way through the fields bordering the northern wall. Her fair hair hung loose and gleaming down her back, stark against the blackness of the greatcoat.

His greatcoat.

His fingers twitched in his lap. He could still feel the liquid smoothness of her hair, softer than anything he'd ever felt. Shining like spun gold in the candlelight. He leaned closer to the window as she tilted her head back to face the drizzling rain. He could see the edge of her smile, even separated by walls and windows. His stomach clenched.

Tender, unwelcome emotions. Lingering where they shouldn't.

He turned back to his book, finding it harder than usual to focus. Praying to the icon had to work, not just to regain his memories, but to erase the strange miasma its presence had settled over him. The incessant headache that had cropped up when Maeve had begun painting hadn't yet abated. His memories felt like colours leaching from a late-winter sky. Growing less and less vivid by the day.

He'd sneaked away to his library each morning to hide his memories in his books, though his magic had felt sluggish to come to the surface, reluctant to answer his call. It was more of a protective measure than anything else – Jude's magic hadn't had the same uncontrollable energy it usually did, writhing under his skin like a hungry beast. It hadn't in a while. Not since he had jumped into Maeve's memories after the bog, now that he thought of it.

Something in him was changing, though he wasn't yet sure if it was down to his new icon or the iconographer lurking in every long-forgotten corner of his soul. Both, maybe. Most likely.

He tried to control the roll of nausea in his belly. The gnawing ache of fear.

His icon was almost finished. When Maeve asked him to pray to it, he'd have to go back to that dark place of devotion he'd tried so hard to move on from. As much as he wanted to regain his memories and free himself from every last tie binding him to the Abbey, he was afraid of what the memories of his child-hood might show. A time characterized not by care and laughter but by blood and steel and salt.

He knew enough by now to call it by its true name.

Abuse.

His abuser's face may have been wiped from his memory, but his body still bore the scars.

Glancing at the window to ensure Maeve was still out on her walk, he carefully pushed back the sleeves of his jumper to bare his forearms. He kept them covered even on the hottest days of summer. The slender inked lines and crudely formed symbols were starkly black in the pale morning light. It would be the same if he lifted his shirt and looked at his stomach and thighs.

Down the insides of his arms and from hip to hip were neatly ordered lines inked for passing weeks. Under his collarbone bore the sainthood symbol. BELONGING marred the hollow of his right hip below the tallies. Small symbols for loyalty, piety, commitment, and devotion were scattered over his arms, legs, and stomach. The largest was at the centre of his chest, a half-circle with three lines fanning from the top. The Abbey's sigil.

A reminder of everything lost and everything taken from him. Tattoos he'd driven into his skin during his weakest moments when he believed he'd deserved the torment he'd endured at the Abbey.

Though his memories were distorted and vague, the rot had long sunk into his marrow. He remembered punishment. Coercion. Venomous words in his ears and words carved into his skin. The hot sting of the knife. The grip of a fist in his once-long hair.

He'd been told to keep the blood and his scars hidden. What would the other acolytes think if they saw? They'd believe he deserved it – a weak, cowardly boy punished for his failings. It had taken Jude a long time to fight the voice that told him his behaviour *did* warrant the abuse. To realize he had been a child, and no child deserved to be harmed by someone meant to protect them, even if he couldn't remember who that person was who had made it their mission to turn his upbringing into a living nightmare.

Now, when he felt the urge to reach for ink and needle, he turned to his books, instead. It was a dreadful practice, maybe – viewing one's pain play out in live action – but it was therapeutic all the same. Jude didn't deserve the abuse. Nor did he deserve to be continually punished for it.

He saw that now.

It had been almost a year since he last pushed the ink into his skin.

His heart thrummed frantic behind his ribs as he saw Maeve turn and start to make her way back to the house. Animal quick, urging him to run. He wasn't sure how he'd feel taking on the role of acolyte once more. It had been almost a decade since he last prayed, longer yet since he believed. He may have been marked a saint in the eyes of the Abbey, but that didn't make him holy.

What would his icon show – a saint or a heretic?

26

Jude

He reread the same page three times before the knock came. His gaze remained on the page for a breath before he looked up. Maeve stood at the door. The ends of her hair lay damp against the coat, the top frizzing with rain. A smile on her face.

'It's done.' Her voice was quiet, hesitant.

He shut the book. 'Your walk? I gathered that myself, funny enough.'

Maeve sat in the armchair across from him. Olive immediately vacated his lap in favour of hers. Little traitor. 'No. The painting. Your icon. It's ready.'

Jude stiffened. That was fast.

'Did you . . .' he hesitated, not wanting to raise her abilities for fear of scaring her. 'Did anything strange happen?' he settled on.

Maeve looked at Olive on her lap, stroking down her back. Unaware she was being used as a distraction, Olive curled tighter, purring with alarming ferocity. Maeve's bottom lip trembled.

'Maeve,' he said gently. 'It's okay if it did. It's nothing to be ashamed of. That's what we wanted to happen, isn't it?'

She levelled his gaze. 'I'm not *ashamed*.'

'No,' he backtracked. 'I just . . . I feel it, too. The Abbey's interest in your magic, their influence – it feels tainted. Like they've corrupted it.' He paused, words escaping him. He didn't want to say that he still felt damaged by it, even now. 'I wanted to reassure you there's nothing wrong with you. Even if the Abbey can take your magic, it's still *yours*.'

He felt the sweep of her eyes as keenly as if she'd touched him directly. After a moment that felt far longer than a few seconds, she blew out a breath. 'Thank you. I know that. It's just hard to see it as something useful and not something . . . Well.' She lifted her hand off Olive and pressed the back to her cheek as if to cool herself down. 'Tainted. As you said.'

Relief coursed through him. 'I know how it feels. But it's not, Maeve. Not at all.'

Not you, his thoughts reminded him. *It only applies to her — not you.*

Jude dropped his eyes, studying the edge of a tattoo on his wrist. It was easy to view Maeve, as sincere, as *golden* as she was, as someone not tainted by the Abbey's touch. But him . . .

'So, yes,' she continued, unaware of the direction of his thoughts. 'Something did happen. The same as when I completed Felix's painting and the sketch of Siobhan. I saw gold, lost track of time, and your icon was done.'

Jude cocked his head. 'That's a good thing, I think.'

'Is it?' Beneath the fall of her skirt, one booted foot bobbed up and down.

'It solidifies a link between your magic and icons,' he explained, sounding more confident than he felt. 'Maybe that will grow once I pray to it.'

Maeve hummed. Her eyes had a glazed, worried look about them. He had grown adept at reading her face over the weeks, finding it almost instinctual how quickly he could parse her thoughts from her expression. She parted her lips, hesitating for a long moment before whispering, 'I'm scared.'

His hands tightened on the armrests, the wood creaking. 'Of what?'

'If it doesn't work . . . praying to your icon.' She shook her head. 'I can tell painting the icon is affecting you. I can see it in your face, in how you've been . . .' she paused. 'Forgetting things.'

Jude palmed the back of his head. Her words were exposing in a way he wasn't ready to address. 'It's eroding, in a way. Like each swipe of your brush is a wave against me. My mind is more—' he waved a hand. 'Loose. Changeable. Like I can't quite nail down my thoughts.'

She studied him closely; looking for what, he didn't know. 'We thought that might happen.'

'And you? As the iconographer?' he asked, rolling the words over on his tongue, tasting the bitterness. 'How do you feel?'

Maeve shrugged. 'I . . . I haven't noticed anything different. Not really. Well. I suppose that's not entirely true.' She closed her eyes, missing the fear Jude knew shone clearly on his face. 'Something doesn't feel quite right. I can't explain it, but I feel an icon isn't complete unless it's done at the Abbey.'

He froze. 'You don't think it will work?'

He hadn't even considered that she might feel this way. It had been largely her idea, after all. She was the one who was sent here to paint him, and it was she who picked up the brush and posed him for his icon. Yet, the resignation painted over her features was undeniable.

The trust he'd decided to place in her wavered. Like a pebble dropped in a quiet pond, its ripples disturbing the stillness beneath. Had he made a mistake? Was this all a ploy to complete her mission after all? After everything he'd told her, every vulnerable inch of himself he'd revealed?

'You want to return to the Abbey,' he said bluntly.

The gaze Maeve pinned on him was unwavering. 'I'm not taking your icon back there. I promise you, that's the last thing I want to do. I just wanted to let you know that . . .' she swallowed roughly. 'Something doesn't feel as it should.'

He pressed her hands into his thighs to still their shaking. 'Explain.'

'When I paint icons in the Abbey, it's almost like it's not really *me* painting them. I'm given a description of the saint, and I work off that. Usually, it's short. Hair, eye, and skin colour. Basic description of their features. Their age and a few lines about their personality. The rest is up to me. Only . . .' she frowned. 'I never really think about it while I'm painting. It's like a face is planted into my mind, and it's my job to transfer it to the canvas. Like I'm a conduit for the magic. My memory magic at work, probably.' Her eyes slid back to his. 'But with you, you're different.'

Jude raised a brow.

She looked briefly uncomfortable. 'I know you.'

'As much as anyone,' he replied, even as warmth stole through his chest.

'No. I mean—' She huffed out a breath. 'You're in front of me. I painted what I saw, not what I was told. That painting up there . . . the icon is of *you*, Jude. Not a portrait based on a description. Not a saint. A man. You're real to me, and I think the painting shows it.'

Her words weren't meant to be affectionate, but he felt their weight all the same. As she looked at him, describing how she had pictured his face, his hands, the set of his mouth, Jude felt a terrible rush of nakedness. Maeve hadn't painted Jude the saint; she had painted *him*. He knew, as he followed her from the room and up the stairs to her studio, he was about to see the most intimate rendition of his personhood he'd ever been allowed.

The very thought of seeing Maeve's portrait terrified him. Yet – he had to see it. Had to see how she saw him, even if the idea of it made his chest ache, his mouth run dry.

Too soon, they were upstairs in the room she was using as a studio, where she'd moved the painting to work on after beginning it in his library. Jude's heart raced, trying to outpace the vicious beast of anxiety as she moved to stand behind the icon. Her knuckles flashed white around the frame. 'Are you sure?'

'Show me,' he murmured. 'Please.'

Squaring her shoulders, Maeve spun the canvas around to face him.

His first thought was one of awe. She was talented, immensely so. The level of detail, the liberties she'd taken with light and shadow – every part of it was masterful. Her work was breathtakingly realistic yet still stylized, displaying her comprehensive knowledge of colour and technique.

He could hardly admit it to himself, but he looked . . . *beautiful* wasn't the word. Striking, maybe. He'd always been ambivalent over his features. He liked his hazel eyes when the sun hit them and didn't mind his dark hair when it was long enough to hold a curl, though he hadn't permitted it to reach that length in years. His nose wasn't his favourite. But the way Maeve had rendered him left him feeling both admired and fully *seen* in a way he'd never been before.

The assertiveness of his gaze in the painting sent a shiver down his neck. He looked untouchable. Something in the angle of his brows and the press of his lips spoke of secret defiance. Like he wanted to be seen, but only as much as he allowed. She'd posed him with the upraised hand of a saint but given him the cool gaze of a dissident.

Jude knelt slowly before it, filled with the strangeness only studying one's face could bring.

She was right. She did know him. The evidence was in the paint. The faint spray of freckles across his nose, the thick slash of his brows, one more curved than the other. Even the way the light sank into the peaks and hollows of his face . . . it was *him*. As he knew himself best.

The realization came torturously slow, an unravelling that started in his chest and wound its way up to his throat where it clenched tight – he couldn't hide from her. Not any longer.

'What do you think?' Maeve asked. Her gaze returned nervously to the icon.

A smile tugged at his lips – she wanted him to like it. 'You're very talented, Maeve,' he said. 'It's like nothing I've ever seen before.' Her cheeks reddened at the praise, and he immediately wanted to see how much more he could make her blush. 'It's beautiful. Truly.'

The colour in her face grew, spreading down her neck. 'Thank you,' she whispered.

Jude remained on his knees, staring up at her. He let himself smile fully.

'Are you going to pray to it?' she asked briskly, getting back to business.

'*Now?*' He hadn't considered that she'd want him to try immediately. He supposed it made sense. Why waste time when both their memories hung in the balance? His stomach clenched at the thought, ripe with fear of what would happen when he finally had the complete picture of his life available. What had he forgotten? What had the Abbey taken from him?

Guilt surged; its grip tenacious despite how hard he tried to shove it down—

If his memories were returned, if all his secrets were laid bare . . . he would have to tell Maeve everything. Every facet of her memory magic that he'd been trying so desperately to hide would be forced into the light. He would have to contradict her ideas, tell her that she was heading in the right direction, but she wasn't there yet. There was still more to learn. Secrets he held the key to but had been reluctant to give her.

He wasn't ready. He couldn't toss her to the storm. Not yet. He needed more time.

Time to ease her into the truth, or time to bask in the denial?

He swallowed the question down, feeling its weight settle in the pit of his stomach.

'Why not?' Maeve asked. 'There's not much to be gained by waiting. For either of us.'

'And what if it doesn't work? What then?'

Her hand slipped into the pocket of her dress, the shape of her fingers racing under the fabric. Jude knew what she was doing, what he'd find if he pulled her hand free and prised her fingers open.

An icon, worn smooth from hours of prayer.

How could she still believe, after everything he'd shown her?

'Maeve,' he urged, louder than he meant. His knees ached, but he stayed on the floor. 'What then?'

'We go back to the Abbey,' she finally whispered. 'And we search for answers there.'

'Is that what you want?'

He had to know. Did she want to go back, despite how they'd treated her? Did she still want to return with her information about memories and the Goddenwood, about *him*? Was her goal still to resume her life, now as lead iconographer?

'I don't know,' she admitted, her voice small. 'Part of me wants to stay here. With you. The other half wants to pretend none of it ever happened.'

Her words stung. He wouldn't pretend otherwise. 'I can't,' he said, louder than he meant.

'Can't what?'

'Go to the Abbey. The repercussions . . .' Jude closed his eyes, head dropping to his chest as his words came out as choked as a confession. 'I don't know what they'll do if I return.'

Maeve laid her hand on his bowed head.

A gift. An offering of a touch he wouldn't normally allow; Jude, the penitent, on his knees before her. The unexpected need to submit to her every wish in the hopes of earning her favour imbued him with a slow-burning warmth. He didn't mind kneeling at her feet. He'd stay as long as she let him.

Her hand slid slowly off his head as she knelt beside him. The faintest hint of green shone in her dark irises. Her mouth parted; the tip of her tongue visible through her teeth.

Words left him entirely.

'Jude,' she whispered. 'You need to pray.'

A choked noise left him, bringing with it the realization that his ability to pray wasn't something he'd broken, merely fled from— 'I don't remember how.'

Maeve folded her hands over his, pressing his palms together. Her hands looked so fragile around his. Paint stained her fingertips, gold dust lingering in the creases of her knuckles. Her touch was a revelation. An unmooring.

'I'll teach you,' she whispered.

Before Jude could even consider bowing his head, before he could search for the words to beseech his icon, the door crashed open.

27

Maeve

A woman stood in the doorway.

Her dark hair was windswept and waterlogged around her face, her light brown skin flushed as she scanned the room, alighting immediately on Jude. She heaved a rapid inhale as she moved swiftly across the threshold. 'Jude.'

Maeve jumped to her feet at the same time as Jude. She stepped in front of him, both arms spread wide. Her loudest thought, her *only* thought, was that this woman was from the Abbey. Terror turned her fingers to ice. Were they not quick enough? Had they somehow got wind of them trying to reverse the memory loss? That his icon was done? The possibilities made her head spin.

The woman froze, her gaze now firmly fixed on Maeve.

'It's okay,' Jude murmured close to Maeve's ear. He gently laid his hands on her upper arms and lowered them back to her sides as he stepped around her. 'It's my neighbour. Bethan.'

'Bethan?' Maeve repeated. The name sounded familiar.

Before Jude or the stranger could speak, Elden appeared. He glanced between the three of them, a frown creasing his brow briefly before it smoothed over with his smile. He clapped Bethan on the shoulder. 'I see you found him.'

Bethan gave herself a brief shake. 'Goodness. Where are my manners.' She thrust a hand towards Maeve, a strained smile already in place. 'Bethan, as Jude said. I live with my mum not too far up the road.'

Maeve shook her hand. Her fingers were like ice, the sleeve of her coat dripping onto the floor.

'You're soaked,' Jude remarked, scanning her up and down. 'Why'd you come all the way in this storm?'

Bethan's eyes flitted to Maeve and back to him. 'It's not so bad out there. And I like the walk.'

Jude smiled. He met Maeve's gaze, nodding encouragingly. 'Let's go downstairs. There should be something you could borrow. And dinner ought to be ready soon.'

Elden levelled Jude with a look Maeve couldn't decipher as he stepped past him towards the door, Bethan already outside. 'Shall I prepare a guest room?' Elden asked, directing his question towards Jude's retreating back.

'That won't be necessary,' Jude called over his shoulder. He disappeared down the hall.

'I didn't realize there were neighbours so close,' Maeve said to Elden once they were alone.

'Not all that close. Past Oakmoor. Maybe an hour's walk,' Elden replied. 'We occasionally meet Bethan and her mum for cards down at the pub.' He hesitated, a strange tension entering his voice. 'Sometimes more when Bethan wants to see Jude alone.'

'Ah.' Maeve swallowed, fingering the edge of her worn, entirely unsuitable chemise and the navy knitted cardigan over it . . . Jude's cardigan. She hadn't seen a need to dress formally when she was just around the house, preferring comfort over fashion. 'I just need to change. I'll meet you downstairs.'

Elden clapped her on the shoulder. His mouth had opened to reply when he abruptly paused, staring past her, towards the icon. 'I thought you weren't going to paint that.'

Maeve drew back, stung even though she knew she shouldn't be. Had Jude discussed his icon with Elden? She certainly hadn't mentioned anything. A worse thought – had Elden read her letter to Ezra, too?

'It's not for the Abbey,' she said, a note of sharpness entering her voice. 'It's for Jude.'

'For Jude?' Elden questioned.

He didn't mean anything by it, Maeve told herself. Elden's fierce protectiveness was one of the things she admired most about him. She laid her hand on his arm. 'It's not to hurt him or to . . . spy. I promise.'

Slowly, Elden nodded. He cast a final look at the icon. 'I'll see you downstairs. Dinner's almost ready.'

Maeve watched him go, her thoughts quickly whipping into a maelstrom.

Bethan.

A knot formed in her stomach as she changed into something more presentable. Were Bethan and Jude . . . she couldn't even think the word. Chewing on the inside of her cheek, Maeve finished buttoning her cardigan and headed down the stairs.

Approaching it like a hot coal, she forced herself to consider the idea that Jude had a lover. A lover who was currently standing in their front hall, one of his jumpers wrapped around her shoulders. She said something, and Jude *laughed*.

Maeve's lungs felt too tight. She studied Bethan from the stairs, taking in what she hadn't had time to in her studio. She was tall, almost Jude's height. Her black hair had dried in messy waves to her shoulders, and her skin gleamed with a healthy glow from the walk.

Undeniably beautiful.

'Maeve.' Jude looked over his shoulder towards where she lurked in the shadows. His smile fell slightly. 'What are you doing halfway up the stairs?'

Her cheeks warmed as she descended the rest of the steps. 'Sorry. I was waiting for Elden.'

On cue, footsteps sounded on the stairs behind her moments before Elden appeared. 'Dinner's ready. Which I'm sure was the plan. Eh, Bethan?' He wrapped an arm congenially around her shoulders and aimed them both towards the kitchen.

'I'm not one to miss a free meal,' Bethan said, 'but I do really need to—'

The rest of her reply was lost down the hall.

Jude lingered behind, his eyes still on Maeve. His expression was unreadable in the soft light from the oil lamps. His mouth opened and shut, a muscle tensing in his jaw. When he spoke, his voice was hoarse. 'She won't stay long.'

'It's fine,' Maeve replied quickly.

He studied her for another long moment before nodding briskly. He headed down the hall towards the kitchen without glancing back.

What was happening? Hadn't they just been kneeling on the floor before Jude's icon, their hearts laid out between them as he had prepared to pray? She looked down, cringing at the mud coating the toes of her boots. Her fingernails were caked with paint, and the hem of her dress was ragged with wear and age.

A mess. Inside and out.

Whatever she thought had been slowly building between them, she needed to tuck it away. She represented everything Jude hated. The Abbey, devotion to the saints, his lost memories. Maeve knew she could be difficult. Ezra had often told her she was naive, her desperation for attention too palpable, turning her into someone exhausting to be around. Words she'd heard often enough to begin to believe them. Jude needed someone different. Someone confident in who they were. Capable and carefree and easy to be around.

Everything she was not.

Feeling like she was gathering the cracked pieces of whatever hope she'd been guarding like a precious jewel, Maeve followed the sound of Jude's laughter towards the little-used dining room at the back of the house.

At Elden's urging, Bethan sat at the head of the table. She

laughed and poked fun at the two men as she ate, though a strange tension lingered around her grip on the fork, her darting gaze. She was also attentive to Maeve, asking her questions about her painting, where she'd got her jumper, and what she did to look after her hair. She found herself warming to the other woman. If it hadn't been for the unwelcome jealousy digging claws into her heart, they might have been friends. If Maeve could push past her feelings, maybe they still could be.

She picked at her food. The malty brown bread, sausages, and mash were more palatable than usual. Not like it made much of a difference. Her appetite had all but disappeared.

'The bread is wonderful,' Bethan remarked. She sipped her wine, sloshing the deep red liquid around in her cup. 'Jude, did you make it?'

He pointed his fork towards Maeve. 'Maeve came up with the recipe. She's quite the baker.'

'Oh!' Bethan exclaimed. 'You must give me the recipe. My mum and I bake bread twice a month to bring to the children's home in Oakmoor. You should join.'

'I'd like that,' Maeve murmured. If she'd been planning on being here long term – which she wasn't – she could have seen herself making a home in the community. Giving back. Searching for the sense of belonging she'd always wanted out of the Abbey. But, like everything good in her life, her time in Jude's home had a quickly approaching expiration date.

Bethan leaned towards Maeve, grinning conspiratorially. 'Elden must be fond of you to allow access to his kitchen.'

Maeve flushed, fiddling with her fork. 'Oh . . . I don't know about that. I've taught him a few recipes, so I reckon I'll be kicked out soon enough.' She forced her lips up in a smile. From across the table, Jude watched her with an unreadable expression.

'As long as it's not Jude in the kitchen, I don't care,' Elden remarked. He propped his hand under his chin and chewed, smiling at Maeve. Her shoulders relaxed somewhat. His ability to settle her with nothing more than a smile or kind comment was uncanny.

'And why is that, Elden?' Jude's voice had turned frosty.

Elden winked at Bethan. 'Think you need to relax, is all. Too uptight.'

Maeve took a sip of wine, swirling it over her teeth as she watched Jude sit back in his seat, hooking one arm over the backrest. 'Hm.'

'I disagree,' Bethan said. Her eyes were fond as she gazed at Jude. 'I rather like that part of him.'

Maeve's fork fell to her plate with a clatter. Jude's eyes swung to hers. She searched his expression for something to pull her from the mire. He brought his glass to his mouth as he raised an eyebrow, fingers tight around the stem. Dark red wine clung to his lower lip. Maeve looked away. Disappointment clamped teeth around her heart.

Bethan was still speaking.

'So, that's why it's just me this time. Mum has been feeling a little under the weather, so I don't know if we'll focus excessively on the herbalism this winter season.'

'Just fortunes and cards, then?' Jude asked.

Maeve tried to listen, she really did, but her mind kept circling back to Bethan and Jude. Part of her, the side that picked at every scab and had long made a habit of eavesdropping on any conversation she could, wanted to know every sordid truth about their relationship. Were Bethan's visits a regular thing? Were they truly lovers or was her jealous mind seeing a connection that wasn't actually there?

A memory surfaced, scoring her mind with the precision of a steel blade.

When she'd been laid up in bed with her monthlies, Jude had brought her tea. He'd given it to her, blushing and stammering, telling her Elden made it for his neighbour to help with similar symptoms.

He also said it prevented pregnancy.

And Maeve had teased him about it, hadn't she? Poked fun and enjoyed his fidgeting.

She stared down at her mostly full plate as pressure built behind her eyes. Carefully, she laid her fork next to her plate, aligning it with the edge of the table. Her fingers moved to fidget with the stem of her wine glass next.

How foolish she'd been. She wasn't the one Jude was worried about protecting.

Bethan laughed, reaching across the table to pat Jude on the wrist. Maeve watched with a sick fascination, unable to look away.

For the first time in days, maybe even weeks, she wanted to be anywhere but his home – but she was a coward. Never one to question her reality until it was too late. Through the buzzing in her ears, she listened to their conversation. It sounded like they were discussing Bethan's foraging. Something with the weather, maybe. It wasn't enough to hold Maeve's attention, nor to keep her gaze from Jude.

He picked at his food almost as slowly as she did. Though he smiled more often than usual, he seemed tense. His occasional laughter sounded forced, almost uncomfortable, though that might've been her own wishful thinking.

Their gazes caught and held across the table.

Jude searched her face with wide eyes. He looked younger. A boy, wondering why his friend was ignoring him. If they were alone, Maeve knew he would ask her what the matter was. She could almost see the question written across his face.

Friends, Maeve reminded herself forcefully. He knew her as a friend, cared for her as a friend. Nothing more and nothing less. She would take it, grateful to have a piece of him at all.

Clearing the plates, Elden urged them to reconvene in the sitting room.

'I think we ought to go upstairs,' Bethan said, eyes on Jude. 'It's getting late.'

Jude pushed back from the table. Maeve tracked his every movement, waiting for his reply. He picked up his cutlery, laying them neatly on his empty plate. Adjusted the hem of his jumper on his hip. He met her eyes for a heartbeat before turning to Bethan and gesturing towards the doorway. 'After you.'

Maeve's lungs emptied in a rush. Though she was no longer sure she had a body, she followed Elden into the kitchen and began filling the sink with hot water. It burned her hands as she scrubbed plate after plate. Try as she might, she couldn't help but listen for every stir in the house. Every creak of footsteps and squeak of furniture. She imagined she could hear the sigh of breath and the slide of skin. She squeezed her eyes shut, surprised to find her lashes damp.

Rejection was a demanding mistress.

'Maeve?' Elden pulled the plate from her hands and gently nudged her aside. He hissed when his hands hit the water, turning the cold tap on and stirring a spoon through the basin to mix it. His movement stilled when he noticed her expression. 'What is it?'

She took a shuddering breath. *Dammit.* She needed to pull herself together. The very thought of Elden sensing the direction of her thoughts sent a frisson of forced calm through her body.

'Just—' she heaved another breath. 'Homesickness.'

'*Homesickness*,' Elden repeated, face sceptical. 'Is that all?'

Maeve nodded, retaking her place at the sink and picking up a plate. Thankfully, Elden didn't prod as he dried every dish she washed. She tried to keep her mind on her task, but— 'How long have they known each other?'

Maeve cringed as Elden's drying motions slowed to a stop. The question had left her lips too quickly to stop. He set the plate down, putting his back to the counter and resting his weight on his hands. 'Bethan and Jude?'

Maeve nodded, watching herself scrub a wine glass as if with someone else's hands.

'A year, maybe,' Elden replied. 'He doesn't have many friends.'

'Is it . . .' she hesitated. Warmth coursed up her neck as she considered how to word her question without outright asking if they were lovers. 'Are they close?'

Elden shrugged. 'Hard to say. I wouldn't say they're friends . . . necessarily. Not close friends. Her presence is more helpful to Jude than anything else.'

Helpful? What did that mean? She chewed on the inside of her lip as she dried the final few dishes, folding the towel neatly on the counter. 'Why did they go upstairs? Where did they go?'

Elden paused. He picked up the drying cloth Maeve had just folded and picked at the hem. 'Jude's bedroom, I believe. But Maeve—'

'I'm going to bed,' she interrupted. 'I'm sorry.'

She'd heard enough, and her emotions were too close to the surface. If she stayed here any longer, she was going to cry. The prospect was too humiliating to consider.

Before Elden could reply, Maeve left the kitchen. She made her way slowly up the stairs, listening to every creak of the house around her. She told herself she didn't care. Her goals may have shifted, but she still had a reason for being here in his home. His memories still hung in the balance, and hers were at risk of slipping every day. She needed to focus on unpicking the link between the icons, the saints, and the artists that created them. The Abbey that stole from them.

After that . . .

Maybe she would return to her family. Maybe she'd rent a cottage by the sea and sell paintings at a village market. She could do anything. Go anywhere.

Jude didn't factor into her decision, her future. He *couldn't*.

She shut her bedroom door behind her and leaned against it.

She wondered if she would've taken this development easier if she'd experienced something similar before. If she'd had friends in the Abbey growing up, maybe she would've grown jealous of them spending time together without her, and learned how to communicate that envy without letting it eat her up inside. Or if she'd had relationships that lasted longer than an evening, maybe she would've learned how to move past those possessive feelings and not let them pummel her confidence into nothing.

But she hadn't. Maeve was at a complete loss at how to cope with the force of both the jealousy and the possessiveness – two emotions foreign to her prior to that evening. She never imagined they could be so strong, so insidious. They demanded all her attention.

She refused to think of Bethan and Jude and the knowledge that she was privileged to see him in ways Maeve had only just begun to dream of. The thought of him, bare, weightless, his hands soft and exploratory. All of his smiles and lingering glances, his bowed head beneath her hand. The look in his eyes as he gazed up at her, a sign of the fragile trust blossoming between them.

It *hurt*. She couldn't pretend that it didn't.

She'd opened up to him in ways she never had with anyone else. Let him see sides of her she didn't know existed. And still, he hid from her. He wouldn't tell her who Bethan truly was to him, wouldn't be honest about all the shades of his heart. He still kept her from his library unless he was with her, still guarded his memories and his magic like he was afraid she would strike when he wasn't looking. As much as he tried to deny it, she knew he still feared she would betray him and take his icon to the Abbey.

Beneath the pain, the hurt, a spark of anger bloomed.

If he didn't trust her now, Maeve feared he never would.

28

Jude

Bethan clicked the lock before turning to face him. All traces of her smiles and laughter from dinner were gone, replaced by the same frantic energy she'd worn when she'd arrived fresh from the storm. Deep grooves were carved beneath her eyes, her normally warm brown skin sallow. Jude recognized that look. He hadn't seen it very often, but when he had . . .

'Bethan?' he asked. Trepidation dropped a weight into his stomach. 'Have you had a dream?'

Bethan was a saint, but she hadn't been raised in the Abbey. In fact, Jude was certain the elders had no idea of her existence. Away from their limestone halls, she'd been able to grow her abilities in ways Jude could only dream of.

Bethan saw her magic not as something to be stolen, but as a gift to be used carefully and thoughtfully. A concept Jude had guarded like a ticking time bomb, to be considered only when he was strong enough to absorb its impact.

A *gift*. Not a burden.

He wasn't sure if he'd ever reach that level of acceptance with himself.

Bethan's mother had fled the Abbey when she'd fallen pregnant, taking the Abbey's secrets with her. According to Bethan, her world had turned into spun gold at a very young age. The manifestation of her abilities outside of the Abbey was a remarkably rare, maybe even singular, occurrence. And perhaps more importantly, her mother had recognized Bethan's talents for what they were — recognized, and chosen to hide them from the Abbey. She knew what title would be placed around Bethan's shoulders and what she would have to sacrifice to bear it.

Bethan had learned to contain her magic within dreams like Jude did with his books, manifesting them in a way that could be useful to herself and others. He often wondered if he ever would be able to harness his magic as Bethan did. She was comfortable with her abilities in a way he wasn't. Greeted it like a friend, where Jude saw only an enemy.

Usually, Bethan's dreams were her own memories, or someone else's she was focusing on, but occasionally, they were of the future. And sometimes, *rarely* . . . her dreams included Jude.

'What have you dreamed?' Jude repeated when she didn't reply. 'Tell me.'

Bethan's throat bobbed. 'Cutting straight to it, then?'

'We just spent almost three hours at dinner,' he replied, barely resisting tapping his foot with nerves.

She sighed in response, lowering herself onto the corner of his bed. He tried not to let his discomfort show on his face. They always used his bedroom whenever she came with a dream to share. He often finished their sessions with a sense of vulnerability he felt was best kept contained somewhere comfortable. But he didn't like people in his space. Ever.

You'd let Maeve in here. Gladly, a voice that sounded suspiciously like Elden whispered.

Jude ignored it.

The thought of *Maeve*, however . . . he couldn't ignore.

She'd been off over dinner. Withdrawn, almost angry. Had he done something? Said something by accident? It wouldn't be the first time his brusqueness had come off as uncaring. Jude drummed his fingers on his thighs. 'Bethan. Tell me what you saw.'

She looked up. Her eyes were red-rimmed and damp with tears. 'Siobhan. She's dead.'

Jude stilled. 'What?'

'Her body was left in the middle of Oakmoor. By the shrine. She'd been strangled. And . . . and— The tattoo on her chest.' Bethan's eyes slammed shut. 'Her saint tattoo. It had been burned. I didn't even recognize what it was at first.'

'Fuck. *Fuck.*' Jude scrubbed his hands over his face. He thought of the saint's frail wrists, her bright blue eyes. Nausea rushed up his throat. 'Were you the one to find her?'

'Mum was. We buried her together.' A flash of confusion crossed Bethan's face. 'Elden was there, too, when we buried her. He helped. Did he not tell you?'

'Elden?' Jude crossed the room, turned, and strode back to the other side, fingers laced behind his head. 'No . . . no, he didn't say. You found her this morning?'

Bethan nodded.

Why wouldn't Elden have said something? He'd been gone all morning, true, and had returned the same time Bethan arrived. Maybe he hadn't a chance . . . but no, that wasn't right. Dinner was already prepared when they went downstairs. Elden had been home for a while.

For whatever reason, he'd chosen not to say anything.

'Jude.' Bethan's voice drew his attention back. 'She wasn't hurting anyone. She was just trying to scrape together what remained of her life. And the Abbey *killed* her.'

Words weren't strong enough to convey the horror rolling through his chest.

'Why?' Jude managed. 'Why would they—' he trailed off, digging his fingers between his brows. The pain was indescribable. 'They've martyred her. It was meant as a statement. Both killing her and burning off her tattoo.'

'I asked around to see if anyone saw anything, but no one knew,' Bethan continued, voice rising in pitch. 'No one even knew who she *was*, Jude. They didn't remember.'

'They were made to forget,' he corrected. Was it possible the same had happened to Elden? 'It wasn't enough for the Abbey to take her life. They needed to erase any part of her that still remained.'

He pulled sharply back, digging the heels of his palms into his eyes.

His fault.

'I shouldn't have taken Maeve to see her,' Jude groaned. 'The Abbey must have learned we were digging into her life. That we know about the Goddenwood, and that I told Maeve about their memory tampering. They martyred her so we would – so we would know that they knew. To remind us that they're watching.'

They never should've created her icon, even if Maeve had burned it after using it. Had that tipped the Abbey off, too? Did they know Maeve had finished painting his icon?

He tipped his head towards the ceiling. What had they *done*?

Bethan rose from the bed and walked towards the window. Rain slapped the glass in an endless staccato, the wind whistling through the gaps. She placed her palm on the pane and her forehead beside it. Her fingers trembled visibly. 'A warning,' she whispered. 'That's what I dreamed.'

He crossed the room to take a small mirror off the wall. He laid it flat on his desk. 'Show me.'

She sat at the desk and placed her hands on either side of the wooden frame. Leaned close enough for her breath to fog the surface. And then, slowly, like snow leaving the heavens above, gold dust materialized in the air. It floated around them in a glowing miasma, settling atop the mirror.

'Here.' She pushed it towards him. 'The first dream. The one I asked it to show me.'

Jude brushed the gold away with his fingertips. For a lingering second, it showed only blackness.

Then, the scene changed. A wall leapt into existence, worn stone peppered with frames in varying sizes. He recognized it, in a distant, far-off kind of way, as the Abbey. The wall of icons. In Bethan's dream, the canvases were painted black — no saints to be seen.

He'd seen this scene before, hadn't he? With kerosene in his nose and heat on his skin.

Suddenly, burning light leapt from the corner, threading its way across the icons like a rope of gold-tinged starlight. It swirled into each frame faster than he could follow, eating away the interior of the canvases until they were empty, showing the stone wall behind them. Vivid blue stained his retinas in its wake. Pressure built inside him with each jump of light. An urge to move — to run, to reach, to do *something—*

And then, a pulsing scream. A fevered, desperate cry that shot from one ear to the next. Jude lurched back just as it faded, his hands clasped over his ears. '*What—*'

Bethan stood over him like a spectral figure. Her hands clamped down on his wrists, holding them to the table. 'Don't look away. Not yet.'

He forced his gaze back to the mirror.

Only a strange, gauzy layer of gold-tinged white remained of the dream. A cloying hum filled the air. A prickle at the back of his neck. He leaned closer.

The mirror showed nothing. *Nothing.*

Yet—

He couldn't breathe. Couldn't look away. The fog was endless. Impenetrable.

Magic, was it magic? It had to be. Air felt funny in his lungs, like it didn't belong in the place it was designed to be. Awareness slid down his spine so suddenly that Jude jerked back, looking over his shoulder. He half expected to see a face there. See *him.* Feel his mentor's hand in his hair, pulling out the strands. A weight on his shoulders, forcing him down. Yelling, whispering, demanding he be better, be anything but what he was designed to be, a saint, an exile, a *martyr*, the only thing he could ever—

'Jude. *Jude!*'

He gasped, eyes flying open as a splash of water hit his face, clinging to his eyelashes, his lips. Bethan stood across from him, the glass from his bedside table in her hands and fear in her eyes.

'What was that? Are you okay?' She grabbed a blanket off the foot of his bed and gave it to him. Jude wiped his face and tried to remember how to breathe. 'I'm sorry about the water. I didn't know how else to bring you out of it.'

His heart thundered like he'd been running for hours. 'It was fog. Only ever fog.'

Her eyebrows drew together. 'Fog? That's not what I saw.'

'What did you see?' He leaned forward. He needed her answer like he'd never needed anything before. 'Please – what did you see, Bethan? What did you dream?'

'I dreamed a man,' she said. 'Well, the back of his head.'

'Who was he?'

'I don't know. I didn't recognize him. He had light hair and was wearing robes, maybe? They were dark brown, some sort of linen. And I saw . . .' She trailed off, pinching the bridge of her nose. 'A chain? I think. Something around his neck. Just a hint of it above his collar.'

Bethan had seen his mentor. The man responsible for Jude's worst memories from the Abbey. He was sure of it. And somehow, the Abbey had altered what he could see of Bethan's dreams. He was weaker than usual after Maeve painted his icon, his mind more susceptible to tampering. But, still . . . the idea that their reach extended so far was concerning. Had they found out about Bethan's existence?

'I only saw fog,' Jude repeated. 'What did you focus on to summon that dream?'

'I'd heard of Maeve's arrival. Mum was concerned about you, about the Abbey's involvement. She wanted me to see if there was anything I could warn you about. And make sure I kept myself safe. I had the dream before Siobhan's death. But what happened to her, Jude—' she sighed. 'It only confirms what I think the dream means.'

'And are you?' he asked. 'Keeping yourself safe?'

She crossed her arms tightly around herself. 'As much as I can.'

'Good. Maybe stay out of Oakmoor for a while,' he said, worry tugging at his chest. If anything happened to Bethan because of him, like it had Siobhan . . .

Jude swallowed, scanning the darkened horizon from the window. The pressure inside his chest worsened, becoming hard to breathe around. He couldn't give in to the agony now. Not yet.

'Your dreams showed you the wall of icons burning,' he said. 'And a man. An elder. You said it was a warning – what do you think it means?'

Bethan's interpretations were as much a work of magic as her dreams. She deciphered symbolism and meaning in a way he couldn't wrap his head around. Whatever she picked up on from the dream he'd seen, if it truly was a warning . . . he feared the worse.

Bethan returned to her seat at the desk. She skimmed her fingers across the gold on the mirror. 'I think the Abbey wants you to know they are watching. They know Siobhan brought the iconographer to the Goddenwood, if only in memory. The icons on the wall were empty, as though they will remain that way until Maeve brings back her creation. The bright light, the flame, I think it represents how the Abbey takes the magic from the icons. She must return, or else—' Her voice cut out. She rubbed her fingertips across her mouth. 'Siobhan was only the beginning. A warning, even more than my dream. If Maeve doesn't bring back an icon to the Abbey, she will be next.'

Jude could do little more than stare, utterly frozen as his world shifted and reformed.

He thought himself safe here, far from the Abbey's reach as long as he led a quiet, lonely life. As long as he didn't run, didn't want more from his existence outside of what they allowed him. He'd protected his memories and reformed his broken body one day at a time. It had been slow. It had *hurt*. And then Maeve had turned his world on its head once more. She'd shown him that freedom wasn't just a dream, it was a possibility he could grasp.

He'd wanted nothing more than to send her back to the Abbey. But not anymore.

'Maeve being here is . . . significant,' Bethan continued, watching him carefully. 'Both to you and to the Abbey. She's brought your life to a crossroads.'

Terror continued to carve a home in his chest. He tried to detach himself. To think of Maeve, and Maeve alone. Her skin against his. Her scent in his nose. How she'd taken things he previously hated – touch, openness, vulnerability – and made him crave them. How she'd come into his life and wholly upended it.

He needed to keep her safe.

Whole.

'Oh.' Bethan's tone had changed as she watched him try to swallow her words. When Jude met her eyes, she levelled him with something both serious and quietly happy. 'Jude.'

He looked away.

Bethan had become like an older sister to him. Sometimes annoying, always caring. She'd long wished for Jude to find someone. Bethan herself had a long-term, casual partner. A sheep farmer called Caleb that Jude had met a handful of times. She claimed neither were interested in leaving their families and marrying, but Jude had his doubts. Bethan had too much love to give to survive on sporadic trysts alone.

If he spoke his feelings for Maeve into existence, he would never recover when she inevitably left him, or if the shadow that had stalked him for over half his life claimed her, too. He feared the Abbey would never let them find peace in each other like he desperately wanted.

Bethan squeezed his arm. 'It's not one-sided.'

Tightness banded across his chest. 'You don't know that.'

'I notice these things. Her feelings for you are written all over her face.' She removed her hand and stood. 'You should tell her. She seems like a rare gem.'

His throat thickened. 'She is.'

And he wouldn't be telling her anything.

Bethan nodded. 'I should go. It's late. And Jude,' she waited for him to meet her eyes. 'Look after yourself. Maeve, too. With Siobhan . . .' she trailed off, shaking her head. 'Oakmoor doesn't feel safe. Not like it used to. And I worry that unless the Abbey is stopped, it's only just beginning.'

After she had gone, Jude pressed the side of his face against the glass, letting it cool his overheated skin. Ánhaga breathed silently around him. Every creak and whisper magnified a hundredfold.

Bethan's words, her dreams, and her warnings, swirled through him like a windstorm, steadily picking up speed. She'd said Maeve's arrival had brought his life to a crossroads. She was right – but what if the crossroads truly was just the start? What if a steeper path awaited them?

He knew, he *knew* in the same uncanny way his body knew when to wake in the mornings, that the Abbey would know the second the prayer crossed his lips.

They would come. And he and Maeve would be at their mercy.

Unless they did something to stop them.

Suddenly, out of the night-pressed darkness, a slamming door startled him upright. Jude's eyes flew open as his heart lurched into his throat with a sickening jolt. He froze, listening intently. Somewhere deep inside the house, floorboards groaned. Footsteps, moving quickly. A door squealed on its hinges.

Directly below his bedroom was his library—

And someone was inside it.

29

Maeve

As the night deepened, Maeve's anger, the prowling insecurity, had only sharpened its teeth. Jude was with Bethan. She heard them only a few doors down. The murmur of voices, the scrape of furniture on naked floorboards. Bethan had said his name, a gasped exclamation loud enough for Maeve's breath to catch in her throat. Hours had passed since dinner, but he would take his time. She'd seen enough of his intensity, his single-mindedness, to know that.

Still, she wasn't quite sure why she had come to the library.

The book she chose was bound in scuffed black leather; the runes inside indecipherable. It didn't matter that she couldn't read it. All she needed to do was open it, and the magic would do the rest. It vibrated in her hands; the pages edged in the gold that would consume her as soon as it opened.

Maeve stood at a crossroads. Continue, and she'd have a piece of Jude he might never have given her. Stop, and the rejected beast inside her would remain hungry.

She placed the book on the floor and laid shaking hands on the cover, deliberating. It pulsed with its own heartbeat. Underneath her closed lids, gold swept into her vision like the unending tide from the sea, staining all it touched. Even with the cover still shut, distorted memories pulsed against her lids. Pain and stifled weeping. Cries smothered into a fist. Blood leaking from slender gashes.

With a choked gasp, she pulled back.

She couldn't do it.

Beneath layers of muscle and bone, her heart fought to be freed from her chest. She had nearly looked at it. She had been so close to opening the cover. Her shaky exhale broke the silence as relief coursed through her. She hadn't done it. She hadn't betrayed his trust.

Around her, the library shifted, drawing breath.

Her eyes snapped open, and suddenly, he was there.

Hands were against her shoulders, pushing her forward towards the book. Maeve's head fell against his chest as she struggled against the movement. '*No.* No, wait, Jude—'

'Do it,' he hissed. 'You came in here for my secrets, so have at them. Read it.'

He pressed against her back, surrounding her, gripping her wrists to draw her hands to his book. She had barely more than a heartbeat to fight back before her palms were against the pages.

Nausea surged up her throat as the memory swept her into its fold.

Damp walls pressed in from all sides. Seawater slapped against the window in a rhythmic pulse. The iron frame rattled, water straining through the edges where fogged glass met stone. Maeve recognized the sound of the sea, the shade of the stone.

She was back at the Abbey. It smelled of brine and blood.

Kneeling on the floor, illuminated by a shaft of weak sunlight, was Jude. Alone. Young – just barely past childhood. His body was frail and shaking, naked from the waist up. One hand was braced on the wet stone floor underneath him, the other banded over his mouth. Tears dripped off his nose and mixed with the salt and reddish stains already coating the floor.

His exposed back leaked blood.

Her head spun, and her tongue felt unwieldy in her mouth. As she moved closer, unable to look away from the horror of

Jude's childhood, she wondered if she would pass out. Her vision wasn't quite right. Hazy, blurring at the edges.

Scratched into his pale flesh, from armpit to armpit, was the word *DEVOTION*.

Blood slunk down the hollow of his spine to collect in the waist of his trousers. The skin around the gashes was purple and bruised. Jude braced both hands on the floor, grunting as he stood. His collarbones were like twin knives, every rib visible, caging the hollowed expanse of his stomach. His face still had some childhood roundness around the cheeks and jaw. Tears streaked down it in messy lines. He wiped his nose with the back of his wrist, taking a deep breath and wincing when the movement pulled at his ravaged skin. The air around him stilled, dust motes freezing in the light, lit with every shade of gold.

His eyes met Maeve's.

She fell backwards out of the memory.

Maeve opened her eyes to Jude standing over her, a spectral figure of pain and embarrassment. His chest rose and fell in rapid, uneven breaths. 'Are you satisfied? Now that you have what you came for?'

'*Jude*—' Maeve heaved. She couldn't stop her tears.

Who would put a *child* through that, tearing a word into his skin? *Devotion?* She felt despicable, the lowest sort of human to think she could claim his nightmares for her own. To even call herself his friend was an abomination. 'I'm sorry. I'm so—'

'Enough.'

She couldn't read his expression, as though an iron mask had descended over every area softness had begun to creep into. '*Why*, Maeve? Why would you come here?' his voice cracked thickly. He pressed his lips together. 'I would have shown you if you just asked. Why did you do it?'

He didn't give her time to speak, crossing the room to the window and bracing against it like he couldn't bear the sight of her face. He opened the lock with shaking fingers. A bracing flush of icy air streamed in. His jumper clung to his back, outlining the wings of his shoulders and the shape of his ribs. The scored word there flashed across her vision.

'Who did it to you?' Maeve whispered.

She could see little more than the side of his jaw, the quick flutter of his lashes. 'I don't know,' he replied, carefully emotionless. 'There's a man in many of my memories who is always blurred. The same person who was behind the door in the memory of my final day at the Abbey. My mentor, most likely.'

'Do you remember anything about him? Was he the one who marked your sainthood?' Maeve asked, rising back to her feet. His mentor had been behind the door – not a nurse like she'd originally thought. She felt a sick need to keep him talking, as if things would return to normal between them if he continued answering her questions.

She caught a whiff of something unfamiliar as he turned to face her. Sweet, like crushed roses with the undercurrent of fresh-cut wood. At her wince, Jude cocked his head. His mouth parted on the precipice of speech, but he seemed to change his mind at the last second.

She wanted him to ask. Give her the chance to find out the truth about him and Bethan.

'Why come here without me?' Jude asked in a low voice.

She raised trembling hands in front of her, palms raised. Jude was a saint, and everything in her screamed to confess. 'Do you want me to beg? Is that what you want? Me begging you to tell me what you were doing tonight?'

Jude stumbled back as his looming anger was replaced by confusion. 'What?'

But she'd already started speaking, and it was far, far too late to stop.

'Bethan. I know you were with her. I don't begrudge your connection, and she's lovely, truly, she is, but I wish—' she hesitated, throat growing thick with unshed tears. Through it all, Jude stared. Maeve ploughed on, 'I wish you would have told me before you had a lover over.'

Horror washed across his face. '*What?*'

'I'm sorry, I shouldn't have broken in,' she wrenched out. 'But these secrets you've kept, Jude. They hurt. I . . . I've come to view this place as somewhat of a home to me, and seeing Bethan with you, how you were with her – so open, when you're not with me. When every inch of give still feels like a battle.' She laid both hands over her heart. Felt its pounding rhythm. 'I thought if I saw some piece of you that you'd kept hidden, it would distract me from whatever was happening in your bedroom. It's wrong. I know it is. And I'm sorry.'

The silence after her words was deafening.

Jude's hand twitched at his side, an abortive reach for her. 'Bethan isn't my lover.'

It was her turn to stare. 'She's . . . not?'

He barked a hoarse, almost disbelieving laugh. 'No. Never.'

'Oh.' She worried the end of her braid.

The guilt worsened. It wasn't as if her feelings of rejection were an excuse for breaking in, but they offered some weak form of justification, however misguided. Now, with Jude studying her like he was suddenly privy to a new side of her character, she had nothing. She'd overreacted, grossly so, and fractured something between them that couldn't be remade.

'Mm.' Jude paused. 'And you were jealous. When you thought we were . . .' He palmed the back of his neck and looked down. 'In bed.'

'Jealous?' Heat stole up her neck. 'I . . . no. Of course not.'

His lips compressed tighter. 'Bethan and I have only ever been friends. She's like a sister.'

'I see,' Maeve replied, studying her socked feet. The wool on her right foot had worn thin, a bit of skin peeking through the weave. Guilt and shame banded tightly around her chest, making breathing difficult. 'I'm sorry,' she murmured again. What more could she say? 'I . . . I could hear you in your bedroom, and I *assumed* – but that's not an excuse. Nothing is.'

Jude didn't reply for a long moment. Maeve met his eyes, seeing only cool detachment in his gaze.

'I think I need to show you something. Address your concerns about my . . . openness. You're right, Maeve.' As Jude stepped towards her, she realized she'd been wrong to think his anger had abated. Hurt played out cleanly across his face, and she feared it was a deliberate choice to let her see it. 'I have kept things from you. Perhaps more than you know. And maybe I haven't trusted you with everything. Maybe I was right not to.'

The air in the library thinned even further. She didn't have a reply, could only watch as Jude moved across the room to a narrow bookcase tucked into the corner and withdrew a book. He pulled something from between its pages before replacing it on the shelf. When he turned back, something murky lingered in his eyes. Like whatever he held would hurt, like giving it to her wasn't a kindness.

He took a step closer. Held out an envelope. 'I'm sorry, Maeve. Truly.'

30

Maeve

Wind stole in through the cracked window, sliding down the loose neck of her dress. Moonlight cut through the storm clouds outside to coat the crisp white of the envelope. The Abbey sigil shone on the still-sealed wax; her carefully penned name.

'What is this?' Maeve breathed. 'When did this arrive?'

A dart of unguarded emotion cracked Jude's mask. It looked, for a moment, like fear.

She took the envelope. He tracked the motion, chest moving shallowly. His fingers curled into a fist as she worked her thumbnail under the wax, freeing the pages within.

The penmanship was familiar. She'd seen it in letters, though never addressed to her. A prickle started at the back of her neck. 'Is this Felix's handwriting?' she asked. Once more, Jude remained silent. His gaze drifted across her face, almost as though he was keeping himself from reading the letter right alongside her. Dread slipped in, deep in her stomach, churning like bile.

Gold shimmered in her peripherals as she began to read.

You might have already discovered the answer to the questions rolling just beneath the surface the last time we saw each other. The questions I saw forming in your eyes as you saw my finished icon. As soon as your world turned gold.

Sainthood is a lie.

You asked what our powers are. I will tell you as best I can. Sainthood is a safeguard for the Abbey's secrets. You're devout. I've seen you pray. But, Maeve, please listen to me when I tell you they are heard by no one. They only serve to manipulate and ruin.

The saints are exiles. All of us. We're sent away when our memory magic is discovered. Sent away, or used. I made a bargain to remain at the Abbey. So did Brigid and every iconographer before her, for you all have the magic the Abbey so dearly loves to use.

I can only hope Jude can explain where I cannot. Even more, I wish I could tell you that you are safe. That you won't be watched.

You must remain vigilant, Maeve. Trust no one in the local villages, even within Jude's household, whoever might be there. Do not let anyone know where you are coming from or what you are tasked to do. And, above all, do not under any circumstances paint Jude's icon. Do not report back on whatever safety he's clawed out for himself in that lonely house.

At the first opportunity, you must run.

Please, trust me. As a saint, if you must. As someone who is trying to help you, even better.

I hope you find the safety we all seek.

For a long, aching moment, Maeve simply stared. Her mind had retreated to a gauzy place. She felt her blood in her veins, the numbness in her fingertips. The steady thrum of her heart. Somewhere along the way of doubting everything she had ever held dear, she'd decided to believe both Jude and the Abbey despite how the two chafed against each other.

What was faith if it wasn't accepting contradictions?

The Abbey could be both an instrument of control and a benevolent force for good. A saint could exist as both a tool of the elders and someone who would listen as she cried, someone who used their abilities like the gift they were. She was an iconographer – and all iconographers had memory magic. Felix just confirmed it. That was the difference between her and Jude. It had to be.

Her breath quickened.

Felix believed memory tampering and the saints' ability to answer prayer were the same thing: equally interchangeable, doubly destructive.

Which meant—

No. *No.*

Maeve cut off the malignant idea before it could develop any further. She wasn't ready. She couldn't view her new reality in its entirety. She needed to protect herself. Running or hiding, what was the difference, really? Both were equally as cowardly.

The saints and the holy mystery of prayer were her bedrock, her safe place when everything else turned to quicksand. She'd come to terms with the elders being little more than figureheads of manipulation, but the saints and their abilities were *real*. She couldn't allow herself to think otherwise.

She wasn't safe here. The realization hit her like a blow to the chest.

She'd spent time in Oakmoor, she'd visited Siobhan and viewed her memories of the Goddenwood. She'd met Bethan and Elden and shopkeepers and bartenders, letting herself enjoy the community in ways she was never permitted to at the Abbey. The last thing she'd been was discreet. Felix's warning had come too late.

The thought gave her pause.

Slowly, her eyes rose to pin onto Jude. 'When did this arrive?'

His throat bobbed roughly. 'Maeve.'

She advanced on him until his back hit the wall. The fact the letter had been unopened was lost on her, the reminder that she had broken into his space first forgotten. There was only the letter and the terrible truths within.

'Did you hide this letter before I could read it?' she asked. 'Why have I never seen it?'

'I took it the night you arrived. From your bag,' he said.

Every smouldering ember of anger burned suddenly to life. She was wholly focused on Jude, the letter's contents messily shoved aside in favour of the man before her. 'As if I wasn't walking around in the dark enough, you thought to keep letters from me, too?'

Jude's chest brushed hers with every sawing breath. 'I didn't know what was in it,' he begged, an unravelling fervour in his eyes. 'I was going to open it, to see what you were hiding from me, but I decided to keep it instead. To open it later. I don't know why, exactly—'

'You *do* know,' Maeve argued. 'You said so earlier. You wanted to keep something from me.'

His nostrils flared, pupils dilating until none of the hazel remained. 'Why would I bother keeping something from you, Maeve? Clearly, you would find my secrets and take them for yourself with or without me.'

'Which I was wrong to do,' she shot back, the guilt gnawing at her stomach still raw, still devouring. 'I wish I hadn't done it. But that doesn't erase the fact that you kept Felix's letter from me. For *weeks*. Who gave you the key to my life, Jude? To my beliefs?'

He didn't reply. His lips parted; words left unspoken.

Snorting an incredulous laugh, she jerked back, stopped by his hand on her wrist, skimming upwards, holding her in place. His hips brushed hers as he pulled her close. 'You're right,' he said. 'You had been sent to take something of mine. I wanted to take something in return.'

'And did I?' Maeve asked. 'Take something?'

Jude paused for a slow, heady breath.

Unwillingly, her gaze fell to his mouth. Her chin tilted upwards. Their noses touched.

She peeled back, stumbling in her haste.

She couldn't bear him any longer. Couldn't listen to the whisper in the back of her head telling her she'd broken his trust by breaking into his library: a far more egregious betrayal. She needed to escape the suffocating closeness of Ánhaga, if only to gain some perspective that only distance could provide. If she didn't leave now, she'd do something she'd regret.

'I'm leaving,' she said. 'Don't follow me.'

'Please,' Jude ground out. He hadn't moved from the wall. Both hands pressed flat behind him as if holding himself in place. A haunted look in his eyes. 'Don't run. Stay and fight with me. Stay and let me explain. Stay and let me *grovel*, Maeve. Let me beg.'

For the span of a heartbeat, she froze. His raw expression picked at the soft places she'd yet to figure out how to hide.

But yet—

She needed to think – about him, about sainthood and the Abbey. About every word Felix had carefully penned. An unmooring she couldn't allow with his nearness clouding her thoughts. With the sting of betrayal still sharp on her tongue.

Without another word, Maeve opened the door and left.

Remaining on the moon-dusted floor behind her was Felix's folded letter.

31

Jude

Jude picked up the letter. Read it quickly.

After he finished, one fact was alarmingly clear. He had fought against it since he first realized that Maeve saw the gold, and held the same memory magic he did, knowing that the truth would wipe the foundation from beneath her feet.

But it was time. It had been selfish, destructive, even for him to hide the truth as long as he did. He'd wanted to ease her in slowly, keep her from falling too fast. But Jude couldn't delay any longer.

He needed to tell her everything.

In the weeks she'd been in his home, as they'd drawn closer, as the walls between them had crumbled and fallen, she'd remained steadfastly loyal to her idea of the saints. A part of him had known she wouldn't allow herself to look any closer, content to keep herself separate from the wretched mess of everything she'd been taught to believe. It was safer that way, and safety was one desire he'd never begrudge her. Safety, *freedom*, was what he wanted above all else, after all.

Jude had watched her develop her theory about iconographers holding memory magic and held his tongue. He'd worried she'd dug the imagined difference between memory altering and answering prayers out of pure self-preservation, choosing not to see the truth behind sainthood in an effort to protect herself. If she knew what she was, what the Abbey and her magic marked her as, what did that mean for her beliefs? For her relationship to the saints?

He'd seen her careful aversion toward the truth and hadn't corrected her, hopeful that she would come to the realization naturally. Hoping she would make the jump herself and he wouldn't have to push her off the ledge. A hidden part of him begged, *prayed*, that the voice of Maeve's doubt would be louder than the part of her that still clung desperately to her beliefs. To the Abbey and to the saints.

But Bethan was right – neither of them were safe. As much as he wanted to continue in their bubble of makeshift peace in his home, they were both in danger. The Abbey drew closer by the day.

He couldn't keep the truth from Maeve any longer. Siobhan's death was proof enough.

So, he'd given her the letter. He'd cast the first stone into her fragile foundation. Now, he would throw himself at her mercy and offer to help piece it together again. He knew better than most the desire to scramble to higher ground when the flood began – but her perch wouldn't remain steady for long.

Jude folded the letter neatly and tucked it in his pocket, moving towards the window. Through the thin wash of moonlight coating the moors beyond, he spotted a thick mass of clouds rolling in the distance. Easing open the catch, he flinched against the bracing rush of winter wind. Though it was late, closer to dawn than dusk, he searched the sky, not knowing how many birds he would need to see to settle him.

A storm was fast approaching. Maeve was out there, alone.

And he knew exactly where she was heading.

32

Maeve

Maeve knelt before Oakmoor's shrine. Rain and wind battered her from every direction, the mud soaking through her dress cold enough to burn. The saint stared back impassively as she bent her head before it. The act felt wrong. Blasphemous, somehow.

Anger fizzled in her throat.

It was all coercion. All manipulation. Stealing memories and calling them answered prayers. A structure built around discrediting the people who'd given their lives to support it. She'd been encouraged to stretch the limits of her piety in every way she could, and for what?

Her whole fucking *life* . . . gone. Taken from her before she even knew what it meant to live.

Digging her hand into her pocket, she withdrew her coined icon and laid it in the mud beneath the shrine. Pressed it deeper into the earth. After fifteen years of devotion, she was as sloughed smooth as the coin.

Footsteps sounded behind her.

She didn't turn and look as she got to her feet; she didn't need to. She knew he'd come. Knew he would follow her into the storm, into the reckoning.

Rain slid down Jude's exposed nape and darkened his collar in splattering bursts as he knelt before the shrine. His knees fitted into the muddied divots hers had left behind. A saint turned penitent.

'I'm sorry,' he whispered. He spoke his apology into the ground, into the shrine that had long governed their lives. It wasn't holy, but it felt like a prayer all the same. 'Maeve, I'm so sorry. Taking the letter was a mistake. I feared what it contained when I took it, and I couldn't *bear*—' his voice broke.

He scraped both hands over the back of his head, fingers digging in. 'I wasn't allowed to be brought gently to the truth. Some part of me, mistaken as it was, hoped to be that safe person for you. Even when I hated you. Even when I wanted you gone. But who was I to be your anchor when I'd been the one to call the waves?'

She stepped closer, sliding her fingers up the back of his neck. A long exhale left his parted lips as he rested his head against her lower stomach, eyes shut. She moved her hand to the side of his throat, felt it as he swallowed. Rain coursed over his face, washing him clean. The moment lengthened and stretched with unspoken possibility. She wanted to pull at it until it unravelled.

'Maeve.' Jude's voice was a harsh whisper. 'I need to say it. I need you to understand fully. No more secrets between us.'

Her chest compressed, panic digging claws into her ribs, her sternum. She *couldn't*.

She wrenched away, putting her back to him as though it could stop the words she *knew* he was preparing to say. Behind her, Jude repeated her name, an edge to his voice this time. Heat brushed against her back. The ghost of his touch skated down her arm, pressing something into her palm and closing her fingers around it. A coined icon.

She uncurled her fingers to look at it. Jude's face stared back at her, etched in metal.

'I don't want you to say it,' she begged. 'Please . . . please don't say it. I don't want to know.'

Jude slid his hand down the sodden rope of her braid, pulling her head back against his shoulder. Around the jut of her hip, his finger dug in. Soft lips went to her ear. 'They've marked you as one of us, sending you here. Nothing less than blasphemy brought you to me.'

Maeve trembled. He was an open flame. Any closer, and she'd burn.

'There's no difference between us,' he said, each word hammering at her carefully erected walls. 'In the eyes of the Abbey, you're a saint, too. Exiled for your ability. The elders take our magic for their own, sacrificing our memories along the way. Prayers aren't real, Maeve. No miracles have happened. It's all memory manipulation masked over with the mark of sainthood.'

She shook her head, pressing back against his shoulder.

'Look at what they did to Siobhan, worn thin by prayers. Look at your own memories. Even before this, before your exile, they were using you,' Jude said against her ear. 'The Abbey chose you long ago.'

A choked sound broke past her guard. 'I'm not marked. I don't have the tattoo. I can't be a saint.'

'The tattoo is a facade like everything else,' he replied. 'The elders can't see who's a saint. They can only see when the gold starts appearing. Then, they take you. They *mark* you as a sign of ownership. It's a brand disguised as an honour. It means nothing. *Nothing.*'

The hand on her braid slipped around to press against her shoulder, right where the mark ought to lie. Rain coated her face, freezing on her overheated skin. 'You're still a saint, with or without the tattoo.'

'Why let me go?' she pleaded. 'Why not mark me?'

Jude paused. For a long moment, only the harsh sound of his breathing filled the empty space around her questions. 'You're an iconographer. They need your skills perhaps more than anyone else, both as an artist and as someone with memory magic. The Abbey knows they can use your work to control us. They sent you here to paint me, didn't they?'

He turned her to face him. She tracked the path of emotion

across his face — desperate for anything he'd give her, even disappointment, even hurt. In a moment of helpless weakness, she thought looking at him would always feel like looking at the moon. The darkest parts hidden behind brilliant light.

His hand brushed hers, their fingers twisting together. Despite the fear in her chest — memories of Siobhan, of the Goddenwood, of everything they stood to lose — Maeve squeezed tight.

'Jude,' she whispered. 'I don't know how to bear it.'

He reached for her again, this time his touch was an offering. Arms banding across her back, pulling her tight to his body. His cheek resting atop her head. Merging them into one beating heart.

A hug. He was *hugging* her.

She pressed her nose under his ear, breathing him in. Her eyes drifted shut, thinking of a hearth long gone cold and wind carried from snow-covered moors. She slid her hand across his ribcage until her palm rested over the words etched into his back. Searching, finding.

'Jude,' she whispered again, pleading this time. For what, she didn't know.

He held her for what felt like hours as she listened to the evenness of his breath. Would she ever have the chance to be in his arms again? Fearing the answer was no, she held him tighter, committing every heartbeat to memory. She wanted to turn her head and place her lips against his neck. Draw so close she would no longer be able to separate where he ended, and she began. But all she could do was hold him.

She, him—

Both of them saints.

Both of them in danger.

33

Jude

Jude had nothing more to say. Nothing more he could give to soften the truth. He could only hold her, and even that wasn't enough. Not for her, not for him. He should pull back and set her free. He had years of experience denying himself touch; Maeve shouldn't be any different. He just needed to slide his hand from her hair, loosen his fingers from her hip. Take a step back and let the sheeting rain fall between them.

He should, he should, he *should*.

It was selfish, maybe. Taking what wasn't his. But he didn't want to miss a single one of her heartbeats, not when they aligned with his. She was safe in his arms; he wouldn't let her drown. He told her as much in whispered words pressed against where her pulse beat frantic in her throat.

Maeve sagged against him, trembling. Slowly, she eased out of his grip. 'A *saint*.'

His arms ached without her, cold in the frigid night air. She wobbled on her feet like a newborn colt. Her eyes shimmered with unshed tears, flashing gold before she looked away.

The watchful confines of Oakmoor surrounded them. He imagined a twitch of a curtain, a whisper passed from ear to ear. If he looked down, would he see Siobhan's blood mixing with the mud?

Unable to help himself, he reached for her hand and curled

his fingers tight around it. Her skin was cold, bones fragile. So human it hurt.

'Felix is right. We're not safe here.' He closed his eyes briefly, gathering strength. 'Siobhan. She's dead. The Abbey killed her.'

Maeve's face slackened as her eyes snapped to his. 'What?'

'That's what Bethan came to tell me. She and her mother found her. Here—' he waved a hand across the shadowed town square. 'Alone. Her dress cut open. Her saint tattoo had been burned from her skin. They martyred her.'

Both hands banded over Maeve's mouth. '*Burned?*'

'No one remembered her.' He took a breath. 'Or knew what happened.'

He didn't tell her Elden was there when she'd been buried. That his memory had been tampered with alongside the villagers' – another victim of Jude's mistakes.

'Why?' Maeve asked. Tears coursed freely down her cheeks. She took another step back as the realization shot across her face. 'Because of us,' she breathed. 'We visited her. I drew her icon. She showed us her memories. Felix . . . Felix *warned* us—'

Both hands clutched the back of her neck as she tilted her head towards the sky, putting her back to him. 'The Abbey will never stop, will they? They take and take and *take*. Nothing is out of reach. To . . . to martyr her, Jude.' She whirled back around, her expression almost deranged. 'It's not the first time. I know it's not. The Abbey has martyred saints before. I've seen it. But *I can't fucking remember.*'

She dug both hands into her hair, her chest heaving. Jude reached out, gently pulling her wrists until she slackened. 'I know. I know, Maeve.' A choked sob left her mouth as she curled against his chest, hands trapped between her face and his body. 'We'll figure it out. We'll fix it.'

She shook her head, voice muffled against her hands. 'You don't know that.'

No – he didn't.

'There's more,' Jude said, hating himself for what he was about to tell her. 'Felix isn't the only one with a warning. Bethan had one to share, too. She has . . . dreams.'

'Dreams,' Maeve echoed, pulling back to look at him.

Jude nodded. As quickly as he could, he told her of the dream Bethan had shared with him and her interpretation of it. The wall of blank icons linked by a rope of gold, how it jumped from icon to icon, consuming all it touched. The Abbey was coming. Siobhan was just the start. Maeve would be next if she didn't bring Jude's icon to the Abbey.

He didn't tell her of the strange fog, the faceless man he guessed was his mentor.

'And these . . . dreams. How do we know they're real? That they aren't just, well—' she shrugged, gripping her arms tight around her torso. 'Dreams.'

Jude let out a long breath. 'Bethan. She's a saint, too. But she wasn't raised in the Abbey.'

Maeve's expression didn't change. Slowly, her hand came up to cup the side of her face. Her pale hair slid in fine tendrils across her cheeks and jaw as her eyes lost focus somewhere between them. 'A saint,' she repeated faintly. 'She has the same memory tampering ability as we have, then?'

'She doesn't see it in quite the same way,' Jude replied. 'She doesn't view it as corrupted or damaged by the Abbey's touch, but as a skill, I suppose. A talent she can use for good.'

'And does she?' Maeve's eyes rose to his. 'Use it for good?'

'Her medium is dreams. Like I have my books, or you have your painting. Bethan dreams. She understands her magic in a way I—' Jude swallowed. 'In a way I haven't learned to. She tells people what she dreams. Beautiful things that bring them hope. Warnings to prevent harm. Everything is . . . it's meant with care in mind, Maeve. Not hurt.'

'Is that a possibility for us, too?'

He wet his lips. Felt the pressure in her words.

Worse — the hope.

'Maybe,' he allowed. 'Maybe.'

The silent *but* hung between them.

'The Abbey won't rest. They'll take our memories. Or worse,' Maeve said. A shiver wracked her body. 'Siobhan's death wasn't just a warning. It was a message. A threat. Like I said — even if I can't remember the specifics, I know the Abbey has made martyrs out of saints before. I feel it in my bones.' She took a deep breath. 'And . . . and we'll never know if our magic is capable of good. Not while the Abbey still exists. Not while they continue to rely on the saints. We need to do whatever we can to stop them.'

Rain fell between them in a sheet of silver. Jude didn't have a reply. He could only nod.

At the touch of her hands, the tension left his body, exhaustion cresting in its wake. A wrung-out towel with nothing left to give.

'First thing tomorrow, you're going to pray to your icon and get your memories back,' Maeve said. 'If that doesn't work, we'll try something else. We'll keep trying, keep fighting. We're not giving up, Jude. Not as long as we're together.'

She stepped back slowly, her hands sliding off his forearms, her fingertips off the undersides of his wrists. And he saw, for the first time, the softest ray of hope streak across her face. Beautiful and heartbreaking in equal measure. For him, and him alone.

34

Jude

Jude jolted upright. The sleety rain hitting his window drowned out the rapid pattern of his breathing. He'd been dreaming something dark and confusing. His wrists had been tied tightly, with his palms sealed together and skin sticky with sweat and blood. Panting, he drew his hands into the air and searched his palms. Mercifully, they were normal in the cold light of a winter's morning.

His vision hazed, darkening at the edges. Dryness coated his throat.

Distantly, he heard a voice, growing louder until soft hands touched his shoulders, his chest. A palm pressed against his pounding heart.

Instinctively, Jude flinched back at the touch before he looked up. Maeve was inches from him, eyes wide, lips parted. 'Breathe,' she whispered. 'Slowly. Push my hand out. Just like that.'

Black spots danced at the edge of his vision. 'What – what happened?'

'I think you had a nightmare. I tried to wake you, several times, in fact . . . but, but, Jude. It's evening already. You've been asleep almost a day.'

He tried to focus past the pounding in his skull, the pressure cinched around his heart. 'What?'

She nodded. He was coherent enough to recognize the fear in her eyes. 'I don't know how—'

'The icon,' Jude cut in. He tipped his head back to stare up at the ceiling, focusing on her hands on him and not the residual panic from the nightmare. They'd returned home from Oakmoor at around three in the morning, agreeing to reconvene just after dawn for Jude to pray to his icon. Somehow, he'd slept for over twelve hours without waking. 'It's the icon. It's affecting me. Headaches, nausea. A strange . . . *pulling*, under my skin. The sleeping, too. The nightmares.'

Maeve eased back, guilt clear on her face. 'I'm sorry,' she murmured. 'Hopefully, once you pray, it'll get better. You'll be yourself again.'

Himself – he hardly knew who that man was anymore.

Her fingers touched his wrist, skating up bare skin. Jude flinched. His long sleeves were pushed back to his elbows, every tattoo visible. Each clumsy stroke he'd marred his flesh with; lines and symbols, crude scratches that he'd never allowed to fully heal.

Maeve stared. Wide-eyed. Saying nothing.

'Don't,' he whispered.

'Jude.'

'It was a long time ago.' He kept his eyes on her face, not wanting to join her in looking at his marked skin. He knew what he looked like.

Her fingers shook slightly as she slid her hand beneath the collar of his shirt. She laid her palm over the symbol for SAINT, transferring her warmth into his frigid skin. A hard press, as though to fuse them. A wish to take the memory of his pain away.

'You can talk about it,' she whispered, surprising him. 'To me. If you ever want to.'

Jude's throat felt thick. He nodded. It wasn't the reaction he'd been expecting. Yet again, Maeve set him completely off-balance. A voice in the back of his mind, sounding suspiciously like Bethan, whispered – *She cares for you.*

He was starting to believe it.

She continued to touch him. A skim of her fingertips across the other tattoos under his collarbones, the lines on his forearm. His skin was sensitive from how often he'd gone over the ink. His heightened awareness of her proximity made it worse. Almost too much to bear. As she brushed her fingertips over the crook of his elbow, he hissed an unsteady breath.

Maeve pulled back. Her throat clicked. 'I'm sorry.'

He caught her hand before she could withdraw entirely. Pressed it back to his skin. When he looked up, he found her staring back with eyes so dark he couldn't make out the pupil. Her lips were parted, and she was breathing shallowly. There was a fogginess to her face he wasn't used to seeing.

Unable to bear the weight of her attention, Jude looked away. He dropped her hand in a pathetic attempt to steady himself. Useless. Like he could be anything but unmoored around her.

His gaze caught on a rectangular shape by the door. *Fuck.* He'd nearly forgotten. 'I should probably get to it. No point putting off the inevitable.'

Maeve followed his gaze. 'Are you sure? I would suggest waiting, but . . .'

'We don't really have the time,' Jude finished.

'Not if we want you awake, that is.'

'And somewhat coherent,' he muttered as he reluctantly pushed himself out of bed. He brushed her shoulder as he moved past her towards the icon. Thin layers of paint feathered the edges of the canvas, the colours deepening as they closed in around his face. For a moment, the vivid gold haloing his head reflected in his painted eyes.

Jude blinked, and it was gone.

Before he could decide how to begin, Maeve dropped to her knees in front of the canvas, pulling him down with her. He bit back a shiver at the casual touch, wondering if he would ever get used to the feeling of his skin on hers. Somehow, he doubted it.

His icon stared back, just as defiant as the first time he beheld it. Just as exposing. It took his breath away. Maeve's talent, her passion and care for her work, shone through every brushstroke. He didn't think he'd ever seen something so beautifully wrought.

'When I pray,' Maeve said, 'I focus on specifically what I want. Peace, absolution, forgiveness, or something more tangible. An event or item, for instance.'

'I remember,' Jude grumbled. He liked the feeling of the wood under his knees less when it was his icon he knelt in front of and not Maeve.

She turned to him and folded his hands between her palms. The back of his neck felt hot. He could almost feel his mentor's hand there, forcing his head lower. But it was Maeve touching him, he reminded himself. Maeve asking him to pray. Maeve's words in his ears. He trusted her. He was safe.

Ever obedient, Jude closed his eyes.

Though he was no longer looking at his icon, he felt it watching. Waiting to hear what he might ask for. Looking down at him and finding him wanting and weak.

He gasped behind his teeth. Maeve tightened her grip.

'You're okay,' she whispered. 'I've got you.'

He didn't believe in sainthood. He *knew* it wasn't real. He couldn't grant requests, couldn't listen to petitions. Yet, there was power in believing. The icons held secrets in their gilded frames. Secrets he was slowly beginning to realize might be very far from their misguided guesses.

Jude asked for guidance, for memory. For the power to go to the Abbey and reclaim what was rightfully his. For strength to do the impossible. Though his tongue formed words indecipherable to any ears but his own, he kept speaking. Maeve kept her hands firmly clasped over his.

He prayed.

He waited.

And nothing happened.

35

Jude

Jude kept his eyes shut. His head bowed. 'It's not working. *Why* isn't it working?'

Maeve's hands tightened around his. 'Maybe it's because you don't truly believe. In prayer. In the saints. In your own magic.'

His eyes cracked open. 'I can't change that. I can't just suddenly *believe*—'

His voice cut off as a lash of vertigo crested over him, the effect so sudden, so breathtaking that he dropped towards the floor. His hearing pulsed in an out, carrying with it the strain of a frantic voice, a strange humming that grew louder and louder.

Pain built at the nape of his neck and wrapped around his jaw. He fought for air, locating his voice somewhere beneath the nauseating dizziness. 'Something's happening—' he hissed through his teeth. He forced himself to look up.

The face in front of him was unfamiliar.

Jude blinked.

He knew her, didn't he?

A thrum started just beneath his breastbone. He placed his hands on his chest, felt the vibration. Deeper than that, a shifting in his marrow. The woman was unknown to his addled brain but familiar in his heart. His fingers glanced off the hem of her dress as she stood.

She cast about the room, gaze darting from one side to the other like she was searching for something. A frenetic energy clung to her limbs. Jude crawled towards her, a name on his lips. He knew her. He couldn't forget her. He couldn't. Not her. Not *her*—

Suddenly, she spun towards the window.

She was moving, running.

Then, she was back, a lit candle in her hand.

Before he could pull himself to his feet, before he could even force his muddled thoughts to remember who she was, she drew the candle to the canvas.

The flame started in the corner. A hole punched through the canvas, the edges slowly peeling back with a ripple of orange embers. It ate slowly across the icon before his painted face began to crumple. His eyes, his upraised hand. The halo behind his head. As though it grew tired of a lazy devouring, the fire suddenly consumed the rest of the canvas in one fell swoop until all that remained was the wooden frame and smouldering edges, tattered and gaping like a hungry maw.

For a long moment, neither of them moved.

Holding his breath, Jude reached one hand towards the burnt icon—

The room dissolved in a flash of blinding light.

A flow of molten metal from the icon rushed towards him. He shouted, scrambling backwards. Every movement felt laborious, as though he was underwater. The strange thrum pulsed at the back of his skull, behind his lids. An unholy hymn of bells and rising voices.

Suddenly, a veil of darkness fell, consuming the gold in a corrosive wave of black.

The ringing intensified. He smelled something pungent and sweet like flesh set alight. Unable to bear the onslaught, Jude banded one hand over his mouth and the other over his eyes, curling down until his brow hit the floor. The bells clanged louder, louder.

He couldn't take it. It was *too much*, far too much.

He was no longer sure the floor was beneath his knees. It was only darkness and pain and endless ringing. Something wet trickled down his neck from his ears as the singing grew swollen with an emotion he didn't yet have a name for.

As quickly as it started, the attack ended.

He awoke on his back, staring up at the ceiling. Silence coated him. He reached up and touched his ears. Nothing; no blood tracing down his neck. He flexed his fingers and wiggled his toes. His body felt like the sea had spat it out.

The sea.

For the first time in eight years, Jude remembered the feel of sand against bare skin. He could recall his glee, childlike and free, as he leapt into the waves. Two boys were beside him in this unfinished memory. He felt their presence, heard their laughter.

His breath hitched.

Some of his memories were there. Some, but not all. Slices of his former life half-returned. A man standing atop an altar, surrounded by cloaked figures, their hands desperate and reaching. Light cutting a slice through the basilica. Tears streaking down his face – from what, *from what?*

The need to close his eyes and examine what was returned nearly consumed him, but the acrid scent of smoke hit his nostrils before he could.

Burning.

He sat up. The smell scratched at a hidden door in his memory, somewhere long forgotten.

Across the room, Maeve was slapping her discarded cardigan against the ground.

Maeve. He hadn't forgotten her. She was here, and he knew her.

The relief faded quickly, replaced with confusion as Maeve stamped on the crumpled mass with one booted foot. The floorboards were blackened underneath. The smoke smelled metallic, like blood or festering seawater.

As she stepped back, Jude remembered what had been burning. His icon.

She turned to face him. Her eyes were wide, lips parted. They stared at each other for a tense heartbeat as Jude remained on the floor. Flames flickered every time he blinked. A thread of memory tugged insistently, still too far to grasp.

There was something there, something on the tip of his tongue—

'You . . . you weren't well,' Maeve said thickly. 'I burned the icon and you started screaming. Looking all around like you could see something I couldn't. Your hands . . .' she searched around, mimicking what she'd seen him do only minutes ago. 'Like you were trying to find something. What did you see?'

He tilted his head up towards the ceiling as he processed her words. The bare plaster between the rafters was stained grey with smoke. What *had* he seen?

'Did you hear the bells? The singing?' he asked.

'I could only hear you screaming.' She rocked forward on her toes like she wanted to go to him but decided against it. 'Did it . . . work? Did you get your memories back?'

'Some,' he replied. 'But not all. But I feel . . . better. My mind. It's much clearer than it was when you were painting. Like a weight has been pulled off me, or a film scraped off my brain.' He tipped his head back and forth. 'It feels like my own again. Or closer to it, at least.' He focused on her. 'What made you burn the icon?'

Maeve knelt down beside him. 'After you prayed, you collapsed. You started . . .' her voice hitched. 'Started convulsing. You looked at me like I wasn't there. It was horrible. Awful, Jude.' She shook her head, gaze falling on the burnt remains of the icon. 'I'd burned Siobhan's icon to try and destroy it. We didn't know if it worked then but I – I had to try. I had to try *something*.'

Wax puddled on the floor next to the icon in a milky-white

crust. The room reeked of smoke, but he didn't care. Not with what he'd just realized.

Jude stood, pacing in a tight circle, thinking. 'This is good. It's very good.'

'It is?' Maeve asked, voice trailing up at the end as she moved back to her feet.

'Praying won't help us return the magic to the saints. Not even praying to ourselves. Although, I do think it serves a purpose. If others praying to icons increases the Abbey's power – if it allows them to steal more magic from us, and therefore more memories – maybe praying to ourselves does something similar.'

'Maybe it increases the magic, too,' Maeve added. Her face had regained some of its colour as her eyes searched his. 'Like a catapult. The harder you pull it back, the further it will go. Maybe that's why praying to your icon affected you like it did. You had to give more of yourself to get more in return once the icon was destroyed.'

Jude ran both hands over his head. 'We should've just destroyed the icon straight away.'

'And ruin all my hard work?'

He caught her eye. 'Hm. True.'

She shrugged, smile still on her lips. 'If you hadn't prayed to your icon first, maybe the effect of burning it wouldn't have been so intense. Maybe you would have had fewer memories returned to you.'

'I wish it was more. But burning the icons . . . I must have learned it worked years ago at the Abbey.' He planted his hands on his hips and surveyed the burnt icon. Now that he was focused on it, the smell was all-consuming. He certainly couldn't sleep here tonight. The tang was heavy in his nose, almost like altar incense—

Jude froze. His mouth dropped open. '*Oh*—'

A memory surged to the surface. Fire, burning hot and bright.

The sound of his footsteps running down stone floors, his chest burning with exertion. *Panic.* He was rushing, frantic to accomplish his task before he was noticed. In his hand, burnt matches.

The Abbey. Fire. *Icons.*

'Maeve,' he gasped, realization slamming into him. 'I tried to burn the Abbey. Tried to burn . . .' he shut his eyes. 'Icons? I think. But I failed. That's why I was exiled. It wasn't just the magic. It was a punishment. But why? Why burn the icons?'

He swung around to face her. 'That's it – burning icons restores memory.'

She inhaled, short and fast. 'Is that what we do, then? Return to the Abbey and burn the icons?'

'Not just the icons. We burn the whole Abbey down.'

'*What?*'

'Is that not what you were thinking?'

'I – no.' She laughed breathlessly. 'Not exactly. I was thinking more along the line of the individual icons. Not . . . arson.'

'Oh.' Jude shrugged. 'What if we accidentally miss some? It all needs to go. If there's even the smallest hope it could restore memories to the saints. To everyone that the Abbey has harmed. Elden. To you, too, Maeve.'

She swayed where she stood. 'If you've tried before, why would this time be any different?'

'We can only make a plan and try again. We have each other, this time. And we know more about how our magic works. How the Abbey works, too,' he replied. 'I don't know what went wrong the first time, but we have to try.' He pulled in an unsteady breath. 'We have to return.'

'Every warning we've heard, from Felix, from Bethan . . . even – even Siobhan's death. It all was to prevent us from returning.' Maeve shook her head. Her face had gone ashen. 'But you're right. I can't see another way.'

The Abbey. Jude saw the promise of it reflected in her gaze. He remembered its facade with near-perfect accuracy now.

Three spires reached towards the heavens, reinforced by flying buttresses embellished with colonnades and carved portraits of saints long passed. Large windows broke up the face of the main basilica, understated compared to the crown jewel of the Abbey – the rose window. Even now, he remembered the intricacies of its glass pattern with nostalgic reverence. He'd spent many mornings kneeling under it, letting its beauty lull him closer to devotion.

Jude was no longer a child. The glory of stained glass wouldn't sway him. But, as he looked at Maeve, he realized he was not so very far from the boy he had once been. Urged to worship the closest thing to divinity he'd ever seen.

'Yes,' he replied hoarsely. 'We go back. Together.'

Maeve wrapped her arms tightly around herself, shoulders bunched close to her ears. Oh, how he ached to hold her. To fold her into his arms and keep her safe.

'Together,' she echoed.

Her eyes met his, and a piece of his armour flaked off to float amongst the rafters.

36

Maeve

They planned to leave for the Abbey at first light.

Maeve sat in front of the mirror in her room, running her brush through her damp hair from roots to end. Slowly, methodically, letting herself sink into the motion. The familiarity.

She examined her face, scouring each faint line, each freckle and crease and shadow for changes. Something that reflected the upheaval she felt within. But her face looked the same as always. Dark eyes, large in her pale face. The gold of her hair smoothed into cornsilk by the brush. She'd decided to indulge in one of her nicer silk chemises for her final night in Jude's home, one she wouldn't dare wear out of her bedroom.

Gently, she pressed the pad of her thumb under one eye, then the other. Slid her forefinger down her nose to her lips. Her gaze bored into her reflection. She'd sat and examined her face in a mirror recently, hadn't she? With the sound of the waves in her ears and limestone surrounding her.

Maeve closed her eyes.

She couldn't remember.

What *could* she remember of the Abbey? She was used to recalling everything with the clarity of a painter: the play of light and dark, the roughness of stone or the fragile glide of silk. How the corridor outside the kitchen smelled in the early morning when the bread was baking or how the kneeler felt digging into her shins.

The shape of the Abbey was still there. Of that, she was certain. The specifics, however . . .

She set her hairbrush on the table and dropped her head into her hands. A shiver coursed down her spine. A part of her had noticed the subtle fade of memories over the past few days, but a larger, louder part had demanded she ignore it. She didn't want to think about what it could mean.

A quiet knock on her door stirred her thoughts.

Maeve sat up. There was only one person it could be. 'Come in,' she called.

Jude entered a moment later. He held up a silver razor with one hand, gliding his palm over his head with the other. 'Would you mind?'

'I don't know what I'm doing,' Maeve replied with a huffed laugh as she took the proffered razor, gesturing for him to sit on the stool. His gaze lingered on her as she moved, pulling away just as quickly. A blush reddened the tips of his ears.

Maeve glanced down. She'd forgotten about the chemise. The silk was fine enough to show every contour beneath the thin fabric. Clearing her throat self-consciously, she caught Jude's eye in the mirror. 'What would you like?'

He felt around the back of his neck, sliding his fingers through his short hair. It was beginning to hold a curl at the ends. 'Just short enough that it can't be grabbed.'

Grabbed?

She swallowed her questions, gently moving the razor across his scalp. Fine, reddish-black hairs dusted his shoulders in her wake. It wasn't as hard as it looked to get his hair back to the length it had been when she arrived. She ran her thumb up the nape of his neck, following the pattern of gooseflesh. 'Cold?'

'No.' Jude tilted his head so she could get around his ear. 'Are you packed?'

'Mostly. I'm leaving my painting things here.'

'Are you planning on returning?' His eyes flicked to hers in the mirror, leaving just as quickly. 'For your supplies?'

Maeve carefully ordered her words. She didn't want to give him anything but the truth, as fragile and uncertain as it was. She coasted her hands over his head to loosen any cut hairs. 'I don't know. I just . . . I don't know what to expect when we return.'

'You said the winter intercession would be happening, correct?' Jude asked.

They had discussed their plan last night after cleaning up the icon's burnt remains. Once they'd obtained the requisite robes and enough materials for a significant, and hopefully fast-catching, fire, they planned to sneak in disguised as pilgrims. If they timed it correctly, they should be able to burn the icons, and potentially the entire Abbey, in between the hymns when the basilica was empty.

'Yes,' Maeve replied. 'It takes place over a week. If we leave in the morning, we'll arrive on the evening of the second-to-last day. The intercession ends with the Call of the Sun.'

'What's that?' he asked, brow furrowed.

'A ritual at the end of the eighth and final hymn,' she said, moving the razor close to his temple. He tipped his head back, throat stretching long. 'A saint is present to hear the prayers. It's said . . .' she hesitated, fighting past the headache blooming behind her eyes. 'The elders tell us that any prayer asked during the Call goes directly into the saint's mind. When they lift their hands and direct the sun into the basilica, all the prayers will be answered.'

Jude kept his eyes downcast as he listened, lashes casting long spikes down his cheeks. 'I remember a little of it, I think. I've tried to pull more of the memory up since you burned my icon.' His eyes rose, skimming over her body before they refocused on her face. 'I was in the basilica. There was a . . . man. A saint,

I believe. He was standing under the rose window. People surrounded him. All wearing habits. They were reaching for him. Like they wanted to, I don't know... pull him off the altar. Like he was a sacrifice.'

'I remember something similar, but not much more,' Maeve replied. She set the razor on the table, scrubbing her hands over her eyes and taking a deep breath.

Each hymn during the intercessions had a meaning. Calls for prayers, for alms, for acts of service and displays of penance. Each designed to bring both acolytes and pilgrims closer to the pulsing heart of the Abbey. Towards something like devotion.

Her memories of the intercessions were hazy at best, buried in the malleable soil her mind had become. Trickles of chanting came through if she really focused. The burn of incense in her nose.

The faint but unmistakable tinge of violence.

How could she plan to face something she couldn't see clearly? How would she know what to expect when they arrived at the Abbey midway through an intercession?

'I don't know what we'll face when we arrive,' Jude continued, echoing her thoughts. 'I can't . . . can't promise safety. I wish I could.'

Maeve nodded. 'I know. But we can't wait any longer.'

She played with the seam of her chemise, rubbing the fine material between her fingers. 'Lately, my memories – you know what you were saying earlier? About your body not feeling like your own. About how you felt eroded. The headaches and the nausea.' Jude made a quiet noise of assent. 'I think it's happening to me, too.'

He stilled. 'What?'

'I wasn't sure at first. Maybe I didn't want to *be* sure. But I can't deny that it's getting worse.'

'Maeve . . .' Jude murmured, anguish in his eyes. He reached out and took her hand, curling his fingers tight around it.

She closed her eyes and forced herself to continue. 'Ever since we burned your icon, since we decided to go to the Abbey,' she shook her head, 'it's all I can think about. And if we thought your symptoms were because I was painting your icon, that can only mean—'

'There's an icon of you at the Abbey,' Jude finished.

'Yes,' she replied. 'I can't think of anything else it could be.'

Jude pushed to his feet. 'I think we should leave now.'

Maeve blinked. 'Now? It's—' she glanced out the window at the pitch-black sky. 'Jude. It's nearly midnight. We can wait a few hours.'

He linked his fingers behind his head, pacing to the window and looking out. His breath fogged the glass. 'You're a saint. An iconographer. They want to control you. Look at Siobhan.' His voice thickened. 'If I hadn't introduced you to her, if I hadn't gone poking around her memories . . . the Abbey would've been content to let her live out her days alone and forgotten. Safe. If they have your icon, they're closing in on you. We can't wait, Maeve. We need to leave now.'

The weight of his words settled heavily over her. She stood, crossing the room to lay her hand on his shoulder. He turned to her, the guilt painted across his features unbearable.

'We're better off confronting them directly than lying in wait,' he continued, searching her face as he spoke. 'If they want to isolate you from me, if they want to use your icon to harm you, we can't just wait for them to do it. I can't keep you here; I can't have something else be my fault.'

'Jude,' she whispered, moving her hand up to cup the side of his neck, tracing his pulse with her thumb. He exhaled heavily, eyes falling shut. 'You cannot blame yourself for their actions. You didn't kill Siobhan. The Abbey did. You were a friend to her, someone who understood what she'd been through. The fault lies with the Abbey, and the Abbey alone. Not you. And if . . . if something happens to me, it won't be your fault either.'

The crease between his brows cinched tighter even as his eyes remained closed. 'I can't let it happen to anyone else. Not to you. Not to Elden.'

Despite her earlier vow to speak only truth to him, Maeve found a lie forming on her tongue. 'It won't. I promise. A few hours aren't going to make a difference. And I want to enjoy the time we have left here.'

Jude's eyes flicked open. He studied her for a long moment, closely, steadily, like he was memorizing her features. Beneath her palm, she felt him swallow roughly.

His eyes dropped, sliding down her neck, lingering on the low dip of her chemise before trailing down her body. The shift in his focus felt deliberate in a way nothing between them had before, as though he was allowing himself to fully look his fill for the first time. Like he wanted to see every part of her, to brand his gaze into her skin. A lungful of air after a lifetime underwater.

Every laboured breath scraped the silk of her dress over her pebbled nipples in a way that nearly hurt. The tension threatened to consume her, obscene, almost, in its power. In that moment, Maeve knew she would've given him anything, *anything*, he wanted.

Jude took a short, quick breath. Then, he moved. Stepped closer. His hand rose, fingers skimming the fine material of her dress, coming to rest lightly against her waist. She felt the fine tremble of his fingers against her skin. The heat was unbearable, both on her skin and from the heavy weight of his eyes on her body. She squeezed her thighs together to alleviate some of the ache.

His gaze dropped, following the movement. His damp lips parted on a low exhale as his thumb brushed the underside of her breast. She bit back a whimper, the sound slipping free to break the silence.

With a rough jolt, Jude stepped back. His hand left her.

Maeve's vision blurred as she swayed on her feet like a newborn colt, trying to orientate herself around the sudden break in contact. When she met Jude's eyes, he looked just as strung-out, just as wrecked.

His gaze dropped to the floor as he cleared his throat. 'I don't mind you lying to me, you know.'

She tried to clear her mind, to remember what they'd been speaking of. She'd promised him nothing was going to happen to them, hadn't she?

A promise she intended to keep.

'I'll try to do it more often, then,' Maeve replied, voice hoarse.

Jude chuckled. Like a moth to a flame, his eyes rose once more to move down her before he turned to the window, visibly gathering himself.

Maeve wished he wouldn't. She wanted to see him unravelled, wholly and completely.

He reached out a hand, trailing it over the wooden frame of the window. 'I never imagined what it would be like to leave,' he said. 'Even when I wanted nothing more, when I was sent here alone and confused, it wasn't something I allowed myself to picture.'

'And now?' Maeve asked. A new kind of ache welled up inside her at the pain in his face. The longing.

'Now,' he replied. 'Now, it's . . . different. Unbearable in a different kind of way.' His smile was soft and drowning as he turned to face her. 'As you said, morning's only a few hours away. You should sleep. We have a long walk ahead of us.'

They'd decided to go alone, hoping Elden wouldn't follow. He was safe here, safe from what waited for them at the Abbey. It would just be the two of them tracing their way across the moors to the Abbey. Back to the place of their creation. The prospect of return felt like an impossible mountain, the summit hidden far beyond sight.

Jude's fingers ghosted around the shell of her ear as he tucked a piece of hair behind it.

Then Maeve watched him go, the mark of his presence fading slower than his whispered goodbye. Lingering, gnawing at the tender spaces between her ribs. She only wished she had time to indulge in the softness between them before the fear was back to swallow it whole.

37

Maeve

Just beyond the gate to Jude's property, in the middle of
two heather-strewn hills, was a single oak tree. Beneath the
soil, its roots spread out in an unseen lattice; above, its riot
of winter-bare branches stretched like naked lungs against the
shape of the horizon. In its long years, it would have faced
countless storms, stretches of droughts and beatings by the relent-
less wind. Yet, it remained unmoved even as it approached the
twilight of its life.

Behind Maeve stood Jude, in front of her, the oak. Both lonely
and still, breathing with the wind. Neither willing to uproot from
the ground that held them fast.

The oak would remain, but Jude would go.

Silhouetted against the violet of the rising sun, a flock of birds
spun in a choreographed dance towards the hills. Maeve turned
to catch him watching them, slack wonder moving in his eyes.

She buried her face deeper into his crimson scarf. It had snowed
overnight, a light dusting that cast their world in white. Beside
them, their meagre possessions were compacted into one bag.
Without horses, they looked at three days on the road on foot.
Two nights spent somewhere new.

Jude eyed the gate like it would burn him if he got too close.
He'd been jumpy since she'd met him in the kitchen that morning,
their movements silent as to not wake Elden. Flinching at the
slightest noises, hardly speaking. Running his hand over his

freshly shorn hair so often that Maeve worried he'd soon begin tearing it out if they didn't get a move on.

Her stomach churned. She didn't know who she was more afraid for – herself or Jude. There didn't seem to be much distinction between them where her heart was involved.

His hand joined hers on the gate. He rested his weight on it, fingers clenched so tightly around the iron that his knuckles bleached white before he pushed it open and stepped through. She wasn't sure where things stood between them, especially after last night. She thought of him often. The wanting didn't seem to be waning. If anything, it was growing stronger. Harder to ignore.

She studied his mouth from the corner of her eye. The pale pre-sunlight painted him in delicate sheets of colour – greens as dark as a night-strewn forest, the hazel of his eyes like lichen. Dusky purples shadowed his jaw and raven hair, flecked with the deepest amber.

He'd had black tea and toast with honey for breakfast. Perhaps he'd taste of that.

The day passed in a slow parade of dewy grass and tumultuous skies. Neither of them said much as they walked, content to simply *be*. In the silence, their worries couldn't be indulged, their fears could be forgotten. It was only the unending, frost-laden hills, their crunching steps, and the thin thread of hope for company.

An hour later, Maeve stopped. She wrapped her fingers around Jude's arm. 'Someone's following us.'

He turned to squint at the black-clad figure behind them for a long moment before he sighed. 'Took him less time than I thought.'

The exposed shape of the moors lent Elden's silhouette a vastness as he approached. A wry look stretched across his face. 'You two are louder than you think you are. Last night's whispering, the liaison in the kitchen this morning. Jude's . . .

packing.' He raised a brow, jostling the bag over his shoulder meaningfully. 'Didn't bring a tarpaulin, did you?'

Jude crossed his arms across his chest. 'Thought we'd find an inn.'

'An *inn*?' Elden repeated, incredulous. 'You're headed back to the Abbey, aren't you? Shall I pipe in your entrance too, then, or will the trail of gossip be enough?'

'What are you doing here, Elden?' Maeve asked. She refused to acknowledge the relief his arrival brought. His steady presence was the antithesis to her and Jude's frantic planning.

'I'm going with you,' Elden replied, nothing in his words a question.

'No,' Jude said. 'Absolutely not.'

He and Elden stared at each other. The mid-morning light cast bluish shadows across the sparse expanse of winter grass between them. A frozen breeze swept through the lone tree to their left, the shake of the naked branches promising more snow.

'Don't think you'd get far across the moors without me,' Elden said softly. 'And Jude.' He squared his shoulders. 'They're my memories, too. I'm going.'

His memories?

Maeve's heart launched into her throat, followed closely by a wave of nausea, as though every second she'd had a headache, had felt like she was treading water over the past few days, had coalesced into something drowning and inescapable. Sweat trickled down her spine as she swayed where she stood.

'Jude—' she murmured weakly. 'Jude, I don't, I can't . . .'

His gaze remained fixed on Elden. 'I can't protect you there. I can't promise you'll get your memories back. I can't promise you'll know *why* your memories were taken.' His voice sounded far away, growing more and more distant. 'Nothing I do will keep you safe, Elden. Can't you see why I don't want you to come?'

Elden's reply was lost as a wave of blackness stole over Maeve's vision. Her knees buckled. Her last view before the darkness claimed her entirely was of Jude, arms extended to catch her.

Maeve awoke to wind whistling through slatted barn walls, drowning out the echo of her heartbeat in her ears. Her jaw ached like she'd been clenching her teeth for hours. A haziness coated her mind, taking minutes to clear as she stared up at an unfamiliar wooden ceiling. Somewhere to her left, blankets rustled. She rubbed her eyes and carefully sat up. She was lying on a pallet of blankets in a small barn. Nothing about the space was familiar.

The man sleeping beside her, however, was.

She shook him awake. 'Jude?' He twitched, burying his face deeper into the pillow. Maeve gently prodded his shoulder. 'Jude.'

'Hm?' He stirred, eyes blinking open wearily. 'Maeve? Why are you awake?'

She noted the lack of worry in his voice, how he relaxed back onto the pillow, one arm thrown over his head. Distantly, a bell of warning chimed at the back of her skull. 'Where are we? What happened?'

'What?' he murmured, scrubbing an eye.

'I passed out, didn't I?' she asked, voice drawing louder. 'After Elden arrived this morning.'

Jude's sleepy, confused expression shifted to one of alarm. He sat up. 'Passed out? No. Nothing happened. Elden joined us, and we walked here. Caleb fed us a meal; Elden fixed his fence. We went to sleep.' He leaned closer, gaze roving her face like he was looking for signs of injury. 'Why? Why do you think you passed out?'

Under her blankets, Maeve pinched her wrist hard. Pain streaked up her arm – proof she was awake. 'I don't . . . I don't remember. Any of it. Elden arrived, I felt ill, and I – I thought I passed out. I *remember* passing out.'

Jude cleared his throat. 'You stumbled a bit after Elden joined us. On a rock, I think. Once you'd steadied though, you were fine.'

Her memory stretched back, searching the gap with a wide-fingered grip. She scoured the edges, looking for anything uneven, anything unusual, finding nothing but an even blackness. She pushed deeper. Pain lanced through her jaw with the effort.

And there, like a trailing hem, *something*—

It disappeared before she could catch it.

Maeve swallowed, smoothing her hand down her throat to feel the motion. 'Was I normal?' she asked. 'On the walk. To Caleb's.' She paused. 'And who *is* Caleb, anyway?'

'Bethan's partner. A sheep farmer. Elden thought it would be a good place to spend the night,' Jude supplied. His voice rose in volume. 'I didn't notice anything amiss. If anything, you were more talkative than normal.'

Well. She didn't like the sound of that one bit. 'What did I say?'

'Not much.' He shrugged. A smile appeared on his lips. 'Professed your undying love for Elden but nothing besides that.'

She snorted, the sliver of humour enough to diffuse the tension. 'Oh, nothing else?'

She could tell he was trying to keep the worry out of his voice, but she saw it in his eyes. In the brush of his hand against hers atop the blanket.

He smiled again, quick and sharp before it faded. 'I wish I had the answers. I wish I knew how to stop the Abbey tampering with our memory without having to return there.'

'Me too.' Maeve sighed, weary at the overwrought conversation. 'Nothing we can do about it tonight. We should try to get some more sleep.'

Gently, she pushed his chest until he toppled back into the pillows. During their conversation, his pillow had somehow made its way to drape halfway over hers. Jude pulled the corner of the blanket back and raised an eyebrow. 'You'd be warmer if you slept closer.'

'Hm.' Maeve fought a smile as she lay down, putting her back to him. Only the regular pattern of Elden's snores on the other side of the pallet of hay kept her nerves at bay as Jude draped an arm over her and pulled her tight to his chest.

'See? It's too cold to sleep alone,' he whispered. His breath was warm on the back of her neck, legs shifting to tangle with hers under the blankets.

'What about Elden?'

Jude's laugh was a faint, sleepy huff. 'Would you rather share with him?'

'No.'

'That's what I thought.'

Maeve buried her smile in the pillow. There was no way she would sleep anytime soon. What did it mean, him holding her like this? Jude had been alone for so long. Perhaps he just wanted to be close to someone. Maybe she was just a warm body on a cold night. Maeve wanted so much more with him, and she wondered, she *worried*, if he felt the same. She needed to find out. It would eat her alive if she didn't know.

'Jude,' Maeve began, a hoarse whisper.

'Not now.' He shifted, tucking tighter against her back. 'Sleep.'

Though her heart was a restless beast thrashing against her ribcage, she closed her eyes. Focused on relaxing one muscle at a time. Despite his unforgettable weight against her, the unsettling blankness where her memories of the afternoon should live, weariness swept in through the cracks. She sank deeper into his arms.

Her final memory was of Jude pressing a kiss to her skin, just under her ear.

38

Jude

Jude woke while it was still dark. He blinked back the last foggy vestiges of sleep before rolling over and stretching one leg close to his chest, then the next. Beside him, Maeve had managed to tuck into a near-perfect ball with arms wrapped around legs and braid strung out behind her. It reminded him, with a fond lurch that had nothing to do with his cat, of Olive settling into a warm patch of sun. An unerring seeker of warmth.

Her cheeks were flushed, lips parted and rosy.

Feeling like a small bird had taken up residence behind his sternum, Jude got up and left the stable. Restlessness chafed at his limbs as he strode up a hill towards where the outline of a church steeple rose against the purpling dawn. The air was crisp in his lungs, each breath beating back his anxiety like a broom to cobwebs. Exhilaration surged in his muscles. A flash of being alive, like the lurch of a dreamt fall in the moments before sleep.

Soon, the countryside spread out before him like a patchwork quilt. He'd never been any further than the Abbey. His existence was narrowed to this — moors and woodlands, memories of the sea and salted wind burning his throat.

The countryside was dotted with tiny hamlets and more populous villages, each an individual community all their own. Except for children leaving home to join the Abbey or occasionally pursue higher education, people rarely left the place of their birth. They married locally, bore children who would have their accents and carry on their trades, dreaming of the same landscape they saw day in and day out. Consistent, steady lives with a comfortable lack of variation. A part of Jude envied them. If he ever managed to free himself from the Abbey, he wouldn't mind a life like theirs.

He lay back on the cold stone of a nearby bench, gazing at the faded stars above. A moment to ground himself, to keep from imploding into a hundred thousand pieces and drifting away. To calm his building worries, all centred around the woman asleep with her head on his pillow.

Jude breathed out, breathed in. Slowly, his muscles loosened. His lids grew heavy. Morning birdsong filled his ears and, in the far-off distance, bells.

He awoke to Maeve's voice. The sun had risen fully, heating his rumpled jumper and drying the dew on the hems of his trousers as he slowly pushed to sit. He scrubbed both palms over his face and squinted down at the path that cut between Caleb's cottage and the church. Surprisingly, Maeve and Elden were there, accompanied by a short, slight man dressed in a sweeping black robe.

Jude leapt to his feet and started down the hill. His heart thundered in his chest. 'Maeve?' he called as he neared.

She stopped, turning to face him. A smile pulled at her lips despite the tension bracketing her eyes. Beside her, Elden's gaze coasted over his head, scouring the oncoming clouds.

'There you are,' Maeve said. 'Mr Peters said he'd give us some of his already split wood and fire-starting supplies after the church service.' She jerked her chin towards the intimidating expanse of hills to her left. The next part of their journey. 'It might be hard to come by out there.' Her mouth twitched. 'Another thing we forgot to pack.'

'Mr Peters?' Jude echoed, gaze on the unfamiliar man. He studied his black robe and congenial smile. Despite his age, his hair was a shiny thatch of honey-brown, absent of grey. Not the

right colour robes for Abbey elders . . . but still. 'Who are you?'
Jude asked, tone sharp.

Mr Peters' smile didn't waver. 'I run the church. Told Maeve
you two were more than welcome to join for the service. We'd
love to have you.'

Jude scowled at his aggressive friendliness. 'We need to get
going. Now.'

'We need fire supplies more,' Elden cut in. He nodded towards
the church. 'Won't take long, then we can be on our way.'

Rolling his lips tightly together, Jude fell into step beside
Maeve. Mr Peters and Elden continued on ahead. Jude didn't
like this one bit. Impatience picked at his seams. He turned
towards her, lowering his voice. 'Is the church connected to the
Abbey?'

'I don't know,' she replied. 'I don't think so. I'm not the most
. . . well-versed on anything outside the Abbey.' She pinned him
with a worried look. 'Surely there are others, right? Other religious institutions?'

Jude returned his gaze to the stranger. 'I don't know. Elden
seems to trust him.'

'I'd like to go to the service,' she whispered, something close
to guilt on her face. 'I just—' she hesitated, worrying her lip. 'I
miss the community, I suppose. The togetherness of a service.'

Jude nodded. Whereas he wanted nothing to do with *anything*
resembling organized religion, he saw how Maeve gravitated
towards it. The saints' loss left a hole in her life, and she wasn't
ready to have her prayers sent up to no one.

'If you want to go more, in the future – I'll go with you,' he
said.

Maeve looked up at him with eyes overbright and glassy.

The four of them entered the church. Despite the unfamiliarity
of the high-ceilinged room with its rows of mahogany pews and
white-plastered walls, a prickle started at the back of Jude's neck.
The subtle scent of incense tickled his nose with every breath.

'Shall I show you around?' Mr Peters asked, sweeping his hand across the space.

Jude frowned. 'No, we need to—'

'Wonderful,' Mr Peters cut in. He made for the stairs. 'I'll show you the organ. It's truly magnificent.'

Jude tried to catch Elden's eye, to signal to him that they needed to get the fire supplies and leave, but he was already halfway up the stairs. Stifling a sigh, he reluctantly followed.

An admittedly stunning section of stained glass bordered the staircase, letting in a wash of diffused light across the steps, blues and greens and reds. Jude stopped. His gaze swept from the leaves and flowers curling around the border towards the middle, lingering there.

A man was depicted with his hands posed in front of him, one raised, the other hovering at his chest. The two fingers curled inwards. *A saint.* The corona around his head was as vibrant and yellow as an egg yolk.

And something about his face—

'Maeve?' he whispered. 'Does he look familiar to you?'

She didn't reply. Jude turned to look at her. Though her eyes were fixed on the stained glass, an odd vacancy lurked in her expression. A blankness he recognized. 'Maeve,' he repeated, a little louder this time. He took hold of her shoulder and gently shook. '*Maeve.* Look at me.'

She inhaled sharply. Her eyes met his. 'Hm?'

Mr Peters' voice broke the fraught silence. 'Are you both following? The organ's just up here.'

'Coming,' Maeve called. Before Jude could say anything else, she brushed past him, heading up the stairs.

He looked once more at the stained glass. Trepidation churned in his stomach.

This constant paranoia was eating him alive. Seeing faces where none watched, sensing danger around every corner. If he couldn't even see a panel of stained glass without getting the

urge to run, what did that mean for the remainder of his life?
Would he forever be waiting for the worst possible outcome?

With a firm word to himself to try to be fucking *normal*, Jude
ascended the stairs to join the group on a narrow balcony looking
out over the empty pews. Mr Peters held a door open to a small,
dimly lit space in the centre of the overlook. 'And here's where
the organist sits. One of the finest instruments in the country.
We're very fortunate to have it here in our modest congregation.'

The metallic glint of organ pipes shone in the hazed light:
silver, then faintly gold. Jude stepped closer, gazing at the instrument.

'You can look if you'd like,' Mr Peters said, catching his
interest.

Jude moved into the stall, Maeve at his back. 'Couldn't wait
your turn?' he murmured, turning to put his back to the shining
pipes. There was something far more interesting before him.

She reached around him to touch one of the ivory keys. A
single, reverberating note echoed through the space. She closed
her eyes, a smile on her lips. 'We used to have a piano,' she said.
'My sister and I would play together. Una was far better than I
was.'

'You remember?' Jude asked.

She shrugged. 'Somewhat. Not as much as . . . before. But I
do remember playing. How the keys felt under my fingers. Una's
shoulder against mine. But that's it.' She lightly dragged her
fingers across the keys, too soft to urge any melody.

'Maybe you'll play with her again someday,' Jude said. She
was so close he could see how her smile rose higher on one side
than the other. The heat of her body pressed into his chest. He
shifted closer.

Bam!

Maeve jumped, the side of her head hitting his jaw. Jude
winced, rubbing it as he tried to turn towards the now-closed
door, shuffling Maeve closer with the movement. The sound of

trailing voices broke through the stillness as Mr Peters continued telling Elden about the merits of mahogany over oak for choir stalls. Their footsteps down the stairs rattled the organ room.

'Did they just leave us?' Jude asked into Maeve's hair. He should probably be more concerned.

She made a quiet humming noise, still pressed against him from chest to hip. Every shift of her body was a very visceral reminder that Jude *desperately* needed to think of something that wasn't the soft curve of her breasts against his chest. His body determinedly reminded him that this level of closeness was a whole new experience, and one he ought to pay closer attention to. He breathed in through his nose, thinking of Elden's compost.

Dammit. All he could smell was Maeve.

'Try the door,' she whispered.

He pulled back as far as he could, reaching for the handle. He'd forgotten there was a door, in all honesty. He tried to turn it. It didn't move. 'I think it's stuck,' he grunted, trying to push against it with his shoulder without jostling Maeve too much. It only pressed them tighter together. She didn't say anything as he continued feeling around the handle.

Stuck, Jude thought, or trapped? He tried the handle again. If the door was jammed, the handle would still turn . . . wouldn't it? But if it had been locked—

Maeve's stifled, panicked breaths broke through the haze of his thoughts. Jude stilled. Looked down at her. Even in the dim light coming through the window overlooking the sanctuary below, he could see the pinkness of her cheeks. Her wide, pupil-blown eyes. 'Are you all right?'

She nodded, jerky. 'Yes. Just . . . tight spaces aren't my favourite.'

'Let me just—' he banged the side of his foot against the door. The sound of protesting wood echoed through the small space. He tried again, harder this time, but it wouldn't budge.

Singing trickled through the organ stall, coming from the

sanctuary below. He looked out over Maeve's head towards where the pews were now filled with congregants. Service was beginning.

Panic cinched tighter around his chest. He couldn't tell Maeve he suspected they'd been locked in here, not while she still trembled against him. He had to figure this out himself.

'Mr Peters is down there,' he said, trying to keep his tone conversational. Why would he lock them in here only to head down and start his church service? Was he waiting for something?

Jude swallowed. Something . . . or *someone?*

Maeve pressed her face tighter to his chest. A small whimper left her lips, muffled against his jumper. Jude laid his head on her crown and tried to think. The scent of his apple soap tickled his nose. More her smell than his by now.

'I'm sorry. I shouldn't have been so interested in the organ,' he said lightly.

She huffed a quiet laugh. The movement jostled her body against his. He hissed a breath in through his teeth. 'As long as my eyes are closed, it's not so bad,' she said.

Jude wrapped his arms around her, sliding his palms flat against her spine. He stroked up and down with his fingertips. 'Elden will find us soon. I promise.'

Wouldn't he? Jude scanned the pews below. Elden was nowhere in sight. Surely, Mr Peters would've given him the fire materials before starting the service. Although, he had said they would be ready after, hadn't he?

Maeve didn't reply. Her hips shifted against his. He bit his lip, wishing the pain was enough to distract him, but then her hands came up and slid around his ribcage. Her nose nudged the side of his neck, a soft inhale filling the space. Every thought and half-dreamt idea about her coloured their proximity deep red. She was so warm, so close. He could feel every inch of her touching him in ways no one had before. He would lose his mind if he allowed himself to dwell on it.

She rocked forward, closer, somehow. And, oh *no*—

'Please stay still,' he managed. He pulled his hips back as far as he could, counting to ten, then twenty.

'Sorry,' Maeve whispered. She didn't sound very apologetic.

He studied the congregants below in an attempt to distract himself. From his vantage point, he could see the tops of their heads, their hands gripping the pews. The bouncing of children's legs and the furtive whispers of back-row patrons. Mr Peters stood at the front, speaking to the crowd in a measured, authoritative voice. His words slid over Jude like a ship over water, its presence inconsequential to the turbulence beneath.

Sometime between leaving them in the organ stall and starting the service, Mr Peters had slid on an ornate white robe, fitted with a shining silver medallion.

Jude's mind fuzzed, a wash of dreamlike stupor eating at his consciousness until he was consumed entirely by the slow sway of the pendant. Gold lapped at the edge of his vision.

Familiar, it was so *familiar.*

He blinked slowly, tipping his head left, right.

'Jude?'

A hand on his chest. His heart, rabbiting against her palm.

'*Jude.*'

He wrenched his eyes from the medallion to find Maeve staring at him. Dark brows furrowed over darker eyes. Her mouth, so close to his.

'What is it?' he breathed. Had they been speaking?

'You were in some sort of daze.' She searched his face, brows furrowing. 'What were you staring at?'

He squeezed the bridge of his nose. The headache was back with a vengeance. 'The medallion Mr Peters is wearing. It looks familiar.'

Maeve rotated until her back was against his chest, an awkward shift in the small space. She rose on her toes and tried to peer out the window. The motion jostled her against the front of his body. Too quickly, Jude remembered his earlier distraction. Warmth rekindled faster than he thought possible.

'Maeve—' he warned. He stilled her with both hands on her hips.

She pressed tighter. 'Sorry.'

'I'm quite sure you're not,' he managed. He tightened his grip on her hips. Her answering inhale made him kick back his head against the wall behind him, closing his eyes. 'Stop it,' he whispered, almost pleading. Her head fell back against his shoulder for a brief heartbeat before she straightened. 'Maeve—' Jude rasped. To say what, he didn't know.

Suddenly, she stilled. 'Is Mr Peters wearing a relic?'

Relic.

The word leapt into existence.

He hadn't thought about relics in a very, very long time, but he'd used to think of them more often, hadn't he? Try as he might, his memory came up empty. A void of carefully placed darkness, fitting itself into a space he'd very much like to see clearly.

'Remind me what a relic is, again?' he asked.

'They're a mark of devotion. Elders wear them as a sign of commitment to the Abbey.'

Deep in his stomach, something sharp and urgent dug in teeth. 'Is there a purpose? Do they do anything?'

She was quiet for a long moment. 'I've heard rumours that they help the elders connect to saints individually. A direct tie to whatever saint the relic represents. I've always thought that it was more . . . metaphorical. A sign of devotion. An outward request for a saint's blessing and protection, but maybe—' her throat clicked. 'Maybe it's more.'

Jude wasn't sure whether his memory of relics had been forgotten, in the way humans naturally filed away information they deemed unimportant, or whether the Abbey had taken it from him. But he couldn't dismiss the feeling there was something to be explored.

He glanced back down at the congregants.

Wait. His heart slammed into his throat. If Mr Peters was wearing a relic—

'Fuck, Maeve. We need to leave. *Now.*'

'Now? Why?' she asked, bobbing on her toes to scan the crowd below. She gasped, spinning to face him. 'Wait. The relic . . . I wasn't sure before, but this *is* an Abbey church, isn't it?' She reached around him and rattled the doorknob. It held fast. 'Did Mr Peters lock it after it shut?'

Jude slammed his shoulder into the door as hard as he could.

It groaned, but didn't budge. He tried again. Sweat beaded at his temples. Maeve jammed the toe of her boot against the hinges. Finally, the door gave with a shattering crack, spilling them both out into the narrow landing. Maeve reached up, steering him by the shoulders towards the stairs. Black crawled in his peripherals. He forced himself to keep moving

Behind him, she whimpered. 'I can't see . . . Jude. My eyes. I can't *see*—'

He spun, putting her in front of him, and guided them both down the stairs as quickly as he could. Wrongness permeated his body. The undeniable ache of violation sent pain throttling across his jaw, the back of his skull. They hadn't just been locked in the organ stall; the Abbey was here, in their minds, eating away at their memories, their sanity.

They careened down the remaining few steps. Beside them, the formerly colourful stained glass was nothing more than an indistinct wash of grey, disappearing entirely when he turned his head to look.

The sound of voices trickled past the pounding in his ears. Shouting.

'Hurry,' Jude urged, looping his arm around Maeve's waist to move her along. She sagged against him, head lolling on his shoulder as they moved across the narthex. The doors were in sight.

'Stop!' a voice called.

Jude didn't turn. Weakness buckled his knees, forcing him to lean heavily against the wall as he inched them towards the exit. The voice called again – his name, this time, and Maeve's. Louder. More desperate. He turned to see Elden barrelling towards them, Mr Peters at his heels.

He kept going. He wouldn't rest until Maeve was outside. Until she was *safe*.

Had Caleb known who Mr Peters was? He didn't know how much the sheep farmer knew of his partner's abilities, if he was aware that in places like this, Bethan would be considered a saint.

Or maybe the Abbey had more unseen eyes than Jude could imagine. Maybe they'd been spotted leaving Ánhaga and followed here. Were there even fire supplies, or had that been Mr Peters' excuse to get them to come this morning? Jude wished he'd been there to witness the man's introduction to Maeve and Elden, to see the manipulation for himself.

Fresh air assaulted every sense as he finally got them outside, the crispness so vivid he shut his eyes tightly against it as he moved them further and further from the church. When he opened them, the world was clear once more. To his relief, Maeve's eyes were open, too. She wriggled out of his arms and turned back to the open church doors.

'Elden!' she cried.

Elden stood in the doorway, blocking the exit with his broad shoulders, his back to them. Jude caught a glimpse of Mr Peters' searching gaze before Elden pushed him back. 'Go!' he shouted over his shoulder. '*Please*, Jude. I'll catch up.'

His gaze locked with Jude's. He recognized the desperation in his friend's eyes. The pleading.

Jude nodded.

Maeve cried out, trying to run back to the church even as he tried to pull her to safety. 'We can't leave him,' she begged, tears in her voice. 'We can't.'

'He'll be okay,' Jude soothed into her hair, trying to quell his own consuming fear. He reached back, fumbling with the cool iron of the gate, and pulling them through. 'He's not a saint. The Abbey has no business with him. He'll be safe.'

The church's doors slammed shut, blocking off their view of Elden and Mr Peters.

Maeve sagged, letting Jude hurry her up the path and away from the church. She looked up at him with eyes red and streaming. 'Don't lie to me,' she whispered.

He pressed his lips tightly together. Trapping lies or truths, he wasn't yet sure.

Ahead of them, the path faded out into the wilds of the moors. Wind tore around them like a beast all its own. Each inhale burned his lungs, his eyes stinging with unshed tears. The weight in her gaze, the accusation in her voice, all of it reminded him that he didn't have an answer. He couldn't protect her or Elden. He couldn't make it go away.

At the end of the day, he was a powerless creature. Stuck under the weight of a boot, just waiting to be crushed.

39

Jude

To their surprise, Elden caught up with them less than an hour after they'd escaped the church.

He was breathing hard, his hat crumpled in his hands, but whole. He even smiled as he approached. 'Told you I'd catch up.'

Maeve hugged him. 'Good to see you.'

'How'd you manage that, then?' Jude asked as they continued walking. He applauded himself for keeping the fondness out of his voice.

Even still, Elden sent him a knowing grin. 'Talked my way out. Told Mr Peters I knew where you were going, and I'd bring you back.'

Jude stopped. 'What?'

He scanned the horizon behind Elden. Nothing. No dark, encroaching shape marred the snow-covered hills. Still, he couldn't deny the shiver that coursed down his spine.

Maeve urged him on with a hand between his shoulders. 'Glad you still have a sense of humour, Elden.'

Elden's gaze remained straight ahead. 'There's a village on the outskirts of Whitebury. About an hour's walk from the town centre. I reckon it'd be safer than going into the town proper. There should be more than a few groups of pilgrims to blend into the closer we get.'

Jude frowned. He didn't remember telling Elden about their plan to pose as pilgrims. Perhaps Maeve had.

As the hours passed, they encountered several other groups trekking through the knee-deep snow towards the Abbey, just as Elden predicted. He did most of the talking each time they encountered a new group, placing his wide-shouldered frame ahead of Maeve and Jude. Mercifully, no one remained close for long, though Jude felt the weight of their eyes heavy upon him long after they'd left. After the episode at the church, he was more suspicious than ever about watchful gazes and too-curious questions.

He scanned each face to see if he recognized anyone from the church. One man, he thought *maybe* . . . something about his gaunt frame looked familiar. Maybe it was the ampulla he had clutched in his fist, or maybe it was the pale shade of his eyes, keenly focused as they roved Maeve's face.

But, like the others, he, too had continued on.

'There's an inn we can stay at once we get into the town,' Elden said as they descended towards the low-slung village in the distance. 'Maeve, you and Jude can hide there while I fetch the robes and whatever else we might need.'

Maeve's dark eyes reflected the pale landscape surrounding them, snow dusting the tips of her lashes. 'Hiding in an inn? Not really how I pictured making my grand return to the Abbey.'

The edge of her smile showed over the red knitted scarf.

His scarf.

'Perhaps not,' Elden replied. 'Safest option, though.'

'Is it?' Jude murmured. He glanced at the new bag slung over Elden's shoulder, its sides bulging. Somehow, in the chaos of fleeing the church, he'd still managed to get the promised fire materials. 'We have the wood and flint now,' he continued. 'Why not find somewhere to bunk down outside where it's safer?'

Maeve's teeth chattered audibly. Elden shook his head. 'Safer where we can get warm. I'll sell the wood if needs be. Some extra coin wouldn't be the worst thing.'

Maeve bobbed her head in agreement. The corners of her eyes were tight, two faint lines between her brows. She'd been unusually jovial today after Elden had rejoined them, teasing and joking with a sort of frantic happiness that worried Jude more than if she'd trudged along in silence. Like she was trying to conceal the sourness of her fear with sugar.

He hated it.

He felt her hidden fear as keenly as his own; had seen her turn to the sky countless times over the hours, blinking rapidly against the headache he *knew* was building behind her eyes. The Abbey's hold grew stronger with each step towards it — why was she so determined to act otherwise?

Yet, as he watched Maeve laugh and gather snow to lob at Elden, he felt himself softening. If she'd rather spend the last few hours of relative safety feigning happiness, the least he could do was play along. No good could come out of dragging her into the pit of worry he was currently luxuriating in.

Jude bent and gathered a snowball of his own. Maeve squealed when it landed directly between her shoulder blades with a wet *splotch*, spinning around and running for him. Her cheeks and nose were rosy, her grin more genuine than he'd seen it all day.

In a flurry of limbs, she tackled him backwards into the snow. It fell around them in a cold drift, flaking into his eyes. She brushed the powder off his cheeks and nose with the tips of her gloved fingers. Her lips turned up in a contagious smile. He allowed himself the span of two breaths before he braced his hands on her hips and prepared to manoeuvre them both back to their feet.

The look in Maeve's eyes stopped him.

'Got you,' she whispered. Her gaze flicked from eye to eye. He drew in a quick breath. Maeve's eyes dropped to his mouth.

Her own lips parted on an exhale. Cold, gloveless fingers touched the corner of his mouth. The side of his jaw. The soft hollow under his ear.

A faint shout sounded in the distance. Elden calling their names.

Maeve's eyes landed on his for a heart-wrenching second before she pulled off him and onto her feet. Icy air slid over him in her place. He gazed at the pearl-grey sky, contemplating the benefits of letting the snow consume him entirely. Arousal faded into nebulous, anticipatory worry. Half want and half fear.

He'd kissed women before – girls, really, since he'd been barely fifteen the last time it had happened and his partner the same age. Forbidden kisses at the back of a pub, little more than a clumsy fumbling of lips and teeth, neither of them knowing what they were doing. Over eight years had passed since the last.

He'd done nothing else. *Nothing*.

If Maeve were to kiss him, if she were to undress and search out pleasure from his body, he'd be clueless. Absolutely, damningly hopeless, just like he'd been in her bedroom when her waist had been warm under his hand, her eyes soft and wanting. If he hadn't been able to take what he wanted, what she'd offered then, would he ever be able to?

Never mind that his body was peppered with scars and tattoos, both from his hand and the elders'. *DEVOTION* was scored into his back, for fuck's sake. Though she knew it was there, he shuddered at the prospect of her seeing it in real life, touching it.

She deserved better than him in every way that counted.

The very idea of that level of vulnerability with another person sent a wash of numbness down his limbs. He couldn't bear to disappoint her.

But yet, he *wanted*. More than anything.

Putting his pathetic mess of worries behind him, Jude rose.

He caught up with Maeve near the path. 'There was a passing group of pilgrims. Two children throwing snowballs.' She studied him, face lapsing into seriousness. 'Are you okay?'

'Fine.' He held out his arm for her to take as they trudged through the snow. 'Well, no. I'm . . . apprehensive,' he amended.

She hummed. 'I don't know what to expect. Especially once the hymns start.'

'No,' he admitted. 'I'll feel more settled when we're indoors.'

Maeve fell silent, squinting up at the heavy clouds above. 'About relics . . .' Jude began, hesitant. He'd been waiting all day to bring it up. 'Do you think it could be how the elders access the magic in the icons? How they can control our memories individually.'

Her face was wholly unreadable. 'Why do you think that?'

Jude tried to piece together his thoughts as quickly as he could. 'You mentioned that they form a connection between the elders and the saints, and it was more metaphorical. But what if it's not? What if it's real? We know that the icons tie us to the Abbey, and that the iconographers' magic is what forges that connection. But what if relics are how the elders *use* the icons?'

'Use how?' Maeve asked.

'Did you ever connect two tins with a string as a child? You hold one side to your ear, give the other side to someone else, and it magnifies your voice,' Jude said. She nodded. 'Maybe it's like that. The saint is one tin, the icon is the other, and the relic is the string between the two.'

'That . . . makes sense,' Maeve hedged. 'I have a memory about it, I think. One from years ago.' Her brows furrowed in concentration. 'I was maybe sixteen when I saw inside one of Ezra's relics. My first icon was waiting to be hung in the basilica, and Ezra was meant to bring me to see it put up. When he didn't show up, I went looking for him.' She paused, eyes losing focus like it took effort to dredge the memory. 'I found him in his study. He was bent over something. A relic. He had the centre, the locket portion, open. I saw a glimpse inside it before he closed it. It was small. Hard to make out against the fabric lining. But unmistakable.'

She stopped. Met his eyes. 'Inside . . . there was hair. A curl of human hair.'

Horror washed over him. He opened his mouth to reply, unsure what to say, but Elden's approach froze the words on his tongue. Maeve pulled back, tucking her face away into her scarf as he arrived.

'I've been doing some thinking,' Elden said. 'About the inn.'

It took Jude a moment to locate his legs to keep walking, his thoughts still circling what Maeve had told him. *A curl of human hair* . . . He shuddered. What did it mean?

'Our funds aren't exactly . . . limitless,' Elden continued.

Jude narrowed his eyes. He was right, but why bring it up now? Besides, Jude had budgeted enough for a few nights in a decent inn, anyway. Vegetable farming was hardly the most lucrative business, but they had enough for food and lodging for perhaps a week if they were frugal. They weren't planning on staying nearly that long, but they needed to be prepared for their plans to go awry.

'I was chatting to some of the pilgrims in that last group,' Elden said. 'There's more coming this time than they expected. Not many rooms left. Not many at all. Prices have gone up, too,' he said with a blithe smile.

Like a distant, horrifying mirage, Jude saw where Elden was steering the conversation.

'We can share a room. It's no problem,' Maeve chirped. 'It'll be a bit unusual, three people together, but I doubt it'll raise too many eyebrows.'

'No – it definitely will,' Jude interrupted, speaking before fully considering where he was going. 'Especially if we're posing as pilgrims. Two men and a woman in a single room? People will *definitely* notice.'

'Aye,' Elden said. 'Jude and I will take one. Maeve, you'll be in the other.'

'She shouldn't be alone,' Jude quickly replied. Her grip tightened on his arm. 'It's not safe, especially with the Abbey so near. We'll share a room instead.'

'An unmarried couple sharing a room?' Elden shook his head. 'That'd be a scandal, too, no doubt. Unless . . .' He tapped his finger on his lip, feigning contemplation. 'You could always pretend to be married.'

Maeve stiffened. 'Is that the best idea?'

Her words were like a dip in an icy river. The last thing he wanted was to force her into something she clearly didn't want. 'No, no, not at all—' Jude backtracked. 'If it makes you uncomfortable, Elden can pose as your husband. Or your father, maybe?'

'I'm not *that* old,' Elden grumbled. 'But if that's the route you prefer, Maeve.'

She didn't reply. The way she looked at him, it was as though she'd heard every shameful thought he'd agonized over earlier. How much he wanted her, how afraid he was to have her. Something in her face softened. 'I'd rather share with Jude if it makes no difference.'

He swallowed against the dryness in his mouth. *Married*. He could do little more than nod.

He needed to keep his wits about him. He couldn't afford to get distracted, not for his sake or anyone else's. Whatever brand of dread the prospect of intimacy surfaced in him wasn't the same as his fear about the Abbey, but he felt its keen sting.

It wasn't the same, he told himself. *Nothing* about it was comparable.

The Abbey had moulded him into something both cowering and devoted; a dog returning to its violent owner again and again, hoping for a gentle touch. Maeve was nothing like that. She'd sought him out for warmth when she'd been cold, light when her world had darkened with the upheaval of her beliefs. She trusted him.

He didn't want to let her down.

His thoughts dissipated like ink into water as he trudged through the snow. He may not have much in this world, but he still had enough left of himself to give to Maeve, which was exactly what he would do.

40

Maeve

Maeve somehow was still surprised the small village a few miles from Whitebury was unfamiliar despite her mind bearing the consistency of wet sand. She was certain she'd been here before, but as they wound their way through the labyrinthine streets, she was shocked to find absolutely nothing jogged her memory. Not the tightly packed buildings, the cobbled streets, or the frost-rimmed windows of the bell tower peeking up over the expanse of shingled roofs.

And especially not the guards they passed on their way into the village. She'd held her breath as they'd picked through their bags, thankful she still had a coined icon tucked into one of the side pockets. Proof of devotion to cling to, one final time.

Elden led the way through the streets, checking over his shoulder to ensure they followed close behind. The motion was so frequent and so twitchy that Maeve was tempted to ask if his neck was all right. Even his steps seemed stilted, jerking along as if pulled by an unknown force.

Jude's hazel eyes shone dark and watchful over the edge of his scarf, more fixed on Maeve than where they were going. If Elden's anxiety manifested in twitchy glances and a quickened pace, Jude's lay in a careful stillness, the weight of his focus like a tangible presence around her.

So far, they'd blended in well enough with the crowds of pilgrims and residents filling the village's cramped streets. She'd thought she'd felt a few lingering eyes but passed them off as no more than human curiosity.

Or so she hoped.

Luckily, and as far as she knew, she could remember everything of the past day, stemming from when she'd awoken in Caleb's barn. Even the moments when she'd lost her vision in the church weren't entirely erased. There had been times during the walk where gauzy buzzing had filled her ears, nausea curdling her belly alongside it, but largely, she'd felt . . . *good* wasn't the word. But it was manageable. For now. She didn't want to think about what might happen when they got to the Abbey.

'This'll do,' Elden called, fumbling with a door under a rugged sign labelled *INN*. The chains screeched as they swung back and forth, rusted where the links connected.

Inside smelled strongly of sour ale and too many bodies, but it was mercifully warm. After two days exposed on the moors, Maeve would gladly sleep here if it meant she didn't fear for the safety of her toes.

She and Jude hung back as Elden sorted the rooms and arranged a meal for them in the tavern. Jude peered around with hawklike concentration, lingering on every face that looked up at their entrance. He stood close behind her, heat washing over her back.

Elden approached a few minutes later with a brass key swinging from his finger, which he handed to Jude. Maeve was relieved to see his posture had relaxed since entering the tavern.

He shifted to cradle his bag to his chest, casting a surreptitious look over his shoulder. 'The innkeeper's devout.' He motioned to his neck, where Abbey followers often wore coin-like icons hanging from slender chains or cords. 'Thought it awfully strange that a married couple would choose this hovel. Especially pilgrims. Might need to sell him on it a bit. Wouldn't want word to get out anywhere, to the guards or otherwise.'

Jude huffed. 'Oh, for the *love*—'

Elden raised his brows. 'Just an opinion. Anyway, I'll go get us some food.'

Jude released another tortured sigh. He moved Maeve to stand in front of him, draping his arms over her shoulders and drawing her close to the front of his body like he had in that damned organist's stall. Also, like then, he kept his hips pulled slightly back from her body. She closed the space, fighting a smile when Elden tossed a wink her way.

Was pretending to be married *truly* necessary? Maybe, maybe not. A woman travelling alone with two men would definitely stand out. But was Maeve enjoying the brief respite from the panic, the worry? Undoubtedly.

Jude's heart pounded against her back. She turned to peer up at him. The strain in his jaw was evident at such close range. 'Don't look so *pained* about it,' she whispered.

He relaxed enough to release a long exhale. His eyes flicked to hers before they returned to scanning the tavern. His throat bobbed. 'That's not exactly how I'd describe it.'

Maeve looked away. Her mouth was uncomfortably dry.

Elden reappeared, balancing three plates of dubious-looking meat pie. Jude released her, leading them to a table tucked into a shadowy corner, out of the eyeline of most of the patrons. He sat slowly, his back to the wall, gaze still roving across the patrons.

Maeve hovered by one of the stools. 'Can we get a drink?'

'Aye,' Elden nodded. He turned to hold up three fingers to the watching barman.

Before she could sit on a stool of her own, Jude cupped his hand on the side of her hip and pulled her down into his lap. His grip loosened slightly as she settled, palm shifting to span her lower stomach. Maeve tried to steady her breathing, certain he could feel its shallow rhythm.

The barman, a grizzled man with an alarming amount of hair growing from his nostrils, slammed three tankards down. His gaze hung on Maeve's face as he waited for Elden to fish coins from his pocket. Even when they were tucked away in his belt, he lingered, still watching her.

'Need something?' Jude barked.

Maeve jumped. He tucked his chin over her shoulder, bringing his pint to his lips. The barman grunted, turning and lumbering back to the taps. Jude drained half his ale in one go before setting it back on the table. His lips went to her ear. 'Perhaps the charade is necessary after all.'

'Oh, yes,' she replied dryly, lifting her tankard. She swished the bitter ale over her teeth. 'If you weren't here, the barman and I would be headed upstairs as we speak.'

Jude's hand tightened on her hip.

'Your type, then?' Elden said, grinning. He'd shed his cloak and hat, rolling up his shirtsleeves. A flush already lit his cheeks under his beard. 'Like them leering and decrepit?'

'As long as they're bringing me drinks, I don't much care.'

The three of them made short work of their dinner. It was hot and filling, more than Maeve could've hoped for after days of scanty provisions. She set down her fork and adjusted herself on Jude's lap. He huffed a quiet breath in response. The thumb against her stomach brushed in a steady circle that wiped her ability to focus on anything that wasn't him as clean as a slate.

Her desperation peaked, consuming every remaining thought but her desire to go upstairs with him. She needed to see where this led. They could have one night, couldn't they? It wasn't selfish to *want*, was it? Before tomorrow came. Before it was too late.

Elden downed the remainder of his pint in one smooth gulp, rising to his feet. He swayed slightly, steadying himself with a hand on the table. His skin looked slightly grey in the scant tavern lighting. Sweat beaded on his temple. 'I'm going to have a look around. You two are going up to the room?'

'Yes,' Jude replied. 'You okay?'

'Barman had a heavy pour. Fresh air will help, I think.'

Maeve felt Jude nod against the side of her head. His hand on her stomach tensed. 'Keep an eye out. We don't know who could be watching.'

Elden studied them in silence, his mouth partially open. He gave himself a brief shake as a smile overtook his face. 'Always am.'

'He finished my pint too, didn't he?' Jude muttered after he'd left. His hand shifted from her stomach to cup the side of her ribs. He pulled her closer into his chest, her backside into his lap.

Maeve strained to focus on his words. Every sense was trained on the feeling of him beneath her. On his lap, to be accurate. On which she was still perched. She inched backwards, squirming against him.

Jude took a strained inhale before abruptly bracing both hands on her hips and levering them both to their feet. He picked up the bag Elden had left behind and slung it over his shoulder. 'Let's go upstairs.'

All she could do was nod.

If Maeve hadn't known him so well, she'd have guessed it was nerves lurking behind his carefully blank eyes, a different variation than the watchfulness he'd employed in the tavern. But he was always so controlled, self-possessed in a way she wasn't. He couldn't be nervous to spend a few hours alone with her . . .

Was he?

Better yet — was *she?*

Together, they ascended the steps of the inn, stopping in front of a door on the second floor. She noticed Jude's hands trembling as he nudged the key into the lock. Maeve wiped her own on her trousers, conscious of the sweat slicking her palms.

The room was small and neatly kept, a fire already burning in the hearth. Choosing to ignore the presence of the single bed entirely, Maeve approached the window. The glass was cold against her palm, tempering the heat in her body. The room looked out to a riot of rooftops. Snow dusted the eaves and collected in thick drifts along the sills. Chimney smoke puffed in white clouds against the blackness of the sky.

Even from miles away, she felt the Abbey's watchful presence like a vapour sliding through the streets, haunting every corner with whispered tales of devotion and deviance. She wondered if she would be tempted to fall back to her knees when she was back inside their halls, or if the reminder of betrayal would urge up a rage she couldn't control.

Only one way to find out.

She resolutely put the window and the Abbey behind her, returning her attention to Jude. He was staring at the bed, worrying the hem of his jumper between his thumb and forefinger. His stilted movements, the silence between them – she'd been wrong to assume he wasn't nervous. Every inch of his body betrayed him, every small tell she'd got so adept at reading told her he was trying very, *very* hard to hold himself together.

'Jude?' she asked, fighting to keep her voice even. She took a single step towards him. Stopped.

He didn't reply, just continued to gaze at the bed like it was a particularly difficult arithmetic question he was trying to solve.

Maeve shed her cloak, unwound her scarf, and pulled the thick knitted hat off her head. Her braid tumbled out, the roots damp with melted snow and sweat. She released it to fall in loose waves over her shoulder.

Still silent, Jude toed off his boots and set them neatly by the door.

Her heart beat in her ears. How could she be expected to sleep next to him like this? With the tension breathing between them like a living thing?

With slow, deliberate movements, Jude began working on the buttons of his jacket. His knitted jumper came next, folded and put away in a drawer. Soon, he stood before her in a thin, long-sleeved undershirt of soft grey linen, his trousers hanging loosely on narrow hips. The hems were damp nearly to his knees and caked with mud. He set his fingers on his trouser button, deliberating.

'You can't sleep in those,' Maeve murmured, her voice husky in the thick silence.

Jude's gaze slid from her loose hair down to where her own trousers, *his* trousers she had borrowed for the walk, were just as filthy. She had rolled the hems several times to accommodate their height difference, but it had only turned them into damp pockets for snow to melt into. Water dripped to the floor, coating the ground beneath her.

'Nor you,' he said.

'No.'

He bent, opening Elden's bag he'd brought up. Frowning, he lifted one book out, then another, tilting the bag to show her the contents. All books. Strange – she was certain that had been the bag he'd taken from the church with the fire-starting materials.

'No clothes,' Jude muttered. 'Or fire materials.'

The line of his throat bobbed as he stood.

All thoughts of the books fled as, slowly, he undid the button of his trousers. Underneath, the black of his undershorts was jarring against the paleness of his lower stomach. He released the final two buttons, stepping out of his trousers and standing before her in shorts that reached mid-thigh. Candlelight gilded the skin newly revealed to her, the thick, uneven lines of his tattoos starkly black.

Like the first time she had beheld his icon, Maeve got a distinct feeling of *other*. Like he was something perfect and holy and she a mere penitent, wishing for nothing but to kneel.

The thin shift she'd tucked into the waist unfurled as she let the trousers fall at her feet, covering from her neck to partly down her thighs. She hadn't donned a new pair of stockings that morning, leaving her skin bare beneath the thin white silk. In the room's darkness, the meagre candlelight had turned it translucent. She held her breath, waiting for him to look like he had in her bedroom, wanting to feel the weight of his eyes just as heavy on her body.

When he didn't, she stepped forward. He held himself so still she wondered if he was breathing at all as she wrapped her hand around his wrist, bringing it to rest over her heart. He could surely feel it trying to flee her chest.

Finally, *finally*, his eyes met hers. The mixture of fear and raw, naked wanting in his gaze took her breath. 'You're beautiful,' she murmured. 'So beautiful. Every part.'

Jude's lips parted slightly. He looked tormented, as though equal parts of himself were at war, and he wasn't yet sure which side would win. The hand over her heart moved to the side of her throat, his thumb resting on the point of her chin. Reverence in his touch.

'Jude—' she began.

'Shh,' he murmured. 'Don't speak.'

Then, he kissed her.

The first thought, the *only* thought, was how indescribably right it felt to have his lips on hers. *Finally.* How long she'd wanted it, how desperately she'd pined for this very moment. How it was both a clarifying baptism and an unmooring.

Nothing else existed except for the feeling of his skin on hers, his tongue in her mouth. Somehow, they'd moved towards the closed door, Jude pushed between it and her body. He cupped her face tightly with both hands. Whatever strung-out feelings she'd experienced earlier were nothing, *nothing* compared to her current desperation.

She wanted him to touch more. To touch all of her.

'Jude,' she murmured, a prayer in his whispered name. She tipped her head back as he kissed down her neck, his mouth open, teeth against her pulse. The sounds he drew from her split the silence.

Maeve pulled him closer by the nape of his neck, whining

when his lips skated back up over her jaw to her mouth. Any last vestige of reason left her entirely as he shoved his thigh between her legs and pressed up. The exquisite pressure bordered on pain, and suddenly, she realized she could come like this. She *wanted* to. Just from his leg between hers and his mouth alone. This was so much better than she had imagined it; it was him and her together, and *Jude* was kissing her, finally—

He released a quiet whimper into her mouth as Maeve slid one hand under his shirt, skating her nails across the warm skin of his stomach. The other went to the hollow of his hip, where she tucked her fingers into his undershorts and pulled downwards.

'Please, Jude,' she whispered. '*Please.*'

He wrenched back, sudden enough to send her stumbling forward. 'Enough.'

Before she could reply, before she could even get a good look at his face, he strode towards the window. When he turned back, his eyes were wild.

'What – what is it?' Maeve breathed. She wrapped her arms tightly around herself as a cold wash of dread coasted across her skin, erasing every inch of the previous heat. 'Are you okay?'

'I'm sorry.' Jude scrubbed his hands over his face. His undershorts hung unevenly on his hips, showing a line of tattooed tallies across his lower stomach. His lips were reddened, and a deep flush trailed down his neck. 'I can't.'

Before Maeve could respond, he was tugging his trousers and jumper back on, pulling his coat over his shoulders. He wouldn't look at her as he moved. She was frozen, unable to do anything but watch as he stumbled back into his clothes.

His hand on the doorknob shocked her into motion. '*Wait –* please, tell me what's the matter.' She stepped closer, stopping when he flinched. Her voice caught in her throat. 'Jude?'

He bowed his head, resting his forehead against the closed door. His fingers tightened around the door handle until the metal creaked. 'It's not you. I just . . . can't.'

He was gone without another word, leaving her alone and half-dressed, her heart spilling into fractured pieces on the floor.

41

Jude

Jude ran.

Panic blurred his vision into pinpoints. He didn't look to see if anyone in the tavern watched him crash through the chairs and tables and fling open the front door, a flurry of snow casting his world in white. The sting of the cold was inconsequential. Only the burn in his lungs remained.

Ropes banded his chest, each knot cinching tighter the further he ran from the inn. From *her*. Shame rushed up, hot and bright. He couldn't breathe. He couldn't fucking *breathe*. How could he have left her, warm and eager, standing alone in that damned room with its single bed, looking at him like he'd just pulled her heart out of her chest and stomped on it?

How he hated himself.

For a beautiful moment, their kiss had been exactly as he had dreamed about in those dark midnights alone in his bedroom. She'd stirred up long-dormant feelings in his body and made him believe, for one shining heartbeat, that he could offer her the love she deserved.

But, then. *Oh*, then – the shattering.

Maeve had slid her hands up his shirt and onto his bare skin. She'd whispered, *begged* him for more, for all of him. She'd pushed herself against him until there could be no confusion about how much he wanted her. Yet, all he could think about were the tattoos under her fingers, and as soon as the fear invaded, it consumed everything else.

He scraped the sleeve of his jumper over his eyes, heaving breath after breath. How could he expect her to want to see his body when he couldn't bear the sight himself? The physical wounds from the Abbey might've healed over the past eight years, but the emotional wounds remained so raw he wondered if he would ever allow himself to be vulnerable.

At that moment, it had felt impossible.

So, Jude had run, and he would keep running.

The village stretched around him in a network of narrow alleys and snow-covered streets. The air smelled of salt and metal. Buildings flashed by in shades of dishwater grey, pale yellow, the faded blue of worn fabric. None of it recognizable, all of it blurry.

He stopped and leaned against a dirt-streaked wall. A sign dangling above him creaked, mixing with the faint whistle of the wind and his panting breath. A creeping thought slipped past the pounding of blood in his ears, somehow more poisonous than all the self-loathing that had come before it.

She knew him. She'd seen him. She'd painted him.

Maeve *wanted* him. His traitorous heart ached with the realization.

It had happened too slowly for him to grasp every moment fully, but somehow, she'd seen the broken, hollow person he was and wanted him still. She'd placed her hand over the tattoos on his arm and offered to shoulder the pain for him. She'd begged against his mouth. She'd had her hands on bare skin and whispered *please*.

Fuck.

Jude opened his eyes. He'd made a mistake.

He would go back and be honest with her — he wanted her desperately, but he was afraid.

Vulnerability wasn't something he took lightly. It had taken months even to have a full conversation with Elden when the other man had first arrived, knowing it was the Abbey who had sent him to keep Jude company. Months of skirting around each other, eating Elden's attempts at meals, watching him as he generously took care of the unpleasant tasks Jude had been avoiding around the house. But slowly, his consistency eroded Jude's hostility. The same tactics he'd used to tame Olive when they'd found her cowering under a bush a few months prior. Maybe Jude was more of a feral cat than he realized.

Jude had let Maeve in quicker than Elden, but his reason for keeping her at a distance had been different than with the other man. Elden might've been found and employed by the Abbey, but he'd come from a life as a woodsman and not from its limestone halls directly. Maeve had been raised the same way he had. Both of them came scarred, visible or not.

She wouldn't laugh at the marks of his upbringing. He had to believe that if he would ever allow her to see him fully. And *dammit*, he wanted to. He wanted to experience everything with her.

If he knew anything about Maeve, it was that she'd listen to him with an open heart, take his hand, and give him exactly what he needed.

A singular lamp flickered sluggishly above, casting the street in oily shadows. He'd seen the lamplighters out earlier – boys running about with their poles, hoisting them up the streetlights to light the flame within. There was no sign of them now, nor anyone else.

The building across from him was boarded with wax paper, a torn corner flapping in the salted wind coming up the narrow alley. The scent gave him pause – hadn't Elden said they were at a village on the outskirts of Whitebury? He shouldn't be able to smell the sea this far inland. The salt dissipated with the next breath, replaced with a slight smokiness.

Snow drifted down in damp flakes to coat his upturned face. He dug his hands into his jacket pockets, thankful he'd had the foresight to re-don his coat. His undershirt chafed his oversensitive skin, reminding him of the feeling of Maeve's nails scraping up his torso. He unhooked the thought before it could embed itself any deeper.

He needed to get moving.

An open sewer ran alongside the cobbled path, smelling uncomfortably like Elden's compost. Wherever he was in the town, Jude hoped he was safe. He hadn't liked the look in the guards' eyes earlier. A frenetic tension lit the air, a watchfulness. If it weren't for the softly falling snow, he'd wonder if a thunderstorm was approaching.

Nearby, a bell tolled.

Jude turned a corner, and there it was – the clock tower. Depictions of bygone saints marred the pale stone, carved around narrow windows of simple stained glass that marched evenly up the side of the tower. The tower reached higher than its neighbouring buildings, its facade older and better looked after. He guessed it had been here long before the other structures, its presence an obstacle for all other infrastructure to build around. That was how the Abbey worked – claiming space even where it wasn't welcome.

He stopped at the base of it, staring up.

Gold flickered at the edge of his vision. He pressed his palms to cold stone, traced the outline of an outstretched arm, the folds of a cloak. He skated the backs of his fingers against the long braid of a saint, picturing Maeve's face in its place. Had artists like her done it – acolytes turned artisans, creating for the Abbey? Giving of themselves to mark their devotion?

The work was nothing like hers. These figures were frozen. Hers breathed with life, with passion and light and devotion to her craft. He pressed his palm flat to the saint's face, covering it to avoid its stone gaze.

Above, light from the belfry flickered and pulsed. His chin tipped slowly skyward. A voice in the back of his mind, growing fainter the longer he stared, whispered that he needed to look away.

He didn't want to.

Suddenly, the gold peeled back, exposing the dark contours of the tower's facade. Each carved face stood out in sharp relief. The texture of the stone-like skin looked softer than flesh. He tried to close his eyes, tried to see anything that wasn't gold and watching, leering faces.

He couldn't.

He couldn't, he couldn't, he couldn't.

The saints under his hands turned to stare at him. Their eyes grew wide, their mouths opening as terror overtook their carved features as effortlessly as if they were human. The tolls pulsed louder, drowning out his thoughts, his heartbeat, the very blood inside him—

'Jude?'

For a harrowing second, Jude didn't recognize the man before him. A hood obscured his face and swamped his frame in a sea of mud-stained black. His sudden appearance ate away the preternatural calm from the bell tower until only panic remained, strong enough to send a shockwave of dizziness through him. The hand reaching for him – unwelcome.

Jude stumbled back as the man grabbed his shoulder, pulling him away from the clock tower.

The hood slid off. All the breath returned to his lungs in a painful burst. 'Elden?' Jude sagged, scraping a hand over his face. 'Fuck.'

Elden's hand tightened on his shoulder before it loosened. 'What are you doing out here? Shouldn't you be with Maeve?'

Jude looked away. He couldn't tell him what had happened, not now. 'I was.'

Elden didn't reply. Jude chanced a glance at his face. He was looking over his shoulder, brows furrowed and lips moving soundlessly. Jude stepped closer. 'Elden?' he repeated.

He shuddered, a rough movement that travelled from head to toe. 'We should go back,' he murmured. 'It's late.'

Jude nodded his assent. Elden wove through the streets like he held a map before him, not checking to see if Jude followed. The village seemed even lonelier than when he'd left the inn, if such a thing was possible. No curtains twitched as they passed, no distant sounds of laughter or arguments coming from nearby taverns and brothels. Only silence padded his ears.

Elden turned a corner, the toe of his boot catching on a loose cobble. Jude hurried to right him, his hand fastening around Elden's bare wrist. His magic hadn't reacted without his consent in weeks, regulated not by the books, but by his own growing acceptance of it. His steadying internal keel. But now, on edge and anxious, it lunged.

Elden's memory shot through him, completely blank but for a deluge of noise.

Fog as grey as ash-fire sank down his throat and obscured his eyes. A hand wrapping around his throat, the words in his ear sweet and unavoidable. He didn't want to, he couldn't—

His lips froze as a silent scream left his throat.

The word wouldn't come.

Jude jerked free. His thoughts spun out. 'What — what was that?'

Elden kept walking, his steps short and jerky. He didn't pause as Jude gaped after him.

'Elden!' he called as he hurried to catch up. What had he just seen? Memory tampering, that much was obvious, but he'd never seen a memory so obscured it was little more than stifled emotions made manifest. Nothing but words in his ear.

Vaguely, Jude recognized the sky had somehow lightened in the minutes since he'd left the bell tower. Streaks of violet and indigo shot through the clouds above. Hadn't the clock just tolled midnight? The sun shouldn't be rising for another eight hours.

Elden finally turned to face him just outside the door to the inn. His eyes flared wide as panting breaths clouded the air around them. In the limpid light, every slack angle of Elden's face was suddenly visible. His eyes were entirely blank, like he wasn't even there, like he no longer inhabited his body at all. Sweat beaded on his temple and the line of his neck.

'I—' Elden choked. Both hands raised to wrench through his hair. His eyes bulged. 'Forgive me.'

Jude didn't have time to reply, didn't even have a second to breathe before they were on them.

Hands on his shoulders, his wrists. Clasped over his eyes. Shouts filled the air alongside the violent sound of retching. A wet rag shoved between his teeth, the sweet smell of incense in his nose. Cloying and searching, wiping away everything that wasn't his final, fading view of Elden, falling to his knees, a puddle of vomit pooling around him.

42

Maeve

Daybreak cracked open over the village, and Jude had still not returned.

Maeve hadn't left her window-side vigil in hours, limbs frozen in a state of forced intermission. She couldn't move forward nor back, simply wait, eyes locked on the street below like Jude's sudden reappearance was the spark that would jog her back to life. The memory of his shadow was yet to leave her alone. Blackness spilled like ink on the snowy cobbles, lingering even when its master had long since vanished. The bedroom glowed violet and cobalt, the crisp white of the sheets untouched. She wouldn't let herself picture Jude there. Embarrassment and hurt dug in claws.

She'd moved too quickly. Asked more than he was ready to give.

Her breath clouded the glass as she leaned closer to the window. Hearth smoke rose in pale columns, fading into a low-hanging, bluish fog. The horizon rippled, the shapes of the far-off buildings vacillating like a quickly moving cloud was rushing to cover it. Maeve rubbed her eyes. The faintest hint of a spire pressed against the visage. The glimmer of a too-familiar rose window—

She shoved to her feet, bracing both hands on the glass to look closer.

The shape of the Abbey was unmistakable.

As soon as she recognized it, it was as though the veil obscuring the village melted away, replaced with razor-sharp clarity. They weren't in a village on the outskirts of Whitebury – they were in the town already. And Maeve hadn't even noticed.

Before she could process any further, two guards crossed the street below, their black cloaks sweeping around their legs. They moved slowly, gazes moving up and down the narrow road. A flash of motion caught her eye. Curtains in a boarding house a few doors closed across the window, the faint yellow of candle-light extinguished.

Maeve held her breath. One of the guards continued on while the other stopped, bending to peer into a gap in the curtained window, hands cupped around his eyes.

What were they looking for?

Suddenly, the guard below looked up. Their gazes locked.

Maeve flew back, heart in her throat. She shifted to sit against the wall, the window to her right. Panic wavered her vision. Surely, he hadn't seen her. She was two floors up and her window was dark . . . and what if he had? She was doing nothing wrong.

Not yet.

She forced a calming breath through her nose. If there were guards below, if they found Jude—

She'd give it an hour, then go out and look for him. She understood needing a walk to clear your head, but all night, in the snow? Did he even know they were in Whitebury? Did Elden, wherever he was?

A sudden shout sent her twisting back to the window. The two guards were still there, but now, they weren't alone. Another had joined them, and they were wresting a man to the ground. Beside them, a fourth person Maeve hadn't noticed at first glance fell to their knees and began vomiting. A horrible pool of bile sank into the gaps between the cobbles. A half-full pint glass sat next to their prostrate form, a puddle of freshly spilled beer and shattered glass beside it.

Had the guards broken up a tavern brawl? She wouldn't be

surprised based on the unsavoury crowd they'd witnessed earlier. She winced as the man bearing the brunt of the fighting suddenly collapsed. The guards bore him backwards, shoving a cloth into his mouth.

Just before a hand clamped over his eyes, Maeve saw his face. *Jude.*

Fear as cold as a knife blade slammed into her. She pummelled her hands on the glass. 'No! *No* – stop! Jude!'

The guards didn't even pause as they hauled him to his feet. Maeve raced for the door. How had the Abbey found him? What were they going to do with him? She froze, hand on the door-knob.

She knew . . . she knew *exactly* what they were going to do.

Half-formed and foggy memories of the intercessions, of the Call of the Sun, swirled in her mind, leaving the stain of violence behind like ash after a fire. She thought of Siobhan, dead, her saint tattoo burned off. A figure on an altar, hands raised. Voices calling higher; blood spilling on the ground. Ecstasy and brutality, hand in hand.

A sacrifice. A martyr.

Her sweat-slicked palm slipped off the doorknob on the first go. She tried again. The door wouldn't budge. Someone had locked it from the outside. She pounded on the wood, crying out for help and rattling the doorknob desperately. Her throat ached with her pleading screams.

No one was coming.

The Abbey had Jude, and she was trapped.

Maeve raced back to the window in time to see the two guards loop Jude's arms over their shoulders and begin walking him towards an alley cutting away from the main thoroughfare. His head lolled back as his limp legs dragged tracks through the muddied snow.

'No,' Maeve begged. '*No.*' She pulled at the latch with numb fingers, prising at it with her nails. If she could open it, she could shimmy down the drainpipe to the slanted roof below and jump down from there. Her fingers slipped against the rusted metal.

The only figure remaining slowly pushed to his feet. A man, broad-shouldered and hooded. His back moved with heaving breaths as he stared at the pool of vomit surrounding him. Slowly, he began shuffling towards the corner where the street split into two opposing roads. Every few seconds, he stopped to look around, the movement mechanical and jerky. It reminded Maeve of a pantomime show she'd sneaked out to see years ago. The overdone looks, the stilted walking.

He stopped when he reached the corner, raising his hands to claw suddenly at his face, fingers sliding deep into his mouth. His hood slid off. Blond stubble coated his jaw, a hank of sandy hair sticking to his forehead. She didn't recognize him. Had his appearance been a coincidence? Maybe he'd come from the tavern, in the wrong place at the wrong time.

She grimaced as another rush of vomit puddled on the ground and redoubled her efforts picking at the lock, jimmying it back and forth while she kept her eyes on the man. He seemed to have recovered somewhat, no longer glued to the wall. Slowly, almost fretfully, he patted himself down from shoulders to waist. He felt around his neck, moving up to palm his nape.

The latch slid open with a metallic squeal just as the man looked up.

Pressure built suddenly behind Maeve's eyes. It took a concerted effort to push it back, to wrestle for clarity because there was something, *someone* she needed to see fully. The small, thrashing part of her brain still her own screamed for her to look.

She pressed both hands hard into her eyes, gritting her teeth against the pain.

She opened them to a face she knew staring up at her from the street below.

Elden.

43

Jude

Jude awoke in increments too small to catalogue. One moment, he was sleeping, dreaming, something dark and lingering on his tongue like overripe fruit; the next, he was awake. Salt flooded his nostrils. Sea air stung his lips and the tender flesh under his eyes.

He groaned. The muscles lining his throat ached. Slowly, he cracked open his eyelids. At first, he could only make out the faintest suggestion of daylight coming from somewhere to his left but as his vision came into focus, so did the reality of his situation.

He remembered bells. Saints, carved and staring, mouths opening to scream. A light, growing with a voracious hunger, so bright it ate him whole. A hand on his shoulder, a cloth between his teeth.

Elden.

Fuck. *Fuck.*

His closest friend, someone he'd slowly come to view as a brother. Someone he had *trusted.*

Had it been an easy decision for Elden to make? Or had he laboured over it, chewing on it like gristle? How Jude longed to ask him. To demand the reason he was so easy to hurt.

He scraped his hands over his face and unpicked the thought, one biting thorn at a time. A spot behind his left ear ached furiously. He probed it gently, wincing when his fingers came back sticky with blood. They must have knocked him out.

Wonderful.

He was in a bed, at least, though the room was barren and cold outside of the thin blanket – rough hand-spun linen in a washed-out blue that reminded him of the sky just before dawn. A glass of water sat beside the bed. He sniffed it carefully before taking a long drink, washing some of the stale taste from his mouth.

A lone window faced the bed. The view – narrow, webbed with iron grating and showing little more than a smooth blanket of cloud – urged him to his feet. Gold spun in the furthest reaches of his vision as he fought to keep his trembling legs underneath him.

Outside, waves crept forward in a steady crawl. Thoughts of escape were little more than a half-realized idea, intangible and lurking too far to grasp. Somewhere in the distance, singing began.

Time passed in a steady trickle. Waves and singing; singing and waves.

He should have known better than to come back. He should have *fucking* known.

Had Elden been in contact with them since they had left Ánhaga? Or, worse, had he always been in their clutches? Was that the reason he'd been sent to Jude in the first place? Not because he begged for company, not as a boon for his continued silence, but to watch him.

In the end, it didn't matter. He'd been dragged back to the place of his unmaking and left to await the final toll of judgement. Letting in the past and all its concealed pain wouldn't change anything, only taint the sweetness he left behind.

He should have stayed. *She* should have stayed.

He felt Maeve in his bones, between his ribs, and it throbbed like a bruise. Jude bit his lip until he tasted blood. He'd abandoned her; left her vulnerable and alone. Had they entered the inn after carting him off, searching for her next?

Maeve – their iconographer turned saint. He couldn't protect her. Not here, not anymore.

Behind him, the door creaked open.

Jude braced himself. He didn't turn from the window, though the back of his neck prickled in warning. Noises. Someone set a plate down, cutlery rattling together. The smell of charred meat turned his stomach despite his hunger.

'Your dinner,' an unfamiliar voice said, the accent as thick and rounded as Elden's.

A middle-aged man stood by the door. His silver hair hung heavy on his brow, faded brown habit stretched over a portly stomach. He regarded Jude with a flat smile. Jude studied him, unable to dismiss the prickle of familiarity sliding down his spine. Something about the way his smile stopped short of his eyes pulled at a memory.

The man turned and uncovered the plate. A chunk of meat, a heap of potatoes. Jude's stomach gave a hungry lurch. It felt like it had been days since he'd last eaten. Still, he kept his back to the wall. Hands pressed flat to the stone.

'How long are you going to pretend, Jude?' the man asked mildly, turning back to face him.

Pretend?

'Ah, of course.' He tilted his head, smile falling as he looked Jude up and down. 'I had wondered if that would be the case. If you'd forget me . . . it has been so many years, hasn't it? At our last meeting, you shut me behind a *door*.' He chuckled. 'Jammed in a piece of wood to keep it in place. But you don't remember that either, do you?'

Suddenly, Jude's knees gave out, sliding him halfway down the wall before he righted himself. The pain behind his ear intensified, throat seizing like a hand pressed upon it. He caught a scream behind his teeth as the man's features doubled, tripled, fracturing for the span of a breath before they reformed with a jolt of recognition.

Jude braced against the wall, panting and weak, as he stared up at the man before him.

The man who had made it his singular purpose to torture him in every way he could, to isolate him until he wasn't even safe in his own mind, to make him hate himself and his magic. Jude remembered him.

Ezra.

Both his mentor and Maeve's.

How had he not known? How hadn't *she*? Had her memories of Ezra been taken from her just as Jude's had? Anger surged up, hot and consuming – had Ezra tortured her, too? Had he taken a knife to her skin? Pressed words to her ear, telling her she was worthless, an embarrassment to both him and the Abbey?

'Oh, there's your memory returned, yes? Very good,' Ezra said.

Before Jude could respond, before he could pull himself fully upright, Ezra was on him. The pale blue eyes that had haunted his dreams were suddenly inches from his face. Ezra's hand pressed against his chest, fingers digging in hard enough to hurt. 'Sainthood, memories . . . why, even the Goddenwood, hm? There are no more secrets between you and the Abbey. Between you and me.'

'Where—' Jude fought for breath '—is Maeve?'

At this, Ezra stepped back. His face melted back into that placid smile. He gestured towards the bed. 'Why don't you sit, and we can talk about the iconographer.'

Jude shook his head, barely resisting baring his teeth.

Ezra shrugged. He grunted as he sat on the edge of the mattress. Underneath his habit, he wore ill-fitting wool trousers, too long on his short legs. The hems were caked in a fine layer of sand. 'Do you mind if I do? These knees aren't what they used to be.' When Jude didn't reply, he continued, 'An interesting conundrum, isn't the little iconographer? She doesn't quite have your . . . rebellion, does she? But my, my, isn't she talented.'

Jude clenched his jaw so hard pain rattled his skull.

'It wasn't my choice to send her away so early. I thought I might have more time to prepare her. Years, even.' Ezra's gaze drifted towards the window, brows pulling together. 'It was naive to expect anything different than exactly what happened.'

'You knew she'd be exiled,' Jude stated, studying his face intently. 'You knew she has memory magic.'

'Exiled . . . such an interesting way of putting it.' Ezra smiled, shaking his head almost indulgently. 'I suppose the elders' holy vision is true in that regard. We know what the gold dust means, at least. I knew your lovely iconographer was a saint long before she realized. We know *all* iconographers have the memory magic, hence why they are chosen to pursue the art.'

'And the spying?' Jude asked.

'Ah, yes. Well.' Ezra lifted a shoulder apologetically. 'The Goddenwood is not so very far away. Did you think we wouldn't know if you tried to pay a visit, all those months ago? Even if the old woman decided to show you anyway.'

This time, the anger was impossible to tamp down. 'Siobhan,' he hissed. '*Siobhan*. And you *murdered*—'

'Jude.' Ezra held up a hand. 'I hardly control the entire Abbey. Whatever happened to her, to Siobhan, was out of my hands.'

Jude didn't believe him for a second. 'Why?' he forced out. 'Why was she killed?'

Ezra studied him for a long moment. 'Sometimes hard decisions need to be made. The sick need to be pruned for the sake of the flock. And sometimes, Jude, the sick go willingly, knowing their sacrifice is for the betterment of the whole.'

'And did she? Go willingly?' Jude spat. 'Or was she manipulated to think she was?'

Ezra sighed. 'If I may be so bold – her business, the Abbey's business, is not always for you to know. Especially as you have made it your mission to turn your back so thoroughly.'

Jude chewed the side of his cheek. He'd never experienced such a consuming longing for violence.

'As I was saying,' Ezra continued. 'Magic is fragile, as you well know. Any . . . tampering is like a misbalanced scale. Instantly recognizable. When you began probing into your abilities, we felt it. Is it not natural for us to want to know why? To want to protect the Abbey and its followers?'

Jude fought to keep his words steady, his emotions at bay. The last thing he wanted was his magic lashing out right now. 'How long have you known?' he asked.

'A year or so,' Ezra replied.

His words confirmed Jude's earlier wonderings – Maeve wasn't the only spy, then. He wondered why they'd thought it best to send Maeve when Elden was already there reporting back. How much had he seen? Had he, too, broken into the library and seen the memory books? Had he realized Jude was looking into iconography? Or had it been more mundane, more *intimate*, reports of long hours spent in the garden, of dawn walks in the moors. Of pints and burnt dinners and arguing over whose turn it was to feed the cat.

Jude tried to swallow the pain, wondering if it would always ache just so violently.

'Our reporting had become spotty, as of late,' Ezra said. 'It seemed our intel had grown too . . . soft to be useful. Hence sending the iconographer.'

'Maeve,' Jude corrected once again, vitriol in his voice. 'Her name is *Maeve*. Who decided to send her away, then, if it wasn't you? To out her as an abomination in the eyes of the Abbey for the magic she unknowingly wielded?' He dug his fingers into the wall to hold himself in place. 'Were you the one to decide not to mark her?'

Ezra's eyes didn't leave his. Pale blue. Guileless. 'The Abbey doesn't view the saints as *abominations*, at least not the way you're imagining. We view them like any other deity, I suppose.'

'I don't understand.'

He didn't. Not even a little. The saints had been the only deity he'd ever been taught to recognize. He knew there were other religions, other gods worshipped outside of the Abbey's prying eyes, but not for Jude.

'When a group commits to a god, if you want to call it that, it's natural to want that *thing* to be set apart. Distanced from the common people,' Ezra explained, adopting an academic tone. 'When something is far away, it's easier to view as perfect. Cracks are only visible from up close, after all, and who wants to devote their lives to something fallible? Even those who are privileged enough to see the saints for what they are—'

'The elders, you mean,' Jude interrupted.

'Yes. The elders. We keep the saints distanced to maintain that fragile equilibrium between those who pray and those who grant. Both magic and religion have their place. Religion is a public endeavour. Belief in the saints binds our community together. It's an expression of structure. And every community needs its scaffolding.'

'And magic?'

'Magic,' Ezra responded patiently, 'is something individualistic we've made communal. By nature, it's a private action. A talent that crops up every so often in individuals. We've simply moved it away from the individual and towards the collective.'

Jude weighed Ezra's words against his own cynical view of religion. He compared it to Bethan's acceptance of her abilities, grown in an environment away from the Abbey and its secretive, white-knuckled hold on saints. She didn't hold the suffocating hatred Jude did for their shared magic, which made him wonder – was his attitude towards his magic down to his personal experience with it or what he'd been taught to believe?

In a way, he understood where Ezra was coming from. Even though Jude's magic felt out of reach on the best of days, he'd always viewed it through a selfish lens. It was *his* magic. The Abbey's touch was what made it feel tainted and wrong.

Yet . . . the elders used that very same magic every day. They'd taken what was personal and made it collective, sacrificing his autonomy in the process.

The thought didn't sit right.

'But you're the ones who steal our abilities to manipulate memories and call it answering prayers,' Jude said slowly.

Ezra made a quiet noise in the back of his throat. 'If it helps you to see it that way, yes.'

'That's not how you see it?'

He weighed his head back and forth. 'Not . . . exactly. We elders view ourselves as more intermediaries. We've trained our entire lives, after all. We're gifted with the discernment to choose when and how we shape memories to answer prayers. The saints—' He paused, inclining his head in Jude's direction. 'Why should acolytes trust you to decide what prayers get answered? You're so young, so volatile with unearned confidence. Why, even my own son—'

Ezra's jaw snapped shut, eyes bulging. His hand slipped up to his neck, moving beneath the collar of his habit. Something flashed silver before it disappeared beneath the brown fabric.

Dizziness swarmed at the edges of Jude's vision. He blinked rapidly as it vanished as quickly as it had come, leaving him unsteady on his feet. When he searched back to the last few seconds of conversation, he couldn't remember what Ezra had said.

'All I mean to say is,' Ezra added before Jude could probe at his memory any further, 'saints are young when their powers manifest. Imagine how catastrophic it would be to give children free rein over their abilities.'

'Why pretend to answer prayers at all?' Jude countered. 'Why intervene and not let life take its natural course? It can't be easy manipulating the memory of so many.'

'Would you let life take its course if you had the power to change it for the better?' Ezra asked. 'Besides . . . we're not altering events. Just how they're remembered. Who does it harm to let them believe in prayers? It's a comfort to know someone is there, someone is listening when they pray.'

Jude hated his tone, hated the false kindness in it. It reeked of wilful delusion. His deep-seated fury at the memories of so *many* under the thumb of the Abbey grew stronger. The members, even the acolytes, had no idea their memories were being altered in the name of answered prayers.

How did the elders justify the theft?

'We're creating peace like any other religion or community,' Ezra continued when Jude didn't respond. 'Even in governments, no leadership framework exists without *some* elements of its function being kept from its followers. Are you saying you need to know how the sausage gets made to enjoy it? Through answering prayer, we can keep our followers happy. Keep the Abbey prosperous. Help our community. The saints are simply our figurehead.'

'Keep the money coming in, you mean,' Jude snapped.

Ezra shrugged, unbothered by the accusation. 'Wealth is a natural consequence of power, not necessarily the goal.'

'Why are you telling me all this?' Jude asked. Nausea surged up from his stomach. He slipped a half-inch further down the wall. 'After all these years, both in and out of the Abbey, why now?'

Ezra pushed to his feet. The joints of his knees cracked under him. 'I have a deal to offer you, Jude, that's why. And I want you to be fully aware of the stakes before you agree.' His smile was gentle, almost saccharine. As though he held a vial of poison prepared to sweeten Jude's tea. 'If you leave now, no further harm will come to you.'

His mouth dropped open. That was the *last* thing he'd expected Ezra to say. 'And Maeve?'

'She's coming here, you know. To the Abbey.' Ezra made a show of checking his wristwatch. 'She should be entering in, oh – an hour's time? She saw you get taken, and I *assumed* she'd come and attempt a rescue.' He cocked his head. 'Would that be the correct assumption?'

'You're using me to *lure* her here?'

Ezra raised a brow. 'Well. It wasn't our original plan. She was meant to be with you when we found you wandering the streets. But this works, too.' He held up a hand before Jude could continue. 'The offer still stands. Leave and return to your home, and you'll be safe.'

'And Maeve? What about her?' Jude repeated. He wanted to spring across the room and wrap his hands around Ezra's throat so badly that his fingers tingled.

'Are you so concerned for the iconographer that you'd risk your own life? Surely, you must know I'd let no harm befall her. She's like a daughter to me.' Ezra drummed his fingers on the opposite wrist. 'It wouldn't be a hard thing, to erase her memories of you, and yours of her. We've done it before.'

Jude could bear anything but that. He tried to slow his breathing at the thought, but it continued to sweep down his body like poison in his bloodstream, promising a bottomless well of despair. His memories of her . . . the most precious thing he owned, gone in an instant.

Why, *why* had he not saved them in a book?

Maeve, staring down at him cross-legged on the floor, the first hint of softness in her eyes. Her pulling him from the bog, the shape of her shoulders under his hands in his library. How she'd captured him wholly and completely on the canvas. He'd knelt before her in the rain and the smoke, promising her his loyalty, his life. She'd seen him like no one ever had, and no one would again.

As surely as he knew the sound of his own heartbeat, he knew Ezra was telling the truth. He would take their memories if they didn't comply. Or worse.

Was it his imagination, or could he hear singing through the thick stone walls? His hearing dipped in and out, leaving a faint ringing behind. He swayed on his feet.

A saint on an altar, the jeering crowd calling for blood.

Jude blinked, and the memory was gone, but the message remained – the Abbey would never allow them to walk in as saints and leave as anything less than martyrs. He had promised himself as a boy, beaten and alone in a room not so very far from here, that he would fight. He'd fought then, and he'd continue fighting now. For as long as he had breath.

'If she's here, then so am I,' Jude said. 'I won't leave her.'

'Ah.' Ezra smiled. 'I thought you might say that.' His eyes fell to the table pushed against the side of the bed. He picked up the glass from it, tilting it to spin the remaining water along the bottom.

For the first time, Jude noticed a faint oily residue in its wake.

He swallowed. The subtle taste of juniper lingered on his tongue.

'You didn't drink the whole glass as I'd hoped, but it should be enough,' Ezra said. He set the cup down. 'Maybe sit before you collapse. It'll be more comfortable.'

Jude swallowed again. Dryness coated his throat. The dizziness at his peripherals crept closer. His legs trembled. 'I . . . I don't—'

Ezra rose. His hands slid under Jude's arms, directing him towards the bed. 'I told you to sit down,' he murmured.

Above, the ceiling flashed briefly gold before it faded entirely into black.

44

Maeve

By the time the Abbey loomed in front of her, Maeve could hardly remember the steps she'd taken between leaving the tavern and hurrying up the steps towards the hulking limestone building. None of the shops had been open, leaving her to break into a piety store and steal a set of pilgrim's robes on her own. It wasn't their original plan – Elden was meant to buy them when they got to Whitebury – nor was it her proudest moment, but the rising sun and sleeping city had forced her hand. At least she'd sneaked in via a back door and left coins on the counter instead of breaking a window.

The fact they had been in Whitebury the entire time didn't sit right with her. Even if the Abbey had her icon and was using it, she should have *known*. Had Elden known the Abbey would take her memories of the town? He'd locked her door without her noticing, after all. Perhaps he'd been the one to orchestrate the Abbey taking Jude, too.

The reminder throbbed like a bruise she couldn't help but prod.

Had Jude realized what was happening in the moments before the hand clapped over his eyes? Maeve pictured him following Elden back to the inn like a lamb to slaughter, thinking only of the safe hand guiding him forward. She rubbed her chest as the ache spread, demanding to be felt.

Her nose dripped. She wiped it with the cuff of her pale grey pilgrim's habit. The cloth smelled of sweat and salt, tinged with the subdued iron of washed-out blood. Bodies pressed in at every side, so tightly they breathed as one as the pilgrims ascended the almost two hundred steps up to the Abbey's yawning entrance. The chord of longing it once pulled had been replaced with icy dread.

Somehow, her home had shifted from salt-crusted limestone and stained glass to a draughty house shaped by wild winds, woodsmoke on her tongue, and *him*.

A pocket of watery blue emerged through the clouds above the tallest spire, visible only for a heartbeat before it was gone. Jude would have liked to see it – that talisman of blue. Rage and grief expanded in her chest like a living thing.

Her toe caught on the final step, forcing her to right herself against the cold iron of the Abbey's inner gate. The pilgrims joined several queues snaking past the guards and through the main doors. Maeve quickly scanned her options, picking the line watched by the least familiar face. She gathered a handful of coins into her palm and prayed the sweat on her skin didn't stick to them.

The guard's eyes narrowed as she approached, focusing on the glint of Maeve's pale braid under her hood. 'Name?' His eyes dropped to the coins nestled in her cupped palm. 'Ah.'

Pilgrims had two options for Abbey entrance – secure a guided tour months in advance, putting their name on a list the guard held between his gloved hands, or pay off the guard directly. One was Abbey-sanctioned. The other less so but arguably more effective.

He dropped the bribe into his pocket with a lazy, incongruous movement. Clearly, he wasn't worried about being seen. His gaze continued to rove boldly over her face. Maeve met his eyes evenly, praying to anyone listening for the guard not to spend any longer wondering why she'd chosen to pay him off instead of getting her name on the list of cleared pilgrims.

Finally, he dipped his chin in a slight nod, waving the next pilgrim forward.

For once, she was grateful corruption didn't stray far from the source.

She moved deeper inside, leaving the vast expanse of the hallway for the cloisters that ran the outer stretch of the Abbey's western wing. The fetid smell of salt and candles left to burn out lingered at the back of her throat as though she'd bitten into something rotten.

She'd expected to feel worse within the Abbey, something similar to the drugging sluggishness she'd felt in Mr Peters' church, or worse – lose track of herself entirely, waking to find large swathes of time lost to memory. It was almost concerning that she felt mostly present in her mind. She worried that it meant the Abbey wanted her here. Wanted her cognizant.

Singing from the basilica trickled down the walkway, hitting her like a punch to the chest. Pulling the sides of her hood close to her face, Maeve drew back from the railing and followed the pilgrims down the cloistered hall. They'd been clicking through hymns like hands on a clock. There'd been at least three since the sunrise that morning, right on schedule for the Call of the Sun to commence at daybreak tomorrow.

She was running out of time.

Ahead of her, the group of pilgrims parted as a figure emerged from around the corner. Dark grey habit – an acolyte or artisan.

Maeve froze. There was nowhere to go. She was about to be seen.

Turning, she hurried back down the corridor, scanning the wall as she went. A small doorway was tucked between two archways, perhaps twenty paces away. Just as she was about to make a run, a voice called her name. Soft, almost choked.

Despite everything in her screaming to run, Maeve turned.

Brigid stood halfway down the cloisters. Her eyes were wide

in her ashen face as she rushed towards Maeve. 'What are you *doing* here?' she hissed. 'Are you stupid? Why would you come back?'

Maeve flinched. 'The memories . . . My icons, *your* icons, Brigid. I couldn't—'

'Hush,' Brigid all but begged. She seemed to have aged a decade in the weeks since Maeve had last seen her. Her normally neat hair hung lank and greasy around her face. 'I know. I know, Maeve, but not here. *Saints*—' she gasped. 'Anywhere but here.'

'You knew about the memory magic?' Maeve asked. Anger pulled at her seams. 'You knew the Abbey uses our icons to manipulate memories? You know that you're a—'

'*Maeve*,' Brigid hissed, eyes wide. 'Yes, I know. I know all of it. But we can't talk about that now. You need to leave.'

'I can't,' Maeve pleaded, stepping closer. 'My . . . Jude. His housekeeper, his *friend*, betrayed him. The elders have him now. He's here somewhere. I have to find him.'

'Who?' Brigid asked, her voice pitching abruptly louder. 'What housekeeper? What friend? The name.'

Maeve blinked, briefly stunned. 'Elden. Do you know him?'

The other woman's eyes slammed shut. She took a deep breath before reopening them. Her gaze pinned Maeve in place. 'Ezra can't know you're here,' Brigid said, ignoring Maeve's question. 'No one can. Actually—' she cast around wildly, gaze locking on the doorway Maeve had spotted minutes earlier. 'There. Go there. Servants' halls. It leads to a storage room. There are icons in there. Burn them. Promise me you'll burn them.'

Icons?

'Burn? Why . . . okay?' Maeve jumbled out. She didn't understand what Brigid was asking, not entirely, but they needed to burn the icons anyway, so Maeve would do what she asked. She nodded, firmer this time. 'Okay, but then I need to—'

'Yes, yes,' Brigid interrupted. 'From there, you can search

for your Jude or whatever else you need. But please, promise me,' she grasped Maeve's hands in both of hers, 'once you find him, you take him and run. You can start a new life. Make new memories.'

Before Maeve could reply, footsteps sounded down the hall. She shoved Maeve towards the doorway, pushing her unceremoniously inside. 'Go. *Now.*'

Brigid shut the door behind her. Silence pressed against Maeve's eardrums, broken up by the steady pounding of her heart and her panting breaths. She pressed her ear to the door. Voices: Brigid's and someone else's. A man, his voice unfamiliar. Reluctantly, she peeled away and descended a short flight of stairs.

How long had Brigid known of the power in her icons, the power in her *blood*? Why would she choose to comply with the Abbey using her abilities to harm? Brigid was an iconographer – a saint. Why had she been allowed to stay at the Abbey? And why couldn't she burn the icons herself?

Maeve turned the questions over in her mind as she walked down the dank tunnel. She couldn't erase the memory of the naked fear on Brigid's face. The warning in her voice.

Regularly spaced openings were dug into the walls, peering into various rooms and hallways. She stopped to look through the closest one. The corridor hung lower than the room she was looking into, putting her eyes at ground level. The faint pounding of the sea trickled through the thick walls. These passages would be the first to flood if the waves ever gained entrance. Their occupants, herself or the maids they'd been built for, wouldn't stand a chance against the tide.

She hurried on.

The path curved to a slender iron staircase jutting up from the floor. A sudden echo of wings flapping slipped down the corridor. Maeve pressed against the wall as her heart leapt into her throat.

Nothing. No birds, no maids.

Her hands trembled. The corners of her eyes glinted metallic as the pressure in her chest increased. She closed her eyes, giving in to the gold, the memories that weren't hers.

Immediately, the passage changed. Lamps now hung from the ceiling, casting the dank surroundings in an oily glow. Cool air came in through the windows above her head, bringing the scent of dusty books and stone wet with seawater. Before she could inspect further, voices sounded from the narrow door at the top of the stairs. Whispering.

'He's asleep,' a male voice mumbled, not a child's voice, but not an adult either. 'It worked.'

A prickle of awareness slid down Maeve's spine as another person laughed. It sounded like *Jude*, his voice younger and higher-pitched than his friend's. His answering whisper confirmed her guess— 'I have the key.'

Their footsteps faded out as the gold leached from her vision. Maeve blinked. Whose memory had she just viewed? It wasn't hers, and she doubted it was Jude's without a book present. How had the memory been triggered?

The urge to slam open the door she leaned against and find him was stronger than anything she'd ever known, even if what she'd just heard was little more than a faded memory. She wished it was real. She wished Jude was here. Safe. *Hers*.

Maeve had little experience with secrets. She knew gossip – where the cook kept the tins of biscuits or who had sneaked out to meet a local boy. She knew the power of hidden words whispered between friends and lovers. She'd never had much reason to keep secrets from herself.

But *this* . . . this feeling like she was drowning, like everything was dull without him, was new. Something she'd kept hoarded away like a precious jewel. It consumed her. Transformed every part of her being until Maeve was rewritten entirely. A new creature made with trembling fingertips upon malleable clay.

She wouldn't put words to it. Not yet.

Holding her breath, Maeve pushed open the door, leaving behind a scatting of gold dust covering what was once dirty and neglected with the gilded remnants of what she would not name.

45

Jude

The next time Jude awoke, he'd been moved. No longer was he in a bed. Chains hung heavy from his arms, holding him to the damp, sandy floor. The walls cried ink-black tears from the creases between the stones. He'd been here before. The wretched stink of blood and sea was one scored into his flesh, words on his skin that would never entirely disappear.

His whole body ached, the juniper in his mouth heavy and lingering. Why, *why* had he drunk the water? Why had he trusted the Abbey for even a second?

Jude clamped his hand over his mouth, the chains squealing with the movement. Fresh tears trickled down his cheeks. He squeezed his fingers tighter to his face, fighting the urge to scream.

Suddenly, he was fifteen again, consumed by the rancid smell of his nervous sweat as he lay on the stone, waiting for his mentor to come and find him.

He'd done something, hadn't he? Something more than try to burn the Abbey's icons, something with a motivation that ran far deeper. He couldn't remember what, only a pounding desperation in his limbs to save someone, to save them *all*. He'd remembered recently pieces of what had got him exiled, but here, in the Abbey, the start of his unravelling . . . . gone. Still out of reach.

He was eight again. He was fifteen, he was *alone*—

'It appears not much has changed, after all, Jude.'

He stopped breathing entirely.

Ezra stood over him once more. A lash of pain forced Jude's eyes back shut. His heart beat behind his lids, aching with a hammer-like pulse. Memory caught him by the throat and squeezed.

All of Ezra's careful explanations earlier, his calm smiles, the false concern for his safety, all culminated in this – Jude flat on his back with salt in his nose and terror in his eyes. A *lie*, just like everything else the Abbey stood for.

'What did you think would happen?' Ezra asked. 'Did you think you could deny my offer and go free anyway? Did you think you could save her? Save yourself?' He laughed. 'You've never been very good at that.'

Before he could move, before he could even breathe, Ezra ground the fingers of Jude's right hand beneath his boot. He screamed, trying to pull away. Pain shot up his arm, hotter than fire.

'Jude.' He pressed harder. 'Tell me.'

'I didn't—' Jude gasped through clenched teeth. 'I thought—'

'No,' Ezra whispered. 'You didn't think. Did you not remember what I told you that day you left the only home you'd ever known? Say it.'

The pain of his broken fingers magnified tenfold. They curled inwards, scrabbling at the roughened leather boot pinning it to the ground. It *burned*. Jude whimpered, trying to leave his body, to rise above the pain, but Erza only pushed down harder.

'My choices have consequences,' Jude gritted out.

The boot left his hand. The tattered remains of his fingers pulsed with their own heartbeat.

'That's right.' Ezra bent down. 'And you don't even remember what you did, do you?'

'Because of you,' Jude gasped. 'You took my memories. You tainted my magic. For *years*, I hated myself. Because of you.'

Silence fell as Ezra rose back to his full height. 'But you came back anyway, didn't you? All three of you are back here. Just as you were always meant to be. Except now, you have that mark on your back. Marks I placed there. Hate me all you like, Jude, but they will always remain.'

All three? Jude wondered, focusing on that part of Ezra's tirade and not the poisoned barbs. He was here, and Maeve must be too — but who else?

Ezra continued, 'And what impeccable timing you have. The pilgrims are here, you know. Wouldn't it be lovely to have a saint for them to pray to? Or had that been your plan all along, to strike when the prayers are at their most potent?'

Jude's mind latched onto his final words, turning them over in his head and comparing them to his scanty memories of the last time he had tried to burn the Abbey. Maybe he had failed because the icons hadn't been at their full potential. Maybe they needed to burn them during the ritual — not before, and not after.

His thoughts swam and dipped feverishly. He closed his eyes to the sound of Ezra moving around the room. Carefully, he stretched his fingers one by one. The stiffness faded with each crack of his knuckles.

They weren't broken. They weren't even bruised.

Maybe he'd dreamed everything. He'd wake in bed to birds streaking across his window and tea boiling in the kettle. Olive would be curled somewhere by his head, silken black fur shining red in the dawn of a new day.

She would be there. He'd roll over and hold her — warm, safe, *happy*.

That dream didn't exist in his head, with the caged nightmares pacing behind iron bars, scoring bleeding lines into his flesh. It lived lower, protected by his ribs and wrapped around his heart. Softer. A dream written in love.

Ezra's footsteps drew closer. Jude opened his eyes to stripes of ochre and russet from the setting sun streaking across the water-stained ceiling, blending into the indigo and violet of the gloaming. Fatigue weighed heavy on his limbs. His breathing barely moved his chest.

A touch on his arm. The crook of his elbow, wrapping oily tendrils around his wrist. It squeezed; it *hurt*. Fire followed the path of his veins up his arm like polluting oil dropped into a fast-moving stream. It bloated his belly and sucked at the blood pooling in the spaces between his ribs, the notch between his collarbones and the hollow of his navel. It dug claws into his tender skin, opening up the blackened lines of his tattoos with familiar precision. Pain served a purpose, even if Jude had long ignored its warning.

He wanted to raise his hands, cover his mouth.

He wanted to go *home*.

Home meant safety. It meant anonymity and choice. It was a lonely house on lonelier moors, taken for granted until the moment he'd give anything to have it back. He would cradle *home* to his fragile chest and slide it between his ribs for safe-keeping. A poisonous delight; one too many, one too gluttonous, and it would end him.

As though accelerant was poured over his skin, the pain magnified tenfold. Jude located his lungs somewhere amongst the viscera and *screamed*.

'You should never have come,' Ezra murmured. 'Why did you return?'

Fingers touched his temple, carding through his hair. Jude flinched; thankful he'd asked Maeve to cut his hair short. He remembered having long strands pulled from his scalp too well to allow it to grow. It used to ache for days. Ezra was keenly interested in punishments that would linger far beyond their gifting.

Jude shook his head, tears dripping down the side of his face. The waves of agony receded enough for him to take a deep breath through his nose and open his eyes, unaware he had closed them again. He lay prostrate on the cold ground, hands folded over his heart.

Was that his body, his hands?

The foreign hands were folded in prayer with palms together. Not foreign, not strange. *His* arms.

'There have been five hymns so far. Three to go,' Ezra murmured. 'The more the pilgrims worship, the higher they urge their voices, the more magic I can use. And your icon is there, Jude. Watching, listening. And I have this.' Something cold brushed Jude's face. 'Know what it is?'

A glint of silver came into focus. A chain. From the end of it, a locket hung open. Inside, cast in resin, was a dark spiral. Jude blinked.

Hair.

Human hair.

Just as Maeve remembered.

It looked familiar; the colour almost black. It'd shine with a reddish tint in the sun.

'Is that mine?' Jude croaked out. He licked moisture back into his lips. His voice sounded like it'd been dragged over hot coals. 'My hair?'

'Mm. Indeed,' Ezra replied. 'A relic.'

A metallic sound, the locket clicking shut. Ezra made a quiet, contemplative noise deep in his throat. The relic swung inches from his nose. 'I'll always have a piece of you, Jude.'

Disgust rolled his stomach. Seeing a curl of his hair stuck forever beneath the resin was horrifying, a disgusting display of invasion.

Ezra sighed, the sound regretful. 'I suppose the *why* of your return doesn't matter anymore. The eighth hymn begins at daybreak, and we need someone to Call the Sun. You'll do perfectly. And with this,' he clicked the relic open again, flashing the hair inside, 'I can keep your mind pliant. Keep your memories trapped.'

Jude's head lolled on his shoulders.

He'd die. They would martyr him.

The darkness of his reality washed over him; a black tide of inescapable despair reminiscent of everything he'd tried so hard to leave behind. A familiar, insidious voice whispered in his head that maybe it was for the best. Maybe he ought to die. Maybe it would be easier to give up.

Desperate, he scrambled for a foothold, a rope to lead his mind back to clarity. He didn't have his garden or books nearby, but he needed a reason to stay alert and keep fighting.

He found it with bloodied fingers and seized.

Anger.

He'd scraped himself up every time Ezra had tried to bury him; he had a life and a home and some semblance of peace, even if it had taken him leaving to realize how rich he truly was. He had Maeve. *His* Maeve, his beating heart, the only saint he could believe in. The Abbey left him in the cold, and he'd be damned if he didn't burn it down to keep himself warm.

He couldn't die. Not yet. Not when he'd promised himself he'd live.

Singing poured through the open door. Ezra manoeuvred Jude to his feet. His body was too weak from the pain and the relic to resist. Somewhere behind him, lingering at the furthest reaches of his vision, gold.

Then, pure blinding white.

46

Maeve

Maeve thought she knew her way around the Abbey, but the room Brigid had pointed her towards was entirely unfamiliar. She tried to quell the nervous shake in her legs as she looked around. The narrow space smelled of neglect and seawater and was filled from end to end with piles of forgotten items. Why had Brigid wanted her to come here?

Her panting breath cut the silence as she crossed the room to where two frames were stacked near the windows. The only paintings she could see amidst the stacks of stools and hampers of crumpled bed linens, a sideboard topped with teetering plates and a low bench covered in a white sheet.

She knelt before them, willing her racing heart to slow.

The wood of the larger one was chipped and aged, paper backing spotted with mould. Her hands shook as she reached for the closest painting and turned it over.

A boy – a young one, too. Perhaps seven or eight.

Very, *very* young to be a saint.

He stared back with a reckless gleam in his bright blue eyes. Something about him looked familiar, but Maeve couldn't place it. The shade of his eyes, maybe, or his sandy curls. Flakes of paint were missing from the gilded halo behind his head. She'd never seen an icon show any kind of age; even the oldest paintings in the basilica were pristine.

An illegible signature marred the left corner of the painting; the boy saint was just as anonymous.

Did Brigid know him? Was that why she wanted his icon burned?

Maeve's throat convulsed, fear gripping her before she forced it back, reaching for the next icon. Its frame was made of rough-hewn wood, the paper backing newer and mould-free. She flipped it over.

For a heartbeat, she could only gape.

Her face stared back at her.

She gently touched the tip of her forefinger to a peak of dusty grey paint in the corner, rubbing it between her fingers. Still wet. The icon was recently finished. No wonder she'd been feeling so awful.

It was odd. She'd expected to feel connected to her icon somehow. She'd seen Jude's expression when he'd sat before his finished icon: the awe, the slack-jawed wonder as his gaze had moved from his icon to her – his iconographer.

All Maeve felt was emptiness. And, if she was being entirely honest, a little offended.

She wouldn't have spared it a second glance if she'd seen the icon in the basilica. It was just so startlingly *average*. Amateurish, even in style. The blending between colours was *just* – she wasn't impressed. Had Brigid refused to paint it, and they'd used an apprentice instead?

She studied the flatness of her hair, hanging in a single braid over her left shoulder. The end of the braid was smooth besides one single strand, a bright slash of near-white against the dark blue of her dress. Everything else about the painting was monotonous, as uninspired as a tracing.

So why was the single hair out of place?

Her nose was a little off, her mouth thinner in the painting than in reality, but they'd got the darkness of her eyes and the point of her chin correct. Whoever had described her face had known her well.

She stilled, fingers still hovering over the icon.

Ezra was the only one who knew her well enough to describe her face so accurately. Even taking the iconographer's magic into account . . . especially for apprentices, the description needed to be accurate. Who else would it have been but Ezra?

The realization sank like iron in her stomach as her gaze returned unwillingly to that damned stray hair. She wanted it gone.

Slowly, Maeve stuck her hand in the pocket of her habit, fingers closing around the slender box of matches. She'd taken them from the piety shop she'd stolen the habit from, desperate for anything that could help her start a fire. Before she'd left the inn, she'd pawed through Elden's bag that Jude had brought up, finding only the books he'd shown her. No fire materials. No fuel, no matches, no wood. Only books. *Gardening* books. Somehow the sight of all those books on urging up plants from the tough winter soil was as much a stab in the back than the fact he'd sabotaged them in the first place.

She slid open the box of altar matches. There were only eight. Eight chances to burn the icons.

Maeve picked one up, hesitating. Should she use one now? She wanted her icon gone . . . but was it worth an entire match? There weren't any candles or lit sconces in the storage room, but there would hopefully be some in the basilica she could grab – if the guards didn't stop her first.

A candle wouldn't be much hope on the higher-up icons on the wall, would it?

But neither would the matches.

She ran her thumb over the tip of the match. Fear tightened her chest. Her eyes locked with their painted replicas. That fucking *stray hair*—

The sharp smell of phosphorous filled the air as the match struck. She raised it to the boy's icon first, but as soon as the flame touched the canvas, it extinguished, leaving nothing more than a singed hole in the painting.

'No,' Maeve gasped. '*No.*' She picked up another match, barely pausing to think before she struck it. She had to burn the icons. She would find other matches, candles, maybe, or fuel somehow, but these icons needed to go first. She had to succeed at *something* if she was going to believe she could burn the entire Abbey.

This time, it caught.

She burned the icon of the boy first, then drew the lit match to her own visage. Her vision grew quickly hazy, prickling against the malleable recess of her mind. She expected to have a reaction like Jude when she'd burned his icon, to pass out or hallucinate, but instead, there was a vivid flash of gold light, a sharp burst of pain behind her eyes, and then – nothing.

But something was different. Her mind felt refined, like copper after the fire, and her magic felt . . . accessible, as if she could have reached out a hand to grab it.

And her memories—

The pressure in her skull was consuming, pulsing, sending a wave of pain across her forehead. She gasped, cradling her head in her hands, and tried to fight back the volume of the memories calling for her attention. Amidst the torrent of the past few days – crossing the bitterly cold moors, Caleb's cottage, Elden's terror-white face at the doors of the church – deeper memories surged to the forefront.

A flash of gold like the sun. A drop of blood like paint.

A groan slipped past her clenched teeth. With a concerted effort, she managed to wrench the memories back, staggering to her feet in the process.

Burning the icons *worked* – the memories pounding fists against the back of her mind were proof enough. But she couldn't let them consume her. Not yet. Not until she found Jude.

Smoke from the still-burning icons was ripe in the air as she made for the door. She would crawl through the Abbey if she had to, bloodied and exhausted. Anything to find him. Anything to save him. She burst from the storage room and froze, her back against the doorframe. Her nails bit into her palms as her gaze locked on a door directly in front of her.

With a quiet *snick*, it clicked open.

Maeve cast around desperately for somewhere to hide, shoving herself into a nearby alcove behind a marble statue of a woman, praying the darkness was enough to hide her.

A figure emerged from the double doors. Brown habit, iron-grey hair—

Ezra. She bit her cheek so hard blood filled her mouth. She wasn't ready to see him. Wasn't ready to explain what she was doing here. He had lied to her. Constantly and without remorse. He was complicit in the Abbey's treatment of Jude. Of *her*.

Ezra closed the doors behind him and turned. Light from his upheld candle cast the beaded seams of his chasuble milky white, the hundreds of gems hoarding the light. An invitation for the fire to eat away at it until all that remained was a tattered hem.

Maeve pressed tighter into the alcove, too frightened even to breathe.

He paused, running his fingers over something hanging from his neck before pushing his hair back from his face. A sheen of sweat on his forehead caught the meagre candlelight. Her gaze dropped downwards, past the reddish stains on his habit to the slim silver locket bouncing on his chest. Two more hung beside it.

Maeve choked back a gasp at the sight of the relics. Three of them – was one of them hers? Disgust welled up in her throat. Deep in her belly, fear gnashed its teeth. Gold flickered in her peripherals.

Ezra looked up. His pale-eyed gaze scoured the hall, sweeping over the alcove Maeve hid inside. His chin lifted as he sniffed the air. She clenched her hands into fists as he moved towards her, gaze fixed on the open door to the storage room on her right.

If he went in there, if he saw the burned icons . . . Maeve had no doubt he'd know she was here, and what they were planning on doing. But if she tried to stop him, he'd find her even faster.

She had no choice but to let him discover the icons and run while he was preoccupied.

She clenched her eyes shut as he passed, turning her face towards the wall. The door to the storage room clicked shut behind him.

She had minutes, if that.

As quietly as she could, Maeve slipped from the alcove and headed towards the door he'd just left. The faint sounds of singing came from the basilica, yet somehow, she knew Jude wouldn't be there yet. If they wanted to use him for the Call of the Sun, they would hide him away until the final moment to create the biggest impact on the already fevered crowd.

Her hand froze on the handle for one, painful heartbeat. The reddish stains on Ezra's habit . . . those had been blood, hadn't they? And the relics he wore around his neck . . .

Had he just come from Jude? Was Ezra responsible for his capture?

She pushed the question down with all the others, letting them fester in her stomach, fuelling her as she pushed open the door. What was one more treachery amidst the wreckage of her entire life?

The door opened to a narrow hall broken up by slender, salt-stained windows. She plucked a lit candle from one of the sconces and used it to light her way. At the end of the corridor was a single doorway which, from her memory of the Abbey's layout, led to the largest classroom in the western wing. She hadn't been there in years but remembered a vast space of stone and glittering windows, acolytes' voices echoing off the arched ceilings above.

The handle spun easily, the door shoving forward into a darkened room. The candle did little to penetrate the thick blackness. The air filling her mouth tasted of salt, underwritten with something sweet and metallic. She swallowed down an acidic rush of nausea.

Something wasn't right. She knew it in her bones.

Maeve turned, braid whipping against her face. The sound of her shoes and the sharp inhale of her breath lit the space. She skidded to a stop in front of the door.

It had shut behind her.

She set her candle by her feet and ran her hands around the edge of the doorframe, searching for the handle. Her testing fingers met a gouged chunk of wood, the sharp sting of disfigured metal.

The door handle was missing, locking the door after it shut.

She knelt to examine the pale glint of naked wood at the base of the door. Thick scratches were scored deep into the door, evenly spaced in five long lines. The shape was familiar...

She raised her hand, fitting her fingers into the shape of the marks.

Human.

Fear sank its teeth in. The scratches continued up the edge in deep, painful gouges, like whoever had made them was willing to sacrifice life and limb if the door would just *open.* Candlelight caught an iridescent gleam. The wood around the upper left corner was chipped, the point missing. Embedded between the grain was a ragged half-moon, transparent and delicate, the edge dark with crusted red.

Maeve covered her mouth.

A fingernail.

She needed to get out.

Rising to her feet, Maeve turned back to the blackened expanse of the room. The cavernous space was an unknown, but it was better than the door. *Anything* was better than the door. She rushed forward, cupping one hand over the candle. Heat singed her palm. Her footsteps echoed through the expansive space like a heartbeat.

Something skidded to her left.

She stopped.

Her lungs burned. 'Jude?' she called, voice thready and weak.

The silence pulsed in reply. She raised her candle to shine towards where she'd heard the noise, half-convinced her terrified brain had imagined it. But, *no—*

There it was again. A light scraping, like fabric against stone.

Maeve edged forward. Inky blackness parted around her. Through the shadow, she made out the shape of something crumpled. Candlelight caught on a pale curve.

An arm. She was looking at an *arm*.

'*Oh*—' she gasped.

With a groan, the mass rolled over.

At first, all she could make out was the livid red of fresh blood streaming from his nose to coat the lower half of his face. Dark hair and angular features, distorted in pain. His eyes, staring blankly towards her, not a hint of recognition on his face.

The picture completed with a series of sickening snaps deep in Maeve's skull.

Jude.

47

Jude

Hands held down his heart to stifle its frantic beating. Pressed down on the peak of his nose and the backs of his eyelids. Against his lips and under his tongue. He tasted salt and iron and *her*.

His eyes were open, though whiteness surrounded him like an eiderdown. It was almost comforting, he thought. But it wouldn't remain that way. Nothing smothering ever did.

For half a tremulous breath, he thought Ezra was back to finish him.

And then he heard her voice.

'*Jude*—' Her voice was muffled and damp, her touch frantic, the press of her body unyielding.

He tried to move his lips, to answer her, reassure her that he was *fine*. He was always fine. How often had he looked in a mirror and told himself those very words? How many faces had he seen staring back? He remembered seeing a child once. Unburdened by the weight of expectation. Then, an acolyte. A young man with shoulders weighed down too heavily for his young body to carry. If Jude were to face a mirror now, who would be there to greet him?

A saint, an exile, a martyr – an unholy triptych armed to fight a holy war.

His fingers twitched. Searching. Her cold hand met his.

Why are you cold? You shouldn't be cold. I gave you my scarf.

Soft fabric rubbed over his face, cleaning the blood from his nose. He blinked, slowly at first, then more quickly the longer the white fog continued to blur his vision. Maybe she was a dream, sent to haunt him, to torture him like pain never could.

'Maeve,' he garbled. Fresh blood trickled down his chin from his nose. 'Is it you? Are you . . . are you really here?' His voice cut out with a wet cough. 'I can't see. My mentor took my vision, somehow. I can't see. At all. Only white.'

'Jude—' she choked. She lifted his hand to her face, let him feel its familiar contours. His fingers slid down her braid, felt its silken weight.

She was real. She was *here*.

Fingers brushed under his eyes, tracing his lash line, skating down his face. Did she think of what had happened between them at the inn? Did she remember how she'd begged, how he'd run?

She brushed his lower lip, and Jude thought *yes*.

He coughed again, fighting to free his voice. He had to tell her about Ezra before anything more was said between them. Nothing was more important. 'My mentor, your mentor – *Ezra*. It's Ezra, Maeve. He was the one who . . . who—'

His voice cut out. The hand on his shoulder convulsed. 'I know,' she said. 'Well, part of it. I saw him leave here and thought maybe – maybe he was the one who captured you. But him being our mentor . . .' her throat clicked. 'I suppose it makes sense, doesn't it?' She loosened a sigh, weary and weighted all at once. 'Fuck. *Fuck*. There's no innocence in complicity, is there?'

He'd never heard her curse. It might have made him laugh if it wasn't for the agony lacing her voice. He scrubbed his hands over his eyes and under his nose, wiping the blood away. The fog across his vision didn't budge. He'd give anything to see her face right now.

'He's more than just complicit,' Jude said. 'He's an instigator. He truly believes in everything the Abbey stands for. The memory manipulation, deceiving the congregation into believing their prayers are answered, exiling saints – all of it.'

'I hate it,' Maeve said, venom thick in her voice. 'I hate it so much, Jude. The Abbey and its constant lies. How deeply the hurt runs. I just want to be free.'

Jude nodded, wishing more than anything to see her expression.

When Maeve spoke again, it wasn't what he'd expected. 'Can I try something?' She touched his face, one finger gently pressing under each eye. 'I don't know if it'll work, but I have an idea for restoring your vision.'

How could he tell her he'd trust her with anything? His vision, his heart, his life.

He couldn't. He could only nod.

She moved closer. The point of her cold nose touched his cheek moments before her mouth did. She kissed him just under his ear. Fresh air. Sunlight. Walks on the moors and paint-covered fingers. He stretched his neck, following her mouth as she drew back.

'Sorry,' Maeve whispered. 'I just missed you.'

'Don't. Don't apologize. I need to tell you, about the inn—'

'Not now,' she interrupted. 'Please. I *can't*—' a muffled inhale. 'I need to focus.'

He rolled his lips together, trapping words behind them.

'Okay . . .' Rustling fabric. 'Will this work? If I—' Maeve continued to mumble as she leaned over him, the arm braced next to his neck brushing against his skin. He shivered. 'Close your eyes.'

She rested her fingertips on his closed lids. Nothing happened for long enough that he started to shift, wondering if there was something he was meant to be doing.

'Don't move,' she scolded. Her voice sounded strained. 'Almost there—'

She gasped, and Jude's world exploded with gold, lasting

less than a blinding second before the white blew away like mist rolling off the coast. He blinked his eyes open as she withdrew her hand from his face. The ceiling opened up above him, dark and endless. Her face appeared perfect in all its angles.

She'd done it.

She smiled, and Jude's heart broke a little further. 'Did it work?'

'How? How did you do it?' He continued to stare at her. He couldn't help it.

'It wasn't that your vision was impaired. Your body couldn't *remember* how to see,' she said. 'Like when I couldn't see for a few minutes at Mr Peters' church. Somehow, Ezra made you believe you lost your vision. He altered your perception of sight. I just removed the blockage, so to speak.'

Jude rubbed at his eye with the back of his hand. 'But . . . how?'

'I found the icon of myself and burned it,' she replied. 'My magic feels closer to the surface now. More accessible. Like I could *use* it if I wanted. Not fully . . . but more.'

She shook her head, light flickering against her face. The candle had less than an inch of wax remaining. A few minutes before it burned out, if that. Hopelessness carved her features into stone as her eyes met his. 'Does it matter though, if we have figured it out? The door locked behind me. We're stuck in here. Trapped. The Call of the Sun is at dawn.'

Jude pushed onto his elbows, wrapping one arm around her waist and drawing her into his side. 'We'll leave,' he said against her ear, not wanting to voice his suspicion that the last thing the Abbey wanted was for them to miss the Call. 'We'll break the door down or find another way. I promise.'

Maeve huffed out a disbelieving breath. Her nose was cold where it pressed into his neck. Just as he was about to move closer, tell her how glad he was to see her, how sorry he was for mixing her up in this mess, she pulled back and laid her hand on his forearm.

'I'm so sorry about Elden. I had no idea. Never even *thought*—' Her voice cracked painfully. 'It's not your fault, Jude. Whatever choices he decided to make to betray you were made long ago. Nothing you did could've stopped it or encouraged the path he took.'

He closed his eyes. Her words were like a balm soothing over the burn beneath. If he gave himself leave to feel the full hurt of Elden's betrayal, he'd never recover, and now wasn't the time.

'Did you see him?' he asked, eyes still shut. 'After they . . . took me. Did he follow?'

'No.' She ran the back of one finger against his jaw, a soothing back and forth. 'I don't know where he went. He wasn't well. Vomiting and lurching around. It was . . . strange.'

Jude opened his eyes. 'Strange how?'

Suddenly, the candle guttered out. Blackness pressed in on all sides.

Maeve inhaled sharply. 'We need to go.'

Pain shot down his legs, lingering in the backs of his knees as he slowly got to his feet. He bit his tongue to keep from groaning. The ache slowly ebbed the longer he remained steady, like it was draining into the ground beneath him. 'It's not—' he gasped, 'as bad as I thought.'

She made a low noise of disagreement, pulling one arm over her shoulder and steadying him with a hand pressed against his lower stomach. Her touch was warm through his jumper.

Suddenly, a low scraping noise moved through the darkness. Both of them stilled.

'What was that?' Maeve whispered.

The penetrating blackness of the room split as a shaft of light cut across the floor. In a slow reveal, a silhouette emerged in the now-open doorway. Jude tensed, pulling Maeve tight to his side. He took one step back, then another, stalled by a ripple of fresh pain up the nape of his neck, gathering around his jaw. Maeve gasped as the figure in the doorway moved closer, his features suddenly in sharp relief. Her hand on his waist convulsed.

Before he could stop her, she moved out from beneath his arm, and headed straight for Ezra.

48

Maeve

There was nowhere to go, nowhere to run. Tension tightened Jude's every muscle, skin over-hot where it was separated from hers by a scant few threads. He smelled of blood and sweat and ash, and she loved him. Maeve *loved* him, and love brought a weight to her decision. There were no limits, nothing she wouldn't sacrifice. She would do anything to protect him.

Anything.

She released her hold on Jude's waist and stepped towards Ezra, ignoring Jude's frantic whisper of her name, the fingers glancing off her wrist. 'I'm so glad you found us,' she called, pitching her voice high, as though she'd been waiting for Ezra to come and save her.

'Maeve?' Ezra replied. 'Is that you? Are you all right?'

She prickled at the false sweetness in his voice. Her footsteps echoed in the high-ceilinged room.

What her plan was, she didn't know, only she had to stop Ezra before he got to Jude. She walked closer, balling her fists at her sides. She wasn't powerless. She could face him, look him in the eye and tell him that she wouldn't comply with the Abbey, wouldn't do as she always did and duck her chin, saying *yes* to whatever he asked. She wasn't that person anymore. Perhaps she never had been.

Ezra met her in the middle of the room. The candle in his left hand guttered, sending waves of deep shadow across his face. The look in his eyes was unmistakable. One she had seen watered down in brief flashes, never in its totality.

Rage – and it was ready to boil.

Maeve froze. Her gaze skittered down to his right hand, clenched just beneath his throat. A flash of silver shone between his fingers. She lurched back, stopped by a glittering wave of pain banding across her head. Somewhere far behind her, Jude gasped.

Before she could take another step, before she could run to Jude and cover him with her body, Ezra struck out towards her with the flat of his palm. In his hand, the relic glinted metallic, open to show a lock of pale hair.

Her vision fuzzed with a wash of golden light before her head split open with pain.

There was no fighting as her world faded to black.

49

Maeve

Maeve opened her eyes.

The basilica ceiling stretched wide overhead. She was lying flat on her back, voices slipping under her skin like a splinter, pulling her from whatever dark and dreamless place she'd been sucked into. Sun from the east sent shards of multicoloured light from the rose window across her supine body. Her vision glazed, urged on by the ache in her head. Fragile peace washed over her like an ocean tide.

She blinked. The fog inched back. She took one breath, then another.

Wait.

What was she doing here, and why was it *morning*?

Singing trickled into her ears. It was nothing more than the hum of disorganized voices, but it was enough to push her onto her elbows and look around. She was boxed into the negative space between the back of the rectangular altar and the curved wall of the basilica behind her. The space didn't seem to serve any particular purpose outside of being a cramped corner of forgotten air, large enough to fit someone and not be seen.

Her left temple thrummed with pain. She touched it with shaking fingers, wincing when they returned sticky with drying blood. Ezra must have knocked her out. Why was she here and not tied up somewhere? And where was Jude?

Scrambling unsteadily to her feet, Maeve tried to look over

the altar's edge, past the chancel and towards the nave where she could hear the chatter of hundreds of voices beginning to shift into organized singing. The altar was a behemoth of wood and marble, large enough to rise a good head taller than her. Where the front was a solid mass of intricately carved wood, the back was perfectly smooth marble, cool under her hands. There wasn't even a jut in the wood for her to use to hoist herself up.

Her nose itched with the heady scent of incense. She looked up, catching the edge of the thuribles in full swing. A horrible realization dawned with each creak of the chains. Her memories, finally loosened from the quicksand of her mind, dredged up a vision both horrifying and startlingly clear.

The eighth hymn was beginning. It wouldn't be long until the Call of the Sun.

As the longest and most involved of all the intercessions, the eighth hymn started at midnight and came to a fevered head a few hours after daybreak. The ritual revolved around the sun – its focus and call, serving as a tangible sign of the power of the saints.

Maeve pressed her back to the altar and looked up at the rose window.

The circle of crystalline glass at the centre was usually kept covered by a metal disc, accessed by twin ropes hanging from the side that, when pulled, would swing it free from the centre of the rose. The Abbey uncovered it only for the eighth hymn during the four seasonal intercessions, directing a blinding shaft of light to cut through the basilica, cradled in the cupped palms of a saint in a perfect mirror of the Abbey's sigil. It was believed that any prayer said during the Call went directly into the mind of the saint performing the ritual, answered upon their death.

And, for the first time in weeks, months, maybe even years, Maeve's memory of the Call was *there* amidst the straining memories, able to be pulled forward.

She lowered to the ground, drawing her legs tight to her chest, knees pressing into her eyes. Light popped and flashed behind her lids as she began the arduous slog through the deepest confines of her memory. It felt like wading through mud, like pulling Jude from the bog. The gripping reeds and sluicing water, growing murkier and murkier the deeper she trod.

The first memory was one of shouting. *Singing.*

Gold laced the memory, tinting everything metallic and dream-like. She remembered the fevered crowd breaking through the low railing guarding the chancel, reaching up towards the saint standing at the altar. Scratching at her until they drew blood, tearing off her robes in a desperate grab for something tangible to press to their lips. Crying and singing merged into one frenzied voice as the crowd pulled the saint off the altar.

The memory ached; it *burned*.

Maeve remembered the saint disappearing into the crush like a stone cast into turbulent waters until all that was left of her was a body broken like bread, blood spilling like wine across the floor.

Suddenly, the crowd cleared. The memory wavered, a new one taking its place, brighter and sharper than the last. Gold dust filled the air.

Maeve was alone. At her feet was a single drop of blood. It was crimson now, shining like a ruby in the clear sunlight, but she knew it would soon be the deep red of rust. She would kneel next to it time and time again as she bowed her head to pray, her thoughts on cadmium yellow and oxide red. She would scrape her nail over it and think it paint.

Her lungs, her marrow, the very heart of her filled with the poisonous vapour of certainty — Jude's blood would be next if she didn't stop it. Already, the edge of the covered circle was beginning to glow with sunlight. It wouldn't be long.

And Maeve *knew*, no matter how much she wished to deny it or how horrifying the idea was to consider, that it would be Jude guiding the sun this time. The crowd would be so frenzied, so desperate for their prayers to be answered, that even the mere thought of a saint being the one to usher in the sun would drive them to new levels of zeal. Personal devotion would no longer be enough; they needed the saints to be a part of them. Their love turned to violence, consuming what it was meant to protect when the emotions became too much to bear.

Jude would be a holy offering. And, just like a meal prepared for a feast, they would devour him.

Adoration and violence – two sides of the same rusted coin.

Maeve crossed the small space to gaze up at the high edge of the altar. If she ran at it and jumped, she might be able to pull herself up. But what then? Every eye in the basilica would be on her. All the elders would be in attendance, never mind the hordes of acolytes and pilgrims who'd flock to the altar as soon as Jude appeared. She could try to pull him down into the corner with her, but then they'd both be trapped.

She needed a plan. Anything that would get her out of this pit and give her some options. If she tried to burn the basilica now, she'd die along with it.

The crowd fell into a softer series of hymns. Waiting for the Call, for that unstoppable flash of sun. She had minutes – if that. She had to do *something*.

Steeling herself, Maeve launched off the far wall, leaping towards the altar's edge with her arms outstretched. Her fingers skimmed the edge, nails catching painfully on the wood before she tumbled back towards the ground. Her head cracked on the stone, shooting tremors through her skull. She pushed to her knees and tried again. Her fingers hooked on the edge this time before they gave out, sending her back to her knees.

Her panting breaths echoed the pulse in her fingertips, the pounding of her heart. She backed up against the wall and studied the altar. Could she lever herself up the side with her foot braced against the wall? No, the limestone was as smooth as the wooden back of the altar.

Just as she moved closer to look for a foothold, a soft scraping layered itself beneath the singing.

The middle of the smooth expanse of the back of the altar split suddenly open, a door appearing on an invisible seam at around waist height. A small opening, barely large enough for a person to fit through.

A wild rush of hope filled her chest as she crouched to peer in. A rush of musty air washed across her face, smelling of earth and salt. It took a second for her eyes to adjust to the darkness. The interior of the altar was entirely hollow. A set of stairs descended sharply downwards from a hole cut into the ground at the centre of the space. It looked almost like the altar had been placed atop the stairs to conceal its existence.

From the depths, something moved.

Maeve shuffled backwards, fear rising sharply before a familiar face emerged— '*Felix?*'

The saint pressed a finger to his lips before gesturing her to come closer. He was halfway up the stairs, kneeling on the steps to keep his tall frame from hitting the low ceiling. He wore a simple black habit, the sleeves pushed up his forearms. Dirt streaked across his forehead, and cobwebs stuck to his short, tightly coiled hair. 'I can help you,' he said in his low, scratchy voice. 'I can help you save Jude. But you have to come now.'

Maeve didn't pause to think, to question, she just followed him down the steps into the waiting dark. The door shut behind them, casting them into sudden blackness. Maeve breathed through her nose, fighting back a wave of claustrophobia as Felix opened another door and ushered her into a low-ceilinged tunnel. Slashes of light from the pinhole windows above were the only illumination.

'Felix,' she whispered urgently as she followed him. 'Where are we going?'

He didn't reply until they reached a small rotunda, lit by a round grate above. They must have been directly under the basilica. The ceiling echoed with the pounding of feet above their head, the faint sound of singing. Felix looked younger than she'd ever seen him as he turned to face her. Not much older than her.

A *saint*. The word no longer scared her.

His chest rose and fell with laboured breaths. 'Too long I have sat idly by. I've watched acolytes become saints, become exiles. That ends today. We're going to save Jude, then burn it all. Is that not what you're here to do too, Maeve? You read my letter. My warning. And still . . . you came back.'

'Yes.' She cleared her throat as one of the tight knots around her chest loosened. Something close to hope lit a flame she wasn't ready to tamp out. 'We came back to destroy it all. To save us from the Abbey. From sainthood.'

Whatever he saw in her face must have settled him, for Felix turned, pulling a heavy tarp off a barrel Maeve hadn't noticed at first glance. She took a startled step back. 'What is it?'

'Kerosene,' he replied. 'I found it a few days ago when I discovered this tunnel. There's a separate door that opens up just behind the confessional booths we can sneak the barrel up through. We're going to soak the lower icons on the wall and hope all of them catch when they go up. It'll be faster than trying to light each icon individually.'

Maeve swallowed, head spinning. Clearly, this was something Felix had been planning for a long time. 'What about all the people in the basilica? There are hundreds of acolytes and pilgrims in there.'

He was quiet for a long moment. His hand came up to rub absently at the burn on the side of his face. 'We'll do our best to warn them. To get them out if it's possible. But I have to advise you they won't be . . . themselves, exactly. Something about the ritual, the singing, the prayers, it erases rationality. Creates a sort of group psychosis. It may prove difficult to get them to leave before the smoke becomes too much to ignore.'

Her own memories of the ritual stretched its legs, reminding her of the haze such a fevered event could bring.

Felix knelt, fiddling with something on the side of the barrel, his familiarity with the object pulling at something in her. Jude had told her he tried to burn the Abbey, that he had help. He'd spoken of a fellow acolyte handing over money in a dank cellar, of his hands damp with kerosene.

Her gaze fell on Felix's scarred throat.

'Felix?' she asked, throwing inhibition to the wind. He glanced up, distracted, wary. 'Did you help Jude start the Abbey fire years ago?'

He flinched. 'I . . . how did you know? Did Jude tell you?'

'No . . .' Maeve shook her head. 'He doesn't remember. At least not fully. I just . . . something he said reminded me, and I thought – *maybe*.'

Felix sighed. 'We used to be friends, he and I. Back when friendships were still somewhat . . . tolerated, not like it is now. I tried to look after him. I didn't realize what was happening with Ezra until it was too late. Jude came to me—' his jaw flexed. 'He wanted out. We both had started showing signs of magic and heard the rumours of what happened to acolytes who became saints. He was . . . scared. More so for Ezra's son than for himself.'

'Ezra's *son*?' Maeve questioned, aghast. She knelt down beside him.

'Yes. I think so. My recollections are . . . not clear.' A slight tremor passed through his body. 'At least where he's involved.'

'Who is he?' she whispered. 'I had no idea Ezra had a son.'

'No one did. He kept it secret. I think Ezra was disappointed when he didn't show signs of memory magic.' Felix picked at one of the knots around the barrel, his voice dropping. 'I wish I remembered his name, his face, anything about him. Gone.' He shook his head. 'Gone. Just like he is.'

'What happened after the fire?' Maeve asked.

'There are parts of it that are mostly lost to me,' Felix said. 'The planning that went into it, *how* we actually started the blaze—' he patted the kerosene barrel. 'I think this is left over from that attempt. Like I said, I found it a few days ago. We must have brought it in all those years ago and didn't use it.' He shrugged. 'I remember the fire being put out fairly swiftly. I don't know what happened to Ezra's son. They'd told us he'd died . . . but I'm not sure. It doesn't add up.'

Above them, the singing grew louder. Maeve glanced up before returning her gaze to Felix. His eyes were unfocused, locked somewhere just behind her as he fought to remember.

'The elders caught Jude. He covered for me. Took the full blame for the incident.' Despair lay heavy in his voice. 'He was exiled, as you know. But me . . . I was offered a deal. Blackmailed into it, really. I'm meant to be a figurehead; an example of the Abbey's power. To encourage devotion to the thing I tried to burn down. And—' he took a deep breath.

Maeve studied him as he spoke. The familiarity in his features was from more than just painting him, more than seeing him stand on the altar, his hands lifted in prayer.

'I was threatened,' Felix continued. 'My mother is still alive. She's in the Goddenwood, but it was made clear to me that could be changed very quickly, should I step out of line. They have ahold of my magic and my memories, as you well know. Everything I do is under their control. Even this—' he swept his hand across the room, the barrel of kerosene '—was only possible because they're distracted by the intercession and by your and Jude's arrival.'

Maeve had viewed Felix almost like an icon himself for much of her upbringing. As a saint, he rarely interacted with the rabble of acolytes who called the Abbey home. He was brought out for important rituals and the seasonal intercessions, always at a distance. Outside of their portrait sessions, most of her view of Felix comprised of hearsay and her own imaginings. She wondered what life had been like for him – a saint forced to live as an exile in his own home.

It was hard to imagine a lonelier existence.

'Why is this time any different?' she asked. 'If you tried to burn the icons, and it didn't work . . . why now? Why will it work *now?*'

'The ritual,' Felix said. 'All the prayers build power in the icons. A ritual wasn't happening when we tried to burn the Abbey as boys. I think that made a difference.' His expression hardened, a strained line appearing between his brows. 'The Call of the Sun is about to begin, and Jude's life is on the line. We can't just sit back and let the Abbey continue to do what they want without care or regard over who is crushed along the way.'

Sometimes, Maeve realized, revolution wasn't down to planning or timing or every facet lining up into the perfect moment; it was about perseverance. Determination to see it through no matter how strongly the odds were stacked against them.

'If this works,' she said carefully. 'You'll no longer be under their control. You'll have your magic back. You can free your mother from the Goddenwood.'

Felix tensed. He gave a short nod.

There was nothing more to say. She helped him wiggle the barrel onto a wheeled trolley, and, together, they started to push the barrel from the room and up the stairs towards the basilica and the sound of singing.

She'd made herself smaller, eating the Abbey's words like she was starving and they were the only things that could make her full. She'd closed her eyes and bowed her head, praying to the saints to make her whole, all while the elders watched, knowing she was offering herself up for *them* to take.

No longer.

She gritted her teeth and pushed harder. Soon, it would all burn.

50

Jude

J ude heard the singing. Felt the touch of many hands guiding
him forward, some friendly, some not at all. How he had
come to rest in this strange, liminal space, he could no
longer remember. Maybe he had never known at all.

He thought of *her*. With every fibre of his fading being, he
hoped she was safe.

A point behind his left ear ached, so tenacious he could think
of little else.

He was no stranger to pain but had never quite learned to
distance himself from it entirely. Perhaps it was for the best, he
thought as his jumper was pulled from his body and the heavy
weight of fabric settled over him in its place. Perhaps he deserved
the hurt, the fire. He'd been a secretive creature. Bowing and
scraping, hiding away in the dark. Cradling his misgivings and
desires tight to his chest. Maybe it was his destiny to have his
ribs cracked open, and his secrets scooped out.

If he were to be a martyr, he'd welcome it with open arms.

A hard shove landed between his shoulder blades, followed
by the snap of a door closing. With concentrated effort, Jude
peeled back his eyelids and tried to focus. Hands pressed to his
shoulders, forcing him to kneel. Ezra's face swam into existence.

They were alone in a dank, low-ceilinged room beside the
main doors to the basilica. The muffled sound of singing came
through the closed door, the faintest strain of incense from the

thuribles hitting his nose. After Ezra had knocked Maeve out, it hadn't taken him long to do the same to Jude in his weakened state, especially not with both of their relics swinging from Ezra's neck. Jude had no idea how he'd moved them from the room or where Maeve was now.

Ezra leaned close. He smelled of drying sweat and incense, the scent alone triggering a rush of nausea in Jude's stomach. A ripe lash of pain shoved fingers down his throat, and he gagged.

'You'll do as you're told,' Ezra said near his ear. 'If you want her to live.'

Jude was nodding before he even realized he was moving.

Ezra tried to conceal the prowling evil that needed violence to be sated, but he'd never done a very good job where Jude was concerned. To the rest of the Abbey, he was a figure of benevolent power. He'd worn his mask well, but Jude wasn't fooled.

As he studied Ezra's face, the familiar blue eyes and the darkness behind them, a question formed on his tongue, one long wondered. 'Why do you hate me?' Jude whispered. 'What did I do?'

Contempt turned Ezra's face into something inhuman. His voice was barely audible – somehow worse than if he'd shouted. 'You took him from me. My son. You set the Abbey fire, nearly burned me alive to do it, and I lost him. He might have been weak, a failure, born without the magic he was always meant to have, but he was my son. *Mine.* You shouldn't have helped him leave.' He huffed a breath, almost a laugh as he pulled back. His gaze fell to the half-open door and the basilica beyond. 'But I found him in the end, didn't I?'

Memories curled at the edge of Jude's mind, frayed like they'd been burned. Something was there, teasing him with its nearness, a realization—

'How you remind me of him, Jude,' Ezra said, drawing his attention back. 'You always have. A disappointment, just like he was. Nothing more than a coward and an embarrassment. Unable to fulfil your purpose. Like him, you too will fall beneath my shoe.'

Jude's knees ached on the stone, matching the pounding in his skull as he tried to parse out meaning from Ezra's spitting threats and his sudden eagerness to talk about his son.

He remembered almost nothing about the Abbey fire. Smoke, a hand clasping his. Running feet and crying, pleading voices. A purpose to his movements, even if Jude couldn't remember what it was. A piece of the memory he trapped in a book of his final day at the Abbey floated to the surface. His mentor – *Ezra* – had told Jude he needed to leave to ensure no one else got hurt. A name was missing from that memory . . . was it Ezra's son?

The only thing Jude knew with absolute certainty was that they had failed. The Abbey remained whole, the icons still watching from the walls. Why had he and Maeve thought this time would be any different? He'd failed to protect Ezra's son – someone Jude guessed had been his friend – all those years ago, and he would fail this time, too.

'What happened to him?' Jude asked, not expecting an answer. 'Where is he now?'

'Why should I tell you? His life doesn't matter, not to the Abbey and . . . and not to me.' Ezra's mouth twisted, bitterness lacing his voice. 'It never has.'

And it was there, in the small tell of emotion across Ezra's face, that Jude saw an opening. Ezra was alone in this life he'd carved for himself, and if there was one thing Jude knew about isolation, it was how eager people were to talk if there was someone, *anyone*, there to listen.

He dropped his voice. 'Why have a child at all if you hated him so much?'

Impatience crested Ezra's face, underwritten by a stifled strain of guilt. A need to confess – just as Jude had hoped.

'An accident. I thought of making the woman . . . take care of it. *Him*. But, the more I considered, the more I saw the merit in a child of my own. One I could raise to follow the Abbey. To learn devotion and obedience. Even if his abilities weren't what I hoped. Even if he wasn't the saint he was meant to be.'

He paused, studying Jude kneeling at his feet. In that moment, in the heartbeat of silence, a flash of disappointment moved across Ezra's face, unmissable and unhidden.

It hit Jude like a punch to the chest.

Had Ezra chosen Jude to be his stand-in-son when his own had failed to produce the magic he coveted? Was that why Jude had been punished time and time again, singled out amidst all the other acolytes, given just enough attention to keep him glued to Ezra's side? For a child raised in the Abbey, attention was a hard-to-get commodity, valuable even when it vacillated from care to punishment with little warning and even less explanation. Was that why he had returned to Ezra time and time again like a beaten dog, hoping that maybe, just *maybe*, this time would be different?

Jude had been so afraid – *still*, he couldn't stifle the instinctual rush of fear when he looked into Ezra's eyes – but he'd grown enough to recognize his mentor for who he was.

A pathetic, crumbling old man.

Darkness ebbed closer in his peripherals, but Jude didn't flinch. 'After the sun sets today, even if my body is cooling in a grave, I will be better off than you, Ezra. You will never run far enough to escape what you did. When you remember me, remember your son – I hope it *burns*.'

For a moment, Jude thought Ezra was going to lunge at him.

He almost hoped he would.

Violence tingled at his fingertips. His mind ran hot, blood coursing with the memory of Ezra's voice. Ezra's hands, carving *DEVOTION* into his skin, as if marking his skin with the word would reap the loyalty and love he desired. Jude imagined rising up from the ground, placing his hands around his mentor's throat and *squeezing*. Life would fade from those cold, pale eyes as he placed his palm over Ezra's mouth to stifle his screams. He'd leave his body here. Let it rot into the Abbey's foundation, where like recognized like.

Maeve, he reminded himself, desperate to keep his knees firmly on the stone beneath him. Ezra could do whatever he liked to him as long as she was kept unharmed.

The air between them thickened, becoming an entity all its own. Ezra looked away first. The hand at his side flexed and released. 'It's time to go.'

Jude turned his gaze upwards as he got to his feet and walked from the room and into the main basilica.

He wouldn't look at the crowd parting around him; their eyes, hazed with longing and hunger. The hands touching his sleeves, the ridges of his spine. Incense in his nose, thick and familiar. The gems and thick ropes of brocade embroidery on his robes whisked against the stone floor behind him. His neck ached with the weight of the sigil swinging from a gilded chain, starkly gold against the black fabric. He was a puppet, and Ezra held the strings.

They moved down the long expanse of the nave, past the low railings guarding the chancel, and towards a ladder at the side of the wood and marble altar at the front of the room. High above his head, the rose window gleamed like a talisman of light.

The crowd's singing grew louder, drowning out even the rush of blood in his ears as he ascended the ladder and stood atop the altar, Ezra by his side. He placed his hand on Jude's neck, saying something in a clear, authoritative voice. Jude didn't bother to listen as he was forced once more to his knees. The hands left his skin, and he was alone once more.

Beneath him, the carved embellishments in the wood dug into his skin. Jude turned his gaze upwards. Every colour he could think of streamed from the rose window, and how beautiful it was. Indigo and crimson, azure and vermilion. He could stare at it forever.

How many years had he spent kneeling under this window, praying for absolution?

He'd picked himself apart in the name of piety, searching out his faults and laying them bare before his mentor and the saints. He'd carved himself to the bone in an attempt to be remade. And what had he gained in return? Tattoos on his flesh and the chance to die as a martyr?

His vision was a fragile thing, hazy around the edges and washed with gold. He was grateful he wasn't able to hear the hymn. If he could stay here, kneeling at the feet of the rose window, he had a chance at maintaining a delicate equilibrium of happiness. At least for a little while.

He moved his gaze towards the back of the room, skimming over the hundreds of faces turned towards him. At the end of the nave, the sloping lines of the basilica coalesced into an expansive mural. A turbulent scene of saints battling beasts, aged by time and altar smoke. Icons hung in gilded frames on the wall next to it. A patchwork of devotion. The Abbey saw nothing wrong with displaying the faces of everyone they'd betrayed; proud of the generations of manipulation.

Jude wanted to burn them all.

Past the crowd, a glint caught his eye.

Her face was visible one moment, gone the next, but it was *her*. Maeve. Unmistakably.

He watched as she grasped a pilgrim by the shoulders, her eyes wide and begging as her mouth moved, words lost in the space between them. The pilgrim wrenched free, leaving Maeve standing alone until another figure appeared behind her – *Felix*. At the back of Jude's mind, memories stretched their limbs. He hadn't realized how tight his chest was until seeing her face gave him space enough to take a full breath.

The buzzing in his ears melted away, replaced with the singing, holy and riotous. Soon, hands pushed at the altar, rocking it on its foundation. The first fingers brushed his robe. He heard the pilgrims chanting, begging *him* to grant their wishes, not knowing they were asking to give up their own memories in return.

Jude couldn't save them. He couldn't even save himself.

He lifted his hands from his thighs, laying them over his heart to feel the beat.

The Call of the Sun was about to begin. They expected him to guide the light into the basilica. With startling accuracy, Jude suddenly remembered witnessing the ritual countless times during his childhood at the Abbey. He remembered how *his* chest had burst open with love and devotion as he watched the shocking violence of the martyrdom. How desperately he'd believed in its power. He would have done anything to lay his hands upon the saint.

And he remembered the shame he felt after the rituals had been completed.

Shame that moved him into action, into rebellion.

He ground his teeth and bowed his head, squeezing his eyes tightly shut until light popped into his vision. *Your choices have consequences.*

He would choose the consequences for himself. He would not complete the ritual. If he were to die today, it wouldn't be following the Abbey's wishes.

Behind his closed lids, he dredged up the memory of the icon Maeve had painted of him. The vulnerability when he'd first beheld it like he stood before her naked, every imperfection visible, every part of him on show for her perusal. Yet, there had been a certain freedom in allowing her to look, to paint him for who he was.

She'd seen him like no one ever had before, and he loved her for it.

Above all, he remembered how she'd painted him as a saint but given him the unmistakable air of a heretic. And that was what he would die as. Not as a saint or an exile or even as a martyr – let Jude be known for his dissidence.

The top of his head warmed with the sun.

The singing changed to shouts as he moved slowly to his feet, the altar shaking violently beneath him as the acolytes tried to climb it to get to him. It wouldn't be long until they succeeded. He gazed over the crowd. It surged towards him, already whipped into a frenzy.

Come tomorrow, the acolytes wouldn't remember how they'd allowed their inhibitions to fall to the wayside. The elders would manipulate their memories from violence to beauty, coloured in every shade of ecstasy, a divine mania. Ezra's words had never been more accurate – the Abbey's reliance on the collective impacted every facet of its rotting core.

He'd never been less a person and more a saint. An object, here to grant their prayers.

A hand grasped his ankle. Jude locked eyes with a pilgrim not much older than him.

'Please,' they shouted. Their mouth was a damp, gaping chasm in their face. Sweat gleamed high on their forehead. '*Please*. My sister. She's not well. Can you just—'

Their hand fell away as they were sucked back into the crowd, leaving their begging to save their sister's life echoing in his skull. He couldn't save her even if he wanted to.

With a metallic screech, the cover across the centre of the rose window tumbled down, ushering in a shaft of pure sunlight. A smile pulled at his lips even as tears wet his cheeks. The sun felt so beautiful on his skin, so *right*.

Yet—

He would not raise his hands. He would not complete the ritual.

More hands grabbed his feet, scraping at his calves, the backs of his knees, his thighs. Nails dug into his tender skin until he bled. He felt their anger and prayers, heard their shouts for him to raise his hands towards the heavens, but Jude remained unchanged. The sun warmed his face, and that was enough. His eyes didn't open, not even when they pulled him from the platform. Not when his robes were ripped from his body as their devotion, their love, turned to violence.

Not even when the first smell of smoke hit his nostrils.

51

Maeve

The young woman wrenched away from under Maeve's hands, her hood slipping free to reveal wide, glazed eyes and a half-open mouth as she spun back to face the altar.

'No—' Maeve cried, reaching for her wrist. To do what, she didn't know.

None of her words seemed to break through the Abbey-induced stupor, no matter how desperately she begged or how ardently she promised that what they were feeling, what they were seeing, were all lies, all manipulation. All that mattered was the intercession. All that mattered was the saint.

Maeve drew her eyes upwards, and there he was.

Jude knelt on the altar with hands palm-up on his thighs and face pointed towards the ceiling. Beside him, Ezra leaned down to whisper in his ear. The hatred she felt at the sight of her former mentor was strong enough to nearly launch Maeve into the crowd. Her fingers itched to wrap around his neck.

They were running out of time.

As soon as the Call began, it wouldn't be long until the crowd pulled Jude off the altar.

She raced to the back of the basilica to where Felix was splashing a kerosene-soaked towel onto the lowest row of icons. The air felt clammy on her skin, the heady smell of the oil fogging her senses. At Felix's urging, Maeve dipped the proffered towel into the barrel and splashed the oil up as high as she could. Would it be enough? She had seven – no, six – matches. How many did Felix have?

Suddenly, the basilica fell silent.

Dropping the towel, Maeve turned to look.

Atop the altar, Ezra raised his hands high above his head. 'Blessed pilgrims, acolytes, and elders. The glory of the Abbey has seen fit to reward your piety today. We have a saint amongst us.'

The crowd pulsed with manic energy, moulding their voices to the thrumming boom of the organ. Drummed up and frantic with devotion. Hundreds of people filled the space.

It was exactly as she'd feared.

She spun back to Felix. 'How long until we light it? Will the icons catch fast enough?'

Felix splashed the oil on the next row of icons. A metallic clang sounded above the voices as she was gearing up to repeat her question. The cover had fallen off the centre of the rose window. Soon, Jude would raise his hands.

'Felix? How long?' she repeated.

'Minutes. Maybe less once we start lighting the matches. You have them, yes?'

Her mind froze, stalling out before it sped forward— 'You didn't bring any? I have . . .' she pulled out the matchbox, dumping them into her palm. 'Six.'

Felix said nothing as he stared down at her cupped palm, the matches so small, so inconsequential next to the hundreds of icons before them. His throat bobbed as he carefully collected three of them. 'The elders keep the altar matches locked away. I couldn't . . . couldn't get any. It was lucky I even found the kerosene barrel.'

Her breath escaped her in a rush. 'Okay,' she whispered. 'Okay. Well. We'll have to do our—'

The volume behind them pitched suddenly louder, the change

so abrupt Maeve's hands clutched convulsively into fists. Both she and Felix swung around to look. The crowd had breached the confines of the chancel to surround the altar. Ezra was no longer standing atop it.

And neither was Jude.

'Where is he?' Maeve shouted above the melee. 'Where did he go?'

'The crowd has him,' Felix said. Sweat beaded on his dark brown skin. 'This fire had better start quickly, or . . .' he shook his head, levelling Maeve with a bleak look.

She didn't want to put a voice to the words rolling around in both of their heads. If the crowd had Jude, they wouldn't be satisfied with his clothing or touch alone.

They'd want his blood.

Forcing her panic down, Maeve turned back to the icons and strained to splash kerosene up as high as she could. Icons stretched a dozen rows high, all of various sizes and age. They'd never be able to get the oil on all of them. Even more, how would they guarantee the fire would reach the highest icons as quickly as they needed?

Felix drew the first match to the lowest icon. It lit quickly, but the fire remained small and contained as it ate away at the canvas, stopped from spreading by the expanse of stone wall between each framed icon. His matches were small, the flame barely more than a spark that quickly petered out.

They needed something bigger.

'You stay here and keep lighting the icons,' Maeve shouted. She gestured towards the door and the hall beyond. The guards were still there, but she had to try *something*. 'I'm going to look for a torch. And see if I can convince people to leave.'

Felix wiped his forehead with his sleeve, nodding. '*Hurry, Maeve—*'

She spun on her heel and shoved through the crowd. It was like facing a solid wall of bodies. She redoubled her force, making for a gap between two pilgrims. 'Go!' she cried. 'Leave – it's going to burn. You need to *leave*!'

Her voice was lost beneath the crowd. No one even looked at her. Hopelessness mixed with the panic. She had to push forward, to accomplish what she'd set out to do, and pray that when the smell of the smoke became too strong to bear, the crowd would finally come to their senses and run for safety.

An elbow jammed painfully into her ribs, forcing her deeper into the crush. Then, from between two bodies, a hand shot out to grab her wrist. Nails scratched against her skin. She wrenched away, but they held fast.

'Enough, Maeve. *Enough.*'

Ezra stood like a stone in a fast-moving river.

His grip on her wrist was like a vice, squeezing, *burning*. The crowd shoved them closer, and despite Maeve's best efforts to free herself from his touch, she found herself face-to-face with her former mentor. He gazed at her like she was little more than a thorn in his side.

He was far from the altar, far from Jude. Almost to the door. Was he planning on fleeing? Did he know they planned to burn it all?

Suddenly, a high-pitched scream echoed above the din, rapturous and frenzied. A scream of gratification. The crowd had what they wanted. They had Jude in their grasp.

'Let go of me,' Maeve snarled, pulling back hard enough that her shoulder ached in protest.

'You're not going to reach him,' Ezra said, redoubling his grip. He was close enough for her to see the whites around his pale irises. Around his neck, the relics swung. She wanted to rip them off and smash them beneath her boot. 'Leave. For your own safety.'

His voice dripped with condescension, and Maeve couldn't stand it. Every time he'd belittled her talents, brushed off her pleas for conversation and reassurance, made her feel small, was suddenly impossible ignore, and *dammit* – she'd had enough.

She reared back and drove her forehead directly into Ezra's nose. It broke in a spectacular splash of blood. His cry of pain was lost beneath the singing. Off-balance by the blow, he stumbled back, releasing her arm to cover his face. The crowd swallowed him up in a fast-moving crush of bodies.

She didn't stick around to see if he'd get back up.

Blinking against the dizzying ache the blow had provided, Maeve stumbled towards the door. Guards stood on either side of it, scanning the crowd. One of them turned to speak with a woman, her head covered by a pale grey hood. The other remained vigilant. Her steps hitched, mind racing for something to say so they'd let her pass.

A commotion sounded behind her, louder than the jeers that had come before it. The smell of smoke abruptly sharpened, becoming thick and pungent in her nose. She spun to look, hoping to see the wall of icons fully engulfed or the flames spreading to the pews.

At first, she was distracted by the dozens of people finally fleeing the basilica in waves. Screams filled the air, more frightened than the euphoria that had preceded it.

Then, her gaze locked on the source of the panic – a figure cutting through the crowd with two burning torches in his upraised hands. His mouth was screwed up in pain and anger as he ran, a desperate cry filling the air.

Elden.

Before she knew it, he launched the first of his flaming torches high into the air. It struck the middle row of icons with a ragged crash. White-hot flame immediately overtook the painting, spreading quickly to its neighbours. Elden held his other torch to the end of the silk cord linking the rows of icons together. The entire rope lit up, urged on by kerosene.

Maeve ran towards it.

All the icons were burning. Smoke blossomed in a heavy, acrid plume. Sparks hit the tapestry on the wall next to it, and soon, it was engulfed in flame, too. Her eyes streamed with smoke and tears.

Bethan hadn't seen a thread of gold in her dream like Jude had described. She'd seen the wall of icons linked in a rope of pure white fire. She'd dreamed the Abbey burning.

Elden's chest rose and fell in ragged breaths. 'It's done,' he said, voice hoarse. 'It's *done.*' His eyes shifted to the crowd behind her as a fresh wave of tears slid down his cheeks. He swayed where he stood. 'Look.'

She turned.

The sight took her breath away.

People were falling to their knees in waves, hands covering their ears. Their eyes were glazed, bodies shaking as pain wrote itself onto their faces. Next to the wall, Felix knelt with his head bent towards the floor. Neither Jude nor Ezra was anywhere to be seen.

Maeve took a hesitant step forward.

The world flashed gold.

Agony shot through her head. It grew and grew until finally, overcome, she toppled to her knees. She placed her forehead between her hands and *screamed* as her brain tried to force its way from her eye sockets, her nose, her mouth.

Her thoughts liquefied, slipping like water through her hands the harder she tried to hold onto them, like someone had cracked open her skull and poured burning coals into it. She slammed her palms on the ground, begging, *praying*, for it to stop.

It went on and on and on.

Memories slipped in, one after the other, too quick to focus on just one.

Maeve, running by the sea, holding her sister's hand and laughing, kicking up saltwater as they went. She was thirteen now, giggling with a friend as they read an illicit book in the back corner of a shop. Fourteen, seeing anger on Ezra's face as he pulled back his hand and slapped her across the jaw. She saw Jude, a young man, standing before her and smiling. She saw him hold out his hand, a paper-wrapped biscuit nestled in his palm. Jude, his head bowed over a notebook, scribbling fervently before angling it towards her to read. Jude, smiling. Jude, crying.

Jude, Jude, Jude.

Maeve came back to herself with a gasp.

The pain had stopped.

Jude.

52

Jude

Sun split the air above Jude's head in a wash of gold-tinged light. It glinted off the rose window, the gleaming organ pipes, the metallic sheen of buttons and hairpins and wretched, glazed eyes. His body no longer belonged to him. He was the property of the masses, just as Ezra had promised. He'd been reduced to the sum of his parts, and everyone wanted a piece.

A hand searched for purchase in his hair, and that, *that*, was the act that ruined him.

He snarled, wrenching back against the acolytes holding him aloft, kicking out with all his strength until he landed flat on his back. The stone was cold and unforgiving but blessedly still.

Of all the eyes searching for him, his focus locked onto one pair.

Fractal sunlight cast the man in triplicate. A ruddy, gaunt face and a shock of reddish hair to match. With a bellow, the man launched onto Jude's chest, tearing and scratching at the fabric over his heart. 'Fix me! *Fix me*,' he screamed. Jude convulsed, trying and failing to push him off. Wetness tracked down into his robes as the man sobbed into his neck. '*Please.*'

A potent mix of fear and pity curled up in his stomach. What had happened to this man to reach such a point of desperation that he'd look at a ruined saint and beg for absolution?

'Who are you?' Jude shouted. Every laboured breath was pure

agony under his weight. For a fraught moment, only the two of them existed – a saint in name alone, and a man who still believed. 'I *can't* – I can't help you,' he choked.

The man pulled back far enough for something to dangle in the space between them. Jude's heart gave an unsteady jolt. *A relic.* The man was an elder, down here amongst the rabble and not up in the balcony with the others. He knew Jude couldn't grant his prayers but yet here he was, desperate enough to ask.

Jude grabbed the relic and pulled it free. The elder howled in response, grasping his neck, but it was too late. The metal burned hot as Jude brought it down to the stone. The pain was irrelevant as it shattered against his palm. All that mattered was that it was destroyed.

Nails scratched against his forearm, digging deep furrows into his skin. Jude convulsed, trying to push the elder off him. His face was crimson, eyes glazed, not with hysteria like the acolytes and pilgrims, but with pain, with misery. 'You, *you little—*'

Jude brought his knee up directly between the elder's legs. He wrenched back with a bitten-off scream. Gasping, Jude rolled as far as he could onto his side and spat. The foamy transparency of stomach acid was tinged with bright, vivid red.

Next to the unsightly puddle was the relic. The metal was twisted, hinges broken beyond repair. A thin strand of reddish-brown stuck out from the broken resin.

Continuing to cough, Jude gazed up, momentarily disorientated.

The air was thick with sweat and screaming, underlaid with the unmistakable scent of smoke. It wouldn't take much for the writhing crush to trample him. Already, his limbs had been trodden over so many times he no longer flinched at the smash of a boot or the jab of an elbow. Unreality coated his mind in cotton. The view overhead – mouths open to scream, tendrils of smoke disappearing between bodies and, high above, a glorious cut of sunlight – doubled, tripled. He floated up towards the rafters.

How easy it would be to close his eyes and never reopen them.

The sickening, damp crunch of something snapping filled the air. The answering scream was blood-curdling. A shudder overtook Jude's body from start to end.

He needed to get *up*.

With a shout between clenched teeth, he forced Maeve's face to the forefront of his mind and fought back to his feet. An arm whirled in front of him, catching him on the side of the jaw before it moved, creating a sliver of space wide enough to force himself into.

He lurched forward, step after aching step.

Tears streamed in hot splashes down his cheeks. If he could just break free of the epicentre, he bore a chance of escaping the basilica before smoke stole the remainder of his breath. Bodies crushed in on all sides, so tightly he couldn't discern where he ended, and they began, turning his torso into nothing but fire and fading air.

'Move,' Jude shouted. Desperation clawed his voice to shreds. '*Move!*'

No one looked at him, even as he sank back beneath the surface of panicked acolytes. His fingers slid off clothing and limbs as he fell. The fear dissolved into engulfing agony, boiling like sulphur beneath his skin. There had been many times Jude had thought he was dying, but he'd never believed it with such certainty before.

This was how it would end.

The Abbey's devotion had bred greed, and greed, where piety failed, had produced a violent focus on nothing but their self-interest. As Jude crumbled beneath the unseeing force of hundreds of acolytes, pilgrims, and elders, he realized Ezra was wrong. It wasn't the collective that would kill him – it was the individual. Each person had chosen to pull him from the altar and crush him beneath their feet. Each of them, in their own mind, had decided not to look down and offer a hand up.

And that selfishness would be the thing that damned him.

His head landed heavily upon the stone.

Pain sliced across his forehead, banding from ear to ear. He didn't flinch as he floated along a plane where nothing – not pain, not fear, not hope – could touch him. Pressure built behind his eyes and against the roof of his mouth. Air filled his lungs in an acrid rush of smoke.

High above, the ceiling swirled. The crowd was gone.

A strange static chipped at his consciousness.

Jude closed his eyes.

Memories spilled out in an uncontrollable rush, like water in a basin, like flame into air. Jude cried out, banding his hands over his ears to keep his brain inside his body.

It didn't help. *Nothing* helped.

His life flashed before his eyes in a series of rapidly clearing images.

Jude, kneeling at Ezra's feet while his mentor sawed a length of twine across his palms until his blood stained the floor. Jude running, laughing, tilting his head back to face the sky as a hand landed on his shoulder, making him look back. A boy, familiar . . . Felix.

His friend. Oh, how he loved him.

Another face, a flash of blond curls—

Jude clawed at his face as the memories shifted forward onto the next.

A stifled bout of girlish laughter cut through the darkness. A door opened, and her face shone between the gap. Maeve, her long hair in twin braids, smiling at him with a space where one of her front teeth ought to be. Later, years maybe, he placed a cup of steaming chocolate in front of her while she sat, twisting her fingers and wiping tears off her face. She took a drink and smiled at him, a sunrise breaking through the storm.

Jude wasn't alone.

He'd *never* been alone.

Ezra had stolen every happy memory. He'd stripped him of

his friends and deprived him of any hand that had ever dared reach through the darkness to pull him to his feet.

The memories continued to come in neat bursts, one on top of the other. Pounding, *pressing* into his head like they were sewing themselves directly onto his brain with a molten needle.

As quickly as it had arrived, the pain ebbed away.

Jude sat up. Blinked against the sudden brightness.

He was kneeling, surrounded by others in similar positions. With the pain gone, he felt like a stone plucked from river water. Everything rough had been sloughed away, leaving him polished and clean. It didn't hurt to think, and, for once, he felt the truth of what it meant to have a mind entirely his own.

Slowly, he got to his feet. His legs trembled under him. Tears welled on his lash line as he scanned the room. Looking, with increasing desperation, for *her*.

And there—

Her head was bowed, and face turned away, but Jude knew her. He'd have recognized her anywhere. Soon, she'd turn and meet his eyes, finding him amidst the melee of pilgrims pushing to their feet and stumbling towards the exit.

She'd come for him.

Jude made his legs move. He'd go to her first. He needed to hold her, to reassure himself that she was whole and unharmed. To tell her that he was there, and he remembered her.

'*Jude.*'

A voice rasped through the thickening cloud of smoke. A wet sound followed, a gasping squelch like a boot pulled from mud.

Jude stilled.

'Please,' the voice called, desperate. '*Help.*'

Several paces away, in a crumpled heap, lay Ezra. His mouth gaped like a fish, eyes glazed and struggling to focus. His purpling hand grasped weakly at his neck. Blood flowed freely between his fingers. His nose was a mangled lump of bone and cartilage.

It seemed somehow wrong that Ezra would bleed the same as him; the arterial redness vivid against the stone.

Jude drifted closer. He knelt, knees dipping into the pool of cooling liquid. The pale blue of his mentor's irises was vivid against the grey of his skin. He didn't have long for this world. Jude felt a flash of watered-down pity, the faint sting of satisfaction, and then, nothing.

'Help me,' Ezra gurgled. Fresh blood spilled from his mouth.

Jude furrowed his brow. 'Why? I have my memories back. We all do. You have nothing over me anymore.'

While Ezra's body and clothes were littered with scrapes and gashes from the stampeding crowd, his neck bore the brunt of it. It looked like a fractured candlestick had been driven straight into his artery. A painful way to go.

Jude couldn't have helped him, even if he'd wanted to. The blood loss was too significant.

Ezra must have known that, but he still searched Jude's face with muted desperation.

Jude watched the blood dribble from between his mentor's fingers with detached interest. His gaze travelled down, over the ornate beading on his chasuble and stole. The sigil of the Abbey in gold and white embroidery, now stained red with blood.

Three relics hung from his neck, cradled in a fold of his cloak like eggs in a nest.

Jude breathed out, breathed in.

He collected the relics and stood, hesitating for less than a heartbeat before he smashed them beneath his boot. They crumpled into a mess of metal, resin, and hair. Maeve's golden hair shone next to his own darker strands. Finally, a curl of darker blond. All crushed beneath his heel.

He brushed the remains away with the toe of his boot before returning his gaze to Ezra.

Fury shone in Ezra's bloodshot eyes. 'You . . . can try to fix me. You're a saint.' He heaved one, panting breath. 'Please.'

'You of all people should know that praying to me is meaningless.'

Ezra coughed, closing his eyes.

As Ezra bled out in front of him, thinking of his son, of Jude, of lives moulded and lost, he made his decision. He was done turning the other cheek.

Jude knelt back down. 'Would your son like to watch you die too, I wonder?' he asked.

He couldn't decipher the look in his mentor's eyes, couldn't dissect the meaning of the emotions playing in his expression. Terror and regret, resignation and a curl of sorrow. His features settled, smoothing into blank unknowingness with one final breath.

Jude rose to his feet, turned his back to Ezra, and left.

53

Jude

Maeve's face was tired and streaked with soot, the pilgrim's habit hanging from her shoulders torn and burnt. She bled freely from a cut above her eyebrow and another just under her jaw. Yet, her eyes were brighter than he'd ever seen.

'Maeve,' he breathed, reaching for her. 'You're all right.'

'You're *alive*.'

She tucked herself into Jude's side, pressing her nose beneath his ear. Her whole body shook. He held her tighter. He ached to place her heart behind his ribs and keep it safe. The numbness broke, ushering in a heavy weight of sadness and relief, undercut by the most resounding wave of hope he'd ever allowed himself to feel.

She was here, and they were alive. It was more than he ever could have wished for.

'My memories . . .' Maeve murmured against his skin.

Jude pressed a hard kiss to her temple. 'Mine too.'

She tilted her head back. Her eyes were clear and dark. Dear and familiar in a way that made his throat convulse. 'We were friends,' Maeve whispered. Her words sent a roll of pain through his chest, grief for what could have been.

Jude cupped the side of her face, running his thumb along her jaw. 'You were always there. Every good memory I have of this place is down to you. It's always been you.'

She opened her mouth, looking like she was about to say more, when a shattering crash broke the air. Jude spun, his arms spread wide, as the rose window collapsed inwards. Glass shattered on the fleeing acolytes and pilgrims as flames licked at the jagged hole it left behind. Black clouds of acrid smoke billowed up from the tapestry and the icons alike.

'Fuck,' he gasped. 'We need to leave.'

Maeve grabbed his hand and began pulling him towards the crush exiting the basilica. It was all he could do to maintain his grip as the flow of people shoved at them. Panic dripped down his spine at the remembered feeling of falling beneath their feet.

Not again, he nearly cried. He couldn't bear it. Not him, not Maeve.

He shouted her name as her hand abruptly went limp in his before slipping out completely.

Thick smoke sent tears to his eyes as the heat grew unbearable. Under it all, his skull continued to pound as memories filled his mind like plaster into a mould. He couldn't make it *stop*. Flashes of midnight sea swims, the feel of paper under his hands as he learned illuminations, the sun's bright glow through a salt-streaked window. A bird silhouetted against an endless blue sky.

Jude stumbled into the stone doorframe.

His heart jerked an unsteady rhythm as he looked up, up. The sculpted cloisters, black smoke against white stone. A flash of movement as a raven took flight ushered in a new memory, more vivid than any that had come before it. At first, it cycled too quickly for him to parse out what he was remembering.

His legs gave out, forcing him to his knees.

Colour and light swirled against his closed lids. Flashes of windswept moors and angry skies. A chipped mug slid across a scuffed table. A snap of frustration at a ruined meal to cover the pathetic gratefulness beneath. A hand on his shoulder to hold him upright, the growing familiarity of laughter on his tongue. Someone who cared for him. Someone who was *there*.

And there, and there, and there.

A choked sob left his throat. The agony of the memory was worse than the pain burrowing into his skull. Elden – his friend, his trusted companion, someone he'd come to view as a brother – Jude couldn't bear it. He couldn't allow the memories to work their way any deeper.

Distantly, he heard Maeve scream his name. Felt his lungs convulse at the smoke, his body cowering uselessly away from the horde leaving the basilica, but he couldn't move. Couldn't command his mind to obey as the memories continued to drown him.

The flashing visions slowed slightly as they moved deeper, older. Childhood memories.

He recognized the now-familiar contours of the Abbey. His old bedroom, his favourite seat in the dining hall. The ache of his knees on the floor echoing the strain at the back of his neck. Maeve, poking him with her paintbrush when he bothered her in her studio.

Felix – Jude marvelled at the sight of the saint.

Not an enemy like the false memories had led him to believe, but a friend. A boy who'd been closer to a brother than anything else.

Memories of laughter, running down the halls, studying in the library and learning their prayers. Pints of cider and barrels of kerosene in a cellar. Gold dust and hands pressed to foreheads.

But that wasn't all the memories showed.

Someone else stood beside them.

The memory echoed Jude's current reality – a burning Abbey and a hungry desperation in his chest. A voice telling him that he was viewing what Ezra had alluded to just before he forced Jude onto the altar, a memory that, above all else, had been stripped from him so completely that even a shadow of it hadn't been allowed to remain—

The memory of Felix and Jude freeing Ezra's son.

Flickers of conversations nudged in at every side. Discussions about burning the elder's quarters to distract Ezra from noticing his son was escaping. Plans to set the whole Abbey on fire to save one person – just *one*. They'd done it, too, succeeded until he and Felix were caught on the outskirts of Whitebury. They were told Ezra's son had died, that it was their fault, but that wasn't true, was it?

The scene turned blurry and dreamlike, whether from the smoke filling his lungs or the force of the memory, he wasn't sure. He didn't care, because Jude recognized the boy smiling at him.

His blond hair was shorter and far curlier in his youth. His blue eyes were his father's. His smile was anything but.

'Elden,' Jude heard himself say in the memory. The Abbey burned behind them. 'You need to go now. Before he notices you're missing.'

Beside him, Felix nodded emphatically. Blood coursed down his face and neck. Elden drew a handkerchief from his pocket and dabbed at it. Felix winced, pulling away, his fingertips lingering on Elden's wrist. 'I can't leave you,' Elden said. His gaze wrenched from Felix's to scour the Abbey with burning blue eyes. 'I won't.'

Whatever Felix said in reply faded into the distance as Jude traced Elden's face with a voracious need for understanding. This version of Elden looked around twenty, with Felix a similar age. Jude would've been around fifteen. They'd orchestrated the Abbey fire to free Elden from his father. Their aim had never been to burn the icons. Learning the Abbey's secret had been an unintended consequence, a realization that had been wiped from his memory alongside every other moment from the fire.

Then, why had Elden betrayed him? Why had he come to Ánhaga in the first place?

He couldn't ask the Elden who lived inside his memories. He could change the past no more than he could write the future.

Before he could delve any deeper, something knocked into his back – hard.

All the air rushed from his lungs, replaced with an urgent burning as he was thrust from the memory and back into reality. His hands came up to search his throat for grasping hands. No matter how hard he fought for breath, it wouldn't come. Black spots danced in his vision, obscuring the tidal rush of the crowd around him, the face coming into view. The hands reaching towards him.

A sudden lightness trickled down his limbs. Jude's eyes slowly shut, his legs curling inwards as his body rose into the air. His head flopped forward onto his chest.

A gentle hand landed on his face, carefully closing his lids.

54

Jude

Jude awoke sprawled out on a patch of scrubby grass. The ceaseless beat of waves came from somewhere nearby and, underneath, the hiss of frantic whispering. He peeled his eyes open. The sky above him wavered as the smell of the sea ate away the lingering smoke in his nose.

'Maeve,' he croaked. His throat *ached*.

Her ashen face appeared above him, the hand on his shoulder stopping him from sitting up. Tears tracked messy streaks down her scrubbed pink cheeks. Her gaze darted between him and something to her left. 'Just . . . just rest a bit longer. Okay?'

His whole body throbbed, a rhythmic pulsing that originated in his lungs to travel down each limb. He turned his neck to better see where he was lying. To his surprise, Elden stood beside the low stone wall separating the grassland from the beach beyond. His shoulders were curled inwards, eyes wide as they searched across the sky. An emptiness blanketed his face.

A look Jude had seen before.

'He's not well,' Maeve whispered. 'We're not sure his memories were returned like everyone else's. He doesn't know where he is. Who I am. He only recognized you.' She moved her hand to his lower ribs, thumb circling lightly until his focus returned to her. Her voice dropped even further. 'He carried you from the basilica. He saved your life.'

Jude swallowed past the burning in his throat. 'What happened?'

She wet her lips. 'I lost you in the crowd leaving the basilica. All the icons were burning. The smoke was impossible to see through, to *breathe*—' Her hand moved further up his stomach to rest over his heart. 'By the time I made it out of the Abbey, you were gone. I couldn't find you anywhere.' She clapped a hand over her mouth as a fresh bout of tears rushed down her cheeks.

'Maeve,' Jude started. Tears brimmed in his own eyes. 'I'm right here. We're both safe.'

She nodded, steadying her voice. 'Then I saw Elden come running out of the basilica with you in his arms. You'd passed out, and he'd found you. He ran right past me like I wasn't even there. He . . . he punched a *guard*.' She loosened a damp laugh. 'Felix and I followed him here. I think he wanted to put you somewhere safe, where the guards or elders wouldn't find us quickly. He won't leave your side.'

Sure enough, Elden had drifted closer as Maeve spoke. His gaze was fixed on Jude, yet he didn't think he really *saw* him. His brows were furrowed tightly, lips moving around silent words.

'His mind has been in the Abbey's grip for a very long time.'

Jude startled, turning to see Felix standing to his left. Felix stared at Elden with a burning, gut-wrenching sadness in his eyes before his gaze peeled free to land on Jude. He knelt by Jude's head.

'Longer, even, than either of us,' Felix continued. 'He doesn't have the magic we do. His mind isn't able to shield against the Abbey's control. There was nothing of him to take, only space to fill.' He scraped his teeth over his lower lip. 'I think we . . . *you* can help to undo it though, Jude.'

'Me?' Jude asked, incredulous.

Felix nodded. 'You . . . you know him best, now.'

Did he, though?

Elden had betrayed him more egregiously, more *painfully* than anyone ever had before, even Ezra. He'd taken the fragile shards of trust Jude had given him and shattered them completely. He'd lied, deceived, and manipulated his way into friendship, only to turn Jude over to the Abbey in the final hour.

But. *But.*

Buried deep beneath the hurt and the anger was the seed of knowledge that just as Jude had been manipulated and deceived, so had Elden. And he needed to know why. Needed to cut off the final thread of the Abbey's malignant touch once and for all. Find a way to move on, if there was even anything remaining to be salvaged.

But how?

It came to him slowly, in bits and pieces, until a picture formed in three parts.

The first was his books. How he'd learned to press his hands to their pages and give of himself. He knew how to search his brain for what he wanted to uncover and dredge it to the surface with the precision of a surgeon. A skill he had won with time and stubbornness and desperation.

The second was of Maeve in that cursed Abbey classroom, laying her hand over his eyes until his vision was restored. Using her magic to help him remember how to see, as she'd put it.

And the third was of Bethan. Her magic, so pure and *good* to her, was a gift she'd long tried to convince him to cherish. He'd never been able to see it as anything less than a burden.

Perhaps it was time to change his outlook. Time to use his magic for good.

His arms trembled as he levered himself upright. 'Elden? Can you come here?'

His eyes drifted across Jude's face. Slowly, as if controlling his body from somewhere far away, he bent his legs and sat. Maeve shifted to give him space, the hand on Jude's chest moving to his thigh. She squeezed encouragingly.

Jude forced himself to take Elden's hand. His work-roughened skin was clammy and cold, fingers slack. Pushing past the discomfort, Jude closed his eyes. Like he did with his books, like he had accidentally done so many times before when his emotions were high, he allowed his magic to leap forward between him and Elden.

At first, he could only see fog. Gold and white with a sickly sweetness that slunk into his nose, down his throat. He fought a gag. Pushing down towards that soft, confusing place where his magic lived inside him, he pictured a strong gale coming from the sea, salt-tinged and refining.

A steady warmth filled him as he called upon his magic. It flowed freely, leaving behind an almost euphoric energy in his limbs. Was this how it was always meant to feel, free from the Abbey's touch? Was it always meant to be something so pure, so clarifying, like the first gasp of air after drowning?

Jude focused, letting it fill him – happy, for once, to be consumed.

Slowly, the fog inched back. Somewhere deep in Elden's brain, his memories trembled.

Real memories.

Jude pressed harder, commanding his magic to remind Elden he had a body, he had a mind – preferences and opinions, likes and dislikes. Pieces of a person that made up a whole. As the haze continued to roll back, a strange sense of peace swept in its place. The steadiness of a cup of tea at bedtime, a walk in the moors. A rag for his hands when he came in from the garden.

You, you, you, Jude begged. *This is you.*

Elden's hand slipped from his, his body jolting. He panted, looking around wildly until his gaze fell on Jude. He stilled as recognition coloured his features.

'Jude,' he murmured.

'Ah good, you're back.' Jude pushed himself fully upright, trying his best to quell the instinctual softness he felt towards Elden and focus only on his anger. If Elden was here, if he was lucid, he could answer his questions. 'I'm owed an explanation, Elden,' he said. 'At the very least.'

Maeve's hand on his thigh stiffened before pulling away completely.

Elden took a deep, shuddering breath. He reached towards Jude, dropping his hand back into his lap when Jude flinched. 'I can't begin to tell you how sorry I am.'

Jude wouldn't let the pain in his voice sway him. 'You're Ezra's son.'

'I – yes. I am.'

'And your memories are back?' Jude asked.

Elden's chest moved roughly up and down. 'Yes. All—' he cleared his throat. 'All of them.'

'What happened once Felix and I helped you escape all those years ago?' Jude asked, pressing forward no matter how much it hurt. 'Did you always plan to betray me, or was that something you decided after getting to know me? A fun little side diversion, perhaps? Something to keep the boredom away?'

Elden's only reaction to his acerbity was a slight tightening of his mouth. 'I was a woodsman for many years. Hiding from the Abbey. From . . . from my father. Then, the winter before I came to Ánhaga, I fell ill. A horrible fever. They found me then, when I was too weak to fight back.' His gaze flicked to Felix's, leaving just as quickly. 'The Abbey's hold was immediate. I couldn't defy it. Couldn't even remember what was happening until just there now.'

Maeve inched closer, laying her hand on his forearm. Elden smiled at her faintly.

Jude cleared his throat. 'And then what?'

'I was sent to Ánhaga as an informant. A spy. I tampered with your research, library, your life. I did all those things, reported them all—' he cut off. His eyes flew heavenward as anguish turned his face briefly unrecognizable. 'There were hours . . . days, even, when I couldn't remember what I'd been doing. My fingers would be ink-stained, or there would be mud on my boots despite not having written anything or left the house. I'd receive mail, open it, and forget immediately what it contained, no matter how many times I reread it. And I couldn't . . . I didn't know how to stop it.'

The full impact hit Jude like a battering ram.

Elden continued doggedly— 'Then, Maeve came, and it only got worse. They were interested in you, Jude, always . . . . But *Maeve*.' His gaze fell to her. 'With your iconography skills, they wanted you somewhere you could be watched. Once I told them you had painted Jude's icon, they wanted you to return to the Abbey as soon as possible. And when it wasn't fast enough, when I told them about what you had figured out, they sent someone to kill Siobhan.' He heaved a breath. 'I tried to stop them, but it was too late. *I* was too late.'

Jude shut his eyes briefly. The worry that Elden had been the one to kill Siobhan had haunted the furthest recesses of his mind, something he had refused to think about too deeply, knowing it would wreck him. Hearing that it hadn't been Elden brought indescribable relief.

'And then, in Whitebury, I had meant to—' Elden's voice cracked with the strain. 'I was supposed to lock you both in the room at the inn. But it didn't work out as planned. Jude was taken, and Maeve was not. And I was too unwell to help any further. I was no longer useful.'

'The Abbey was controlling your memory? Your actions?' Jude clarified.

'Not the Abbey,' Felix whispered. 'Ezra. His father.'

Jude whipped around towards him. 'You knew?'

Felix paused. His throat worked with a swallow. The gut-wrenching anguish was back in his eyes as he stared at Elden, a downturned softness to the corners of his mouth that Jude remembered from when they were boys. It seemed to take effort for him to clear it away and focus on Jude's question.

'I knew,' Felix replied. 'My mother is . . . *was* living in the Goddenwood. Each day there worsened her mind, and there was nothing I could do. *Nothing.* But if I complied and helped Ezra find Elden, convinced him to go to Ánhaga and inform on you, they told me they would cease praying to her icon. She would be allowed to leave.' He studied the ground beneath him. 'It was a lie, of course. She'd been dead for over a decade. I thought she was alive all this time. I only just remembered . . .' he trailed off, clearing his throat.

Jude rolled his lip between his teeth. Felix's involvement stung like a thorn just under his skin. He understood what it was like to be manipulated, to be trapped under the Abbey's thumb, but he couldn't deny hearing about his role in Elden's deception was a difficult reality to swallow.

'*Saints*,' Maeve whispered. 'Is there no limit?'

'What happened after the Abbey guards took me?' Jude asked.

At this, an unexpected smile pulled at Elden's mouth as his gaze shifted to Felix, like his words were for him alone. 'Brigid found me. She used her magic to break some of the Abbey's control, at least for a little while. I got some of my . . . best memories back.' He shifted, rubbing a hand over his chest. 'There's something else. Brigid – she's my mum.'

'*What?*' This time, it was Felix who gasped. 'I had no idea. This whole time?'

'That's generally how it works, yes,' Elden remarked with a smile. 'No one knew. Not even me. Her continued loyalty to the Abbey and her promise to keep quiet about my parentage were the only things that kept Ezra from seeking me after I escaped. If she remained at the Abbey and did her work, didn't try to harm the Abbey with her knowledge, I would be safe.' He raised a brow. 'Until, of course, Ezra decided to find me anyway. Keeping promises isn't one of his strong points, I'd reckon.'

'Brigid,' Maeve whispered, wonder in her voice. 'Elden,

that's . . .' she checked his face. 'Good, right? She's family. Someone to rebuild your life with.'

He nodded. 'Yes. Yes, I think it is.'

Silence weighed down, heavy and suffocating.

The weight of betrayal hadn't left Jude's chest. He didn't know if it ever would, both towards Elden and Felix for his involvement. But neither would the view of Elden, laying his darkest secrets out for his forgiveness, unflinching in his honesty. Jude wanted to believe him, wanted to believe that the Elden he knew hadn't been a fabrication. The memories they held together, both as boys at the Abbey and as men at Ánhaga, weren't a lie.

He could learn to trust him again. It might even be easy.

The part of Jude that longed to forgive stretched its limbs. It hadn't been Elden's fault. Like Jude, like Maeve and Felix and every saint who had come before them, every person the Abbey had crushed beneath their feet, Elden was a victim, too.

Slowly, Jude reached out a hand.

Elden's warm palm met his, squeezing tight.

55

Jude

Elden brought them to a cottage a few hours' walk away from the Abbey. A quaint, sea-worn structure nestled in a quiet cove outside Little Westworth he claimed had once belonged to his grandmother, Brigid's mother. It had a small dock jutting into the sea where a two-person boat bobbed, a rusted fishing contraption secured to the back of it. The sides of the cottage were whitewashed plaster; the roof, door, and windows framed in dark wood. As Elden pushed open the door and ushered them inside, Jude felt something in him break off and release.

This was Elden's home. Not Jude's house. Not Ánhaga – *here*.

It was all his, from the stack of hand-stitched quilts in a basket by the oversized, frayed sofa to the scored wood of the small dining table. It smelled of dried flowers and sea breeze and something unmistakably Elden.

He'd been forced to leave all this to come to Jude. Guilt dug talons into his stomach.

Elden lowered himself onto the sofa with a groan, propping his socked feet on the table in front of him. A contented smile hung on his lips. The rest of them stood in the small kitchen, exchanging confused glances with each other as he prepared to settle in for a long, well-earned nap.

'Shall I . . .' Maeve trailed off. She turned, opening a cupboard at random. Glass cups sat in a neat row, covered in a faint sheen of dust. 'Right.'

Jude watched her stilted movements, a lump of uncertainty forming in his throat.

She'd been . . . *off* on the walk here. Felix had asked them both their plans now that they were free from the Abbey, with Maeve replying that she'd like to find her family as soon as she could. Immediately, if she could help it. There was a finality in her tone; a stress on her singularity that he wasn't sure if he'd imagined.

He'd turned her words over in his head again and again, nudging them like a sore tooth.

He wanted them to stay together. More than anything. But he needed her to choose – choose *him*. To stay or to go or anything in between. He was hers entirely. He'd felt what it was like to be nearly ripped apart, and he'd come out the other side a changed man. She'd taken someone broken beyond repair and would leave behind someone . . . not quite whole, but getting there. It was more than he could have asked for when he'd considered what his recovery might look like.

No more running, no more hiding. Jude wanted her. In every way she would have him. And so, when Felix had asked him what his plans were, he'd replied in the simplest way he could. He wanted to go *home*.

Home was Ánhaga; home was Maeve.

If she wished to hear him beg her to stay or to allow him to go with her to find her family, he would. He would *gladly* get down on his knees and give her anything she asked for.

She just needed to look at him first.

'There should be something to eat around here somewhere.' Elden pushed back to his feet with a grunt. 'I'll go to the village tomorrow and get something that hasn't been preserved.'

He disappeared through the back door. The sound of clanging jars and muted muttering followed. Maeve busied herself filling the kettle with water, making tea with short, jerky movements. Felix caught his eye after she closed a cupboard with startling force, raising an eyebrow.

Before he could muster a response, Elden returned with his arms full. Soon, they were gulping down bowls of sticky porridge and chewing on hunks of dried salted cod. The porridge was virtually tasteless without sugar or milk, but it eased the ache in their bellies. After their dishes were cleaned, Elden pulled blankets from a cupboard under the narrow, rickety set of stairs leading up to the loft.

'Here,' he shoved a quilt into Jude's hands, eyes jumping between him and Maeve. 'I have a bedroom, there's the sofa and my grandmother's old room—' he jerked his chin up the stairs '—up there.'

'I'll sleep down here,' Felix said quickly. His eyes danced with a faint amusement at the staunch distance between Jude and Maeve. She shifted, gaze moving to the floor.

'I'll be in my room down the hall,' Elden said. 'You two . . .'

Jude swallowed down the nervousness that had begun to collect somewhere behind his breastbone. Did Maeve even want to be alone with him? He risked a glance in her direction. She hadn't looked up from the ground. Redness had begun to trace its way down her neck, disappearing down the front of her soot-stained habit.

'There's a bath upstairs, should you like to use it,' Elden continued, breaking the fraught silence. With that, he spun on his heel and disappeared down the hall, clearly wanting to escape the palpable tension. Maeve startled at the faint snick of the door that followed.

He turned to her. 'I can sleep here on the floor if you'd rather be alone.'

Dark eyes met his, faintly glassy in the candlelight. 'Why would I want that?'

Jude shrugged helplessly.

The candle between her clenched fingers cast the stairs in a honey glow as they ascended. He was reminded of their first night together. A night full of storms, inside and out. How she'd stood in her shift made sheer by rainwater with fire in her eyes. How he'd known, from that moment onward, that he was completely and irrevocably fucked.

Maeve eased open the door. The bedroom was larger than he'd expected. Its roof was peaked in the middle, the slatted wood a faded white. A window looked out towards the sea beyond. Just under it, lit by a shaft of moonlight, was a single large bed.

Through a door on the left, he glimpsed a bathroom fitted with a sink, a mirror rusted around the edges, and a copper tub placed under a round window. It was a luxurious contraption for a sea cottage, big enough that he reckoned he could lie flat along the bottom.

He knelt beside the tub and flicked on one of the taps. After a heaving groan and a concerning amount of gurgling, water thundered down to hit the base of the tub. He tested it with his fingers, adjusting the taps until the mixture coming out was a comfortable temperature.

Clothing rustled behind him. Moonlight turned the stream to silver.

'Jude.'

Maeve's voice was little more than a whisper, but he flinched all the same.

He thought he knew her by now. Knew her mannerisms, her habits. How her voice sounded when she was nervous or angry or joyful. But now . . . he had no idea what to expect from her.

'Jude,' she repeated louder. Her footsteps came closer. He remained with both hands braced on the side of the tub, his head bowed in the space between them. He closed his eyes when her fingers brushed the back of his neck.

'I want you to come with me to find my family. And then I want to go home with you.' Her exhale sent shivers up and down his back. 'If that's what you want, too.'

Relief flooded him. 'You do?'

'I don't want to go anywhere without you,' she admitted.

The heat of her body brushed against his side, and Jude wanted to look, he *did*, but the vicious lump in his throat held him in place. There was so much he wanted to say to her, but the thought of looking into her eyes while he did so terrified him more than anything else.

But he had to say something. He had to access that hidden well of bravery – for her.

'Maeve,' he began. He kept his eyes cinched shut, even when her hand drifted up to palm the back of his skull, her fingernails raking through the short strands. She was the only one he'd let touch him there. 'About the inn.'

'No, please, wait,' she interrupted. 'I want to apologize. I pushed you far more than I should have that night. I shouldn't have just *mauled* you—'

'I did want . . . I *do* want that with you,' Jude said. 'I want everything. I was just afraid. Overwhelmed. I wasn't sure how to handle it. And—' he hesitated, huffing out a short breath. 'I haven't before. Ever.'

Though he desperately wanted to see her face, the weight of her silence kept his eyes closed.

The air shifted as Maeve knelt beside him. He finally allowed himself to look at her. Her eyes were wide, mouth parted. The depth of feeling on her face was enough to take his breath away.

'Do you have any idea what you mean to me?' she murmured. 'Even if you never wanted to go further than holding hands—' Jude snorted, shaking his head, but she pressed on '—it would be enough. *You* are enough.'

He kissed the back of her hand, resting next to his. Her lashes fluttered against her cheeks. 'I don't want to disappoint you,' he whispered. It hurt to admit, but he didn't want anything between them, even something as uncomfortable as his insecurities.

'Not possible.' Her mouth was only a breath away. 'Trust me. I've never . . . never cared for someone like I do you. Never wanted someone more than I want you. It scares me too, you know.' He raised an eyebrow, and she nodded. 'It's a frightening thing, opening yourself up to that kind of vulnerability with another person. But it's also a gift.'

'I want that,' Jude whispered.

Maeve stood. She'd shed her habit back in the bedroom, wrapping a quilt around her shoulders in its stead. She held it together with a hand clamped between her breasts. Candlelight gilded her pale skin, sliding into every hollow, every smooth plane in the same way Jude wanted to. With his hands, his mouth.

The light was golden, but this was a different kind of magic.

She smiled. 'Do you remember how we used to sneak into the kitchens every Thursday and steal the honey biscuits? I was always nervous we'd get caught, and that time we did—' she laughed, covering her mouth with her palm. 'You told the cook you thought you heard mice in your room. You wanted mint leaves to get rid of them because they hated the smell. *Mint leaves*, Jude. Of all the things.'

'It worked though, didn't it?' he replied, grinning. 'We didn't get in trouble. And, if I remember correctly—' he pushed to his feet and moved towards her. Her breath hitched as he neared. 'You got your biscuits anyway, didn't you?'

'Yes. And the whole Abbey was checked for mice.'

'Sounds like everything worked out perfectly, then.'

Her smile widened. 'Yes, it did.'

He took another step closer. Let himself fully sink into the moment, into the reality of her. Everything he dreamed of and everything he would finally let himself have. Without guilt, or fear, or insecurity – any of those cloying emotions that had festered at the bottom of the lightless well alongside him. He'd lived so many years in the dark. No more.

He brought his hands to his collar. Every movement felt fluid, dreamlike as he pulled off the habit Ezra had forced him into and let it fall to his feet. Beneath, he wore a simple white shirt and the same trousers he'd left his home in.

Maeve picked up the candle and blew it out. Their eyes met and held; a thousand promises and whispered words filling the space between them.

She let the quilt drop to the floor.

56

Maeve

Maeve was no stranger to trysts. Quick exploits, often hurried and rarely satisfactory. Nothing more than an itch scratched. She'd liked most of the people she'd been with enough to share that part of herself with them, enough to risk the Abbey's retribution should she be caught. But she'd never let any sort of vulnerability permeate the equation.

But this, *this*, standing wholly naked while Jude looked at her with reverence in his eyes, was something she'd never experienced. She studied the part of his lips, the moonlight painting him with a delicate touch. His eyes took on an unfocused sheen as his gaze travelled across her collarbones, lingering on her breasts, her navel, down even further. He tilted his head, meeting her eyes from beneath his lashes.

At her sides, Maeve's fingers twitched. She wanted to touch him. *Badly.*

Slowly, he began unbuttoning his shirt.

His bravery wasn't lost on her – she knew he found this difficult. Tattoos littered his torso, layered thickly on his inner arms and the thin skin over the jut of his hipbones, tallied in even lines across his lower stomach. She stepped forward and gently pulled the shirt from his grip, taking over the task of undoing the buttons. She traced down his chest with her fingertips, lingering on the tattoo for *SAINT*. His pulse beat in his throat, a rapid thrumming just below his skin.

Maeve pressed her lips to his neck, sucking gently at his skin. He inhaled sharply. She chuckled, pulling back as his shirt fell to the floor. 'Let's get in the bath.'

She lowered herself in slowly, hissing at the sting of the water on her various scrapes and burns. It passed quickly, the heat working the tension from her muscles. She pooled water in her palms, rubbing away the remnants of smoke and sweat, giving Jude privacy as he finished undressing. The soft sound of shucking fabric sent goosebumps down her back.

'Move up,' he murmured, stepping into the tub behind her. She complied, water sloshing close to the edge as he got in. His fingertips ghosted down her spine before curling around her hip. She felt his mouth beside her ear, his scent in her nose. 'Now come closer?'

Her heart felt ready to launch from her throat as she moved until her back was against his chest, his legs bracketing hers. The feeling of his bare skin was feverish. Overwhelming. He pressed a lingering kiss to the juncture between her shoulder and neck. Maeve shivered. 'Jude?'

'Yes?'

He'd moved one hand to her right thigh, the other to her stomach, where he traced slow circles with his fingertips. The point of his nose skimmed up her neck as he breathed her in. The wanting turned her to liquid. Maeve's breath hitched. She pressed her thighs tightly together to relieve some of the ache. 'You know we can do whatever you want,' she said. She prayed the desperation didn't leak into her voice. 'I'll like it. Anything. Everything.'

'And what if I want to do it all?' he asked with his mouth still against her skin. The hand on her stomach shifted infinitesimally lower.

She swallowed. 'As I said.'

The backs of his fingers brushed the underside of her breast. Maeve laid her hand on his under the water, tracing the delicate bones of his fingers, the raised shape of his veins and the contours of his wrist. The sight of his hands on her threatened every shred of control still available to her.

'Are you . . .' Jude began, shifting behind her. His chest had gone still. She looked at him over her shoulder, catching the edge of hesitation in his gaze.

'Am I what?'

'The tea,' he replied succinctly.

It took her a moment to gather what he meant. When she did, she laughed, planting one hand on his bent leg to lever herself around to face him. Jude's gaze quickly darted to her chest and back to her face like he feared she'd catch him looking. 'Am I protected from pregnancy, you mean?'

He nodded.

'The tea lasts a month. And I haven't had my next monthly, so . . .'

He made a quiet noise in the back of his throat, pulling her back around and tight to his chest. 'That's . . . good. Very good.'

'Don't want children?' Maeve asked as he began washing her hair with a small vial of soap they'd found perched on the windowsill. The smell of summer mint filled the air. She caught a sigh behind her teeth as Jude worked her strands into a lather.

'Never really thought about it, to be honest.'

'Me neither. Maybe someday, but not anytime soon.'

He pressed a kiss against the back of her neck in reply.

'When you first arrived, even though you made me angry—' he chuckled, running his hands down the length of her hair. '*So* angry, I couldn't stop thinking of you. Couldn't get myself to quit picturing your face, your hair, and the way your eyes shone when you glared at me. Every bit of your frustration and, eventually, your smiles. Those I could never forget.'

She smiled then; she couldn't help it. Jude pressed his face into her neck as he spoke. 'And all those shifts, Maeve. The nightgowns.' He groaned. 'They about killed me. Did you realize how see-through they were?'

'Maybe.'

'I thought so.'

She turned her head to press a kiss to the underside of his jaw. Unlike past times she'd experienced happiness, the shimmering vein of it she felt here, *now*, was of a more solid variation. Like her limbs were dipped in gold, a steadfast coating of something that wouldn't be easily shed.

She'd often wondered whether she'd find someone who saw every one of her dark corners and wanted her still – a dream she rarely allowed herself to indulge in. The fear it would never come true was too much to bear, so she'd pushed it to the back of her mind into the space that occupied the vulnerable hours between sleeping and waking.

She hadn't been lying when she'd told Jude she'd like whatever they did. She couldn't imagine anything that might pass between them as less than a perfect representation of everything she felt for him come to life. Like the heady feeling of her magic when she painted, something almost religious in strength of her joy, so euphoric she'd commit her life to it in an instant.

They took turns washing in the slow, comfortable quiet of the moonlit bathtub. He had yet to kiss her lips, though he'd mapped across her neck and shoulders enough to make her shivery with want every time his mouth touched her overheated skin. He seemed content to take his time, exploring her body with his usual careful, observant precision.

Finally, when she thought she could bear the teasing no longer, Jude drew his hand up her thigh. She released a breath. 'Took you long enough.'

He chuckled, a bitten-off sound that shifted to a sigh as he slid his fingers through her, slow and languid. Behind her, his chest stilled. 'Maeve,' he breathed. 'Fuck.'

She closed her eyes and pushed her legs wider, moving his

hand where she wanted him. His other hand fastened tightly around her hip, holding her still. Their panting breaths filled the silence. Her nails dug into his skin, even when she no longer needed to guide him. All the while, he whispered into her hair, telling her how beautiful he found her, how well she was doing. Admonishing her when she looked away from where they connected.

'That's it,' he murmured against her neck when her head dropped back at the feeling of his fingers sliding inside her. Maeve reached for him, fastening her hand around the back of his neck. She needed to touch him as she came, the bliss a slow-moving wave that left her gasping and trembling in its wake.

Their breathing didn't slow for a long while after. Jude continued to touch her like he didn't quite know how to stop – slow, lazy passes of his hands up her thighs, over her breasts, a featherlight brush between her legs where he'd left her wrecked. She shuddered in his arms.

The cooling water eventually urged them apart.

He wrapped an oversized towel around her shoulders, kissing her forehead before grabbing one of his own. Maeve took the opportunity to study him as he moved, as both an artist and a lover. She'd known he was tall and slim, with graceful limbs and a certain elegance she'd enjoyed capturing in paint, but she hadn't been prepared for the reality. She wet her lips, trailing her gaze down to his narrow hips, his legs' long expanse, the subtle definition of his chest and abdomen. The harsh lines of his tattoos only emphasized his beauty, their existence a tangible reminder of all he had survived.

Emboldened, she moved closer, placing her palm flat on his chest, directly over the SAINT tattoo, and kissed his throat.

Jude stilled. He sucked in a tight inhale, pulling his towel closer around his hips.

Maeve continued her path downwards, pressing her lips against the line of his collarbone, the swell of his chest where it rose and fell. Ran her fingers over his ribs, the soft insides of his arms. At his sides, his hands grasped and released.

'Is this okay?' she murmured as she lowered to her knees.

Jude stared down at her, his eyes so wide it was nearly comical. She concealed her smile against the edge of his hip. If she'd read him correctly, he was going to like this. His mouth parted, but nothing came out.

'Jude?' Maeve asked, kissing the soft skin just above the towel, featherlight touches across each inked tally on his lower stomach. She pressed her tongue to the point of his hip, nearly moaning with the taste. He threaded his fingers through the hair at her nape, angling her head to meet his gaze.

'I—' his throat bobbed. 'I mean – yes? Please.'

Before she could lose her nerve, she pulled off his towel and took him into her mouth. She'd never done this before, never wanted to, really, but she wanted to see Jude come undone, knowing *she* was behind it. She wanted to hear the noises from his mouth as he dug fingertips into her scalp, his sharp intake of breath as she took him deeper. Feel him pull her away when he got close.

'I don't want to . . .' he shook his head, guiding her back to her feet. His cheeks were flushed, a wash of colour that extended down his chest. 'Not yet.'

'Well, that's one way to keep you around,' Maeve said, smiling as he pulled her tight to his chest. His breathing had yet to slow.

'Come on,' he said into her hair.

He divested her of her towel and laid her flat against the bed. She laughed, skating her palms up and down his sides as he moved to hover over her, accidentally setting his hand down on her loose hair in the process. It pulled sharply at her scalp.

'*Ow*—' she winced, pulling at her trapped hair.

Jude drew back so rapidly that he nearly toppled over. 'Are you all right?' He massaged his fingertips into her scalp, eyes wide with concern.

Maeve fought a grin as she pulled him down on top of her. 'I'll survive. Maybe.'

An answering smile moved quickly to his lips. 'Funny,' he murmured, sliding his hand into the hair at her nape to angle her face towards his. Their gazes locked and held, something heady passing between them. Emotion welled up in her chest at seeing him like this – allowed to be free, unconcerned with anything that wasn't his present moment. She leaned up and kissed him.

As he moved his hand to wrap around the side of her throat with his thumb against her pulse, Maeve realized this would be nothing like their last kiss. The kiss at the inn had been all desperation and a wild reach for connection. They'd been starving for each other, wanting one moment of happiness amidst their rapidly crumbling reality. It was no wonder it had played out the way it had. Whenever she had thought of kissing Jude, sleeping with him, even, she'd pictured something slow. Reverent, almost.

She'd admitted to herself once, when she'd been out of her mind with jealousy at the thought of him and Bethan as lovers, that Jude would take his time. As his lips moved over hers, his thigh pressing between hers and sliding up, the friction more than perfect, she knew she was right.

He was going to make a slow study of her, and she was going to let him.

Jude released her mouth to kiss down her neck, across her collarbone. He pressed his nose to the underside of her breast, fitting his thumbs into the hollow of her hips. Slid his tongue over her nipples until she began to gasp before kissing over her ribs and sternum, each brush as light as a feather. He drank in her every reaction, lingering when she arched against him, mouthing at her skin. Love, she thought as he made a careful catalogue of everywhere he could reach, was everything and nothing, indefinable in a world she tried to keep safely contained. Love was this – sacrifice and survival.

Maeve watched him move downwards, trying to control her heart rate.

She'd never craved a lover's eyes like this. Certainly not *during*, when she was vulnerable, open, him between her legs. But when Jude kissed the soft hollow where her hip met her thigh and looked up at her, she wanted nothing more than *him*. Memorizing her with his eyes and with his mouth.

'You will need to instruct me,' Jude whispered.

'I think—' she cut off, squeezing her eyes shut when he pressed his nose to her inner thigh, followed by his tongue. 'I think you'll be fine.'

She slid the short strands of his hair through her fingers, feeling him shudder in response. Desperation filled her as he lingered at her hip, kissing her skin with barely-there touches. He pulled back to study her, running his fingers lightly between her legs until she squirmed.

'Jude,' Maeve said, breathier than she would've liked. 'Please.'

He smiled, mumbling something against her skin that sounded suspiciously like *patience*. She memorized the sight of his head between her legs, his fingers pressing indents into her hip. His panting breaths against where she needed him the most.

She couldn't take it anymore.

Maeve skated her hand over his head to pull his mouth closer. Her eyes fell shut as he finally pressed his tongue to her skin. Her body was strung-out and eager, her heart beating in time with his touch. For a moment that seemed endless, it was as though she didn't inhabit her body at all. It was only Jude, his mouth between her legs, his fingers inside her, and the heavy weight of his hand against her thigh.

Like in the bath, she guided him with a hand in his hair, back arching upwards when he pressed his face closer, groaning into her. He didn't let up until she lay spent, her breaths coming in rapid pulls. Even then, she had to pull him back, laughing when he whined and placed a final, open-mouthed kiss between her thighs.

'How very enjoyable,' he said, wrapping his arms tight around her waist and burying his face in her belly. 'Marvellous.'

'*Marvellous?*' Maeve laughed, a breathless thing. 'You've never used that word in your life.' She stretched the stiffness from her fingers on the quilt as he chuckled, rubbing the stubble on his cheek against her skin until she squirmed. 'I am very glad you think so, though. Extraordinarily glad, even.'

He shifted downwards. 'Again, perhaps?'

'There are other things, you know,' she said, regretfully tugging him back up.

'Are there?'

His voice was light, teasing. Maeve didn't think she'd ever seen his smile so unencumbered. She kissed the side of it and rolled him onto his back. His hazel eyes were clear and dark as he gazed up at her. The fringe of his lashes covered them as he tilted his head to watch her fingertips skip down the planes of his stomach, lips parted. She traced the runic tattoo on the hollow of his right hip, stopping when he stifled a gasp.

'It's sensitive,' he said. 'But don't stop.'

She flattened her hand, covering the lines before running her palm up his side and tracing the largest tattoo on his chest – a half-circle surrounded by three lines like the rays of a sun. The sign of the Abbey, forever marked on his skin, just like it was on both of their hearts and minds. It might never leave them entirely, but perhaps it could be reclaimed.

She leaned down and kissed it. Jude shuddered.

Fighting a tremble, she drew her hand back down the centre of his stomach and slowly wrapped it around him. He made a keening noise, gripping her waist as she moved her hand up and down. A light sheen of sweat dewed his chest. She rubbed her thumb across him, smiled when he whimpered. She drew closer, sliding him against the wetness between her legs. Fought a gasp of her own at the feeling of it, at the way his head tipped back with a moan.

'Jude,' Maeve whispered.

His throat bobbed with a rough swallow. 'Yeah?'

'Is this what you want?'

'Yes,' he breathed, nodding. 'Please.'

Steadying herself with a hand on his chest, Maeve rose on her knees and slowly sank onto him. His fingers convulsed on her hips, the tendons in his neck stretching tight. She paused there, letting them both adjust. She wished they had more light – the sun, a candle, *anything*. She wanted to see him, see where they connected.

Finally, he let out a long breath, shifting his hips beneath her and pressing his head back deeper into the mattress. He wanted her to move. She wouldn't – not yet. Instead, she leaned forward, sliding her nose up his neck and sucking a kiss into the soft skin just beneath his ear, not quite hard enough to leave a mark. 'Okay?'

His whole body jerked in response. She pulled back to look, worried she'd done something he hadn't liked, but his face was slack, lips parted. He slid both palms up the line of her spine, one coming to rest around the back of her head as he brought their foreheads together.

'Can you do that again?' he asked, their lips brushing together.

His brows were knitted tightly, eyes half-open, almost in pain. A deep flush was working its way down his neck. She gave a few rolls of her hips, just to see him shudder. *Saints*, he felt good. 'Do what?'

He brushed his fingertips lightly under his collarbone. 'Mark me. Here.' His voice took on a soft, pleading cadence. 'I want to see it later.'

It was her turn to shudder, leaning down to press her mouth exactly where he'd touched, sucking until a deep purple mark bloomed on his skin. 'Like that?' she asked.

Jude nodded. He rested his palm over it when she was done, his face relaxing like she'd unknotted something inside him.

Before she could return to unravelling him completely, his hands were on her hips, moving her over him. Her legs trembled with the strain. She braced her hands on his chest, leaning down over him. His gaze was clear, his face inches from her.

And Maeve couldn't focus, not on anything that wasn't him. The way he felt inside her, the tender pressure of her chest sliding against his. The liquid heat travelling down her limbs was too much to bear.

'Maeve.' Jude made a stifled noise at the back of his throat, almost a whine. Sweat dewed on his chest, his throat. The mark she'd left. 'Maeve, you—' he swallowed. 'Please. *Please.*'

'I know,' she murmured, fighting for control as much as he was. He skated trembling palms up and down her flank, pushing his head back into the pillow. He was close, but not close enough. She wanted to see him unravel. Wholly and completely, and for her alone. She brought her lips to his ear. 'You can do it. For me.'

His whole body tightened before he released a half-gasped noise next to her ear. She drew back just far enough to see his face. The flush on his cheeks, his tightly squeezed eyes. The way he caught his lip between his teeth.

Her heart swelled with a vibrant swell of emotion as she fell forward onto his chest, burying her face against the side of his neck. The sheer reality of him was enough to take her breath away. Enough to make her thankful, a hundred times over, for the gift of the man in her arms. A gift she would hold tight for as long as she had strength.

For a long moment, the only sound was their breathing, the soft rasp of skin. Then Jude laughed, exhilarated and shocked, before rolling them over and draping himself on top of her.

'You're heavy,' Maeve mumbled, huffing a laugh as she playfully shoved at him. Jude pressed a final kiss to where her neck met her shoulder before shifting enough for her to curl into his side. She turned to look at him. Both dimples were out on full display. He hugged her, pressing a kiss to her hair.

'I knew you'd be the death of me,' Jude murmured. 'One way or the other.'

57

Jude

Jude awoke slowly. His thoughts unspooled in downy
ribbons, knotting, untangling, and knotting again. He
blinked lazily as warmth diffused down his limbs. Buttery-
yellow light streaked across the worn quilt, lingering in the
hollows between their bodies. Contentment stole through the
gaps in the gauzy curtains on a sea breeze.

Maeve was tucked under his arm with her cheek pillowed
against his bare chest. Dawn sunlight played greedily in her
spun-gold hair. Last night's delicate flush turned her skin luminescent, catching on the faint sheen still clinging to her
cheekbones. Inside his chest, in the place reserved only for her,
his heart gave a tremulous squeeze.

He never considered himself someone who needed another
person, but he needed *her.*

Needed her laughter, her sighs. He needed her argumentative,
and he needed her forgiving. Just like he didn't know how much
he needed her head against his chest until it was there, Jude
hadn't realized how much he'd desperately craved for someone
to be his until she stood before him.

The memories of the night before came flooding in, sending
a rush of heat down his body.

Maeve had been right – vulnerability was a beautiful thing.
He'd stood bare before her with every ragged tattoo in plain

view, every inch available for her steady gaze. And it had been freeing in ways he hadn't known were possible.

He ran the backs of his fingers down the curve of her hip, soft enough that she wouldn't wake. He wanted her again, fiercer now that he knew what he was asking for. What he'd give. He touched the mark her mouth had left on his chest, the subtle ache it left behind.

He'd needed that, too. A sign of love imprinted on his skin, freely asked for and freely given.

He had not been given the privilege of calling many things his own, but if the fierce longing to mould himself into Maeve's skin and never leave told him anything, it was that the gift of loving her wouldn't be one he'd let sift through his fingers.

He moved his mouth to her temple. 'Maeve.'

She stirred, rolling until her back was against his chest. Their legs tangled together. Jude rested his forehead on the nape of her neck. Penitence, he thought. Of the truest kind.

'Good morning,' she whispered, voice husky with sleep.

She turned in his arms, hitching her leg over his hip. A flash of heat from the previous night had him rolling her onto her back and kissing a line down her neck. He licked her collarbone, pressing his mouth against her pulse. 'Morning.'

'What a way to wake up,' she murmured, a smile in her voice.

He loved her like this, sleep-warmed and affectionate. She dug her hands into his hair, pulling his face to hers. Jude went gladly. Her mouth was warm and sweet. He could kiss her forever.

Sometime later, Maeve pulled back. 'Last night . . .' her flush deepened.

'Good?'

She nodded.

He kissed the side of her smile, pressed his lips to her ear. 'I'll always be good to you.'

The morning quickly slipped away from them. Before long,

the sunrise had brightened, filling the room with the clear light of day. With her head pillowed against his stomach, Maeve turned to look at him. Her fingers skated across his forearm, a delicate touch that meant more than he could put into words. Breathlessly, he studied her, the need to confess stronger than anything he'd ever known. The words lingered on the tip of his tongue, promising relief once he released them into the open air. Sunlight refracted in her dark eyes, painting them in the deepest shades of emerald and quartz.

Beloved, his mind supplied.

He could wait no longer— 'I love you.'

Her eyes fluttered shut. 'Jude.'

He'd never tire of the sound of his name on her lips. Both hands cradled the back of his head as she buried her face in his neck. 'I love you, too,' she whispered against his skin. She moved to kiss the corner of his mouth. Once, twice. 'Of course I do.'

His face ached with how wide he was smiling. Every beat of his heart was for her alone.

He never wanted to move, but eventually, the muted gurgle of his stomach caused them to pull back. Maeve skated her fingers across his jaw. Their noses touched. 'Ready to get up?' she asked.

'Not yet.'

A look of deliberation marred her brow. 'How do you feel?'

Jude eased back. He wanted to see her whole face for this conversation. It needed to happen, despite how little he wanted to dwell on it. The Abbey. The fire. Memories and saints and bright golden magic. *Ezra.*

'I feel . . .' he hesitated. Words came in a slow trickle. 'Weightless. Like there's nothing to worry about. It's just me. You. And whatever we'd like to do next.'

The corner of her mouth flicked up, though her eyes were heavy. She looked away, towards the window. Clouds rushed high overhead, spots of blue emerging through the tumble of grey.

'Ezra died,' he murmured, watching her expression carefully. 'I need to tell Elden.'

'Ah.' Her only tell was a brief tightening of her mouth. 'How?'

'Candlestick through the neck. It was too late to do anything by the time I reached him.'

'Hm.'

Jude didn't know what else to say. Almost desperately, he asked, 'And you? How do you feel?'

She sighed. 'The same, I think. More unmoored than anything else. The fire was necessary, and I'm glad for it, even if I wish you hadn't been forced up on that altar. I'm glad we have our memories back, and the Abbey is no longer taking our magic. That we can do whatever we want, *be* whoever we want, is a gift I won't take for granted. It's just . . .' she grimaced.

'You're not used to living without a guidebook,' he supplied.

'Something like that. It's not so much the religious side of it – it's more the fallback. The idea that there's someone else there watching over me. Listening when I pray.'

His heart gave an unsteady thump. He had become so accustomed to living without a safety net that inviting one back into his life was more frightening than continuing alone. Where Maeve saw a safety net, he saw a shackle.

'Did I ever tell you the meaning behind my house's name?' he asked suddenly.

Maeve cut her gaze to his. 'Ánhaga?'

'It means a solitary being,' he said. 'A dwelling for one.'

Her brows knitted. 'Why would anyone give a house that sort of name?'

'I don't know.' Beneath the blanket, their fingers twined together. 'It made me think, though. If it was built to be somewhere without community, without companionship . . . what happens when it becomes exactly that? Does the house lose its name? Its identity? Or does the meaning of *Ánhaga* get rewritten into something new entirely?'

Maeve blinked. 'Its roots remain the same, but the growth takes a new direction.'

Jude smiled. 'Exactly. As with you and me, Maeve. Our foundation is the Abbey. The good and the bad. But that doesn't mean our futures can't grow into something new.'

58

Jude

'Look who decided to grace us with their presence,' Elden remarked with a sly smile as they made their way down the stairs. The smell of frying bacon greeted them, reminding Jude of one of the few meals Elden was wonderfully proficient in.

'Eggs, too?' Jude asked, stealing a strip of bacon. He leaned his back against the counter. 'When did you head out this morning?'

'Early enough.' Elden slid the fried eggs onto the waiting plates. 'Met my great-aunt. Some cousins, too.' He smiled, sadness lingering around his eyes. 'They were surprised to see me, and happy to hear Brigid was still alive and planning to visit soon. Offered us dinner tomorrow, should we like it. It was—' he blew out a breath. 'Nice. Good. Really good.'

Jude fought for an answering smile as he debated how to tell Elden about Ezra. Before he could, Elden was already speaking. 'I know about him, that he died. Ezra. My . . . father.'

Maeve half-rose from her seat, stopped by a raise of Elden's hand.

'No, don't worry. He hadn't been a father in a long time. Maybe ever. Not when he took me from my mum, or when he realized I didn't hold the magic he wanted me to and decided to turn to Jude in my place. Not when he decided I could be someone he could use.' His throat bobbed, and Jude sensed there was a lot he wasn't saying. As badly as Ezra had treated him, Elden had suffered worse. 'I don't want any pity. Don't need it, okay?'

He waited for Jude and Maeve's nods before his expression softened. He pointed the frying pan towards Felix. 'We both went into the village. Thought Felix ought to have a good look at Little Westworth.'

Felix kept his gaze on his mug as he turned it round and round by its handle.

Jude still wasn't certain how to approach the other man, not with the weight of their childhood friendship lying heavy behind them, his involvement in Elden's manipulation still bitter on his tongue. Years had passed since, years when Jude had falsely believed Felix to be his enemy. Now, they were little more than strangers.

He picked up his plate and moved to sit next to the former saint. Perhaps he could move a step in the right direction. 'Why's that?' he asked.

Felix glanced at him once before turning back to his mug. Black tea swirled in the bottom, smelling of bergamot and bitter citrus. 'I might stay here for a little while. Elden offered, and well . . .' he hesitated, shifting in his seat. 'I thought the quiet might do me some good. After, I'm going to see what's become of the Goddenwood. Brigid said that's where she was going, and I want to join her. See what happened to my mother. Maybe I can—' his throat worked. 'Maybe I can bury her.'

Elden sat down next to him, warmth in his eyes as he smiled at the other man. He reached out and patted Felix's wrist, lingering for a long moment before retreating. Felix tracked the movement.

'Aye,' Elden said. 'Told him he's welcome 'long as he likes. And I'll go with him to the Goddenwood whenever he's ready. I want to spend more time with Brigid, too.' His voice dropped. 'With my mum.'

Maeve cleared her throat, clinking her fork on her plate as she cut into her egg. 'We'll head out tomorrow morning if that's okay. My family lives only a few more hours' walk north. It's been a few years since I was last there, but I think I remember the way.' She smiled at Elden. 'Maybe you could lend me a map.'

Elden nodded. 'Sure, I have one around here somewhere.'

Jude tucked into his breakfast. They'd discussed their plans earlier, deciding to take their time on the journey to Maeve's family. Neither of them had much experience of the world outside the Abbey and Jude's home, and they were eager to see more of it. After they spent time with her family, they'd head back to his home. *Their* home. Ánhaga.

As Elden began describing a farm they'd pass by that offered fresh-baked scones every morning, Jude studied Maeve. Though she smiled and offered quips when needed, her fingers tapped an anxious beat on the table next to her discarded mug. Her gaze kept flitting to Felix. He wondered if her thoughts were wandering to their earlier conversation about religion.

Finally, Maeve took a deep breath, flattening both hands on the table. 'Felix.'

He looked up. 'Yes?'

Under the table, Jude placed his hand on her thigh.

'I was wondering,' she began. 'Do you still believe? In the saints.' At his raised eyebrow, she hurried on. 'Not in the way the Abbey does, but . . . well, in prayer, I guess. In someone listening when you ask for something.'

Elden stood and collected the dishes, leaving them to their conversation. Jude wished he'd stayed, thinking that maybe Elden could do with hashing out his relationship to the Abbey, too, but decided to keep quiet. He'd approach it in his own time.

'Yes and no,' Felix replied slowly, every word a product of careful deliberation.

Maeve leaned forward in her chair. 'How do you mean?'

'While I think the saints' power, all of our power, that is—' he gestured between the three of them '—is something very real and very potent, I don't look at it like the Abbey had always taught us to believe.'

Jude found himself asking, 'How do you look at it, then?'

'Well, to fully answer your question, we're best off examining how the Abbey dissects and uses the saints' power and, thus, how they've taught acolytes to view it for generations,' Felix replied in his smoke-stained voice. Jude's mouth twitched at the familiarity in his professorial tone, remembering it from more than a few lectures growing up.

Felix held two fingers up. 'Firstly, the Abbey views the saints' ability to access and change memory as a commodity. An exchange. Prayer equals power. It was only ever a vessel. Something to pour into the icons and fuel them, which, in turn, bound the saints to the Abbey.' He folded one finger down.

'Secondly, their focus was never on making the acolytes feel *heard*. It was always about control. If you convince the people that for their prayers to be granted, they needed to give of themselves – their devotion and time and money – you have a method of control.' He ticked down the second finger.

'So praying was virtually meaningless in the grand scheme of things, outside of fuelling the magic in the icons?' Maeve asked. Her face was very pale, and her eyes very dark. Jude pressed the side of his leg against hers.

Felix shrugged. 'You can look at it that way.'

'But you don't?'

'Not exactly. Even though the saints never heard prayers, I still view their devotion, *all* of our devotion, as something to be honoured. It's a beautiful thing, to release the deepest contents of your heart into the universe in the hopes that someone might be listening.' He smiled at Maeve. 'I still pray, you know.'

She blinked. 'You do?'

'Yes. All the time.' Felix laid his hands flat on the table, studying the gaps between his fingers. 'Belief and institution are not married. They can exist separately from each other. I can still pray, maybe not to the saints, but to anyone who might be listening, call it the universe or energy or whatever you'd like, and keep that belief separate from the Abbey.'

She nodded slowly. The stiff angle of her spine relaxed alongside the haunted look she'd worn for most of their conversation. Jude saw the refuge offered by Felix's encouragement in her face. It unknotted one of the ropes around his chest, seeing her reform part of her identity.

'Thank you,' Maeve murmured. 'Even at the Abbey . . . the letter. Your warning. I can see now that you were looking out for me.'

Felix shook his head. 'It wasn't enough. Not even to distract Ezra. I didn't protect you from exile.' His eyes caught Jude's. 'Nor you.'

Something vital lurched inside Jude at his words. 'No,' he insisted. 'You can't put that weight on yourself, Felix. You were barely an adult when I was exiled. And we can only guess the kind of life you were forced to live at the Abbey as a saint. You did everything you could.'

Felix shot him a look, half pleading and half guilty. 'The house . . . Ánhaga. I was the one who decided that's where you should be sent.'

Jude stilled. His belly performed an odd, swooping dip. 'What?'

'It was my father's house. He was an elder. I was born there.'

Jude paused, trying to meld together the home he'd slowly begun to claim as his own to what Felix was telling him. And – he felt dizzy at the thought – the *library*. He rubbed a hand over his scalp, collecting his thoughts. It made sense. He'd always wondered if someone from the Abbey owned the house. He remembered the strange feeling he sometimes got in the library, like there was someone else with him, their memories imprinted onto the walls.

'The books,' Jude all but whispered. 'You knew about the library.'

'I did,' Felix confirmed. 'Though I hadn't been back to Ánhaga since I was a boy, I remembered my father's collection, both the Abbey books and the sketchbooks. I thought there might be something in there you'd find useful.' He drummed his fingers on the table. '. . . Was there? Anything useful?'

Jude smiled. 'You could say that. My magic, it . . .' he hesitated, wondering how much to say. 'It found its outlet in books. In the . . . sketchbooks, I suppose. The blank pages.'

Felix smiled. 'So, you have your books, Maeve's magic loves her paintings, and I have the birds.'

'Birds?' Jude echoed, voice slightly faint.

He nodded. 'It's different to how both of your magic manifests. It's less of an outlet and more of a reminder. I can work memories into the sight of a bird. It's . . . complicated. Hard to describe and even harder to demonstrate. Like how a certain smell will remind you of an event, in a way.' Suddenly, his eyes flashed to Jude's. 'Are you okay? You look pale.'

Jude pictured one, two, three birds on the horizon. His heart gave a tremulous lurch.

'Fine,' he murmured.

Felix met his gaze. A familiar current passed between them, harkening back to boyhood antics and secrets shared between friends. 'You can tell me some other time,' he said. A rare, shy smile pulled at his lips.

'Do you want it back?' Maeve asked. Her cheeks were faintly pink. 'The house.'

Felix raised a brow. 'Ánhaga? Absolutely not.'

Maeve laughed. 'Not a fan of crumbling old houses, I take it?'

He chuckled and shook his head. 'Nor the ghost of my father.'

'Understandable,' Jude said. 'Nevertheless . . . thank you. Both for sending me there and for letting us stay. I know it's been a long time, Felix, but ah—' he cleared his throat, feeling somewhat awkward. Felix had gone back to studying the grain of the table. 'It's good to have those memories back. Maybe we can return to them someday.'

Felix looked up. Smiled. 'I'd like that.'

Maeve reached across the table to squeeze Felix's hand. A wash of resolve passed over the three of them. They'd been wounded, but they were healing. Life stretched out in a clean sweep of possibility, in a way it never had before. The Abbey would fade away, its advocates slinking back to nurse their wounds and look for ways to knit back together what they'd lost, but ultimately, they didn't hold a candle to what burned brightly inside them.

Hope.

EPILOGUE

Jude

Only fifteen days had passed since Jude last laid eyes on Ánhaga, yet he felt like a completely different man from the half-formed figure who'd left. He used to imagine turning his back on it entirely, with mouth bitter and teeth gritted. He'd picture how he'd slam the iron gate and stride away with the wind at his heels and freedom in his lungs. Never, ever to return.

Yet, here he was. Returning. And *excitedly* at that. Not a dog to its whip-wielding master, but a migratory bird returning to its nest after a long winter.

Not alone, but with her.

Maeve's shoulder brushed his, softly at first, then harder, purposeful. Jude caught the edge of her smile before she tucked it into the red wool of her scarf.

'Thoughts?' she asked as Jude pushed open the gate.

He stepped aside to let her through first. 'About?'

'Coming home.'

He cast his gaze over her head. The house stood tall and imposing, the windows impossibly dark. Ivy grew up in reaching tendrils that spread like fingers over the curve of the front door. Frost clung to the meagre path snaking towards the house, crunching underfoot. He smiled.

Home.

The first place he went was the kitchen.

'Really?' Maeve's voice was thick with laughter. '*This* is your priority?'

'It's all I could think about,' he grumbled, dumping out the contents of the cutlery drawer onto the counter. Spoons, knives, and forks went everywhere with a metallic rattle. He arranged the divider back in the drawer and neatly replaced the cutlery in their assigned section. No more of Elden's seemingly random toss of knives and teaspoons together. He was putting his foot down.

Maeve came up behind him, resting her hands on his hips and notching her chin over his shoulder. 'I thought the kitchen would be my domain now that it's only the two of us. Since I've never actually seen you cook.'

'Very funny. We can share. If you respect the sanctity of the space, of course.'

'Naturally.'

She laid her cheek between his shoulder blades. Her breath warmed his skin through his thin jumper, trailing goosebumps across the word etched into his skin. Jude closed his eyes. He could stay here forever, basking in the warmth of her, a haven of peace.

His stomach grumbled.

Maeve laughed, pulling back. 'Toast?'

Soon, they were seated in front of the merrily burning fire in the front room, eating fresh bread Maeve's sister Una had made them for their journey, honey dripping down the thick crusts. Their teacups sat on the scuffed floor with handles slotted together. Besides Elden, only Olive was missing from the happy picture. He'd go collect her from Bethan's tomorrow.

Warmth from the fire stole over his face. Outside, a light pattering of rain traced rivulets down the window. He tracked a figuration of birds streaking across the blanket of clouds, outstretched wings curving into points against the wind. Perhaps the library would tell him what a dozen birds signified. Maybe he'd just ask Felix.

Jude set his half-eaten toast on top of his mug to warm. 'It's strange having nothing to do. No looming presence or shadowy task to complete.' Maeve quirked a brow, and he sighed. 'I'm happy for it, of course . . . but it is odd. Like I need to learn to relax.'

'I'm sure you'll find something to occupy your time. Vegetables and the like. Maybe knitting.' She chuckled, angling her head to catch a trail of honey sliding down her wrist. Jude drew one knee close to his chest. His stomach clenched.

Well. There was *one* thing they could do.

They'd only had the one night together, burned forever in his memory. He didn't think anything could erase how she tasted. His only regret was their severe lack of alone time since leaving Elden's. After they'd found Maeve's family, they'd stayed a little over a week at Una and her husband's house, sleeping on the two sofas in the small house's main room. Not exactly conducive to continuing his study of Maeve and her sighs.

But now . . . they were alone. His bedroom was only a few floors up. Too far, really.

Why didn't he place a bed here, next to the fire? He wanted to see how the orange flame gilded her skin and drew out the spun gold of her hair, the emerald lurking in her eyes. His fingers ached to reach for her. He knew she at least somewhat enjoyed herself last time, but would she welcome his touch again? Did she look at him and *want*, as he did her?

Jude was going mad with desire. Just to be known by her. Seen, touched.

He took an unsteady sip of tea. The honey lingered on his tongue. Sweet, so sweet. He couldn't look at her lest she see the naked desire on his face. He didn't want to frighten her with its force.

A soft touch on his wrist. A fine tremble to her fingers. He looked up.

Her eyes were dark, lips parted and damp. 'Let's go upstairs.'

'Upstairs?' His voice sounded thready, even to his own ears. Maeve nodded, leaning imperceptibly closer, and he realized that as he'd been fighting his desire for her, she was tracking along the same path. He slid his hand up her bare forearm and squeezed.

'No,' he murmured. 'Upstairs is too far.'

He wasn't sure who kissed who first, only the next moment, Maeve's lips were against his, her breath in his lungs. He fell backwards in a graceless slump, laughing against her mouth as her thighs bracketed his hips. 'I couldn't wait,' she said, kissing the sensitive corner of his mouth, under his ear. 'Days, Jude. *Days*. I can't stand it any longer.'

His heart leapt into his throat. 'You have no idea.'

She leaned back to shove her hands under his shirt. Her palms were as hot as a brand on his skin. He wanted her nails, her teeth. The mark on his chest had been too long faded. 'I think I have *some* idea,' she said, shifting against him.

He trembled, already too close, and stilled her restless hips. He levered himself on his elbows, nodding to the chair facing the fire. 'Sit on the chair.'

A dark blush traced its way down her throat, bringing out the pinkness of her lips as she got to her feet and lowered onto the chair. She crossed one leg tightly over the other as she watched him make his way over to her.

Well. That certainly wouldn't do.

He braced his hands on the chair's arms and leaned down. Her eyes were glassy with want as she stared up at him. A dull buzzing settled deep in his skull, erasing everything that wasn't her.

'Here's what's going to happen,' he said, dipping down to run his nose up her neck, taking in her scent. 'I'm going to get on my knees. You're going to tell me when to stop. Okay?'

He wasn't sure she was breathing as she nodded. He wasn't sure *his* lungs were functioning. Wherever this untested confidence was coming from, he would use it while it was here.

A memory floated to the surface as he lowered to the ground.

Weeks ago, kneeling in front of Oakmoor's shrine. Maeve's hand on his throat, the trembling in his thighs as rain coated them both. How he'd thought, desperate and weak, that he'd do anything to remain kneeling at her feet.

So much had changed, but not that. Never that.

Jude inched her dress up her thighs, kissing her black stocking-covered calf. He stared at the curve of flesh over the top of the sock on her thigh, momentarily entranced. Last time, this had gone quickly. He hadn't had the time to truly learn her like he wanted to. Pulling down her sock, he rubbed the short stubble on his jaw against her until she sighed, skin reddened. Somehow, the sight of her bare thighs was the thing to end him.

'Jude,' she whispered, voice strained.

He urged her knees wider before looking up. 'Yes?'

'Hurry up.'

He kissed her thigh. 'You know, I don't think I will.'

Smiling at her annoyed huff, he slid her final layer off, dropping the thin fabric behind him. He pulled one leg over his shoulder, leaned in, and stopped.

'*Jude.*' Her leg tightened over his back. 'Stop being a tease.'

Her skin was dewed with a fine sheen. The long rope of her hair hung down the side of her neck, gilded in the firelight. Jude couldn't look away from her mouth. He'd kissed her. He was on his knees for her. She begged for his touch with low, murmured words.

Look at you, he wanted to say.

Instead, he gave her what she wanted.

Her thighs didn't take long to clench up around his ears as soon as his mouth was between her legs. He remembered what she liked from last time, angling his head, sliding his fingers inside her. He forced himself to pull back when she groaned.

Her eyes snapped open. 'Why'd you stop?' He kissed her lightly between the legs, deciding not to answer. She tried to pull him closer with her leg. 'Not nice.'

'Very nice.'

'Jude. Please.'

He decided he liked the desperation in her voice and leaned in for another taste. Immediately, Maeve's legs began to tremble, trying to spread wider. He felt her touch on the crown of his head, skating back to palm the base of his skull. She pulled his mouth closer, moaning. Too close. 'Jude, I'm—'

He sat back on his heels.

'No, no . . . *why?*' Maeve whined. Her eyes were wild. 'I thought I got to tell you when to stop. How can I when you won't—'

He ran his tongue back over her, not stopping this time. The silence of the room pressed in around them, broken only by her panting breaths and the crackle of the fire. He neither noticed nor cared if his knees ached on the floorboards beneath him. Only her, her taste, her sounds, the feeling of her coming on his tongue, mattered.

Her legs went boneless as she came back down to earth.

'Took you long enough,' Maeve mumbled, still managing to sound grumpy even with the mess she'd made of his face. She collapsed back in the chair, covering her eyes with the crook of her elbow.

Jude kissed her knee. 'Hm.'

He watched her as her breathing slowly evened out, her body going lax. One leg was still around his shoulder. His eyes skated down to where she was still open for him. 'I don't think you're quite done.'

She moved her arm to look down at him as he resumed sliding his thumb back and forth over her. Her head dropped back. She tried to close her legs, stopped by his shoulders. He kept his touch light, pace steady, as her face scrunched.

He'd meant what he said – he'd stop when she asked.

'Another?' Jude asked as her cheeks grew more and more flushed. She took a deep breath, holding it in. Her back arched. He didn't vary his touch, content to watch her crumble.

And crumble, she did.

He was only half aware his mouth was on her again. He closed his eyes, reaching down to press on himself, staving off the end. *Fuck*. He could stay forever.

His head swam. Drunk, almost.

Finally, Maeve pushed him back. She looked utterly wrecked as he wiped his mouth on his wrist. 'That's,' she paused, catching her breath, 'enough.'

He smirked.

She rolled her eyes. 'I would tease you about that smug look but . . . I suppose it's deserved.'

He laid his head on her thigh to hide how his smile widened.

The afternoon seemed to pause, a hushed reverence falling over the room as Maeve ran her fingers through his hair, pulling gently. Perhaps it was time to let it grow longer again.

'Let's go upstairs,' she said, breaking the comfortable silence. 'I want to be in your bed.'

Jude pressed a final kiss to her thigh before he stood, leaning down to bring his lips close to her ear. 'I thought about you there, Maeve. Many, *many* times.'

Maeve shoved to her feet, grabbing him by the hand.

Their laughter filled the house as they ran up the stairs, breathing life into the walls. Jude paused on the way to his bedroom to open the door to her studio. He smiled at the contents. 'Maeve?' He caught her hand, pulling her back. 'Look.'

She curled into his side, grinning up at him until he directed her to look into the room with a jerk of his chin. She turned in his arms. It took her a moment to take in what filled the room. Then—

'*Oh*. Jude!' she squealed, leaving his arms to race towards the easel. 'When did this arrive?'

Maeve crouched beside the solid oak easel arranged by the window to examine the tray of oil paints, the cup beside it full of silky brushes. All new, handcrafted by an artisan in Oakmoor or sent from one of the larger towns nearby. Jude had arranged it all through a letter to Bethan, sent while he and Maeve were at her family's.

All for this very moment – the smile on her face better than he imagined.

'Do you like it?' he asked, approaching to sift his fingers through the fine hair at her temple. 'I thought you might want something new to paint with.'

'I *love* it,' she said, standing to throw her arms around him. 'So much. Thank you.'

'You're welcome.' He drew back, taking both her hands in his. 'Bethan told me there's a group in Oakmoor that meets every few weeks to paint together, if you'd like to join. Her mother goes.'

Her eyes lit up even further. 'I'd love to.' She turned, sweeping a hand across the room and the view beyond. 'I want to paint this – our home. Our life. All of this.'

A lump formed in his throat. 'I can't wait to see.'

She squeezed his hands, dragging him bodily from the room and towards his bedroom. Jude laughed. 'Eager, are we? I thought you learned your lesson about patience.'

Maeve shot him a *look* as she shoved open the door and unceremoniously pushed him onto the bed. Her eyes were bright as she gazed down at him sprawled against the sheets. 'Is teasing me a good idea right now?'

'But it worked out so well last time,' he said, raising a brow suggestively.

Her lips pursed as she toyed with the button on his trousers. Her fingers brushed the bare skin of his lower stomach. He shivered. How such a small touch could affect him so drastically was unfathomable. She tilted her head, gazing at him from beneath her lashes. 'Show me?'

'Show you what?'

She undid the button. 'You said you thought of me . . .'

He swallowed, nodding.

'I want to see what you did when you pictured me here.'

Oh.

Her smile was sly, catlike. Jude's heart pounded in his ears. Somehow, this was so much more vulnerable than anything that had come before. To touch himself and think of her, knowing she was watching . . . the thought nearly stunned him into inaction.

But he trusted her.

He would give her what she asked.

His fingers shook as he set them on the next button on his trousers. At the same time, Maeve pulled her jumper over her head, leaving her in her chemise and skirt. Before he could undo another button, she had the skirt off and on the ground. Light poured through the thin material of the chemise, illuminating the curve of her breasts, the dip of her waist, just like it had all those days ago in her bedroom.

Those *damn* chemises. She knew exactly what she was doing.

Jude pushed down his trousers, keenly aware of her rapt attention. Slowly, he wrapped his hand around himself. Maeve hissed a shuddering breath as his own breathing grew rapid. He couldn't look away from her face. There was something reverent in her dark eyes, almost disbelieving. How many times had he pictured her here – maybe not like this, stroking himself while she watched – but *here*. Wanting him. If she couldn't quite believe what blossomed between them, then he was the same. Overwhelmed and utterly undone.

His stomach tensed, and Jude closed his eyes. 'Fuck.'

'What did you think about?' Maeve's voice was thick, raspy.

'You. Here.' His voice was hoarse, bitten-off.

Maeve laid her hand on his wrist, hastening his movement until it bordered on too much. 'What else? Tell me.'

'How you'd taste. How you'd sound. If you'd shut your eyes

or keep them open,' he choked as she urged his hand faster. He gazed desperately into her face. 'Do you, do you want me to—'

Abruptly, she stilled his hand. 'No. Not yet.'

A breathless laugh escaped him. 'This is punishment, isn't it? For earlier.'

Her smile grew sharper, more feline. 'Now, why would you say that?'

'Cruel,' Jude replied.

'Deserved.'

He laughed, levering up to kiss her. There was too much fabric between them. He voiced his concern, and soon, nothing remained but layers of anticipation. Maeve scratched her nails down his back, whispering in his ear. 'I love this. I love you.'

Jude ran his thumb along her jaw, kissing the tops of her cheeks, her eyelids, the tip of her nose. He wondered if happiness had a limit and, if so, if his allotment was more than everyone else's. It certainly felt that way.

He ghosted his lips over the shell of her ear, smiling when she shivered. She wrapped both legs around his waist. The feeling of her against him was enough to make his brain stall out.

She shifted her hips impatiently. 'Get on with it, would you?'

'You sure are demanding today,' he remarked, giving her what she wanted. The heat, the pressure . . . it was almost too much. He wasn't certain how long he'd last. Her lids fluttered shut. He lost track of every place they touched. Her lashes were dark on her pink cheeks.

'Let's stay like this always,' she whispered.

He searched for a reply. 'That . . . wouldn't be practical.'

She drew her legs higher up his back, cupping the side of his neck to draw their foreheads together. He revelled in each minute response, hoarding them like precious gems. The brush of her breath against his mouth, the tensing of her thighs around his waist. How his name sounded when gasped from her lips.

Nothing else mattered. He could spend decades learning her and still find something new to discover, which was exactly what he planned to do.

Jude awoke to Maeve curled against his chest, her breath slow with sleep. Moonlight cut an ivory ribbon across his quilt. The night was at its blackest, yet he was suddenly wide awake. Something tugged at him, blanketing his vision with flecks of silver like dancing dust motes. He blinked. A memory floated to the forefront. New, but . . . not new. As fragile as a pearl and just as rare.

In the memory, he was sitting in the crack of a half-open window, one leg dangling over the steep drop to the sea below, the other curled close to his chest. Cold air buffeted his face. When he licked his lips, he tasted salt. Despite the wind creeping off the whitecaps below and the icy limestone bricks against his back, he was warm. His heart was full.

Behind him, the door to his bedroom creaked open, and there was Maeve. Young, maybe thirteen or fourteen.

You only have a year left.

Jude brushed the worry aside as she crept closer. Her face was full of youth, eyes just as bright as he knew them best. Her thick flannel nightgown swept the top of her socked feet. She had her hands cupped gingerly in front of her, like she was afraid of what she held between her palms.

'What is it?' he heard himself ask.

Maeve scrunched her nose as she extended her hands towards him. 'Open the window wider.'

Pulling his hanging leg in, he slid from the windowsill and did as she asked. The iron was cold under his too-warm fingers. Maeve stepped past him to gaze at the night sky above. Stars winked against the inky blackness. He didn't think he'd ever seen something so lovely.

Slowly, she opened her hands.

A small, brownish bird sat perched between her palms. Its silky feathers were dappled with fine black lines, tiny beak needle-sharp as it cocked its head to gaze at them. Jude held his breath, wondering if Maeve was doing the same.

'A wren,' she whispered. 'I found him in the hall. He was surprisingly easy to catch.'

'I think he likes you,' he replied, his voice just as quiet. If Ezra caught her in his room, they'd both be in trouble, but for now, it was just them and the bird.

The wren's wings snapped open. Almost too quick to follow, it rose into the air, disappearing into the night. Her shoulders brushed his with her exhale. She lifted a hand, waving to the wren's barely visible silhouette. 'You know what Felix likes to say about birds, don't you?'

He shook his head.

Maeve smiled at him, squeezing his hand once before releasing. 'One bird for courage.'

ACKNOWLEDGEMENTS

Like all good stories, my journey from idea to finished book is full of all of the twists and turns, the heart-wrenching highs and the tear-filled lows. I can't put into words how lucky I am to have such a wonderful group of people around me. Truly – I am so grateful, humbled, and very, very lucky.

Firstly, to my wonderful husband, Gregg. My first reader and biggest supporter. From reading this book chapter by chapter while I was drafting (including reading the same chapter over and over because I changed the *slightest something* and it made a BIG difference, trust me) to brainstorming on walks and dealing with my various meltdowns, you never gave up on me or wavered in your belief in this book.

I am so grateful, always.

To my family for the support and encouragement, even from 4,000+ miles away. It's not easy living so far from most of the closest people in your life, but the constant love and care truly made the distance feel like nothing at all. To my dearest mother, Kristi, especially, for dipping your toes into the wild world of fantasy novels, and for the constant book promotion to literally every person you meet. I think I can credit every sale in the US to you, personally. To my sister Ashley, for being a general menace, and (lovingly, of course), forcing me to be a better writer to pass your rigorous quality control. I was always nervous sending something to you, but I think it's because I value your opinion so much, both as a sister and a reader. You're the best – don't let it go to your head.

To my non-bookish friends, thank you for all the pints and the unwavering support. I don't know which was needed more. And to my cat Dorothy, for stepping on my keyboard at the most critical moments and being generally the cutest and most annoying companion I could ask for.

Writer friends truly make the world go round. To Rachael A. Edwards, your mentorship on my first book all those years ago changed my writing forever. So grateful for you and the friendship we've made since. To Jenny Kiffer, Mariana Coelho, Elian J. Morgan, Norees Gaspar, Lucy Rose, Laura R. Samotin, Jamie Pacton, and Tarah DeWitt for being the *most* excellent author friends and always willing to offer advice and encouragement, read disjointed first drafts, and deal with my various spirals. To those who read *Sacred Space* in its various pre-publication forms – Hannah, Louise, Maddy, Healey, Bailey, Ellen, Sara, Taylor, Sierra, Meg, Monique, Megan, Kalie, Maddie, Liz, Emma, Sophie, Rhian, Ellie, Sarah, and Jen – thank you SO much. And to the welcoming, supportive community I've found on BookTok, I love you all.

For anyone who has shown support and excitement for Jude and Maeve, please envision me planting the LARGEST kiss on your forehead. Thank you!

Alongside such a wonderful group of friends and family, I am beyond thankful to have the best team of literary professionals behind *Sacred Space*. To my first agent, Alice Caprio: you're the best. The absolute best. Without your hard work, determination, and belief in me and this book, it would still be a document on my computer. I can't tell you how much I appreciate your endless enthusiasm and all of our (slightly unhinged) WhatsApp's throughout every stage of the journey. To my current agent, Maddy Belton, thank you so, so much for your dedication to seeing me live out all my career hopes and dreams and for your enthusiasm and care for Jude and Maeve. I can't wait to see where our partnership goes! I'd also love to thank the wonderful Victoria Marini for helping bring *Sacred Space* to the US – thank you so much for your tireless effort and determination!

To the teams at Harper Voyager UK and Little, Brown in the US, thank you so much for seeing the potential in *Sacred Space* and making every dream I didn't even know I had come true. To my editors, Rachel Winterbottom, Elizabeth Vaziri, and Julia DeVarti, thank you for your keen editorial vision and all the hours spent making this book into the best version of itself. As soon as I saw Rachel's note in the offer letter about making my beloved characters suffer more, I knew I was in good hands!

I'd love to thank everyone who had a hand in every aspect of bringing *Sacred Space* into the world. On the UK side: Natasha Bardon, Fleur Clarke, Chloe Gough, Catherine Perks, Emily Chan, Robyn Watts, Sian Richefond, Angelica Bowden-Jones, Hannah Gillingham and Megan Smith, and on the US, Sally Kim, Gregg Kulick, Gabby Leporati, and Kathleen Quinlan. Thank you so much!

At its heart, *The Sacred Space Between* is a story about belonging. It's about making careful inroads through loneliness and isolation, about walls crumbling in the face of love, and the brightness dawning just over the horizon. Much of it (as you may have guessed) stemmed from my own experience of the grappling that comes alongside deconstructing long-held beliefs. Writing Jude and Maeve's journey was cathartic, to say the least, and I hope some of my readers see themselves in their journey, too.

Finally, I want to express every bit of gratitude to everyone who will pick up *The Sacred Space Between* – a forehead kiss, too, for making a debut author's dreams come true. I hope you enjoy!